SHARDS

IN THE

VOID

FATE OF THE DEHMI: BOOK TWO

— K.T. HOST —

Table of Contents

CONTENT WARNINGS

This book is written for adults ages 18+. It is not suitable for children.

This novel contains the following situations that may be uncomfortable for some readers: recollections of sexual assault (in the form of memories from the first book in the series), vulgar language, explicit sexual content, detailed descriptions of gory violence, hallucinogenic images of horror, severe emotional distress, on-page descriptions of anxiety and depression from a first person point of view, and death. I understand that these situations and terms are upsetting to some readers. Sensitivity readers have been consulted, but you as the reader reserve the final judgment on what you are comfortable with. This list is not exhaustive and other triggering circumstances or topics may be present within the work without any further warning beyond this point.

Please prioritize your own mental health and read at your own risk.

Thank you and take care.

This is for anyone who has ever teetered on the edge of giving up.
Keep going. Run. Walk. Crawl if you have to.
Drag your body up over that hill you're climbing.
Cut yourself some slack; take your time. Rest a bit, then start again.
Do whatever it takes to get to the summit—just don't stop.
There's something beautiful waiting on the other side.

Prologue: A Meeting

With heavy hearts and pounding heads, Esraa and Amon strode down the hall towards where the golden doors of the Council chamber sat ajar. The overlapping voices of the nine lower Paragons echoed throughout the corridor despite the muting effect of the rich navy carpet beneath their feet—hers clad in silk slippers the color of dawn, his in pristine black boots, their gold buckles glinting in the glow of the enchanted sconces spaced evenly along the deep red walls.

Explaining the death and impending resurrection of Valorie Vargas was not going to be easy.

The dual Paragons of the Underworld, the King and Queen of Death itself, paused at the threshold to the chamber. A shield of shadow pulsed around the pair, obscuring their presence from the others gathered within. Through the doorway, a predictable chaos reigned, the same volatile collision of alliances and personalities which ensued every time the full Council was convened. It was the reason Esraa and Amon so rarely pulled their rank in this manner. The results typically weren't worth the subsequent headache.

Today, however, they had information that needed to be shared. Needed to be shared *now*, not in the two weeks it would likely take for the nine lower Paragons to deign to read their portal missives. In truth, half of the Paragons would answer immediately. The others, through arrogance, laziness, or sheer work volume, would take days to open the message. Days they did not have to lose.

Esraa and Amon surveyed their fellow Avalleans from the entryway. Within the marble depths of the circular room, beneath vaulted ceilings hewn from the same swirling ivory, rose and sky blue stone as the walls and floor, the Paragons awaited the news that would change the course of Avallea. That already *had* changed it. They simply were not aware of it yet.

Andrew lounged against a pillar carved with a placid forest scene, his charcoal suit accenting his bright crimson hair and pale eyes. He played with his fingernails, studiously ignoring his eternal enemy, Callista, who sat in her seat across the room and pretended not to notice him in turn. The Paragon of Technology and the Paragon of Arts and Skies could prove a formidable match, if their animosity ever turned into the lust several Paragons believed roamed underneath their cold interactions.

In the trio of thrones next to Callista, Zoe, the Paragon of Family and Fertility, regaled George and Deacon with an outlandish tale of trickery she performed against some band of rogues during her days as a dehmi. Her tawny skin and wild mass of coils glowed beneath the cool-toned lighting, head thrown back in laughter alongside the brawn of the Paragons of Plants and the Paragon of Healing.

Deep within the shadowed recesses of the room's outer edge, Aretha and Zahur sat with their foreheads pressed together in quiet conversation. Their matching jet-black ponytails and slight, secretive smiles gave the impression the two were siblings, though their bond was of an entirely different nature. The Paragons of Justice and Food were not historically close allies, but this cycle had seen the two form a deep connection beneath their near-silent exteriors.

Their pairing left Rhea and Leander alone in their chairs, neither choosing to join the others in their plotting or reminiscing. The Paragon of Water sat straight-backed in her golden throne, a match to the eight others arrayed around the circular table. The final two chairs differed. Twin thrones of blackest night sat together at the northern curve of the table, across the room from the door where their owners stood unnoticed.

Rhea's brilliant blue eyes were staring straight into the hole in the table's center. Her silver hair fell in a cascade over one shoulder and her long fingers were steepled together, tapping against each other in a pattern as she waited. At her side, Leander feigned slumber, his head resting on his muscled forearms. A single one of the Paragon of Animal's bronze orbs remained cracked open above his folded arms, surveying his colleagues with a feral wariness that edged closer to the animals he oversaw than to the other Avalleans.

Esraa cast her gaze across her left shoulder, searching for her eternal companion. Amon stood a heartbeat away, always within reach. As he promised he would be when they were Bonded nearly four centuries ago. Her fingers twined together with his, sunset pastels on midnight skin, and a small sigh slipped from her full lips before the two swept into the room as one.

The moment their feet crossed the line where carpet met marble, the room became silent but for the quiet whisper of feet against the bare floors. Only when the Council was seated around their table did the Rulers of Death settle into their obsidian thrones. Nine sharp gazes met around the ring of opalescent wood carved from Avallean faelms, trees said to contain threads of the Web of Fate itself. In the table's hollow center, a shimmering web of magical threads slowly rotated. The mass floated freely in the hole, its colors shifting from golds to reds and blues, with several tenuous strands of pure white woven through. A physical representation of the state of Fate itself, the Fate Manifest was the closest Avalleans had to a holy relic.

Under its ever-changing glow, the meeting was called to order.

"Thank you for gathering on such short notice." Esraa greeted the assembled Paragons with a soft smile that did not touch the sadness in her gaze.

George leaned forward, bracing his large arms on the table. Corded muscle under tan skin rippled as he replied, "You don't call us together in this manner often. Figured it must be important."

Esraa gave a single firm nod. "It is. We're here to discuss certain recent events, ones specifically involving the Fate-touched human Valorie Vargas and a Haven team from Earth."

"Is this the same human girl from your memo several months ago?" Deacon ruffled a stack of papers pulled from some unknown pocket. They were largely for show, given the fact his memory was near-perfect when it came to Council matters. "The one meant to be Bonded to a dehmi and Ascended? I hope there weren't any complications from the Ascension. It's a rare transition, but not unheard of." He fluttered his sheets once more before muttering, mostly to himself, "Although, if it were a matter of complications, you likely would have been able to handle them yourselves, or contacted me directly for guidance. A meeting of the Council would not have been necessary."

"Yes," Amon replied in a clear, booming voice. Deacon's rambling was cut short before it could derail the meeting entirely. An inevitability which would surely happen soon enough without his hastening the process. "However, the ceremony was...waylaid."

"Poor girl." Zoe's coils bounced as she cocked her head to one side. "Did she have second thoughts?"

"She was murdered."

At Amon's clipped statement, a shocked buzz ran through the lower Paragons.

With his next revelation, the buzzing became a roar. "By one of our own."

Amon allowed the shouting to crest before slamming his fist onto the shimmering table. "Enough." He did not raise his voice. He didn't need to. The room collapsed into tense, razor-sharp silence as soon as he demanded it. Several minutes passed, filled only with wide-eyed stares and shocked intakes of breath as the Council brought themselves to order.

It was Zoe's abnormally subdued voice that finally broke the shocked spell hanging over the Paragons with a single, shaking word: "Who?"

"A visiting dehmi from another Earth Haven, Joran Straught. He and the girl met during a party at the Haven Domenic and Marguerite oversee, the one the male she was to be Bonded with was assigned to."

"Do we have a method? A motive? Anything?" Andrew this time, his formerly carefully coiffed appearance rumpled by fidgeting fingers. Several other Paragons were also uncharacteristically jittery, their eyes darting to and fro while their hands played with hems or gripped the table's rounded edge to keep still. Gone were the vibrant personalities and confident unflappability worn like cloaks around the shoulders of the Paragons in their daily lives. The mantles of a people steeped in benevolent power, both mystical and political. This news, the concept of one of their own veering so far astray, was unheard of, and it showed.

Amon dipped his chin, locking eyes with several of the less composed members of the Council as he spoke. His stern visage seemed to comfort them, to draw them back to the present. "Both, in fact. Method more than motive, but enough of both to begin planning. Joran, evidently, is a talker. He met with Domenic the night before the party where he first encountered Valorie. Spoke to him at some length about his beliefs—beliefs revolving around changes Joran believes should be implemented in our core systems. Joran apparently thinks young dehmi are being somehow wasted in their service on mortal worlds, that they could better solve Avallea in 'other ways'. He did not get a chance to mention what these ways might be before Domenic dismissed the conversation as the ramblings of a disgruntled dehmi on a long journey and invited him to rest and refresh himself.

"It was Marguerite who noticed the glares Joran directed at Valorie during their party the following evening, but she thought nothing of it at the time. 'Joran is not typically a male given to smiles,' she reported. In the following days, Domenic said Joran asked several questions about Valorie's usual habits and whereabouts, but disguised them as a desire to know the woman Conall Raoult was to Bond with. In hindsight, we believe he was canvassing for information to end her life."

Aretha's slender fingers raised in a questioning gesture. At the dip of Amon's chin, the Paragon of Justice said, "So, there are the bones of a motive. An abhorrent one, to be sure. But the method? And any evidence?"

Esraa's soft, clear voice replied, "Valorie Vargas was found dead in a forest a small distance from the home of her mortal friend on the morning of her planned ceremony. The two dehmi who were planning to help her prepare had become worried when she would not answer any messages, so they searched the area. She had been beaten horrifically, her broken, bloodied body left in the churned mud made by dirt mixing with her life's blood in her fight for survival. In her hand, she held a scrap of fabric torn from Joran Straught's denim pants."

"And where is he now?" Aretha asked, her hands now clenched into fists atop the polished faelm surface.

At this, Esraa's face fell, and she shrank back minutely in her throne, lips pressed tight together. "He escaped," Amon answered for her, his palm making soothing strokes on her knee beneath the table. He knew she felt this was a personal failure, despite being nowhere near Earth at the time. Conall's happiness was especially important to her. To them both. "Domenic and Marguerite are already scouring for information on his whereabouts and possible co-conspirators. But, they need our help." His torso angled to better face Andrew around the shifting glow of the Fate Manifest. "We have access to systems and resources they do not. Resources which could make this process much faster."

Andrew gave a firm nod, his eyes icy in the light from the Web's threads between them.

"What about the boy?" Zoe asked. "I'm sure he's crushed. His beloved is dead, and in such a horrid manner."

Amon leaned against the straight back of his throne. "Initially, his grief was overwhelming. We came close to having to restrain him within the bowels of his Haven for fear of him harming himself or others. You know how volatile the healing gifts can be under the wrong mental state."

Zoe nodded, her brows drawn over a pitying frown. It was well known those who could heal were also able to siphon the life force of others. What was able to be manipulated could be bolstered or destroyed.

"However," Amon continued, "I would assume he's currently feeling a great many things. He and his siblings are in our domain, searching for her soul before her current...*condition* becomes permanent."

For the third time this evening, shock rolled through the Council chambers. Under different circumstances, Esraa would have found it amusing. Amon always said the lower Paragons reminded him of birds, with their posturing and preening. Seeing them flustered, their proverbial feathers rustled, gave merit to his description. She was sure she would hear those exact words from his lips later, if they could only keep the conversation on track and get this meeting over with before she began pulling her hair out in frustration.

Esraa cleared her throat, the quiet sound calling the Paragons back to order once more. "We figured it was only right to offer a way to rectify the situation, should they meet the parameters. I have sent one of our own to intercept the girl and lead her to their home."

"And your plans for the pair? Do they remain unchanged?" Andrew asked, referencing the meeting they had in this same room several months ago.

Esraa smiled. "They are already underway. In a way, this may result in a more streamlined process."

The Paragon of Information smiled knowingly, his straight teeth reflecting the Web Manifest in a strange mix of colors. "You do enjoy efficiency, don't you, Esraa?"

She shrugged one shoulder, the billowing strap of her Grecian gown sliding along her skin with the action. "If something can be simple, let it be simple."

For the first time that night, Leander leaned forward to speak. All eyes turned to the Paragon of Animals, who rarely contributed more than a few words in a meeting unless directly called on for his expertise. "So, now what?" He asked in his lion's growl.

"For now, we help find this Joran, ideally before he manages to do more damage," Amon said, glaring at a thin strand of red weaving through the vibrant golds of the living Web in front of them as though he could force its color to change with his will alone.

"And what about your dehmi? What of them?" Leander continued, shaggy golden locks glinting as his head tilted to the left to meet Esraa's gaze.

The room itself seemed to inhale as Esraa replied, "They try to survive."

Chapter 1
The End is the Beginning

- Valorie -

Ironically, it's the silence that wakes me.

Silence this complete and total doesn't exist on Earth. There are wellness clinics on billboards in the city advertising fancy sensory deprivation chambers built for meditation and relaxation, but I highly doubt even they've perfected the utter lack of sound my mind is currently struggling to comprehend. It scratches at my muddled brain, uncomfortable in its strangeness. No birds, no wind, no vibrating *whoosh* of my blood rushing in my ears. No pulsing thrum of my own heart to mark the seconds.

Wait.

No *pulse*.

In flickers and flashes, the memories creep their way back to me. A moonlit forest seen from an awkward, broken angle. Xavier's rage and fear, my desperate fight, and his escape into the forest's depths. Joran passionately regaling me with his fanatic dreams of a new, restored cosmos—one where mortals are subjugated and the Avalleans live as deities instead of peacemakers. The crunch and snap of bones, *my* bones, sharp against the muffled sounds of the night. Silent pleas for my friends, my family, to know I love them and tried so damned hard to survive.

Conall.

My lids snap open and I catapult into consciousness. Everything is shrouded in the hazy blur of eyes that have gone unused for...who knows how long. I pant and scrub my clumsy, sleep-deadened fists across my eyelids, tearing out a week's worth of eyelashes in my haste to know where the hell I am. If Mom could see me now, she'd *tsk* and remind me it takes up to four months to grow lashes back. But Mom is out there somewhere, blissfully alive, and I'm...

...in a meadow?

Soft, verdant grasses caress my waist, crushing under my weight as I shift. Wildflowers in shades of blue and purple and cream speckle the circular, tree-lined hollow, their perfume subtle and inviting. As the buttery sunlight plays across my skin, I am drenched in confused relief.

"It was all a dream," I breathe, unwilling to break the quiet magic of this space. "A horrible, awful dream. Way to give yourself a heart attack over nothing, Val. Wait 'til David finds out about this."

I press my hand against my chest and chuckle at my overactive imagination, picturing my best friend's face when he hears I took a nap in the woods and thought I died.

But my giddy joy sours as the laughter rolls through my otherwise-silent chest and out into the clear blue sky of this soundless world.

No pulse, no sounds.

No *life*.

"What the hell is going on with me? Where am I?"

I jump to my feet and tear my way through the entrancing glen, cursing the thick vegetation and loamy soil for impeding my ability to easily pace back and forth. My breathing accelerates, ramping up at breakneck speed as I struggle until only sheer force of will keeps me from hyperventilating and fainting. Can someone even faint if they're already dead? Because I'm back to being pretty damn sure I'm dead. I died and now I'm dead and I'll always be dead and Conall—

Conall will be waiting at the Haven for a bride who never comes.

Tears bubble up in the corners of my lids and flow in rivers down my cheeks, drenching the collar of the plain black tee shirt I'm wearing, the soft cotton unbearably similar to the dozens lining Conall's closet. I pull it to my nose and drag in a hiccuping sob, praying for the fabric to somehow smell of pine and lavender and the man I love, but all I get is sweet, clinging grass and cursed flowers.

My grief drags me back to the meadow's floor, the warmth and softness of the dirt a parody of the blood-soaked ground where I lost my life some unknown time ago. Has it been minutes? Are Finn and Gabrielle waiting for me, the idling of Finn's giant truck rumbling over their anxiety as my phone goes to voicemail again and again? Has it been decades? Are my parents and friends buried in their own plots of churned earth, their hearts as unmoving as mine? Are the Avalleans the only ones left to suffer with the pain of my ghost, or did they move on, forgetting the pitiful human girl who was allowed to peek behind their curtain and into their secrets for a blink of time?

Which would be worse: being forgotten, or being remembered?

My sobs echo for what feels like hours, vacillating between waves of misery and useless anger while the sun crosses the circle of sky high above me. It isn't until the branches at the treeline start to tremble I realize my shuddering is being caused by more than my own weary breaths. The leaves crunch and crackle across the glade, urging me to get my ass up and *move*, but there's nowhere to hide in the clearing. I make myself as small as possible, crouching down below the stems and blades of grass while I wait for the next horror of the day to appear.

It doesn't disappoint.

With one final, ominous step, a magnificent nightmare emerges from the shade of the trees.

"A *dragon*," I mouth, momentarily forgetting my terror. If tween Val was here, she'd be pissing herself for an entirely different reason than the one I'm currently experiencing. The girl who spent her days dreaming of mystical creatures from realms filled with magic grew up, but her desire never truly faded. I funneled it into biology, the closest I could get to the feeling of wondrous amazement back when life was mundane. Even now, the scientist section of my brain is rejoicing while the rest of me trembles against the earth.

With a heavy inhale, the beast swings its horned head in my direction, catapulting me out of my musing. Its nostrils flare as it catches my scent among the flora. I crouch lower, but its eyes are set in a regal visage so far above my head, I know it has no problems seeing where I'm hidden. Standing twice as tall as the Clydesdale I worked with during my animal husbandry course, it somehow manages to be incredibly muscular and practically silent. I have a horrible feeling that, had the trees' shifting limbs not given it away, it could have easily been peering over my shoulder before I noticed I was no longer alone.

Massive scales in varying shades of cerulean cover its hide and reflect pinpricks of light across the glade, a reptilian Hope Diamond. The larger ones across its spinal column are the darkest, fading subtly down its flanks to the underside, where there is a dense, short form of fur instead of scales. Twin horns protrude from an impressive brow ridge alongside tufted ears which somehow manage to not be out of place on a lizard's head. I spy ivory fangs within its partially opened mouth. The resulting image is terrifying and captivating in equal measure.

The beast pads towards me, slow and steady, as though I'm a small animal it's trying not to frighten. I guess in this case, I am. If it's even intelligent enough to care about my mental state. More likely, it's trying to figure out if I'm worth turning into a meal. Does it eat ghosts? I feel intensely corporeal right now, but this doesn't mean much. I'm sure that's what all the recently murdered girls say when they're being stared down by a lizard the size of a small barn.

The dragon sinks to its electric-blue belly a few feet in front of me, claws gouging deep furrows in the ground. Its topaz dinner-plate eyes focus on me with a lazy blink, lids large enough to ensure I hear the *snick* of their membranes at this distance.

I did not expect to find you awake.

The rumbling voice fills my head and I jump halfway out of my skin. What was *that*?

My apologies. I did not mean to frighten you. My previous interactions with your kind have been sparse.

"Wait a second. Hold the phone. Are you *talking* to me? Inside my *skull*?" I scrunch my eyes shut and shake my head. "This is the final straw. Now I know I'm still asleep. This can't be real, no way. Conall mentioned a lot of things, but nobody ever said anything about telepathic dragons. Wake up, Valorie, because this is insane."

Another slow blink, this time accompanied by a trio of puffing exhales.

"Are you laughing at me? I dream up a dragon and it has sass? Seriously?"

His caramel iris reflects a warped image of my disheveled self back at me. *You have been asleep for many turns of time,* kynaira, *but you slumber no longer.*

The strange, untranslated name he calls me barely registers next to the rest of his statement. "I'm not asleep? There's no dream or concussion or life support system in a hospital causing me to imagine a partially-telepathic conversation with a creature who could eat me for a snack? This is...real?"

Yes.

"So if I'm not asleep, does that mean I'm—" I attempt—and fail—to clear the lump from my throat before choking out, "—dead?" I'm desperately hoping there's a secret third option. I don't want to be dead in general, but especially not if it gives Xavier and Joran the satisfaction of being the ones who killed me.

The clicking shutter of his massive eyelid fills the oppressive silence, a gate sliding shut to stifle my last fragile hopes of an easy reunion as his answer reverberates through my psyche. *In some ways, yes, but not in others.*

Well, isn't *that* comforting.

Deep breaths, Val. I begin to pace again, this time in a circle around his massive body. Now that I'm reasonably certain I won't be his next meal, I want to burn diagrams of him into my brain so I can analyze them later. "Listen, Mr. Dragon—"

Ceraun.

I pause my examination of his gently curving sapphire horns. "I'm sorry?"

He shifts on his haunches, throwing sparks of blue from his scales across the grasses like a living disco ball. *My name is Ceraun, Valorie Vargas. What is this "dragon"?*

"Well, they're...you?" His huff of breath warms my side, and I hurry to explain before he turns out to be hungry after all. The last thing I need right now is to alienate the only other sentient being I've found here. Wherever "here" is. "They're a legendary creature on Earth. A giant, serpentine or reptilian beast with mythical powers. These days, children are usually obsessed with them, but sometimes adults, too. They're seen as fantasy creatures, not real animals."

He snorts again, and I'm unsure if my harried explanation helped or hurt my case. *I am clearly no imaginary beast used to amuse nestlings. I'm a wyrok, native inhabitant of the myriad realms known collectively as the Underworld and attendant to the wishes of its ruling Paragons, Esraa and Amon.*

"I'll be honest, there's entirely too much to unpack there. Let's break this down, all right?" I circle back around and sit in a patch of refracted sunlight a few feet in front of his snout. "You're telling me I'm in the Underworld? Like, 'realm of the dead', that Underworld? But I thought you said I wasn't dead?"

I said you weren't entirely dead.

Oh, now the giant lizard has a sense of humor. "Listen. I've had an awful day this far, Ceraun. I was beaten to death by my ex boyfriend and a sycophantic Avallean, missed my basically-wedding, woke up in a weird storybook glen with the sound turned off, and now you're here telling me I'm dead-but-not and talking like I should know what you mean, but I can assure you I do *not*. So, can you help me or not, because I really need to get help and figure out what I'm even supposed to be doing here!" By the time I finish, I'm panting and yelling into Ceraun's impassive face. Shouting at a creature who could snort me into oblivion isn't my smartest choice, but it's definitely a cathartic one.

Before I can react, Ceraun darts his head forward and nudges me with his nose, hard enough to knock me over but not to injure. I thump to the earth, the wind knocked out of both my lungs and my proverbial sail.

"What the hell, Ceraun?" I wheeze. Only my pride is injured, but it still wasn't a pleasant experience.

I had to calm you somehow. You wouldn't listen in that state.

He's right, but I don't admit it aloud. My fingers trace patterns in the scuffs where my feet wore through the grass, and I wait.

After another beat of silence, he continues. *Yes, wyrok are the only living inhabitants of the Underworld, which is where we currently are. We serve as the facilitators of the Paragons' will and laws, which is why I was sent here by Esraa and Amon to assist you on your journey. I will guide you to my home, deep within the Crystal Forest, and they will attempt to restore your form and return you to your living realm.*

"I can go home? Back to Conall and my friends?" I bounce to my feet, dusting dirt and clumps of grass from my shorts. "Ceraun, if you can get me back to being alive, I'll push David and Charlie out of the way and make you my new best friend."

I'm positive he has no idea what I'm babbling about, but I don't care. I might be able to go *home.* "Lead the way, boss, I'm yours to command. What do we do now?"

Ceraun unfurls himself and stands, the underside of his chin a full two feet above my head. His strange, furred stomach brushes the tips of the long fronds beside me. *Now, we walk.*

CHAPTER 2
And Off We Go

- VALORIE -

Ceraun prowls towards the dim green expanse of trees lining the glen where a path materializes through the gloom. His massive frame slinks silently over the dark, packed loam, his giant footsteps whisper-quiet. My own stumbling jog is a herd of elephants in comparison, made even louder by the ever-present lack of ambient noise.

"Hey, Ceraun," I pant, trying and failing to keep pace with him. "Why is everything so quiet here? Shouldn't there be, I don't know, magic birds or something?"

Hmm? Oh. A self-conscious chuckle rolls through my mind, and I get the distinct impression Ceraun is embarrassed. *I forgot. Apologies.*

He hums, and a sudden cacophony of animal calls, whistling winds, and crackling underbrush bombards my eardrums. The multicolored birds hopping along the branches behind us, tiny puffs of feathers who cleverly hid when Ceraun ambled by, peep and twitter to one another. Insects whir and buzz in front of my nose faster than I can swat them aside. What was a silent crypt is now a bustling ecosystem. The amount of life in this place beyond death is fascinating.

"How?" I murmur. I'm falling behind him worse than I was in the quiet, but I can't bear to hurry through the sudden onslaught of sound. My brain needs a moment to process the changes around me.

Ceraun's head swings around, and he lopes back to my side. *I did not wish for the forest to wake you prematurely,* kynaira. *Your spirit needed rest. But, in my shock, I forgot to reverse the change. Keep up,* he says crisply, turning forward and resuming his trek, *we have a fair distance to cover before dark.*

I do my best to comply, ignoring the vibrant flora and fauna around us as much as possible in order to focus on my feet. "Oh, sure, because *turning off all the sound* is a normal, everyday occurrence. So, you're not just a dragon, you're a magical, mind-altering dragon?"

Not a dragon. A wyrok. His disgust at being called a dragon again is palpable. I chuckle, but it turns into a squeal when he swings his head around and bathes me in a flood of steam from his nostrils. My hair blows back behind me with the force of his exhale. I cough twice, frantically waving my hands in front of my face. He may not be a dragon, but his breath reeks like a carnivore's.

I hold my hands up and placate, "Fine, you're not a dragon." Anything to avoid another trip to the Ceraun sauna. The stench still hasn't entirely dissipated. "You don't need to light me on fire. Doing so would be awfully draconic of you, and you don't want to hurt your image." The jab is juvenile, but I can't resist. My euphoria over finding out I might not be trapped here still hasn't completely faded. Frankly, I'm clinging to the last wispy remnants of my joy. Once it leaves, the anxiety will set in again. I'll be no good for traveling when that happens.

Another mental scoff, but I count my blessings when his head stays facing forward. *I don't breathe fire, either. I am not one of your children's tales.* His tail swishes behind him in a steady rhythm as he walks, swiping leaves and detritus from my path. At first, I think it's coincidental, until I spot it flicking out of the pattern to shift a thorny piece of bramble away from my ankles. Maybe the grumpy lizard isn't as much of a curmudgeon as he pretends to be.

"What *do* you do, then?" I ask. I'm curious from a biological standpoint, but also on a personal level. Ceraun fascinates me. He's surly and formal, but I've barely spent any time with him and his prickly exterior has already shown a few cracks.

Ceraun rustles the brilliant cobalt wings tucked in tight along either side of his back. *Different wyrok have different abilities, but we all have some level of mastery over the various components of nature.* One large eye fixes itself on me over his shoulder. *This does* not *make me one of your fire-breathing mythical lizards. I prefer lightning, but can manifest the other elements if the necessity arises.*

His description abruptly reminds me of sitting in a pristine, sunlit kitchen, learning about the elemental affinities of the Avalleans I dreamed of joining. My heart squeezes painfully at the memory. I clench my fists until my nails dig into my palms and my traitorous tears crawl back into their ducts. I file the new information away in my lexicon of Ceraun, determined to coax out more tidbits as our journey continues. If we're going to be companions all the way to wherever he lives, I'd rather us travel as friends. Which reminds me...

"Hey, Ceraun," I call, "where are we going, anyway? You mentioned your home, some crystal place? Is it far?"

Yes, especially if you get distracted by every insect and sprig along the way.

For a moment, I'm offended. Until the low rumble simultaneously vibrating in my ears and the soles of my shoes registers as laughter instead of a small earthquake. Shocked, I crack up along with him. "Wow, I didn't know you were capable of humor, Ceraun. This is quite the development in our relationship."

His deep laughter fades away into the slowly waning sunlight. We walk in a significantly more companionable silence for a while before he speaks again. *The Crystal Forest is as it sounds, and my people hail from a city within its depths. The Hearth, it would be called in your tongue. You will understand when you see. Are you aware of the structure of the Underworld,* kynaira?

I jump at the sudden, still-unexpected voice in my skull and almost turn my ankle on a loose stone. We've been hiking for a few hours; my legs are beginning to fumble and protest. "No. I've heard of Esraa and Amon, but that's about it."

The Underworld is an enigmatic space, a layered expanse of smaller realms crafted to mimic the mortal worlds their inhabitants lived in while alive. A fork appears in the path before us. Ceraun takes the left branch without hesitation, his explanation unbroken as he adjusts our route. *A network of portals manned and guarded by my brethren serves to connect the pocket realms, with only wyrok being allowed to pass freely between them, and only for official reasons or the traditional journey all young wyrok take to learn about the lands before reaching adulthood. We would be poor stewards of the realms if we did not know their ins and outs before we took up our ancestors' mantles.*

Something he glossed over snags in my brain. "Wait, if only wyrok are allowed through the portals, how will I go through them? I'm guessing we didn't happen to get lucky and end up in the exact corner of the

Underworld we would need to be in for the meeting. My life doesn't tend to work that way." The last sentence twists its bitter way out of my lips. What an understatement. Being beaten and murdered while lying alone in a muddy forest is much more than your average stint of bad luck.

No, we did not, he answers, his mental voice humorless once again. *There were several locations your spirit could have landed upon arrival, and this was one of the furthest from my home. It is not the worst possible location, but we do have a significant journey ahead.*

"Wonderful. I get the scenic route through the land of ghosts instead of the express train."

Dense branches scrape against his scales, the last rays of yellow sunlight shimmering in the gaps between the foliage. *Not ghosts. Spirits.*

A snort of my own escapes around my somewhat labored breaths. After all this walking, I'm seriously regretting passing on the cardio course David wanted me to take with him last spring. In my defense, how would I have known I'd be trudging behind a definitely-not-a-dragon through the damned wilderness? "Not really seeing the difference there, big guy, but sure."

We stop for a moment to rest beneath a large willow, its drooping branches keeping most other foliage away from the softer earth under the tree's canopy. Far above us, between the leaves and bark, the sky is a powder blue that reminds me of sultry summers at home, of backyard parties and families mixing, of proposals and group hugs and hilariously-timed afternoon picnics with my new sister.

Nails bite into my palms within tightly clenched fists. I should be in Avallea right now, wrapped in Conall's arms while we learn about his childhood home and my new existence.

One phone call in David's upstairs hall changed everything. Now nothing is certain.

When Ceraun asks if I've rested long enough, I don't have the energy to answer. I rise and let my feet carry me away from the memories.

Eventually, the dirt beneath our feet becomes studded with dry clay and rocks. I glance away from my uneven steps to ask, "Ceraun, why do we need to travel all the way to the Crystal Forest, anyway? Don't Esraa and Amon have power over the entire realm?" There are enough questions rattling in my head to last us days, and talking is keeping my brain off the fact I haven't had any water or food since I woke up. I don't know if "spirits" need to eat or drink, but I'd rather obtain that information before I faint from dehydration.

He doesn't turn around. The poor stones beneath his feet crumble into dust with each quiet tread without any hope of resistance. *My home, the Hearth, is the point in the Underworld where the barrier between this world and others is the thinnest. Esraa and Amon could traverse at any point with relative ease, yes, but the greatest concern is your soul's fortitude. A thin barrier gives your spirit the best chance of surviving reconnection with your mortal form. Time is also a factor, which is why we shall hurry to the best of your ability.*

Sure would be nice if he expanded on his last point, but it seems he's done talking. *Of course he is.* "And are we planning to walk the whole way there?" I snipe at the back of his head. I've always hated not knowing what's going on, and today has been one giant question mark. It has me on edge and uncomfortable. Blame it on the anxiety, but it's the exhaustion making me short-tempered to the point of rudeness.

Ceraun would have to be more dead than I am to not sense my tone, but it rolls off him. *Patience,* kynaira. *Eager for our trek to be over already?*

He chuckles, pulling a grudging smile from me. *Take heart—there's a supply cache nearby with everything we could need for this stretch. We will gather materials and make camp there for the night before resuming our journey in the morning.*

My smile stretches wide at the promise of food and a place to rest, and I follow my new best friend into the unknown with a spring in my step.

CHAPTER 3
Solail, The Mapmaker

– CONALL –

"We came through that Fate-forsaken portal forty-five minutes ago and Solail still has us waiting out here in the gutters," I grumble. My toe strikes one of the moss covered rocks at the edge of the deeply rutted gravel thoroughfare. It flops over once and rests in the waterlogged muck with a *thud*.

The sound isn't satisfying enough. With a grunt, my boot connects with the same rock and sends it splashing into the misty river at the end of the road. Three more follow in quick succession, each one a little larger, a little louder, a little more useless.

"Conall," Gabrielle admonishes. Her voice is a whisper, low enough our brothers can't hear her from their spots at the opposite end of the small house's exterior, but the tone comes through all the same. She's concerned, afraid I'll jeopardize this mission from its outset. But I won't let that happen. I'll keep it together, even if I'm boiling over inside.

I'll do anything to bring Valorie back. *Anything.* Standing here in this dull void of a town, fog leaching the colors from every surface while the ever-present dampness pulls the warmth from my bones, is a mere drop in the bucket of penance I owe her for my failure. And Valorie would want me to pull myself together and play nice with my siblings,

25

no matter how deeply I long to throw my fists into the wall of roughly masoned stones at my back.

I unclench my jaw and take two deep breaths, holding each for a handful of seconds before letting them *whoosh* from my protesting lungs. The exercise does nothing for my impatience, but it makes Gabby smile. She's been having a difficult time Seeing since we entered this world, but she doesn't need her powers to know how I'm feeling.

Gabby rests her tiny hand on my shoulder and squeezes hard. "We're all worried, Con. But you won't do her any favors by falling apart."

The creak of rusted hinges saves me from replying. Solail's weathered face pokes from the equally ancient entryway of her home, her glare harsh enough you'd think *she* was the one waiting in the cold and damp for close to an hour. The puff of white atop her head is near translucent in the firelight emanating from behind her, giving her the glow of an angel. Her voice, however, carries all the bite of a disgruntled demon.

"Well, get in here," she barks, already turning away from the entrance and heading back into her home.

I'm through the heavily decorated wooden door before Finn and Gaius have time to catch up to us, eager for the assistance Esraa and Amon promised we would find at the hands of the old mapmaker.

The interior of the tiny home isn't as much of a hovel as the facade would have you believe. Papers and trinkets cover every flat surface and crowd the shelves and pockets of storage space lining the walls, but there's a sense of organization to the chaos. A fire crackles merrily in the hearth, its warmth thriving in opposition to its mistress' frostiness. Small tiles carved in intricate designs make up the flooring, while the walls are paneled with wooden planks bleached near-white with age. Through a darkened doorway at the far end of the room, the edge of a bed and well-made dresser are visible. A small kitchen encompasses the front right side of the main space; it's there Solail heads first, snatching up a tea tray as though it personally offended her, before leading us towards a set of plush chairs near the fire.

We spread around a small, finely crafted round table covered in ink stains and scratches. Gabrielle and I perch on the edge of a pair of adjacent chairs, while Gaius and Finn flop into theirs with matching sighs.

"This is a nice little place, ma'am," Finn says, his trademark smile turned up to eleven under his twinkling blue eyes. He can't hide the lines under them, however—he's not as carefree as he strives to appear. He's been blaming himself since they found Valorie in those woods, as has Gabrielle.

I'd be lying if I denied a small, horrid part of myself blames them, too.

Solail grants Finn a small tilt of her lips before turning to Gaius, who is busy dangling his long legs over the arm of his chair. "Get your feet on the floor and pour the tea, boy, and I'll forget you ever treated my chairs like they're your sweat-covered bedroom furniture," she snaps, all evidence of good humor gone in an instant.

Finn chokes on a laugh as Gaius snaps to attention. "Yes, ma'am. Sorry," he mumbles, grabbing the finely-painted kettle and pouring five cups of rich black tea.

"So," I begin once the drinks are distributed, "are you able to give us a map or not?"

"Nope," the old woman says, casually stirring sugar into her flowered teacup.

My heart plummets. "I'm sorry, *what*?" I blurt. Surely she must have misheard my question. The Paragons sent us to Solail specifically—Esraa and Amon wouldn't screw around with something this important. Solail must be mistaken, that's all. She's obviously old—her mind must be addled.

Before I can repeat my question more slowly, the old woman drives another dagger through our carefully laid plans. "There are no maps of the Underworld," she says with a prim sip of her tea. Steam wreaths her head, roiling as she speaks. "Save those within the heads of the wyrok, that is. The pocket realms are too complex, too layered. A map would be hopelessly jumbled, like reading one hundred sheets of parchment glued on top of one another in a stack. Pointless."

Every word leaks out of my head and I'm left in stunned, horrified silence. Gaius gingerly raises his hand into the air. The motion is slow and cautious, as if he's worried Solail will rip the limb from his body. "Uh, ma'am?" he asks in a small voice, "why do they call you 'The Mapmaker' if you don't make maps?"

It's a legitimate question, one I would very much like to know the answer to myself. This trip is beginning to feel futile, and every second we spend here with this old woman nattering on is another step closer to losing Valorie forever.

Solail scoffs. "It keeps nosy busybodies with nothing better to do with their eternities from knowing the truth," she replies. "If the creatures of this world knew every bit and bob about me, they'd be hammering at my door like—well, like you lot!" She cackles with mirth at her own joke, tea sloshing dangerously close to the rim of her cup.

My razor-thin patience reaches its limit. "You're saying you can't help us?" I'm halfway out of my chair, ready to either fight everyone in this room or flee into the mist outside and lose myself to the endless wailing in my skull. I don't know which.

"Of course I can help you," Solail answers with a roll of her eyes. They're surprisingly sharp, pieces of ice-blue flint nestled within her heavily lined face. The rheumy film of age doesn't dare to touch them. "The question is whether you're smart enough to take what I can give you and know what it's worth."

I clench my fists around my backpack, settle back into my chair, and try to keep from screaming. "Listen, we don't have time for riddles—"

"What Conall *means*," Gabrielle says loudly, cutting me off with a pointed glare and saving me from my own anger for the second time today, "is we will be grateful for any information you can give us. However, our mission is also incredibly time-sensitive. We would appreciate it if we could get started so we can be on our way."

Solail settles back into her chair with a *humph*. "The first thing you need to learn is how this realm works. Otherwise, you'll roam around in circles until the muscular one has to drag you back to my house." She points a gnarled finger in Finn's direction. He chuckles and flexes his biceps at her with a wink.

My nerves grow taut as bowstrings and my jaw clenches ever tighter as Solail spends the next twenty minutes on the intricacies of the layered realms comprising the Underworld. She explains in great detail how each miniature world is crafted and maintained by the Paragons and their assistants—a dragonesque race called the wyrok—in order to match the mortal world its inhabitants lived in before their deaths. Under normal circumstances, I'd be as fascinated by the crash course in the mystery-shrouded Underworld as my siblings. But all I can think about are the minutes slipping away while we learn about portals and climates and the best way to avoid trouble inside the myriad locations we'll be visiting on the way to Valorie.

"Wait a minute," Gabrielle interrupts, worried lines creasing her forehead. "If only the wyrok are allowed to use the portals, how will we get through them?"

Solail's etched face creases even further into a devilish smile that makes the hairs on the back of my neck stand at attention. She has all the mischief of Gaius, but I have the intense feeling her brand of mayhem would be much more volatile if it were unleashed. I make a mental note not to leave the two of them alone together. Gaius doesn't need any more lessons in chaos, especially not from a woman who lives in the realm of death itself.

"Why, you'll have to trick the portal magic with a little help from this," she says, pulling a wrapped package from a dangerously cramped shelf behind her head. Several small items rain down onto the jumbled mass on the shelves below, but she pays them no mind, brandishing the dinner-plate-sized oval of beige fabric with a flourish.

Gaius leans in, his rose-colored irises narrowing as he scrutinizes the plain parcel before asking with a small snicker, "Okay, we're going to...wear this dusty old cloth? Wow, what a magic trick."

Quick as lightning, Solail's gnarled hand whips out and *thwaps* against the back of Gaius' head with enough force to bounce his nose off the mystery package. Finn howls with laughter—his first real laugh since *that* day—as Gaius rubs his nose and glares daggers at Solail. Even Gabby manages a slight lift of her lips. As Gaius' twin, she's spared the worst of his antics, but it doesn't mean she doesn't enjoy seeing him get his just desserts on occasion. Gabrielle knows her brother is much closer to imp than angel.

"No, you twit," Solail barks. "Shut up and try to keep those two brain cells of yours focused for a minute, or I'll tie you to your chair and muzzle you."

Her threat sends Finn into another overly loud fit. His joy causes my fists to clench until my nails threaten to pierce my palms. Every muscle in my body strains to let loose, to pummel into his smiling face until he's as battered as Valorie was atop the stone table beneath the Haven on what should have been our wedding day. Until he bleeds the way she bled out on the muddy forest floor, alone and in pain because our leader's *friend* murdered her and my family wasn't there. Until he feels as betrayed by his fellow dehmi as I do.

"*Conall,*" Gabrielle hisses, always watching for the moment I finally snap. I sigh and give her what she's waiting for.

Two long, slow breaths in.

Two futile, time-wasting breaths out.

To think, I used to be the calm, composed sibling. Now I'm the loose cannon, the liability. The fragile thread in our web, all because *the* Web saw fit to take my battered, beautiful love and rip her to shreds.

Gabby nudges my boot with hers, the movement subtle enough to go unnoticed by the rest of the room. "Pay attention," she mutters, cocking her head towards Solail, who appears torn between telling Finn to shut his mouth and laughing along with him. "If we're going to save Val, we need whatever is under that cloth. Now's not the time for hysterics."

I bite my tongue against the flood of vitriol that threatens to spew from my lips and clear my throat until Finn finally quiets. "What *is* it, Solail?"

Her smile is sharp enough to cut, and I'm again struck with the thought that Solail would be a formidable, terrifying enemy. "Something so valuable, so illegal, any denizen of the realm caught with one without permission gets a one-way ticket to the endless nightmare of the Pit. Which, my clueless dehmi children, is a fate worse than any death you can imagine."

Satisfied she has our full attention, the crone straightens her spine and unwraps her bundle. The four of us lean in, wide-eyed and breathless at the spectacle nestled in her lap. "Behold," she says with all the pompous regality of a circus grandmaster, "a wyrok scale."

Chapter 4
Scales and Stories

- Conall -

Approximately a foot long from rounded base to tapered tip, the wyrok scale gleams brighter than a polished gemstone in its canvas nest. Its surface shimmers and shudders in a million shades of rich brown, from the darkest earthen umber to liquid bronze. The warm firelight hits its broad, flat face and the light refracts into shards that bounce off every surface in Solail's cluttered home. The space is instantly transformed into a glowing hybrid of a disco ball and a tapestry, colors seeming to become richer, more *real* under the scale's shine.

Several quiet gasps fill the stunned silence of the room. Finn and Gaius stare open-mouthed—even Gabby's gaze is filled with wonder. Her malfunctioning Sight must have missed forewarning her of this event, but she doesn't appear to be upset at its failure this time. Perhaps pleasant surprise is a novel experience for her.

"It's beautiful," my sister breathes. Gabby twists her arms to watch the scale's sparkle set her plum skin ablaze. She's not wrong; the massive slice of keratin is indeed magnificent. However, its captivating beauty is inconsequential if it can't help us reach our destination: the mysterious depths of the Crystal Forest and whatever they contain that could—that *will*—save Valorie.

33

As if she hears my thoughts, Solail folds the cloth back over the scale, muting its brilliance and drawing our attention back to her. "It's more than some pretty trinket," she says. "This scale is your ticket through the portals."

Another tangentially helpful statement. I drum my fingers back and forth against the arm of my chair and seethe. *Tap tap tap, tap tap tap*, a rolling beat to ward off the monster roaring in my gut.

Gabby's slender hand covers my own—another silent reminder and reprimand. "And how do we use it, Solail?" she asks firmly, her fingers clenching and unclenching against mine as she speaks. Something is going on inside her head, but Gabby never tells any of us about what she's Seen until she believes the time is right.

The old woman rolls her eyes. "Well, that's easy," she scoffs as though we're naughty students who should have these answers already memorized. "You simply take it with you through the portals, and the magic that prevents entrance into the portal will recognize the scale the same as it would a live wyrok. Imprecise magic, those portal wards. Anyway," she continues, waving a hand across the wrapped scale, "you don't need to *do* anything. This here's your ticket through, simple as sin."

Lids closed, I breathe a small sigh of relief. A tiny crack appears in the mountain of anxiety resting on my lungs. We have our key through the portals—a small step forward, but an important one.

Valorie's face swims through my turbulent mind—stormcloud irises with crinkles at the edges, full lips stretched into a carefree grin, wild curls tangled in a summer breeze. Something flips, and the colors drain away like rain down a window, leaving her wan and faded. Half dream, half nightmare, she's a mixture of the vibrant woman I was willing to throw the universe away for and the sallow, lifeless facsimile I left behind at the

Haven. I snap my eyes open and shudder, willing the image to fade. It does not comply.

I'm coming for you, Wildcat. I won't let you down again, I swear it.

"That's great and all," Gaius drawls, a lick of flame dancing leisurely between his knuckles, "except we have no map and therefore no way to even *get* to the portals in the first place, not to mention a method of knowing which one to go *through* if we were to find a portal entrance."

Solail licks her fingertips and slowly leans across the table towards Gaius. She pinches the jumping ember, leaving it nothing but smoke drifting in the inches of space between her icy glare and Gaius' smirk. "If you were twice as quick to listen and half as quick to jump in with that mouth of yours, you'd be much better company," she whispers through the swirling gray.

Quick as the cat catching the canary, Gaius leans into Solail's ear and murmurs, "I can promise you, my mouth makes me *fantastic* company."

Gabrielle squeaks, horrified. Before she can apologize, the crone jerks away from Gaius until her spine slams against the plush backing of her chair. A hoarse, braying laugh wheezes from Solail, loud and grating and full of surprised delight.

"Now *that*, you soot-loving little urchin," she gasps, wiping a stray tear, "was quite amusing. Keep it up and I might end up enjoying your visit after all. Anyway, back to business." Solail takes far too long to adjust herself in her seat, and my teeth continue their attempt to grind each other into dust.

When she finally continues her explanation, I hang on every word as if it's a lifeline directly to Valorie. "The scale of a wyrok does not carry the magic of its original host. You'll find no flashy displays of elemental magic or shapeshifting when you touch its surface. But, that's no bother, for the bit of power left hidden within is precisely what you need to find your way to the depths of the Crystal Forest. Hold tight to the scale and think of your destination, and—provided your intent is pure—the magic in its depths will guide you. Follow its lead and you need not fear getting lost among the treacherous wilds of the realms."

My siblings talk amongst themselves, murmuring their interest and appreciation. We're no strangers to powerful mystic objects, but never before has one meant this much to a mission. At once both key and compass—the wyrok scale is valuable indeed. My fingertips itch to grab the unassuming bundle from Solail's lap and hoard it away before something falls from the sky to shatter my hopes into dust.

A chime sounds from within the depths of the cozy kitchen to our right, accompanied by the rich smell of meat and bread. Solail places the scale in my lap with a gentle reverence which belies her barked order to Gaius. His lanky frame at her heels, the pair heads into the kitchen and returns several minutes later with a steaming pot pie wrapped in a checkered cloth between Gaius' hands. Fragrant steam rises in curls from the caramelized crust, its surface decorated as intricately as the rest of the house. Mourning doves and centaurs crafted in crisp pastry dance across the pie in a scene almost too tranquil to eat.

Solail has no such qualms. She pulls a large butcher's knife from her dress' sash and carves a giant portion into bowls for each of us, ladling the rich inner stew until the massacred pastry creatures are drowning in a delicious flood. Utensils and napkins make their way around the group and we tuck in.

She may be a prickly, short-tempered old crow, but Solail cooks with the skill of a goddess. The simple meal is bursting with flavor—tender chunks of meat and vegetables melt between crispy, salted crust and savory gravy. The experience is made more delicious by the knowledge we have weeks worth of dried trail rations and hunting ahead of us, dotted sparsely with civilized meals in whatever towns we might come across.

Finn shatters the quiet to ask around a massive mouthful, "Hey, Solail, remember how you said the super-powerful wyrok scale is also super illegal? Why do you have one, then? And how do we know you're not so irritated by all of Gaius' antics, you're giving us some contraband and sending us off to be arrested and thrown in this 'pit' place?"

"You don't," she replies, waving her spoon in his direction. "But, you'll trust me anyway, and you'll get where you're going. As for the tale of how I became one of the few non-wyrok owners of a legal scale? It was a gift—a 'thank you' for my hard work, both in the past and now. A show of trust from the wyrok and the Paragons."

"What do you do?" the words are out of my mouth before I can stop them. I don't *want* to listen to her story—I don't want to do anything to prolong our time here. But, part of me thinks maybe, when we finally find her, Valorie might ask about the details of the old woman in the house by the foggy river. It would prick at the researcher inside her, the part that yearns for every scrap of information. If she finds out I was too impatient to ask, she'll scrunch up her brow and *tsk* at me like a teacher, disappointed I wouldn't have gathered every detail for her perusal. The scene is bittersweet, vivid enough in my mind I could almost lean in and kiss the furrow from between her eyebrows.

It aches.

Solail sets her empty bowl on the low table. "When young wyrok reach their age of maturity, they're sent on an expedition with one goal: journey to a set destination, gather an object as proof, and then make their way back home in one piece without getting lost. It's meant to prove their prowess over the intricacies of the Underworld. Make it back to the Crystal Forest, present your token, and become an adult with full rights and responsibilities in their society. This—" she gestures around us, "—is their midpoint. They enter my home, make much less of a ruckus than you all, and then leave with a little something to prove they stopped by. I enjoy the polite company, and the wyrok elders take comfort knowing I'm here to look out for their young ones."

"Here I thought you had a bit of a hoarding problem," Gaius muses as he scrapes the last bits of food onto his spoon.

There's one small detail not adding up in Solail's story. "And the wyrok chose you to help them instead of one of their own people because...?"

"Because she's the first Seer," Gabrielle interrupts quietly. "Aren't you, Solail? You're the one who created Avallea."

CHAPTER 5
Gifts

- CONALL -

"**I** had heard you were a bright one," Solail says to Gabrielle, a genuine grin lighting up her creased visage and making her appear much younger, "I'm glad to see Esraa and Amon weren't wrong."

"Wait, what?" I blurt. "There's no way." The first Avallean, here in a shadowy corner of nowhere at the edge of death's domain? Impossible.

The old crow's icepick eyes bore into mine. "There is exactly one way, obviously, since I'm sitting right in front of you. Esraa and Amon sent you to me for a reason. Would they send you on a wild goose chase to waste your time? To waste the life of your precious human? You know they would not. So, if it isn't true, then who's the liar: the Paragons who sent you here, or your pretty sister and her Sight?"

Pure silence descends on the room. Finn gapes as if seeing Solail for the first time, and I've half a mind to join him. The snippy, hard-assed old woman we've been trading attitudes with all evening is the legendary Seer responsible for the creation of our homeworld? I'm torn between demanding insight into our future and groveling on the floor for forgiveness.

Gaius leans over and ruffles his sister's hair, pride gleaming in his eyes. "Good show, sis," he says. "Nothing gets by you, not even a crotchety old woman with fantastic pie-making skills."

"Watch it, boy, or I'll string you up outside and let the mist creatures have at you," Solail barks. "Seer or no Seer, age won't stop me from shoving my foot down your throat."

I'd like to learn exactly what kind of creatures live in this mist, but Gaius merely slips her another sarcastic smile and remarks, "Solail, honey, I'm not into feet." He wiggles his booted foot in her direction. "Mine could use a rub, though, if you're offering. But you probably knew that, didn't you? You being a famous Seer and all."

"Gai!" Gabrielle screeches, hands flying to her mouth. "Have some respect!"

"Oh, it's fine, honey," Solail replies, "He's harmless. Plus, I think he's growing on me. Like a tumor, or an abscess."

"I don't understand," Finn cuts in, all smiles and bashful, dimpled charm. "Why live here? No offense ma'am, but I would think a legendary hero would be entitled to something more...palatial."

"I didn't want to live in some golden tower, eating fruit while a legion of servants primps and pampers me. I grew up in the mud—having a roof over my head is still a miracle to a small part of me. Here, I get my privacy, and I get to have a purpose. Given the choice, would you want to go from capable dehmi to soft, sheltered nothings? Would you trade a hard yet happy life full of fulfilling work for a well-earned bland existence after everything you've been through?"

The room grows quiet, each of us searching inward for answers to her question. I gaze around and let my siblings filter through my field of view, imagining how each of them would respond in an effort to ignore my own churning mind.

Gabrielle barely gets a choice, blessed and cursed to always live at the mercy of her powers. She would sooner rip her own arm off than hold her tongue if she Saw something which could help someone. I'd pay a hefty sum to give her a reprieve, but the closest she'll get is the fog obscuring her inner eye while in this realm. She's stuck, and I'd bet good money part of her curses the twist of the Web which chose her for this life.

Finn shifts uncomfortably in his chair, catching the corner of my vision. He's harder to place than Gabby. He loves helping others, but he would likely be equally content to spend his days baking bread and training climbing vines to ensconce him in a world of his own making, only emerging when he was bored of solitude. Finn's jokes and sweet temper would be a boon whenever he chose to show his face in public—he's the most beloved of our foursome for a reason.

My final sibling—the mischief-maker and king of chaos himself—blows tiny sparks at his sister and revels in her small laugh and playful swat. Gaius presents himself as crass and unfeeling, but I watched him sneak out of the Haven on more than one occasion when we were younger to fight neighborhood fires when the humans weren't able to handle them. His heart may be buried under layers of soot and weighted dice, but it's genuine. Nothing matters more to Gaius than Gabrielle, though. His answer would depend on hers—he would follow his twin to the ends of the universe and find ways to be useful wherever she settled, or fade into smoke and obscurity if she preferred.

As for me? I'd forfeit every shred of magic and immortality and live in this realm of death forever if it meant seeing Valorie's smile light up my world again.

"We need to go," I toss the words into the room, buttoning up my coat. I carefully place the scale into a quilted front pocket on my pack where it will be easily accessible on the trail and rise to my feet. "Come on, quickly now. Valorie can't wait forever." Turning to Solail, I extend my hand towards her seated form. "Thank you for your hospitality and your help. It's been an honor."

She reaches to meet me, but where I expect a frail handshake, I instead find a firm shove against my forearm. I stumble backward, unprepared for the force. The backs of my knees hit the lip of the chair and I clatter into my seat, the full pack crunching uncomfortably between my spine and the cushion. My heart pounds, and I whip my bag around to open the padded front flap. If Solail has broken the scale, I'll kill her. Or get as close as possible to killing someone who is presumably already dead.

My lungs deflate with relief—the bronzed sliver twinkles merrily at me in the low lights, completely unscathed.

"Sit down, everyone," she orders, at once both casual and firm. "You didn't think I'd let you leave without a parting gift, did you?"

Twenty minutes pass, and Solail has not emerged from her bedroom. After proclaiming she had "gifts" we simply couldn't leave without, she retreated into the darkened rear room without any further explanation. Muffled shuffling and rustling sounds have periodically emerged, but no sign of the crone. I have no clue what these surprises could be, but they couldn't possibly be worth losing half an hour of travel time and counting. We'll already be working our way through the mists to find a place for our camp in the darkness at this point; I'll be damned if I waste my whole night waiting for an old woman's castoffs.

At last, Solail's even footsteps grow closer. Her slight figure appears in the doorway, lit by the firelight and carrying a leather bag seemingly older than myself and my siblings put together. She slings the weathered sack onto the table and upends it, dumping the contents onto the wood. A smaller bag made of black fabric and full to near bursting, a battered ocarina, and a meter-long string of pearls fashioned into a loop at one end.

Not a single one of them makes any sort of sense, a fact I'm positive Solail is aware of.

"These are only half of what I'm able to give to you," she says, gesturing to the messy display. "But, this half I can explain somewhat. All three of these items will help you on your journey in particular ways—ways I'm sure you haven't got solutions for inside those fancy packs."

She points towards the lumpy black sack, its contents straining against the drawstring closure. Small, brightly colored corners poke out of the gap at its mouth, like a geode's innards. "This is a bag full of polished Narvian sea-glass. There is a hamlet on your way which would have nothing to do with your coins and bills. They deal purely in nature's spoils, both as currency and faith offerings. This is enough to obtain whatever you should be lacking by that point in your trip."

Solail's picks up the ocarina and turns it over in her lined palms as she speaks. "Deep within a forest, not too far from here, lies a special manner of many-limbed beast. Large, yet wily, with glowing orange eyes and bright blue fangs. They're vicious and territorial, but a quick tune will have them eating out of your hands. Beware, however, for their sister species has black fangs and becomes enraged by music. The two look identical except for the fangs, so mind the color. I'd hate to have some wyrok stripling bring this ocarina back to me in splinters a few months from now."

Gabrielle shudders, her fists clenched in her lap. Logically, I know it would be best if we were to avoid conflict with these monsters entirely. But, there's a feral energy in my locked muscles begging to be let free, to finally be able to unleash my pent up fear and anger upon something I could rend and destroy without restraint. I won't seek these beasts, but I also won't be disappointed if we cross paths with the black-fanged variety. Surely, they would fall quickly to a pack of dehmi on high alert, especially ones harboring a monster of their own, howling for release.

We shift our attention to the final item on the table. Solail lifts the long, glimmering strand from the wood, twining the pearls through her gnarled fingers in the soft light until they seem to glow from within. "Now these," she says softly, "are some of my favorites. I hate to part with them, and I'm expecting you four to find a way to get them back to me. These are all loans, you hear me?" At our rapid nods, she continues with a *humph*, "When you come to an impassable lake—you'll know the one, it's absolutely massive—dip your toes into the water and wait. Then, use the pearls to hitch a ride to the far banks."

"That's it?" Finn asks, incredulous. "How exactly do we use the pearls? What is this ride? If we trade the pearls away for safe passage, how will we bring them back to you?"

Solail chuckles and begins to put the three gifts back into her bag. "If I told you everything, you wouldn't have to work at all. And, more importantly, I'd have much less fun."

I open my mouth to demand more information, determined to ensure the fastest passage possible, but Gabrielle covers my lips with her palm to muffle my protests. "Thank you, Solail. We're honored, and we promise to return your items." Gabby removes her hand, fixes me with a glare, then turns to our brothers. "Let's go, boys."

"Always so quick to be off," Solail croons. The hair on the back of my neck rises at her tone and the silky smile she's wearing. "There's one more present I have waiting for you, if you're interested. But, this one might be less welcome than the rest. It takes a strong heart to hold a prophecy until it comes to pass."

A prophecy? Prophecies are dangerous business, a double-bladed phenomenon every dehmi is warned about from a young age. While Seers like Gabrielle and Solail are rare compared to the elemental affinities, most dehmi will meet at least one during their life. The temptation to beg or barter for insight into your future is strong, but a prophecy destroys as often as it helps. They're much more ephemeral than a normal glimpse into the Web, often leaving their receiver with more questions than answers for years to come. Horror stories of dehmi who are driven mad or into early, reckless graves in their desire to fulfill—or escape—their prophecies are no mere fictitious cautionary tales. In the right minds, knowing a tidbit of your future can lead to greatness. But, for a feeble consciousness, it can kill far faster than ignorance ever could.

A prophecy could be the edge I need to save Valorie.

"I'm in," I say without hesitation.

Gaius nods. "Me too. Why not? I can handle it," he says with his trademark smirk. He might fool Solail, but I know he's thought the decision through. We all have, with a Seer for a sister.

Finn and Gabrielle both follow suit, agreeing to shoulder whatever the Web deigns to show tonight. I'm initially surprised by Gabrielle's choice, but then I recall a conversation with her from our teenage years, one where she explained how a Seer has trouble Seeing themselves clearly. This could be her only chance for a clear view from an outside perspective—and from the first Seer, no less.

Solail claps, delighted. "You children are much more interesting than I thought you'd be. All right, let's start with the burly one. No time to waste, else the angry one might finally escape his chains." She cocks her head in my direction before focusing intently on Finn. Her expression drifts into vacancy for several long seconds. Small beads of sweat form on Finn's forehead as we wait, the only sign of his nervousness. I doubt he's regretting his choice, but it wouldn't matter at this point. Once the process has started, it can't be stopped.

Three slow blinks, then Solail begins to speak in a low, unsettling monotone with her eyes half-open and hazy. "Creature of leaves and loam: In a land of green and gold, justice will bring you to what you seek most within your soul."

Finn jerks in his seat, a small motion I'm not sure my siblings notice. Their gazes are locked on Solail as she emerges from her trance and turns towards Gaius, the next in line. Finn takes several deep breaths and fixes me with a wobbly half-smile that doesn't come close to being believable. I know Finn, and he'll be mulling over the prophecy's single sentence for a long while. At least his sounds pleasant—no blood or gore involved.

Solail has already returned to her stupor by the time I turn in her direction. Gaius fidgets minutely, nervous sparks flitting around his shoulders while he picks at a loose thread on his dark denim pants. "Creature of smoke and cinders: The fire who travels in shadows should beware the glare of the enemy, lest his hubris find him caught in the sun with nowhere to hide."

Now *that* is a foreboding prophecy.

With a small scoff and a wave of his hand, Gaius glances into the fire and brushes the words away like flies. The wooden armchair creaks as he slings his legs over its arm and pulls an enameled switchblade from his pants pocket. The small blade blurs, whirling through the air between his outstretched hands as though taking flight. His aloof, unaffected performance is next to flawless—I'd believe him myself, if it weren't for those same motes of flame shuddering around his hairline.

Gabrielle blanches, her skin ashen with worry as Solail slowly comes to and shifts into my sister's space. Wrinkled hands meet the flawless skin of youth as she gently takes hold of Gabby's wrists. After the last foretelling, we're all visibly less enthused about the prospect of dealing with two more. Gaius still refuses to look at anyone, and Finn's head is in his hands. I catch him peeking at our side of the room from between his interlocked fingers. He gives a tiny, practically inaudible groan as Solail begins to speak once again.

"Creature of secrets and starlight," Solail croons, her voice softer for my sister than for the others. The entire room leans in to hear the power of two Seers collide—even the flames in the hearth seem to gutter with anticipation. "When two become one, turn to the right hand of death, man and not man, for there lies salvation."

Death and salvation united. And the promise of a joining, or a loss? A prophecy as enigmatic as its recipient, who nods her thanks at the old crone. Solail graces her with a gentle smile, warm and fleeting.

And then it's my turn.

Locking stares with the first Seer, I expect an experience resembling the countless times I've asked Gabrielle for a glimpse into the Web. As her consciousness fades into somewhere I cannot follow, however, a chill covers my skin in goosebumps. Where my sister's Sight is gentle yet unavoidable, this is a winter's gale to Gabby's summer breeze. It's nothing like what I'm used to, and a primitive part of my brain screams I'm not ready for what is about to happen.

"Creature of fate defied and remade," Solail's voice is a trap without a safety latch. I'm a fish on a line, powerless as it reels me in for the killing blow. "To heal is but the twin face of death, as love is twin to hate, and help is twin to hurt. Be careful not to flip your coins in your haste, for Fate does not return what has been paid."

As though a switch flicks with her final word, she leans back in her chair, lids closed and face waxy. I am gifted with no further useful information, only enumerable questions. "Two sides to every coin" is a human phrase I'm familiar with, but this went beyond simple idiom. Who is being hurt or healed? Is it Valorie? If another soul hurts her after all of this, I'll kill them. If they're dead, I'll kill them twice. And what price is being paid? The two of us have paid enough already, but the Web obviously doesn't agree.

"Con," Gabby murmurs, nudging my knee with hers, "Let's go." I didn't even notice my siblings rising, but they're already packed and ready to leave. Finn and Gaius wait by the open front door, expressions closed off and devoid of their usual jokes.

With a quick recheck to ensure the scale is still resting safely in its pocket, I clutch the straps of my pack in a white-knuckled grip and meet my brothers at the door. As we head into the night, Solail calls through the foggy darkness, "May the Web weave your path straight and simple, children. And don't forget to return my trinkets, or I'll bake you into pies."

I'm not entirely sure she's joking.

49

CHAPTER 6
The Cyribaum

- VALORIE -

We've been walking for ten thousand years.

If I asked Ceraun, I'm sure he would say it's only been a few hours since we left the glen where he found me. He'd point out how easy it is to tell the approximate time based on the sun's pattern across the sky, the glowing ball's movement showing it's been a mere four hours and not a small eternity of endless, dragging footsteps.

But I wouldn't agree. Maybe days here are longer than on Earth, or maybe the sun only moves when I want it to, or time passes in leaps and stutters here depending on someone's mood. Who knows?

Something has to be off, because even Charlie would be struggling by now, especially as the soft dirt of the deep woods has given way to the firmer, rockier ground of lightly forested screes. We've stopped at the edge of yet another sloping valley, and I don't know how much longer I can force my legs to move before they revolt.

"Ceraun," I pant, too tired to be embarrassed at the way my voice wheezes into the wind, "you said…cache was 'nearby'…it's been hours…"

His majestic, stupid blue head swivels around to face me. My reflection in his iris shows exactly how disheveled I've become during our little hike. Sweat-soaked tee smudged more brown than black by a collage of

50

dirt and dust, frizzy, puffy mass of black curls doing its best impression of a sheep atop my head, and knees stained green from the two times I fell over slick patches of moss I failed to notice until my feet were sliding out from under me. I'm a mess. All I want is to get to this damned cache Ceraun keeps dangling like a proverbial carrot whenever I falter or need to rest.

I expect a scoff, but his mental voice is surprisingly gentle after my endless weakness and complaining. *Peace*, kynaira, he reassures the sluggish mush of my brain. *The walking is not agreeing with you, but we truly are nearly at our destination.* He points his tail across our path and down a nearby slope. *Look at the base of the far ridge.*

I have to squint against the setting sun, but finally his destination comes into view. The windswept cliff we're on arches over a flat expanse of land, studded by large boulders and scrub brush for what must be a mile before it reaches the edge of a copse of gray-barked trees. At first glance, all appears to be normal, but—

"There," I call, "those piled rocks. They're where we're heading, aren't they?"

Ceraun's hum is unmistakably pleased. *You have a good eye*, kynaira.

"The rest of the stones in the area are in small groups—ones and twos, the occasional group of three. But, that pile has at least four stacked up. Plus, it's a perfect spot to conceal a burrow or warren. If it wasn't you using the space, some animal would undoubtedly be living in there." I give him a side-eyed glance and raise one eyebrow. "You don't seem the type to want competition around, so I figured it was a safe guess."

He snorts, a trail of putrid smoke drifting from one nostril. *No creature around here would be competition for a wyrok.*

My chuckle turns into a groan as it rattles my aching muscles. "All right, you can beat your chest later, big guy."

Why would I do that? Ceraun asks. *What purpose would hitting my own chest serve?*

"It's an expression. On Earth, it's used when a guy is trying to act tough. Guess it doesn't translate well over here, huh?"

A dizzying wave of despair and homesickness hits me with the force of a monsoon, sending my knees to the dusty ground. For a moment, I had forgotten this wasn't a simple hike through the Alleghenies with David and Charlie, tossing jokes around to keep our minds off how much we would rather be eating takeout on the couch. I'm in the middle of nowhere with a mind-reading dragon who glitters in the sun the way my dad's sun catcher collection sparkles in his office window. We're on our way to some secret stash to get supplies for a trip to his hometown, and then two god-people I've never actually met are going to squish me back into my corpse so I can get married. Oh, and then I'll stop being human entirely, if I still even count as human in whatever zombie-ghost state I'm in now.

My shoulders sag under the weight of everything I've lost, everything I have yet to face. How the hell am I going to do this? It's all too much.

A soft slithering sound filters through the numbness a moment before a heavy pressure bands around my midsection. Ceraun's sun-warmed tail is draped across my lap, its tapered tip curved to rest along my spine in a gentle, lizard-like hug. His snout taps against the top of my head with a soft chuff. *Peace,* kynaira, he says. *You may be lonely, but I will not leave you alone. Let your feelings become your armor, not your enemy.*

He's right. I can't afford to fall apart, not when there's still so far to go. Ceraun and I will make it through this journey to his home, then I'll become a burr in everyone's sides until Esraa and Amon fix all of this mess. I'm going to reunite with Conall and the others if it's the last thing I do. But none of it can happen if I'm blubbering on the ground, lost in memories of a past I cannot change.

"Let your feelings become your armor," he said—and I will.

I stumble to my feet, dust my hands off onto my equally dirty pants, and square my shoulders against the setting sun. With each deep inhale, I picture everyone I left behind—family and friends, human and dehmi. David, Charlie, Mom, Dad, Gabrielle, Finn, Gaius, even Marguerite and Domenic. And Conall, his expression beatific on the night I promised my forever to him. Love and loss, pain and pleasure, hope and hurt swirl together until they become my blood, my heartbeat, my strength. No matter what, the only way back to them is forward.

"How do we get to the cache, Ceraun?" I ask, toes curved over the cliff's edge. There is no visible path down this side of the incline. I have a sinking feeling I know what his answer will be, and it isn't going to involve an elevator.

Sure enough, he points a sled-sized forepaw straight down the slope. *You're looking at it,* he chuckles. The tip of his tail flicks in front of my nose, a taunt. *Hold on tight, we don't have time for tending to injuries.*

I give his wide back a longing stare. "There's no chance of you giving me a ride, is there?" No harm in asking, right?

Another patronizing chuckle, and I remind myself punching a dragon would likely hurt me more than him. *The center strip of my spine is covered in reverse-set, razored scales meant to protect against attacks from above. We aren't made for being ridden—our younglings are born able to cling to our underbelly fur in emergencies. I can assure you, without proper padding, you'd rather walk.*

My already-sore inner thighs tense at the mental image of the chafing a ride full of bladed scales would cause. *No, thanks.* I guess I'm walking.

Grumbling about the uselessness of dragon companions who aren't able to be ridden, I grab hold of my makeshift scaled guide-rope and begin the descent.

When Ceraun said he needed to gather more wood before dark, it didn't occur to me he meant *without me*. As in, "Stay here in this creepy, Stonehenge-esque pile of rubble, Val, while I go off and disappear into the trees to find things to light on fire for the night." If my brain wasn't overchurned mush, I would have caught on in time to put up more of a coherent argument against being left to fend for myself. As it is, I barely managed a squeak in protest towards his retreating rear legs, his body already halfway lost in the branches and brush.

He assured me there are no predators within miles before padding off into the copse, but my heart refuses to settle for at least fifteen minutes after his departure. Every creak or rattle is an alien beast skulking through the undergrowth, waiting to pounce. The strange, pin-straight trees become spindly beings creeping closer when my back is turned. I fling myself around to check time and time again, then giggle breathlessly at my own childish fright. Eventually, the gloom of deep twilight fades into the mundane, and I busy myself with peeking into the bags and boxes Ceraun left hidden cleverly between the rocks. My fingers itch to organize, to take inventory, to help somehow, but the contents of each bag are already meticulously packaged. Plus, half the items are mysteries to me, and breaking a tool we cannot proceed without isn't on my shortlist of plans for the evening.

With nothing else to do, the comfort of a few minutes off my feet and the intrigue of an unknown nightfall beckon in a siren song. Heels tapping against the boulder beneath me, I watch as the last dregs of evening melt down to meet the horizon. The sun gives up its battle with a final wave of orange and violet, and then we're plunged into a dark so deep I'd believe Ceraun if he said the sky had fallen while he was away.

I stare into the black, marveling at the lack of moon or other celestial bodies. Whatever place served as inspiration for this slice of the Underworld must have existed in a lonely corner of the cosmos. The absence of stars is unnerving. My eyes squint, searching for familiar pinpricks of light in the velvety darkness.

And then it peels apart into a riot of colors which puts the Aurora Borealis to shame.

Wild licks of blue and purple ripple upwards from the horizon in great swaths. Greens in shades of emerald and chartreuse smear down to meet them, colors blurring into unnameable hues where they touch. Fiery reds and their milder coral cousins dance merrily between the cooler tones, flipping and swirling in an entrancing almost-dance. Between the quiet rasps of my own breaths, I swear I hear a lilting combination of music and laughter.

The Cyribaum dance merrily tonight.

I squeal, barely managing to catch myself before I tumble off my makeshift chair. The magic of the sky had me captivated, allowing Ceraun to approach completely undetected. Imaginary tree gremlins and crackling sticks? They don't have a chance against me, I'm Mr. Miyagi. Surprisingly real giant dragons who could swallow me whole? They can peek right over my shoulder and I evidently won't even notice.

"Ceraun, wear a bell or something!" I gasp, clutching my silent chest.

Unperturbed, he blows a ring of smoke directly into my face. Can smoke be snarky? Judging by the quirk on the corner of his reptilian mouth, the answer is yes.

I settle once again against the rock, my eyes cast back towards the heavens. "What are the Cyribaum?" I ask with a small shiver. Without the sun, the stone is no longer warm and comfortable beneath me. My thin layers aren't enough to shield me from the chill, but finding a warmer spot would require me to stop watching the performance overhead.

Ceraun, ever watchful, settles his cheek against my side. The warmth rolling off his skin instantly brings me back to a comfortable temperature. My personal scaled space heater.

The Cyribaum are a race, he answers quietly, as captivated as I am by the show. *A species of elemental spirits who choose to weave themselves amongst the skies after death instead of being beholden to an earthen home. In life, they are largely terrestrial, tied to their individual elements, but in death, they become what you see before you.*

"So they're not a 'what', they're a 'who'?" I whisper. Something about the magic overhead demands hushed voices.

Yes.

"Where do they go during the day? Is there somewhere else where it's night at that time, like on a planet, or do all the spaces operate on the same day-night cycle?" My scientific interest is piqued, the overworked emotional section of my brain gratefully acquiescing control to the biologist inside who's slavering for facts about this strange new world.

He butts his brow ridge against my side affectionately, and I tell myself it's his version of a giant dragon hug. I hope he doesn't stop—I could really use a hug, or ten, today. *Think of the Underworld as less of a single world and more of a universe unto itself, fashioned of billions of tiny planets, each with their own cycles. The sentient beings inhabiting this place exist with an awareness of the magic of the realm, but the Underworld's power works to emulate their homes as accurately as possible, only on a smaller scale. And with less hardship.* He snuffles, a small sound for such a large creature. *As for the Cyribaum, not even my elders know where they go when the night is over. We don't concern ourselves with their secrets. They cause no conflicts, start no wars, break no laws. They simply...exist.*

We sit together in the quiet for some time, until the real question burning in my gut works its way to the surface in a tremulous voice, fragile as a bubble from a child's wand. "Do you think they're afraid when their time comes to an end, Ceraun?" I ask the hulking mass beside me, his scales oil-hued in the multicolored darkness of the night. "Do you think they worry about taking that step off the edge of everything and into the open sky?"

If it were me, would I have the courage to take the leap, alone at the edge of eternity? To leave everything I knew and become something beautiful, but strange? All with the hopes my people would be waiting for me when it was over?

In a way, it doesn't sound much different than the path I've already chosen.

High above my head, the Cyribaum paint the dome of the universe in their wild glow. They're chaotic, yet there's unmistakable patterns to their movement, resembling steps of a dance I'll never quite grasp. It looks like...

Freedom.

"They seem happy, don't you think?" I whisper to Ceraun.

He rubs his nose against my arm, scales scraping gently along my now-warm skin. *I think so,* kynaira. *But, not even a wyrok's wings are powerful enough to reach their domain and ask. And even if I could, I do not think I would. I'd hate to interrupt them just to sate my own curiosity.*

We fade once again into a peaceful silence, content to watch the Cyribaum dance and listen to their strange, laughing music until not even Ceraun's presence is enough to keep the chill at bay.

Come. Ceraun's mental voice breaks the silence, startling another small jump from me. *I came across a stream while I was gathering wood. It's not far—you can bathe while I make camp and get the fire settled.*

I slide down from the boulder, blessedly landing on my feet and not flat on my ass. "And what about you? You get to stay stinky and warm while I play in a cold river in the dark?" I force a chuckle, but part of me truly balks at the idea of bathing alone in a random body of water, especially one where I won't even recognize the calls of local fauna in time to know whether they'd want to make a meal of me. I'd much rather stick around and help set up camp.

A bark of laughter reverberates through my head and into my bones. *I already bathed. Nice try, though. Now, follow me—I want you washed up and back here before it's too late to eat.*

"Yes, dad," I grumble. So much for staying at camp. Guess I'm going swimming.

My footsteps rustle and crunch through the underbrush, obscenely loud next to his silent footfalls. The fact I'm heavily dragging my feet probably doesn't help with their volume, but how else would I show Ceraun exactly how enthused I am about this part of his plan?

Maturity, who? She wasn't invited on this little walk.

Entirely too quickly for my liking, the gurgling of water reaches my eardrums, and we round a tree to find a slowly flowing stream with a bank pebbled in smooth, gray stones. Through a gap in the treetops, the dance of the Cyribaum provides ample light. The whirling colors create the intense sensation of being instructed to bathe in the middle of a rave, but at least it isn't pitch black.

Ceraun nudges a soft, dark bundle in my direction before turning towards the cache. *Check there first,* he says, then he's gone, tail giving one last flick in front of my nose before it follows him into the trees.

"Bye then," I grunt, irritated. What if some sort of river monster is waiting for me? He didn't even check to make sure the water was safe before he left. I'm no damsel in distress, expecting him to bend over backward to carry me over puddles and cut my food for me, but there is a clear disparity between us when it comes to lethality.

Eager to be done as quickly as possible, I jog the ten feet to where Ceraun left his bundle. The sack is filled to the brim with layers of soft, dark-colored clothing, their true shade impossible to discern in the ever-shifting light of the Cyribaum. At the bottom, a length of plush fabric roughly my height is rolled tightly around itself in a log, and a chunk of something pale and mildly waxy is nestled underneath. Its edges crumble and smear in my hands, pods of some type of plant studding the brick in uniform patterns.

I inhale deeply, then smile. It's soap—a thick piece of milky-colored soap resembling those found in any artisanal shop on Earth, creamy smooth and smelling strongly of citrus notes akin to lemon or bergamot.

The plant bits dotting the surface don't are softer than their counterparts on Earth, but the scent is close enough to lavender to conjure up the memories of Conall constantly lurking near the surface of my subconscious. Maybe this bath won't be terrible after all.

Gathering my spoils, I lay them on a flat rock near the shore, then tiptoe towards the water. To my surprise, the gentle current doesn't freeze my feet when I reach the edge and step in. It's a far cry from the near-boiling temperature I would choose for a bath, but "not freezing" is better than I expected. Still unpleasant, but bearable.

I bathe quickly, longing for the fire's warmth and the company I've already grown to rely on. Ceraun is occasionally prickly and often strange in a way that makes it intensely obvious we're from completely different worlds, but he's kind and surprisingly funny. In my eyes, we're fast friends, the type I'd want to somehow keep after this is all over. I can only hope he feels the same—I'll probably never be brave enough to ask him myself.

Hair dripping and skin knobbly with goosebumps, I turn back to our makeshift camp. The light of Ceraun's newly stoked fire is a flickering beacon in the night. It flits between the trees, guiding me back to the stacked stones and my companion. A happy hum—a pleasant version of "Johanna" from *Sweeney Todd*—works its way from my throat as I jog to the edge of the copse.

And then freeze, because, although Ceraun is nowhere in sight, I'm not the only one by the fireside.

"Who the fuck are you?" I shout. If I am able to keep the intruder at bay, Ceraun will return before long. I hope.

The interloper turns, his slightly choppy, shoulder-length electric blue locks tinged green at the ends by the fire's glow. A faint dusting of fuzz, the same strange color as what tops his head, coats the backs of his muscled arms—over a pattern oddly akin to scales—and down the center of his chest until it meets a pair of loose-fitting black pants. At his back, a pair of bat-like wings rustle. A smug grin tilts the edges of his lips beneath a strong nose and topaz eyes. Familiar eyes.

"Hello, *kynaira*," he rumbles in a voice I've only heard inside my own head.

"How? Wha-? You're supposed to be a *dragon*!" I'm a spluttering mess, but can you blame me? The last thing I needed on such an exhausting day was another surprise. I don't know if my currently-silent heart can still arrest, but Ceraun has clearly decided to test it and find out.

His laugh is soft yet full-bodied, somehow realer now I'm hearing it in the open air. "A wyrok is a being of two forms: the native, which you like to refer to as a dragon despite my objections, and the upright." He spreads his arms to his sides, *clawed* fingers open and palms facing in my direction. "I'm assuming you can figure out which one I've decided to take for the time being."

Stupid, smug dragon-who-isn't-even-always-a-dragon. "You don't think this is something you maybe could have *told* me before you sprung it on me at the end of the world's longest day ever?"

"Which world had this 'longest day ever'?" He asks with faux innocence.

A wordless shriek forces itself through my pressed lips and gritted teeth. I stomp to the edge of the circle of firelight, torn between laughing and screaming and yet smart enough to know this as far as my tantrum can take me. The fire means safety. Ceraun may be on my shit list right now, but I don't want to run. I need a single moment where I feel like I know my up from down. Everything has been topsy-turvy since I woke up dead, and I'd enjoy nothing more than to push a button and have this merry-go-round *stop* for a minute.

Several deep breaths later, I turn back to my new friend and quietly ask, "Why didn't you tell me?"

Ceraun appears chagrined. His hands are clasped before his taut stomach, his head bowed. "I have not spent much time around humans. Most Underworld inhabitants know of the wyrok; we're no secret. It didn't cross my mind until I was setting up camp and decided it would make a fun surprise, a small trick. I see now I have misstepped. My deepest apologies." He punctuates his statement with a deep bow, and the last of my anger slips away into the dark.

From his perspective, it's understandable. He couldn't have known this would be too much, couldn't have known my brain would be too frazzled to see the humor in the situation. It wouldn't be fair to either of us to turn tonight sour over an accident. "It's all good, Ceraun. No harm, no foul."

We settle shoulder to shoulder beside the fire, exhaustion weighing heavily around my neck. Ceraun doles a rich stew from a large pouch over the fire into two smaller pouches, one for each of us. They're strange to eat from, but I guess carrying bowls would be cumbersome over long journeys where space is at a premium.

Between bites, I muse, "I thought the Underworld would be a bit less 'camping trip' and a bit more 'fire and brimstone.'"

Ceraun snorts into his stew pouch. "The Underworld is everything you could imagine. This includes fire and brimstone, although it's mostly relegated to a few volcanic realms and the Pit."

"The Pit?"

He nods. "The Pit is a place of eternal torment, where the worst dregs of life are cast upon their deaths. It is designed to maximize suffering—both lava-filled and yet somehow icy, a magical dome covers the entire area and analyzes the minds of the inhabitants to make sure they never experience an ounce of comfort. The entire space is a massive ravine of jagged shale and glassy ice which never melts even under the lava flowing through the center and down its sheer walls."

I shudder, nearly dropping my half-empty dinner. *Sounds like Hell.* "Sure hope you aren't planning on adding this place to our little tour, Ceraun. I'd like to stay in the friendly part of the Underworld, please and thanks."

"No, but the Pit does not mean the rest of the Underworld is without danger. No system is perfect, and what one species considers horrible may be completely normal to another. It's best to always keep your eyes open and stay cautious. You're unfamiliar with this world—you wouldn't know whether a tribe is friendly or marauding until it's too late." He thumps a fist against his chest. "And travel with a wyrok, of course. It's our job to keep the realms and their inhabitants separate and peaceful, to whatever extent that applies."

A jaw-cracking yawn interrupts my thirst for more knowledge about this fascinating jigsaw puzzle of a world. Ceraun's yellow gaze narrows, as though he's concerned by my exhaustion. "Are you well, *kynaira*?"

I hum, suddenly too weary to form complete sentences. I need to find out what this word means, but I can't muster up the effort to ask. "Just sleepy. Long day, lots of walking."

He smiles, but it doesn't reach the worry in his eyes. Cocking his head towards the piled stones, where two bedrolls—complete with pillows—wait, he says, "Then we'll sleep. My magic will warn us if someone approaches."

Stumbling drunkenly, I somehow make my way across the camp without falling. As I tuck myself into one of the rolls, my eyes swivel upwards and return to the Cyribaum high above. I drift away under their whirling colors while the sounds of strings and merriment blend into a lullaby.

CHAPTER 7

The Wanderer

- VALORIE -

The rough scraping of a calloused palm over my lips heaves me out of unconsciousness and directly into panic. Darkness blankets the campsite, blurred into meaningless shapes by my exhaustion and the shadowy figure hovering above me. My shallow gasp only serves to suction the palm further against my mouth, forcing a small, ineffectual cough from my lungs. I frantically blink the film of sleep away and the empty hole that once held my heartbeat settles somewhat when Ceraun comes into focus, crouched over the head of my makeshift bed. His wings blot out the Cyribaum and leave us in utter blackness until he pulls them in behind his back.

"Shhh," he breathes, quieter than a whisper. A finger rests against his pressed lips, his talon's edge highlighted by the light of the Cyribaum continuing to dance overhead, oblivious to whatever danger lurks beyond Ceraun's protective stance. He pulls his hand slowly from my face, as though afraid I'll scream the moment my mouth is freed. Ceraun doesn't know I've had plenty of practice with keeping quiet. Too much practice.

Another message wrapped in a breath, one that chills my skin: "Someone is here."

As though summoned by Ceraun's statement, a rustling permeates the camp. I can't discern much beyond the dull glow of the coals where our roaring fire once blazed, but the sound continues to emanate from the dense tangle of brush along the trees' edge. My eyes strain between the vague lumps I know are bushes and Ceraun's wide, slitted pupils, flying back and forth in a desperate attempt at communication.

Now would be a great time to turn your mind-speak shit back on, Ceraun! I seethe internally. My damp palms press against the warm inner lining of my blanket as I wait to learn who, or what, has decided to infiltrate our space. Is it an animal? A person? Another wyrok? Whoever it is, they're unfamiliar enough to have his hackles up, and the dragon being concerned does not bode well for me. Our conversation over last night's dinner filters through my brain: *What one species considers horrible may be completely normal to another.*

I hope this encounter lands on my side of "normal".

The noise intensifies, morphing into the quiet thud of footsteps and harsh breathing. A smack, followed by pained muttering, accompanies the roll of a softball-sized stone across the middle of camp. It hits the smoldering coals and sparks fly, illuminating the profile of a man.

Judging by his sudden grin, the fire has given away our huddled hiding place as well.

"Ho there!" He calls, his friendly voice at odds with Ceraun's hostile crouch. The difference in their demeanors would be comical if I wasn't close to being smothered by my guardian. The man's arm raises in a little wave, one quickly shot dead when he moves close enough to notice the malice in Ceraun's golden irises and the way his half-clothed body is practically crushing me into the dirt.

"Ah, a wyrok. Fear not, friend. I would have to be an imbecile to try and come between you and your mate."

Ceraun shakes his head and growls a denial, his glare honed to the sharpness of a dagger's edge. I groan and make a half-hearted attempt to throw him off my sleeping bag. My back is screaming from the contorted position it's spent the last fifteen minutes trapped in—my friend may be content to keep up his caveman act all night, but my bones are not.

"Ceraun," I croak, my attempt at wriggling from the sleeping sack succeeding only in getting my feet tangled up within the fabric's folds. "He can't possibly hurt me when you're going to smother me first." I swivel my head to face the newcomer. "And we aren't mates. Ceraun is a friend. He's helping me with—something important." Perhaps we don't tell the mystery stranger about our trip to the Crystal Forest five minutes after he's birthed from nowhere. It's entirely possible other people aren't supposed to know about Ceraun's home. I shudder as a vivid mental image of a secret fortress filled to the brim with snarling dragons who wouldn't take kindly to me spilling their business forms inside my skull.

Ceraun shifts enough for me to sit up, but no further. "We do not know him, *kynaira*. A poor guardian I'd be to let him slip past my defenses with a wave and a pretty smile."

The man's laugh is almost bright enough to cover the way his eyes bulge when he hears Ceraun's nickname for me. I file his reaction away, but soon I'll make the time to investigate what my so-called guardian has been saying. "I assure you, I have no intentions of harming your...*kynaira*. I merely saw you from up on the ridge and thought you seemed like fine company." He points over our heads towards a section of scree near where Ceraun and I climbed down yesterday afternoon, then returns his earnest stare to the two of us. "Maybe a fun-loving pair such as yourselves has room for one more? The roads are lonesome and dangerous, but you'll surely add a sense of levity."

A wink punctuates his tongue-in-cheek comment, one I can't help but reward with a reluctant chuckle. Ceraun is currently the farthest thing from "fun-loving", all brooding and snarling in the rippling rainbow lights. He's doing a fabulous impression of a grumpy dad at a child's princess birthday party.

I shove at Ceraun's side, launching myself back onto my pillow when he doesn't move an inch. "Come on, dragon-man," I groan, "Light the fire and we can talk without you pissing a circle around my bed."

The stranger springs towards the coals. "Here, let me help," he says, poking a forked stick into the center of the dimly glowing pile.

Ceraun stalks to the fire, his stormy attitude looming over the center of camp as he bends down and sets the half-burned logs ablaze with a hard breath. "A wyrok needs no assistance with fire," he spits at the stranger. "Come, *kynaira*," he calls in a kinder tone, pupils never leaving the newcomer's face, "Warm yourself."

He doesn't need to tell me twice. I scramble to free myself from the bedroll and settle next to Ceraun at the fire's rock-lined edge. The warmth sinks into my bones the way the first sip of coffee warms your chest on a winter morning. As I bask before the blaze the way a lizard does in the sun, I get my first true glimpse of the male requesting to join us.

His age strikes me first—falling somewhere in the gray area between your twenties and thirties where everyone is far too mature and bogged down by life to be a teen but not old enough to feel truly "adult". He's close to my age, alarmingly young to be dead—but yet here we both are, traipsing through the Underworld. I wonder if the chain of events that lead him to this campfire are as horrific as my own.

The fire gilds his edges in oranges and golds, highlighting a choppy, dark brown mop falling close to his glinting black irises. It's mussed but not unkempt, shaggy in an artfully disheveled way models pay large sums for back on Earth. His hard jaw would make him unapproachable and cold if not for the constant smirk playing across his lips. He's seated, but I'd bet the contents of my long-gone wallet he's over six feet tall without his scuffed black boots, with a build closer to Gaius' slim wiriness than Finn's burly brawn.

When my gaze lands back on the stranger's face, his raised eyebrows make it apparent he caught my perusal. "Like what you see?" he asks, flexing dramatically.

I scoff, choosing to ignore him. It's self-preservation. If we don't figure this situation out in the next few minutes, Ceraun is liable to explode. "Let's start at the beginning. What's your name? Are you a human? An Avallean?" If there's a way to tell the two apart on sight alone, I have not been informed of it.

"Dennick, a humble Avallean, at your service," the stranger replies with a flourishing bow. It's impressive considering he remains seated throughout the exchange. His smile spreads as though this is no more than an enjoyable icebreaker. Glancing sideways at the fuming wyrok beside me, I question Dennick's sanity.

Ceraun grunts his derision and breaks into the conversation with a gruff, "Why should we allow you to travel with us, transient?"

"Transient?" I ask. "What do you mean?" The word implies a wanderer, a person passing through without a permanent home. Is this what Dennick is? Someone ephemeral, someone lost?

Ceraun turns towards me, but his eyes never leave Dennick's face. "Remember our talks about the makeup of this world? Inhabitants are instructed to stay within their realms unless accompanied by a wyrok through the portals. Exceedingly rare exceptions are made, mostly for people deemed trustworthy by the elders, and even they are not allowed unfettered travel. Otherwise, movement between realms is prohibited for the safety and tranquility of each realm's occupants. Mental fortitude is of the utmost importance when a being is destined to stay in this place forever."

The glare returns, boring into Dennick hard enough to burn a hole straight into his gut. "*Transients,*" Ceraun sneers, "are lawless heathens who spurn the rules of the Paragons and flit through realms illegally, often with pieces of desecrated wyrok corpses as their false pass through the portals' magics. They care not for the ramifications of their actions, or the futility of their schemes. The entirety of their own assigned realm is not enough majesty to sate their greed."

"And that is all abhorrent, I'm sure, " Dennick replies, his smile faltering for the first time since he entered our camp, "but I opened my eyes to *this* slice of the Underworld's sky. Not another."

"Impossible," Ceraun says. "This realm is supposed to be uninhabited by sentient life; it's why the drop-off points are stationed throughout this area."

Dennick shrugs. "Well, then something went wrong. Do you scent another wyrok on me? If I were using the scale or bone of your kin, would you not be able to tell?" At Ceraun's reluctant silence, he continues. "I awoke here, alone, so long ago I could not count the weeks if you asked it of me. At first, I wandered in hopes I would find other Avalleans, but I found nothing but beasts. The occasional cadre of young wyrok appeared, but I didn't trust them, and so I remained hidden. The Pit is the last place I want to be sent, and a jumped-up youngster with a fire in his belly would surely haul me there before listening to my tale."

His earnest expression bores into me. "But you're a strange pair, a wyrok and something new, so I took my chance. I don't want to be here forever, lost to my own dreams and memories."

Dennick's explanation raises as many questions as it answers. I want to trust him, but I know there's secrets stirring behind his friendly face. I've been burned before—I'm not rushing to put my hand back over the flames. Still, I don't know if I could handle leaving him here to waste away into madness when we are able to assist him.

"Ceraun?" I ask quietly. "Is he telling the truth?"

"He does not smell of lies," is his begrudging reply. "I am loath to take him with us, but it would be wrong to leave him here. This journey is yours, *kynaira*. You decide."

I decide? Of course the overgrown lizard couldn't make the decision for us. My brain is soup, my muscles are jelly, and the only decision I want to be making is how late we're going to be able to sleep before we pack up and start another long day of traveling. Whether or not to let a complete stranger into our group? One who could be lying through his teeth, spinning a story so tangled even Ceraun can't decipher it? That's beyond my pay grade.

But, leaving him here in this cold patch of forest would make me no better than Joran and Xavier.

"Dennick," I sigh, attempting to ignore how his chin tips up like a puppy's does when its food bowl rattles, "Welcome aboard. *But—*" I point a finger at his face "—if you screw us over, I'll have Ceraun throw you so far into the Pit, you'll never see the sky again."

The dark chuckle to my right confirms this would be no strain on Ceraun's conscience.

Dennick nods, solemn at last. "I'd prefer to keep my body in one piece and far from the Pit's crags. Consider the message well received."

I leave Ceraun to fill our newest teammate in on the specifications for our journey and stumble in the general direction of the bedrolls. My only goal is crawling back into my bed and reclaiming my slumber, whatever's left of it.

"*Kynaira?*" Ceraun calls, his low voice laced with concern. "Are you well?"

My head hits the pillow, eyes already closed. I mumble my garbled question into the furred blankets: "What does that even mean, Ceraun? What's a *kynaira?*"

But the jaws of sleep consume me before he gives his answer.

CHAPTER 8
Frayed Ties

- CONALL -

"**I** think we're making pretty good time, if I do say so myself. Steady on to the next portal—hopefully we'll arrive by tomorrow morning." Finn's voice floats back to the rest of our group. He marches on, eyes on the line where the clear afternoon sky meets swaths of green and white and pink.

Traversing the portal between Solail's fog-shrouded land and this one was a surreal experience, one I'm not looking forward to repeating. After two hours of silent walking, we came upon the site the crone had described. A ten foot tall rectangle of swirling blues, golds and creams stood alone in a clearing. It was flanked by two guardians, the portal's churning light painting them in unnatural chiaroscuro. On the left, a humanoid wyrok with armor made of bark and shadows waited as though born from the gloom of the world itself. On the right stood his massive draconic companion, muted crimson and larger than the greenhouse behind our Haven. It was he who interrogated us, his mental presence overwhelming in its strength.

For close to an hour we answered question after question, each of us subject to the scrutiny of the giant wyrok. Once he was satisfied with our story, his companion stepped forward to inspect the scale. She traced

73

its inner edge for several minutes with a soft, faraway gaze, and I had the distinct impression she knew the dragon who grew the shimmering oval. She swaddled it tightly in the plain canvas wrapping before returning it to my pack and beckoning us through the portal itself. The universe itself seemed to bend and warp into a sickening reversal of every law of science. Paltry things like "down" and "up" ceased to exist as our very atoms revolted and turned on each other in their haste to escape the portal. We arrived in this world an instant later with a bright flash, stumbling out of empty air and into the warm light of day painted on white and yellow wildflowers.

Behind us was nothing but unbroken miles of grasses, swaying gently in a warm breeze.

Finn demanded to be our scout, barely explaining his plan before forging on ahead of the rest of us to inspect the endless, sloping fields blanketed with blossoms. The wispy smoke of distant villages dots the horizon on either side, but Finn keeps us on a straight course between them. Dozens of feet ahead, his straight, tense spine is a desperate flag, signaling his pain even though he refuses to speak of it. Fragrant blossoms sprout up and bend in to touch him with every step he takes, called to attention by his innate magic over them.

My heart twists in my chest, the tense bar of his spine an arrow through my ribs. I worry he's succumbing to the twisted call of this particular realm. It's a fell spirit we discovered after our arrival. A fell wind roams these hills, whispering into our ears as we walk ever onward. Sometimes, the voices are young and jovial, promising endless mirth and merriment if we'll only stay with them and play until our bones become dust for them to carry away. Other times, the voices on the breeze turn sinister, recalling your worst transgressions and muttering how you deserve to lose yourself to the creatures of the grass and dirt.

I know I should comfort my brother, tell him I forgive him, tell him there's nothing *to* forgive, but the words have lodged themselves in my throat and taken root. Valorie would be furious at how I've alienated my family. I should be ashamed, but I only wish she was here to chastise me. Some small part of me wonders if my outbursts come from a misguided, childish hope this bad behavior could somehow *make* her appear in front of me, reprimand at the ready. Maybe it's madness, maybe it's love. Are the two truly so different?

"Maybe we should walk slower, take our sweet time," Gaius calls over the swishing of calf-high grasses, "I'm not exactly eager for another portal after how freakish our first one was. This is a nice place for an extended stay." He shifts his eyes in my direction, palms up in front of his face in a placating gesture. "Before you decide to murder me in my sleep, I'm joking. You should try it again some time soon. Maybe even add in a smile, if you remember how. Otherwise, your bride might take one look at your sorry mug and run away after we go through all this effort to find her."

I suck in a deep breath and make a conscious effort to rearrange the scowl which has been etched into my skin long enough to become permanent. It does nothing to stop another cold chunk of fear from burrowing its way into the bottom of my gut. To go through all of this and still lose Valorie—no, it's not worth thinking of scenarios which will never come to pass.

A vine—the creeping tendril certainly not native to the open, rolling hills we're traversing—snakes up from the dirt and wraps itself around Gaius' ankle mid-stride. With a yelp, his leg flies from under him and he slams into the lush grass beneath his feet. Shocked silence reigns for a single moment before laughter permeates our entire group.

Gaius, dirt and broken blades of grass rolling down his forehead, aims a golf ball of flame at the vine. It curls and shrivels to a fine ash. "What the hell was that?"

"Don't be a dick, Gai. I know it's your default state, but strive for some personal growth." Finn's eyes meet mine. His normally smile-softened blue irises have darkened to stormy pools, turbulent and troubled. With a sharp nod, he turns back to his self-imposed exile before I can thank him for always having my back. For having *Val's* back.

She's mine, but I struggle to remember she is not *only* mine. My brothers and sister bonded with my wildcat during those weeks last spring. They became her friends, her family, as they did for me years ago. Finn saved her from Xavier and taught her to fight and laugh over Margie's famous cinnamon bread. Gabrielle explained our world and its mysteries under a canopy of early summer leaves. Gaius charmed her with a drink and a peek at the sparks behind his smoking shadows. She fit herself into our little band, made us complete.

The loss of her has shattered us all. Now we're planets on misshapen orbits, trapped in a system littered with the pointed, fragmented reminders of what we're missing.

I clear my throat, the sound echoing away into the open air. "You're right." Three heads whip to face me. "That portal was about as fun as those all-day training sessions Dom used to hold. Remember the one where Finn sneaked down to the kitchen beforehand and then vomited banana nut muffins all over the yard?"

Gabrielle's wind chime laugh chases my voice over the hills. "We had to move to the indoor practice rooms for two weeks before all the birds cleared away and we could go back outside."

"It was worth it—those muffins were perfect," Finn says with a pleased sigh. I catch the quirk of his mouth before he can turn away again, and it eases my tightly coiled innards by a minute degree.

Gaius snorts. "At least the wyrok were cool. Shame they were scary assholes, though."

Gabby's shoulders shake in a delicate shudder.

I'm inclined to agree.

"Do you think it freaked Valorie out, the first time she saw a wyrok? I hope she wasn't too scared." The distance between myself and Finn does nothing to dull the pain in his words, nor the agony they leave in their wake.

My fragile smile snaps in two. "Come on." I clap my hands together and quicken my stride until my shoulder bumps Finn's. "We'll never get to the next realm at this pace."

The plan works. When we're focused on marching our way across the plains, there's no energy left for talking.

"Conall, put it away and come eat. You won't get anywhere on an empty stomach." The smell of roasted meats is carried on the neverending breeze, straight to my perch at the edge of our fire's glow. It's as though the world itself agrees with Finn's assessment and demands my presence at the fireside.

Night fell suddenly on this world, the creamsicle sunset abruptly trading for a brilliant navy sky swathed in stars and splashes of celestial color. With no sign of natural shelter to use for the night, we settled for making camp in the shallow dip between two gently sloped knolls. My siblings settled quickly into habits honed by training, unpacking rations and bedding and removing the heaviest of their travel clothes before gathering around Gaius' roaring fire. I know Gabrielle expected—hoped—I would join in, but instead I gave a shallow tilt of my chin, trudged to the top of one side of the camp's meager fortifications, and flopped to the grass.

I had something more pressing to attend to.

Eighty-nine percent. The white numbers in the screen's top right corner are a comfort and a taunt. Plenty of time, and yet nowhere near enough. Another timer ticking down the minutes until I lose this lifeline too.

Soft swishing, barely audible over this world's strange wind, announces Gabby's approach seconds before she takes a seat beside me on the hilltop. "That's a pretty one," she says, tracing a finger down the tempered glass. "She looks happy."

"She was." Valorie smiles up at us from beneath a faded gray ball cap, black spirals curling around the rim in attempted escape. Her gray eyes are hidden behind mirrored sunglasses reflecting a minuscule version of myself, phone in hand and grinning from ear to ear. Behind her, a pristine beach sparkles under a perfect late-May sky, waves frozen mid-crash and sand peppered with seagulls. "It was the day after I asked her to marry me. She said"—my throat sticks around the words—"she said she wanted to take me to see everything one last time before we left."

Gabrielle's voice is hoarse as she rests her cheek against my shoulder. "We'll find her, Con. I swear it."

For the next several minutes, we flip our way through my entire gallery. Valorie dances her way through a slideshow of the year we spent together. Hair stuffed into a beanie, pupils blown wide in the light of a Christmas village display. Head thrown back with a mouth full of laughter as Finn tumbles from his chair in the kitchen. Sleeping soundly on a chair in a sunny patch of the training yard after a workout, oblivious to the fact Gaius had drawn a mustache on her upper lip in thick, black marker. Posed pictures, candid shots, group panoramas, all slowly winding their way backward in leaps and spurts of time until we land on the first picture I ever snapped of Valorie: a tired smile beneath haunted eyes, hands resting against a ripped paper as she reads a note I had written for a girl who seemed too broken to ever be repaired. The girl I was supposed to destroy, but who ended up making me whole.

A single drop of liquid blurs the image, startling me back into the present. "Gabs," I whisper, afraid speaking too loudly will break the bubble we've created here. "Could you try to See her? Please?"

"Conall," she sighs, her voice both placating and concerned, "it's not—"

"I know it's not working correctly," I'm rushing through the words, desperate to finish my plea before she can say no. "And I promise I won't be upset if you can't get anything. I just want you to *try*."

Gabrielle heaves a heavy sigh and closes her lids, slumping forward before straightening her spine. "The vision is unclear, but she's there," she murmurs in a low monotone.

"Is she all right?" I breathe, afraid to break her concentration yet unable to keep silent.

A small nod. "She isn't alone. There are two others with her, both males. Judging by the colors, they're near a portal."

Males? "Who is with her? What do they look like?"

Her brow furrows for a handful of tense seconds before she shakes her head, lids opening. "That's all I can See, Con. She's safe, and she isn't alone. That's all I've got."

My fists clench and unclench against the knees of my jeans.

You promised you wouldn't get angry, Gabrielle's stern gaze seems to say, and she's correct. Chagrined, I force my fingers to unfurl and rest against the rough fabric. I knew going into this the vision likely wouldn't be perfect.

But if I learn another male had his hands on her, I'll end them.

"If you two aren't going to eat, can I have your shares?" Finn's shout carries up the side of the knoll. He stands by the fire, waving a fork in our direction.

Gabrielle and I share a small smile before I slip my phone into a pocket and call, "Only if you want it to be the last meal you eat."

We race down the hillside, skidding to a stop a hair's breadth from the crackling flames. Nestled close enough to keep warm are two stainless steel plates lined with cured meats, hunks of sharp cheese, crusty slices of a thick, brown bread dripping with honey and butter, and a rainbow of root vegetables Finn likely grew himself while we were reminiscing. It's simple fare, but the scent hits my nostrils and my stomach roars to life. Gabrielle and I descend on the food like vultures, devouring our meals with a lack of table manners I guarantee would turn Marguerite apoplectic. I won't tell her about our feral behavior, but I will make sure to thank her some day for stuffing our packs with more than the standard travel rations before we left home.

Finn settles on the grass next to Gabrielle. "Save me some, eh Gabs? I'm a growing boy," he says, giving her shoulder a jostle. She feints a stab at his hand, wielding her fork as one might a dagger.

"Go eat a flower, Finnegan," Gabrielle mumbles around a mouthful of parsnips and carrots, but she tosses him the last crust of her bread. He snaps it out of midair with his teeth, swallows the chunk whole, and nearly chokes.

Across the fire, Gaius snorts as Finn splutters and chugs water from a canteen. He's busy coaxing the flames into complex whorls and helices in an attempt to keep himself awake for a while longer. "Do you think Margie and Dom have managed to track down Joran yet?" Gaius asks.

Thick silence blankets the camp in the wake of his unexpected question. At the mere mention of the traitor, my blood howls. It rushes through my ears, yet it is not loud enough to drown out the eerie, whispering winds taunting me with how I failed to catch Valorie's killer. They don't need to remind me—that particular fact plays on constant repeat whether I'm awake or asleep. My dreams are haunted with scenes where I arrive in time to witness her last breath leave her lungs. Without fail, Joran disappears into the twisted fog of nightmares before I can rip his throat from his neck.

"I hope they did, and I hope he's still alive. His lifeblood belongs to Valorie." The venom in my voice is matched within my siblings' eyes. Two sets of pale pink irises and one of deepest blue stare at me in the flickering light. Six chips of pure determination, six promises of retribution.

"And she'll have it, brother," Finn swears, raising his flask to the night sky. Gaius, Gabrielle and I match the gesture. Our cheer roars loud enough to wake the stars themselves.

"For Valorie! For revenge!"

Chapter 9
Stings and Stones

- Valorie -

I've never considered myself to be particularly religious, but when I contemplated an afterlife, it most certainly did not include a locale populated by stinging, bloodsucking insects.

"If everything here is dead—well, except the wyrok," I grumble, swatting mercilessly at one of the dragonfly-sized, segmented creatures when it attempts to land on my arm, proboscis primed and ready to drain another of my veins. "Then how the hell are these bugs finding things to suck on around here? Shouldn't we be bloodless or something?"

Dennick's chuckle at my side morphs into a grunt when a needle-sharp stinger pierces his sweaty neck. "It's the magic of the realms, Princess. The Underworld attempts to make things as normal as possible for its residents. Some animal probably eats these insufferable pests, which means they needed to be included in their afterlife. The pests obviously need a food source too, then, and this means..."

"Yeah, I get it. Trust me." I crush another beneath the heel of my palm, wiping its greenish guts onto my pants. *Avallea better be bug-free, I swear.* "But did they have to make them *hurt*?"

Another laugh, another wet *thwap* of skin against moist skin. "That's just a gift from the Underworld."

If it's a gift, I need to find my receipt.

I was a fool to believe every plane of this death-world would be charming and filled with merry little woodland creatures with smiling faces. Every squelching step through this marsh has proved my idiocy tenfold.

At the front of our little band, Ceraun marches through the muck as though it's a freshly paved thoroughfare. His steps are silent and even, navy blue wings bobbing with each footfall. Not a single one of the accursed insects has tried to make a meal out of *him*. I know, because I've been glaring at him for hours, peevishly waiting for one to strike. But no, he's somehow immune, and the bugs are taking their anger over this out on me and Dennick.

"Why aren't the little buggers bothering you, Ceraun? Give us your secret tricks; sharing is caring." He could tell me he dances naked around the fire every night for enchanted bug repellent—I'd do anything for relief at this point.

He turns his head to peer at me over his shoulder, electric blue strands shining even in the hazy light through the lichen-strung boughs. "If they drank from me, the magic flowing through my blood would turn them to dust."

Seems the best possible scenario to me. I shoo the three monsters currently buzzing around my head in his direction, but they don't take the bait.

"Maybe you're too sweet to resist," Dennick says as we pick our way over mossy boulders to cross a fetid stretch of stagnant water. Bile rises in my throat with each inhale—what I wouldn't give for fresh, clean air.

I roll my eyes, unamused, then gasp. Slick mud proves an unreliable surface, sending my left foot sliding. Luckily, my other boot holds and keeps me from ending up face-first in the muck. "I'd be more inclined to believe you if they weren't sucking you dry too, Dennick."

"That's obviously because I'm sweet as honey. Impossible to resist." The wanderer hops around my stumbling path with a wink, nimble as a goat on the slimy rocks. He's annoyingly capable where I'm struggling to stay dry. A small, irrationally jealous part of me itches to give him a shove into the murk and wash the ever-present grin from his face. Why is he always smiling?

I might actually do it, if I wasn't likely to lose my balance and end up soaking wet myself.

Mercifully, the ground slopes gradually upward and becomes marginally drier once we're beyond our ungodly hopscotch session. The mix of putrid mud and lank grasses still squishes beneath my soles, but I no longer feel as though I'm battling against the sucking hold of the dirt itself with every step. Unfortunately, the insects don't notice or care we've left the worst of the marsh behind, hopefully permanently. They're along for the long haul, it seems.

"We're almost there," Ceraun calls from several feet in front of me, breaking the drone of buzzing wings and the faint plinking of condensation from somewhere high above. Not rain, if the shafts of sunlight highlighting the humid air are any indication. I hustle forward, hoping the mystery liquid keeps itself away from my curls.

My steps quicken until they bring me close enough to be able to reach out and touch the trail of deep blue scales and fur lining his spine, if I dared. Which I don't. Despite the ironic specifics of our current location, I don't have a death wish. Startling the only member of our party capable of turning into a creature big enough to swallow me whole isn't exactly a self-preserving move.

My vision strains to its limit, but there's no sign of the telltale shimmer in the distance. "Where's the portal, Ceraun? I thought you said we were close."

He shakes his head. "Not to the portal. Close to *that*."

I squint to follow the path of his outstretched finger through a gap between gnarled trees dripping vines in matted, green ropes. There, where the speckled shadows blend into the distance—

"No," I groan, head thrown back in sweat-soaked despair. Dennick chuckles at my misery. I throw him a withering glare. "Another swamp? And this one's even bigger than the last one!"

Several steps closer, the ferns part and the swamp looms before us in plain sight. It's horrifyingly large, a torpid plane of liquid stretching across my entire field of view, unbroken except for the occasional drooping fern or purple-mouthed flytrap. No conveniently placed stepping stones to be found this time.

The toes of my now-scuffed, sturdy boots stop short of the water's edge. Not even the barest breath of a breeze touches the still surface, as though the air itself shies away from the stench and sludge. Dreadful, it will be absolutely dreadful to spend hours slogging across this mess.

"Over here, Princess," Dennick's cheerful call is muted in strange ways by the humidity. To my left, he and Ceraun stand before a dark hole in the soil. Roughly seven feet tall and four feet wide, the rectangular hole reminds me of the entryway down into my grandmother's cellar. Those rusted metal doors and their gaping tunnel into the earth always terrified me as a child. The basement was a dark creature, its creaking jaws stretched to swallow me whole.

Judging by the chill creeping down my spine, those feelings have not faded.

Ceraun begins to lead the way down the stone steps, but I balk as the darkness starts to engulf him. My knees lock against my will. I can't go in there, I *can't*. "Wait," I call, my hands raised. "Why do we have to tunnel under? Can't we cross it above ground?" If someone would have told me ten minutes ago I'd be begging to slosh my way through another swamp, I'd have called them insane. How the tables turn.

"Take a peek around, Vally." David's nickname from Dennick's lips is at once comforting and distressing, as the first glimpse in a mirror often jars a person after a drastic haircut. It's endlessly familiar, yet twisted into something new. I don't enjoy the sensation. "Those plants are huge, and you're, well, not." He gestures up and down, encompassing my barely-over-five-foot frame with a single casual wave. "I don't think they'd be above taking a snap out of you."

I shudder, vividly recalling the mechanisms by which a flytrap devours its prey back on Earth. I have no desire to end up being slowly dissolved in the maw of a much-too-large plant.

Ceraun's face peers from the gloom below to add, "The fish are carnivorous, too."

Oh, joy. Well, that settles things. I force my feet forward, one after the other, and begin my descent.

Three steps into the tunnel, the darkness begins to win its battle with the sun. Five steps, and its victory is absolute. The last tendrils of humid, sun-soaked air give up all at once, and the damp coolness of the underground swoops in to take their place.

My determination flees with the light. For the first time, I'm aware of the fact that, on some level, I am dead. Dead and now buried, here in the soil of some forgotten corner of the Underworld. No coffin, no urn, only endless worms and dirt to cocoon my soul and suffocate me until I go mad.

My breathing quickens from quiet inhales to rasping wheezes.

I can't, My vision fizzles at the edges like an old television set, trembling knees giving way as I sink to the cold ground. *I need air, can't breathe. I can't—*

"Hey, hey," Dennick's blurred features are barely recognizable. His hands, warm against my frigid arms through my sleeves, squeeze gently as he croons, "Come on now, Princess. Rein it in. It's nothing more than a little dirt and darkness."

"Don't call me that," I pant. My stomach heaves in time with my lungs, and I fight the urge to vomit on his boots. "I'm not your princess. You barely even know me."

He chuckles, callused palms rasping against the supple leather of my jacket as he helps me into it. "Would you prefer *kynaira?*"

"I have no clue what *kynaria* even means. Ceraun never answers."

Flame explodes into being, throwing Dennick's face into sharp relief for a moment before Ceraun shoves him aside, a blazing torch in his hand. "It's nothing to concern yourself over," Ceraun murmurs. He spears Dennick's sprawled form with a glare. The torchlight gilds his wingtips in orange-tinted-green where they peek over his shoulder blades. "Just a wyrok term for a silly girl who has no reason to be afraid. Remember our goal, *kynaira.*" The quirk of his lip and softened eyes keep me from being offended, and his gentle reminder bolsters my resolve, even if I doubt he's giving me the full truth. He can keep his secret sayings for now—I'll uncover it eventually.

Ceraun pulls me up on legs wobblier than a newborn fawn's. "Here," he says, "Maybe this will help."

A cooling breeze filled with the faint scent of fresh spring whispers through the dank cavern. For a moment, memories of Finn's flower-filled pathways woven across the Haven's grounds fill my mind, banishing my fear. Intense longing swoops in to replace it. Longing, and determination. I'll never hold my new family—or David, Charlie, my parents—again if I let this defeat me. If I collapse here and waste away in my own terror, I'll never fall back into Conall's embrace. My heart clenches at the thought, trying its best to force me back to the dirt. But I stand tall. If dying didn't break me, neither will this.

"There she is! 'Atta girl!" Dennick mock cheers when I take my first lurching step forward into the tunnel. He's dusted himself off and appears no worse for wear after his mild, inexplicable scuffle with Ceraun. He howls with laughter at my one-fingered response as we trod off into the earthen gloom.

In the warm, inconsistent light of the torch, I examine our surroundings. Ceraun leads the way deeper into the tunnel. He keeps those sapphire wings tucked in tight, away from the dirt pressing in on all sides. The walls are rough and uneven, as though excavated by hand. Approximately two feet above my mass of surely-knotted-beyond-all-help curls, the ceiling is surprisingly evenly carved in comparison. The occasional scraggly root system or variably-hued slab of rock disturbs its monotony. It offers confirmation we are in fact making progress through the myriad of twists and turns and not walking in circles for all eternity. The floor is solid stone, carved with strange symbols and lines. Some are simple scratches in the ancient surface, while others gleam with inlaid colors in a rainbow of shades. Try as I might, I fail to discover any discernible pattern in their chaos.

"Ceraun," Dennick calls from his usual spot at the rear of our line after yet another left turn sends us back in the direction we came from, "Did you pick the longest route possible? What kind of tunnel is this twisted, anyway? They need a new architect."

The torchlight swirls and shivers as Ceraun takes a sharp right at a fork. "It's not a tunnel," he replies without looking back. "This realm is a common pass-through between strings of portals. It's a labyrinth, designed to make overconfident, unapproved travelers lose their way and succumb to the creatures who inhabit this place before they can reach another realm."

Lose their way? Creatures? My palms slicken despite the cold dampness of the underground. A strange creaking wheeze fills my ears. Only after Ceraun stops and swings around, concern plastered across his furrowed brow, do I realize the sound is coming from me.

Ceraun's gentle hand around my upper arm leads me to his side. He points down at the etched floor. "Do you see these markings, *kynaira*?"

They're the ones I've been examining for hours.

At my shaky confirmation, he releases my arm and continues, "They've been left here by my people, a code for wyrok travelers to make their way safely from end to end. We are no mere transient wanderers, unwelcome by the laws of this place." The message in his sideways glance towards Dennick is clear—his "we" doesn't necessarily encompass all three of us. Despite Dennick's repeated assurances, Ceraun is still hesitant to believe his origin story. If Dennick continues to be helpful, I don't care where he came from. This mission is too important to be picky. I've told Ceraun as much.

"All right," I breathe, motioning for him to continue our journey. My chest eases with the knowledge we aren't blindly fumbling through the darkness. We have a plan, a map laid by wyrok who survived this place and lived to tell the tale. We will do the same.

The first pile of bones shows up four turns later.

Polished to an unnerving ivory shine, two femurs, a single ulna, and a rib cage lay atop one another in the center of the aisle, impossible to miss. They would have sent me sprawling, were it not for the warning glow of the torch reflecting off of their rounded edges. I flip the closest femur with one booted toe, searching for a sign of what sort of creature it used to belong to. My dusty, exhausted face reflects back in a funhouse approximation. It's been picked mirror-clean.

"Wangeir worms," Ceraun says with a hiss, eyes on me from across the bonepile. "The true residents of this place. Horrid beasts only focused on their next meal. They make the perfect deterrent—we'll be better off if we avoid them entirely. They have little in the way of intellect and will not discriminate between us and criminals." He motions for us to continue on, and I oblige with a shudder.

We trudge on in relative quiet, the steady beat of our shuffling feet on the dusty stones only broken when Ceraun pauses to decode the markings at each intersection. Every drip or crumble in the distance morphs into the sounds of man-eating horrors in my mind. I stick close to Dennick and Ceraun and beg the never-ending dark for some sign it's planning to spit us out before a worm makes a meal of us.

With nothing to do but put one foot in front of the other, my mind is free to wander—a blessing and a curse. Shadows morph into visions of Conall in the corners we pass. Everywhere I look, there he is, lurking close enough to ache but never to hold. Tears pool in the crinkled edges of my lids, fracturing his image into a painful kaleidoscope. I shake my head and banish him into the past—and the future. *I love you,* I cast the thought into the universe in hopes it might reach him, wherever he is. Maybe he's as hopelessly consumed as I am.

"So, Ceraun." Dennick finally breaks the silence, kicking aside another wayward bone—a skull. "Why choose this path? Correct me if I'm wrong, but there must be an easier route somewhere?"

Another brief pause at a crossroads dotted with sparkling red and turquoise symbols. "No," Ceraun replies, choosing the left path. "This is the fastest route."

"Ah," Dennick presses, inching his way around a pile of stinking *something* in the center of the aisle. I pull my shirt over my nose, but the distinctly fetid stench of the large fecal pile follows us long after we've turned the next corner. "'Fastest' does not mean easiest, though. Why prioritize speed over comfort? I'm sure Valorie would appreciate a more comfortable journey."

While part of me—specifically my lower half—longs to agree with him, I'll hike for days on end if it means we reach the Crystal Forest in time. Ceraun and I have decided to wait to explain our entire reason for traveling until he feels confident Dennick can be trusted. He's afraid, were Dennick to show his hand and turn on us, I could become a hostage—or worse. Dennick doesn't seem the type, but I've been wrong before when it comes to trusting people.

It's how I ended up in this mess, after all.

A wave of crushing fatigue barrels into me without warning. My vision blurs momentarily. I stumble into the crumbling dirt wall. Fluttering motes of black drift across my vision, following me as I slide down the packed earth to the floor.

What the hell is wrong with me? Everything was fine thirty seconds ago. Searching for anything to explain this sudden lightheadedness, I have to assume it's related to the bloodsuckers from the marsh. If those mutant mosquitoes gave me the Underworld version of Lyme, I'm coming back here with a flamethrower.

Dennick crouches beside me. He grasps my limp hand before Ceraun can elbow him away. "See, Ceraun? She needs calm, not a mad rush across the realms."

I scoff, pulling away and pushing to my feet with a groan. Spare me the annoyances of men who think they know me better than I know myself. "Shove it, Den. I'm no gentle lady from bygone days, afraid to get dirty. I'm just a little drained—literally—thanks to those bugs turning me into a human juice box a few hours ago. I'll be fine once we're out of here."

He sketches a bow, amusement written plainly across his smirk. "As the lady wishes." His playful chuckle morphs into a hiss, courtesy of my foot connecting with his shin. I know he's only trying to lighten the strained mood. We're all beyond done with playing moles, scurrying around in the tunnels.

My stalwart dragon companion falls back until he's walking at my side. Our steps sync, and the rhythmic thumping is so soothing, it takes me a moment to notice the bundle held in his hand.

"For you," he murmurs, shaking the parcel. I open it to find a small roll of sweetbread and his waterskin. "Keep your energy up, *kynaira.* Tell me if the tiredness does not cease."

"Is there something you aren't telling me, Ceraun?"

He presses his gift into my chest, only removing his hand once I wrap my own fingers around the bundle. "Just keep me informed," he says quietly. With a gentle brush of my shoulder, he returns to the front of our line, eyes once again on the markings only he can decipher.

At the next intersection, Ceraun's fist flies up for us to halt. Dennick and I crowd in around him.

"What's wrong?" I ask. We've stopped before, but never more than a few seconds while Ceraun cleared away some rubble to properly read the markings.

He gestures at the ground, eyes glued to the place where the three possible paths converge. "We should be nearly to the exit, but—" Ceraun sweeps the torch close enough to the floor to send sparks skittering across the bare stones until they collide with another rank pile of dung in the corner.

Bare stones. Where there should be a smattering of multicolored symbols, there are only strange scrapes. It's as though a giant's broom has swept the wyrok code away.

Far too late, it occurs to me the mounds of scat nearby have been as large as I am tall. And fresh enough to reek. Fresh enough to steam in the cool of the labyrinth.

It's around this time the scuttling registers.

Ceraun's head whips in our direction. His wide eyes collide with Dennick's. "*Run!*"

They're off like rockets, all squabbling forgotten as we sprint down the central path. Why Ceraun picked this one, I have no clue. I'm praying it was more than a blind guess.

The clicking of a thousand limbs against stone draws my attention faster than a hypnotist's chant. It forces my head to swivel even as my feet fly down the corridor. Behind us, a monster from the deepest dregs of childhood nightmares emerges from the gloom. Roughly ten feet long and taller than Ceraun, the wangier worm's gargantuan, centipede-esque body scrapes against the walls and roof, sending small avalanches of dirt and shale tumbling as it advances. Rings of serrated teeth line its gaping mouth, bringing forth memories of the lamprey exhibit at our local aquarium. I've seen a lamprey latch on and suck a fish dry in record time, but this beast would simply swallow the three of us whole without pausing its rampage.

"It's gaining on us!" My scream reverberates through the tunnel. The worm screeches, gnashing its teeth as though the sound offends it. Maybe a creature used to skulking beneath the soil can't handle noise. Maybe it's simply pissed off at the prospect of losing a meal. I don't plan on waiting around to ask.

Ceraun gives a wordless shout and flings a hand forward, pointing down the straight, wide tunnel.

My eyes strain to discern what his spy easily, but—*there!* In the distance, the blackness we've become so familiar with lightens to a shadowy brown.

The surface.

Dennick and Ceraun grab my elbows and we fly across the floor, the whorls and symbols blurring beneath our feet. Brighter and brighter, the surface beckons us forward. The wangier roars its rage at our heels. With a final sucking snap, it retreats into the dungeon's depths and we tumble into the waning sunlight of late afternoon.

For a long while, the three of us fail to talk, only able to force ragged pants through our throats. The sun continues to set, dipping below the horizon before Ceraun finally says we'll be camping here tonight. As long as that worm stays in its hole, I'll camp in the swamp itself if it means we don't have to move until sunrise. My reserves are shot—I wouldn't have enough energy left in me to kill a fly. Thankfully, the insects from earlier don't appear to inhabit this side of the labyrinth.

We start a small fire to warm up a quick meal and soothe our aching, frigid limbs. I shovel meat and bread into my mouth on autopilot, going through the motions until my hunger is sated as I can finally crawl into bed.

Dinner finished and the fire banked for the night, I flop onto my bedroll without enough strength left to unroll my blanket. Freezing in my sleep is more appealing than moving. "Ceraun?" I call, eyes half closed.

He places his bedding down next to mine and tosses my blanket over me, the mother hen. "Yes, *kynaira?*"

"If you send me into another damn maze again, I'll pick your scales off in your sleep."

He chuckles, a sleepy sound filled with relieved humor. "I wouldn't blame you."

I collapse into one of the wrought-iron chairs dotted around Sycamore University's campus and melt onto the sun-warmed garden table, pulling a chuckle from David. I fold my arms around my backpack to make myself a pillow and snuggle in. The heady mix of chrysanthemums and black-eyed Susans on the hot breeze is a lullaby to my exhausted brain.

"Vally, you have to be part cat, I swear. If you don't get your nap you turn feral." His chuckle turns into full blown laughter at my unintelligible, growled response. He's not wrong; I do require several daily siestas to function at peak performance. And today, I haven't finished a single one.

I barely manage to nestle into my arm cocoon when a low, melodic voice drifts to my ear from beside me. "Valorie Vargas?"

My head tilts enough to peek one bleary eye from the blissful darkness of my crossed forearms. I quickly sit up and crane my neck back to take in the bronzed, green-eyed man in front of me, his full lips pursed into a shy, concerned pout.

It's Conall. I'd recognize him anywhere. This is the day we met, last summer after our first class together.

My heart cracks open, overflowing with a mixture of joy and pain. I try desperately to open my mouth, to respond to him somehow, but I'm caught in the grip of the dream. A powerless observer.

I clear my throat, blood rushing to my face and tinting my cheeks pink. "That would be me. Can I help you with something?"

His hand scrapes through his wavy hair as he replies, his low, clear voice rolling straight through me, "I'm new. Got here today, actually, and I haven't a clue where most things are on campus. I know I'm looking for you, though."

"Me?" I ask. Surely he's mistaken. Why would he be looking for me?

His smile stretches wide, kind and inviting. The type of smile a girl would trade her life for. "Because you're my salvation."

What? This isn't how our introductions went at all.

"I'm sorry, I don't understand." My brow furrows. Exhaustion must be making my imagination run wild. "We don't even know each other."

"Oh, but we will."

Chapter 10
A Ballad for Beasts

- Conall -

"*Welcome to the jungle, we've got fun and games.*"

"Welcome" stopped being applicable several hours ago, but this fact hasn't hampered Finn in any way. He's once again leading our pack, both because he refuses to let anyone else take charge and because his magic is especially useful in this corner of the Underworld.

We stepped from our last portal into the steaming, thick air of a world reminiscent of Earth's Amazon rainforest. Blanketed in a thick carpet of green and brown and cloaked in warm mist, the tangled jumble of flora is practically oppressive after the open slopes of the previous realm. Near the forest floor, ferns congregate into masses of feathery leaves longer than my arm. They leave a sweet-smelling, waxy residue on our clothes which causes the air's moisture to bead and roll down the fabric instead of soaking in. Nature's waterproofing.

Above the bobbing ferns, bromeliads, with their long rosettes in shades of crimson and violet, adhere themselves to the long roots of walking palms. Orchids large enough to dwarf my head are scattered along the dead wood littering the ground and speckle the trunks of trees, a woodland giant's pale freckles.

It's the trees themselves which serve as a constant reminder of the strangeness of this land. Their twisted trunks spiral and angle themselves into knots. The branches are tipped, not with leaves, but with long, jade pods the size of baguettes. These seedpods rattle and hiss against each other like rattlesnakes despite the lack of breeze. They lend this stretch of our journey a foreboding soundtrack Finn is determined to combat.

If only he would choose more than one song as his weapon.

"Finn," Gaius shouts over his horrible Axl Rose impression, "If you don't shut up, I'm going to incinerate you."

Finn strolls through the undergrowth, parting the sea of green. The rest of us follow through the path he carves, thankful we don't have to spend hours hacking our way across the jungle. As Gaius passes a particularly ropy vine wrapped around a root near the forest floor, the tendril reaches and twines around his ankle.

The underbrush muffles the sound of his impact.

"Again?" He splutters, bits of discarded leaves and petals flying from his lips as he brushes himself off. "Get a new trick, Finn."

"I will when you stop falling for this one," Finn replies. His off-key singing resumes, miraculously louder than before.

I chuckle despite myself. My mood has been much improved today, a far cry from the miserable bastard I know I've inflicted upon my family these past few weeks. I'm sure he'll return soon enough. For now, I'm savoring the speck of lightness within my chest. It's all thanks to one small change.

I heard Valorie last night.

She was faint, a mere thread of her voice whispering through sightless dreams for only a moment as I tossed in my sleeping bag. The things she said were a warped, nonsensical version of the day we met. I was unable to speak to her, to let her know I was there in the clouded darkness, but I could hear her.

My siblings, were they to find out, would tell me it was only my imagination. They'd paste on bland smiles that never reached worried eyes and tell me I need to focus. But I know the truth. I've dreamed of Valorie every night since well before we left Earth. This time was different. This Valorie wasn't a memory, a facsimile created by my subconscious. It was *her*. And that's enough of a raft for me to cling to for now.

With the sun high in the hazy, far-off sky, we break for a cold midday meal in a gap between the closely packed trunks. Gabrielle crouches to smell a pearlescent orchid, light reflecting off of its petals and painting her in shades of silvery white until she resembles a living moon "Remember the time you filled the whole foyer with those humongous sunflowers, Finn? And Margie complained she was finding sunflower seeds in corners for weeks?"

We all burst into laughter. Finn was assigned extra cleaning duties for an entire month as a result of his stunt. Marguerite and Domenic never learned the reasoning behind Finn's sudden desire to bring his greenhouse project into our home. They'll never know the truth: if Finn had been fast enough to win our race, they would have discovered the house wallpapered with embarrassing pictures of me instead.

Gabby sighs as we gather our supplies and resume our walk. "I wonder how they're doing."

"Margie and Dom? They're fine," Gaius replies with a nonchalant flap of his left hand. He throws an arm around his twin sister's shoulder. "They lived for, like, a century before we came along, remember? It's not like they're inexperienced."

"True, but that was before"—She waves her hands in a circle, the motion hampered by Gaius' arm—"*everything*, you know?"

We enter another small clearing, the trees thinning to reveal a pocket-sized pond, little more than a puddle with a strip of mossy shore between it and the encroaching flora. "I bet they're lonely. Dom would probably never admit it, but he's as soft as Margie. They'll be fine, but I'm sure they're worried about us. About Val, too. She's one of us now." Finn's voice is soft and full of sadness.

Nods and murmured agreement meet his words. My heart swells to have my siblings accept my wildcat as their own. It was not long ago—a mere blip in our lifespans—we were discussing how I would end her life.

Now, we're fighting to save it.

We keep our heads on swivels as we cross the pond's shoreline. The odd, ever-present rattling of the seedpods is louder in this space, seemingly increasing in volume as we make our way towards the trees on the other side of the clearing. As we pass the halfway point, the din becomes oppressive. I fight the urge to cover my ears. Ahead of me, Finn checks his own ears for signs of bleeding, his face screwed up in agony.

It's a painful distraction. One which nearly spells the end for us.

A massive blur streaks across the clearing, next to invisible until it stops directly in front of our group. Four slightly smaller creatures emerge from the trees, flanking us in a slowly tightening circle. The beasts are menacingly wonderful, their panther bodies shimmering with an oily rainbow against the endless black of their fur. Muscles bunch and stretch beneath their skin as their paths criss-cross back and forth, thin tails whipping rapidly. Five tails barbed with large, razor-sharp stingers glint in the dappled sunlight. Five pairs of molten orange eyes glow with a foreboding gleam in the shadows above jaws unhinged like the large snake I once saw Valorie tend to back at the Conservatory, but much less friendly. And I was convinced Noodles wanted to take a bite of me on more than one occasion.

The largest cat sinks onto its haunches, glare focused on Finn. It's clearly decided the largest of our group is the greatest threat. For Finn's sake, I hope it's not wrong.

"Brace yourself!" I scream, praying to the Web any of them hear me over the crushing rattle still assaulting us. My knives flash into my palms half a second before the pack descends.

The weight of the closest beast barrels into me with the force of a jet engine, doing its best to bowl me over. I drive my right hand forward, knife locking between its fangs to keep them from ripping my jugular wide open. The damned thing cranks its jaw wider and my knife falls free in time for me to fling it at the barbed tail in my periphery. An enraged screech and Gabrielle's grateful shout let me know it found its mark.

Down one weapon and struggling against the feeling of my brain splitting in half, I lunge desperately at my own creature. Half-blind with the pain of the incessant noise, the attempt is sloppy. My swing flies embarrassingly wide. It snags on muscle and sinew in the beast's right flank instead of vital organs. The monstrous feline bares its unholy mess of teeth and the rattling increases twofold as it circles once more, right side streaming blood from a thin, deep line of torn flesh.

Revelation strikes faster than the beast. "They're creating the sound!" My voice is ragged, desperate, but it's all I can get out before the scorpion-snake-panther thing launches itself into my side once again. We orbit one another for a handful of tense seconds, each searching for an opening to give us the upper hand. The creature yowls its frustration in a higher pitched, whining clatter, but isn't enraged enough to lose all sense. Yet.

It isn't until the sun reflects off the turbulent water of the pond and blinds me that I realize I've played right into the creature's plan. A lucky swipe of a clawed paw catches the gap between my thick trail pants and my reinforced vest while I blink spots from my view. The blow leaves a hot lick of fiery pain in its wake. I mentally siphon only enough strength into my healing magic to staunch the bleeding. Any more could leave me vulnerable and sluggish until my body recovers.

The beast jerks to my right, sunlight dappling its sleek pelt. Prismatic rainbows dance across its short, sleek fur. Its attack veers towards my weaponless side, but the surprisingly intelligent move leaves its own still-dripping injury unprotected.

Blinking against the slide of sweat down my face, I bury my knife to the hilt between its ribs, deepening the wound and praying the thing has a heart where one would be expected. And that it has only *one* heart.

Blood pours around the hilt and down my wrist, but I don't remove the blade until the glow of the creature's eyes dims to a glassy blankness. Too slowly, it slumps to the mossy floor. I wrench my weapon free and wipe it on the beautiful coat of the creature who tried to kill me. *Well met, warrior.*

Raising my gore-spattered face, I take stock of the scene raging around me. My courage quails in my chest.

A single pile of fur rests at the water's edge, vines constricted tightly enough to partially embed themselves in the corpse. It isn't the alpha of the pack—the one who began this whole debacle when it chose my brother as its prey—yet Finn was certainly the cause of death. Blood tints the water pink where thorns have punctured its pelt in multiple locations. One orange eye lies in ruins beneath a barbed snarl of twig-like protuberances.

My own eyes scan the churned dirt of the formerly tranquil glen, but the obviously asphyxiated feline is the only casualty besides my own adversary. All my siblings remain on their feet, but so do the other three panther beasts. One has several singed patches in its hide, a clear sign of its battle with Gaius. Another favors its bleeding right forelimb, but none are near enough to death for my liking. They've formed a tight unit, each beast surging forward only long enough to swipe or nip at whichever of my siblings is within reach of their claws, tail barbs, and bright, cyanic fangs.

Wait.

As another of the demons rakes its claws across Gabrielle's leather-covered sword arm, our conversation with Solail floats back into my brain.

Blue fangs, never black.

Glowing, orange eyes.

"Gabby," I call hoarsely, sprinting to her side. If I'm correct, this will change everything. If not, we hope our strands aren't cut from the Web today. "Do you think four limbs and a long-ass tail count as 'many-limbed' or not?"

After a second of confusion, her tired expression brightens. "Normally," she says, parrying a tail as it whips towards her neck, "I'd say no, but when it comes to Solail...."

"Exactly." I pivot on one heel and slide myself in front of my sister to block her from the fray while giving her access to my backpack. "Front pocket, hurry."

The bag jostles as she flips open the pocket's flap and slides the ocarina into her hands. It glints dully in the varied lighting, shadows and sun playing across the pitted brown lacquer. Twelve holes of varying sizes are arrayed across the top of the teardrop-shaped instrument. Gabrielle covers three with her long fingers and blows the first clear note.

Silence descends upon the chaos of the battlefield. The horrible rattling cuts off as three hinged jaws snap shut—and remain closed—for the first time in a small eternity.

My brothers sidle around to our side as Gabby's stilted, amateur jumble of notes captivates the monsters. The three sink onto their bellies, eyes half-mast beneath heavy lids like house cats at midday. Overgrown house cats with scorpion stingers I won't be checking for venom. Valorie will have to speculate without evidence when I recount this tale to her—there's no way I'm harvesting a sample from any of these, even the dead ones. She'll stomp about it, but I'll kiss her until she forgets how to even spell "science". The thought brings a soft smile to my blood-caked face, cracking the dried crimson streaks across my cheeks.

"She won't win any awards for being in tune, will she?" Gaius whispers when we're finally shoulder-to-shoulder behind Gabrielle. Her discordant melody is more soothing than the demonic rattle of the beasts, but only marginally.

I snort. "I'll make her one with my bare hands if this is what gets us out of here."

Finn shores up the other side of our rear guard. "Between the twin assailants," he says a hair too loudly, his index finger flicking between Gabrielle and the now-docile cats resting comfortably on the forest floor, "I don't think my eardrums will ever be the same. Do you think Val will kiss them and make them better when we rescue her?"

This bastard. My blood bursts into sickening flames in my veins. I manage to keep my voice steady and low enough to slip beneath the ocarina's music as I seethe, "If you *ever* ask my wife to put her lips anywhere near your—"

Finn's face closes off. His eyes become glassy and cold as his smile falls into a frown. "I love Valorie the same way I love Gabby, and you know it, you overbearing psycho." He turns forward and faces Gabrielle. The golden sunlight highlights his furious profile. Obscuring half his face doesn't lessen the sting of his next line. "But remember who you're talking about. Valorie was a man's plaything before—she won't appreciate being caged again, even if you think you're doing it out of love. You may want to channel those feelings of possession into something more useful before we find her, brother."

He takes a step towards Gabrielle and the panthers, who have finally succumbed to their slumber, but stops when my fingers close around his elbow. "I'm sorry," I mutter, my gut now filled with sick dread where fury boiled seconds ago. "It's hard to quell the rage. She should be here, with us, and not knowing where she is or whether she's safe...it eats at me. It tears me up and shreds me into bits inside, until everything I am feels as though it could seep from my pores and I'd be left as nothing more than a husk. But it's no excuse. Would you find it horribly ironic if I said 'it's not you, it's me' by way of apology?"

When his signature smile spreads across his face, the chokehold on my heart eases. "I know it's you, idiot. We all do. And we understand, to an extent, because we love her too. But remember who the enemy is. It's none of us. We don't want you to find her and look back to realize you've burned every bridge on the way to where she is. She would hate you for it." He grips my shoulder with a firm squeeze, then resumes his place at my side without another word.

I say nothing because he's right. The realization is another knife through my skin. I've been quick to anger, greeting them with vitriol when all they've tried to do is help me rescue the one I love. We're a team, yet I've turned on each of them along this road. Domenic and Marguerite would be ashamed of me.

My head bows under the weight of the cruelty I've let override my relationships with my siblings. It may have been born of love and fear, but it was cruelty all the same. A beast far more dangerous than the ones we creep past, resting on the moss-softened ground as our group leaves the pond and its glen behind. And I worry I won't have the strength to keep it at bay if we don't find Valorie soon.

Once we're deep enough into the trees the battleground and its inhabitants are no longer visible through the weave of branches and trunks, Gabrielle lets the last note of the ocarina fade alone into a low finish. She approaches my pack, flipping the pocket open to nestle Solail's instrument safely back into its nest. The crone's wrath is a fear none of us wishes to experience.

"I heard the two of you." Gabrielle's murmur is barely above a whisper, but my gaze snaps to where Finn and Gaius lounge against two trees several feet away. "He's right, but I expect you know this as much as I do."

At my nod, she pats my backpack and moves to my front. "Good. Then enough has been said. I'd hate to lecture you when it's not necessary. I'll save it until the next time one of you falls out of line." She winks one cerise eye and extends a hand for me to take. We rejoin our brothers under the dappled shadows of the strange seedpods. The dry rattle I expect I'll hear in my dreams wends its way into our ears on a warm, moist breeze as we march on into the jungle.

CHAPTER 11

Hide and Seek

A flurry of Technicolor spores rains down upon us, dusting my shoulders and Dennick's in specks of light. Deep in the shadows, the dust glimmers on his locks the way a galaxy shines in a starlit sky. A sea of grayish cream stalks rises around us to disappear into the misty nothingness high above. Their color is the pale gray of a grove of birch trees I visited as a child, but we haven't encountered a single tree since we arrived in this corner of the Underworld.

Mushrooms in every shape and size populate this forest—likely this entire pocket realm. Where one would expect to find trunks and branches, there are smooth stipes curving gradually on their upward path, their bone-colored skin broken only by a ruffled ring three quarters of the way towards the sky. It's impossible to tell if there truly *is* a sky beyond the layer of enormous caps. Their distant details are softened by cloudy fog. The largest of the fungi dwarf California's redwoods by dozens of feet at least, while smaller ones the size of oaks and elms are scattered between them under the canopy of pale periwinkle gills which line the undersides of the umbrella shaped caps. These smaller—though still massive—mushrooms are topped in shiny shades of swirling yellow, purple, or crimson.

The ground beneath us is blanketed in a spongy layer of thick moss, the only plant in this place. The green carpet squishes beneath our steps, the subtle bounce soothing my sore leg muscles. Smaller fungi protrude from the moss in brightly colored clusters. Their ruffled edges remind me of flowers. The entire scene is magical. Ethereal. A setting fit for a fantasy, but lately I've lived in a horror movie.

"Is it dangerous to inhale these?" I ask Ceraun as I catch up to him. My finger swipes through a trail of the shimmering powder on his wing. The mushroom spores coat his hair and turn his head into a gilded neon beacon glowing faintly in the dimness. For an instant, I'm reminded of another shock of highlighter blue from the life I lived eons ago. David's may have been a result of dye and not draconic genetics, but the colors are similar enough to sting. My heart clenches beneath the fist of grief clogging my chest. Will I ever see David again?

"No, *kynaira*." Ceraun's voice breaks through my thoughts. I jump and my foot catches on something buried in the moss beneath our feet. Down I go, hands scrabbling wildly for purchase and finding nothing.

Dennick's chuckle comes from behind as Ceraun guides me back to my feet. A concerned furrow forms between his brows, but he doesn't bring up the fact I've stumbled three times this morning.

I know he's keeping count.

I make a mental note to resume the strength and balance routines Finn taught me last spring. He'll toss me on my ass if I'm this uncoordinated when we reunite.

Ceraun continues, "The mushrooms' spores are largely harmless. Mildly stimulating, but not to a dangerous degree."

"Huh. Reminds me of coffee. On Earth, they have coffee made from mushrooms, you know," I reply, absentmindedly catching another rain of the soft dust on my upturned palms. The giant mushrooms exhale clouds of it every few minutes in a giant's slow, puffing breaths.

I soak up the magic of the land around us. The endless glitter that catches and refracts the bits of light lucky enough to make it this far beyond the canopy. The groves of towering fungi, their glowing caps reaching into the mist high above our heads. Nothing close to this exists on Earth. Not that I should be surprised after the other worlds we've already been through. Although, the place where the three of us met would have been at home on Earth, were it not for the strange inhabitants. The same could be said for the swamps around the labyrinth.

I shudder at the cold, damp memories. The wangier worm is a nightmare I hope has no equal on any planet.

"I want to go explore. Can we, please?" I turn my brightest smile on my companions. I'm desperate for a bit of fun after the struggles of the past two weeks.

It's been four days since I awoke from my dream of the day Conall and I met. Exhausted despite the full night's sleep, I explained the strangeness of it to Ceraun and Dennick.

I was met with two entirely different reactions.

Dennick immediately brushed it off as nothing more than the bizarre workings of an overtired mind. Ceraun was harder to convince. By the end of the long, arduous conversation, he had agreed it was likely nothing more than the typical weirdness of unconsciousness. But, he made me promise to speak up if I experienced any more discomfiting dreams. I haven't had any concrete dreams at all these past nights, but the foreboding feeling of *something* has been woven through my sleep every night since then.

Ceraun sighs. I know what his answer will be before he says a word. "*Kynaira*," he murmurs in a placating tone.

Dennick's arm flops around my shoulders. His thumb brushes my clavicle as he grins down at me. "Sure we can, Princess." He glares at Ceraun as though daring him to comment.

Ceraun takes the bait. With cold eyes and thinned lips, he advances on Dennick. The two are nose to nose before he speaks. "We don't have time to dawdle. She needs to get to the Hearth as quickly as possible."

"Taking an hour or two to have a look around won't hurt her. What's the harm in living a little? She's already dead, *dragon*." Dennick scoffs. He throws the last word at Ceraun with a sneer.

Ceraun's response hisses through bared fangs. "You know quite well what the harm is, I believe. And I'm trying to make sure she doesn't stay that way, *transient*." One wrong move, and Dennick may snap the tether holding Ceraun into this form. For the first time in this journey, I worry Ceraun may lose control.

I desperately want to do something other than walking from portal to portal, but it isn't worth the arguing. Ceraun and Dennick barely get along on the best of days. The prospect of a rampaging dragon crushing the beauty around us is worse than continuing this endless plodding. "It's fine, Ceraun. Forget I said anything. I only wanted to have a chance to explore a bit, since I'll likely never experience anything like this again. But we can go, it's fine." I offer him a small smile. I'm not angry at him, not truly. He's only doing what we both know needs to be done. And I should want to get to the Hearth as soon as possible. I do, truly.

It's just—I think I'd trade a piece of my soul for a reprieve and consider it a fair price.

Something strange flits across Ceraun's expression before it settles into one of fond, resigned indulgence. With a small tilt of the corners of his lips and a soft sigh, he says, "Two hours, *kynaira*. That's all I can offer. Even that is pushing things. We'll have to make up the time later if we're to stay at our current pace."

A high-pitched squeal breaks from my lips. I lunge forward and wrap my arms around Ceraun. "Thank you," I gush. "I'll only take an hour, promise. Then we won't be too far behind your super secret schedule." I wink up at the slitted pupils peering down at me.

Ceraun cocks his head and returns my wink with a contemplative smile. I turn away before he has a chance to analyze my expression and change his mind. If he gets even an inkling something's wrong, he'll whisk us off towards the next portal without delay. I need to keep things light. Effortless. Sometimes, I swear Ceraun can see right through to the tired wreck I'm burying deep within.

"So," I call, clapping my hands. "What should we do with our free hour?" I probably should have had a plan already formulated, but I didn't dare dream Ceraun would relent. He's been driving us harder than sled dogs from portal to portal without more than a handful of short rests and our nightly camp. Even those frequently aren't set until well after nightfall. I fall into my bedroll each night and sleep like the dead—no surprises there, since I technically am one—but wake each morning with my energy levels hovering barely above empty. Likely because sleeping on the ground with only a few layers of fur and fabric between you and the dirt doesn't lend itself to regenerative slumber.

Dennick pushes off the oak-sized mushroom he's been lounging against. A shower of golden spores flutters down with the movement and momentarily shrouds his face from view behind a glittering curtain.

They disperse as he sneezes twice in quick succession. "How about a game of hide and seek?" he says, throwing his arm around my shoulders once again and knocking his hip into mine. The bare skin of his arm is warm and firm against the back of my neck beneath the cool shade of the toadstools. But the comforting weight feels wrong when it's not Conall's lavender and pine scent filling my lungs on my shaky inhale. I've never had an issue with physical intimacy with David or Charlie, but something about Dennick's charming air of mystery feels...different.

I shrug out of his embrace, flashing him a grin to soften the movement. Relief fills me when he responds with one of his own. No hard lines of rage mar his confident features. "Hide and seek, Den? What are we, children?"

He chuckles, challenge glimmering behind his dark irises. "I'm never too old for the thrill of the chase, Princess. And the capture."

I scoff and dismiss him with a wave of my hand. Turning to my other, more surly companion, I ask, "Ceraun, you'll play too, right? I can explain the rules."

"Of course, *kynaira*. Judging by the title, it's likely similar to a game young wyrok play in order to develop their detection skills." He offers an arrogant grin of his own. "I assure you, I won't lose."

We spend a few moments hashing out the particulars of the game. It turns out Ceraun's version is almost identical to the Avallean and human version, except wyrok hide and seek involves rules against shapeshifting and flight.

"Pinky promise you won't change into a humongous lizard and find us in a heartbeat?" I ask him with a false frown plastered on my twitching cheeks. At his confused head tilt, I lose the battle against my smile. I hold my pinky up between us and wait for him. Slowly, his own hand rises to mirror mine. "It's a human thing," I explain, guiding him through the motions. "You twist your smallest fingers together, and it means you're making a promise you'll never break. It's mostly a joke to ask for one, but some people take them very seriously."

Ceraun's long finger twines around mine. His other hand reaches up to clasp my forearm and holds fast as his stare bores straight into me. "I will never break a promise to you, *kynaira*."

"No pinkies for me, Princess?" Dennick asks. His signature cocky tilt of his lips is firmly in place, but a cloud lingers in his eyes. He blinks, and it's gone before I can decipher it.

We gather around one of the medium-sized mushrooms. "You want to pinky promise not to cheat? Be my guest."

He leans forward and flicks my nose. With a hiss, I swat his hand away, his fingers glowing where they swiped spores from the tip of my nose. "I want to promise never to let you down. Or is Ceraun the only one who can be your guardian?"

I blink, flabbergasted by his sudden change in demeanor. Where did that come from?

Before I can respond, Ceraun shoulders between us, a slight frown carved into his face. "Are we playing or are we continuing on? We can talk while we walk, if you're giving up before you've even attempted to win against me. It's understandable you'd be afraid."

His jab is all it takes to have the three of us back in competition mode. Dennick volunteers to seek first. Ceraun and I sprint into the stalks to find our hiding spots. We split up and head in opposite directions to make things more difficult for Dennick. Deep within the shadows of the cap of a thick-stalked 'shroom slightly taller than me, I smother my excited, ragged breaths with my hand and wait.

The squashy moss beneath our feet lends itself to stealth. It's the perfect environment for seeking—I'm sure Dennick will take full advantage. Small forest sounds creep in without our voices to cover them. They fill the late-morning air and mask any residual footfalls the moss hasn't smothered, making it impossible to tell whether Dennick is coming this way or not. I press my back further into the soft flesh of the fungus and cross the fingers of the hand not plastered to my lips.

Suddenly, a faint "*Hah!*" fills the air. I spin around, certain Dennick must be right behind me. It takes me a solid five seconds to understand the exclamation was faint because it came from across the stretch of forest we've chosen to play within.

Somehow, Ceraun has been found first.

My muffled whoop of victory is swallowed by the misty heights and dense stipes surrounding us, but the lack of volume doesn't dampen my excitement. I won a game of stealth against an Avallean and a wyrok? An magical warrior with super senses, and a freaking dragon shifter with magic of his own? Wait until Gaius and Finn hear about this. They'll swear I cheated.

I pop back to the center of the area and meet up with the boys for round two. Ceraun covers his eyes and begins counting while Dennick and I scatter. This time, I'm found first, and in half the time it took Dennick to find Ceraun. Another two rounds pass in much the same way, the three of us coming together only to rush off again to find new hiding spots before someone prowls through the shining spores to hunt the others down.

By the end of round four, my stupid human legs are trembling and my breaths are coming in gasping pants. The moss may be more soothing than hard-packed earth, but it takes more energy to run across such a squashy surface. My knees wobble as I sink down to crawl beneath a short, purple-capped mushroom. The pale blue gills are much too low for me to stand. Even sitting upright is out of the question—an ideal spot when my opponents have a foot of height on me.

I roll onto my side with a pleased sigh. The moss cushions my body and the cap blocks most of the glowing light from the ever-present rain of spores. Finally, a chance to relax. At least, until someone is found.

Apparently, that someone is me. The next thing I know, two wide, frantically roving pairs of eyes—one black, one topaz—are peering under the brim of my hiding place. Behind them, a curtain of veined blue obscures the view.

"That was fast. At least I wasn't the first one found this round," I mumble in a scratchy voice.

Ceraun scowls. Even Dennick's trademark smirk is subdued as he says, "We've been searching for you for half an hour, Princess."

Half an hour? I crawl from under the cap. Small bits of green fluff cling to my clothes. "Strange," I muse. "I could've sworn I only crawled under there a minute or two ago. Must've fallen asleep." As if in confirmation, a jaw-creaking yawn splits my face in two. "Sorry, guys. My bad. Another round? Or is it time to get going?"

Ceraun's gaze narrows as it roves over me, presumably checking for injuries. I straighten before him and ignore the protesting of every one of my muscles. I'm fairly sure I've grown a few extra muscles simply for the purpose of them protesting the movement. "We'll rest for the day and resume tomorrow," he suddenly states. His tone leaves no room for argument.

Too bad for him. "Ceraun," I protest, "you're the one who was worried about us losing time. Let's just move on. I'm fine." Exhausted, but fine. Even if my body is pleading for me to agree with him.

"The two of you bicker like siblings. Who will win, I wonder? Big brother, or little sister?" Dennick's laugh-laced comment enters the conversation from a few feet away, where his back has found another large stalk to lean against. His black eyes sparkle, vibrant chips of onyx. His enjoyment at seeing me get under Ceraun's skin is palpable. It's usually his job.

Ceraun's teeth grit hard enough I can hear them grinding against one another through his tightly pressed lips. "A few hours, *kynaira*. Take a nap, eat a meal, and we will resume later. No predators wander here. We will be fine to continue into the night before stopping to sleep."

It's a fair compromise, and I'll be better equipped to pull my own weight after a rest and some food. Being the tired, clumsy burden grates on my confidence. My companions may have me beat in both stamina and strength—not to mention them both being beyond mere mortals—but this isn't my first rodeo when it comes to being the sole human hanging with mythical beings.

"Ceraun," I murmur as we begin setting up a small camp within a gap between a few of the towering fungi. He raises an eyebrow, and I finish with, "Sorry again for the delay."

"If it gets too late, I'll carry you," is his only response.

Dennick tosses a green-and-pink speckled fruit my way and snickers, "I'll carry you instead, Princess. I'd be much better company than old Grumpy Guts over there." When Ceraun glares at him over his open pack, acting every bit the grump he's been dubbed, Dennick and I burst into laughter around mouthfuls of tart pulp.

After half an hour spent lounging on the soft moss and munching on a light meal of fruits and seeds, I tell Ceraun my energy is replenished enough to continue. He refuses, adamant we'll stay put until after the evening meal. No amount of me pointing out *he* was the one who was against a detour in the first place sways him. I know he's part dragon, but the male is stubborn as a mule.

The forest teems around us, full of the quiet noises of unseen life and the shifting glow of the spores perpetually falling to the green floor. It's soothing in a simple way few things are in life. No expectations or conditions, just vitality in its purest form.

Until that purity is broken by an equally quiet, yet wholly jarring sound.

"*Kynaira*," Ceraun whispers, his stare locked on something behind my left ear. His catlike pupils expand and contract as they focus on his target. "Do not make any sudden movements."

Every muscle in my body turns to stone. My eyes snap to Ceraun's face. I strain my thoughts, trying to silently ask him what kind of horrid mystery beast is creeping up behind me. He slinks to my side, his moments fluid and soundless in a way no human could achieve. Even the dehmi would make *some* type of noise, but I would have no idea Ceraun had made a movement if my panicked gaze wasn't currently boring a hole into his. I remain frozen while his hand slips behind his back to where I know he keeps a small knife stashed on a hook attached to his belt. His arm tenses and moves from behind him, fist securely wrapped around the base of—

A mushroom?

My eyelids close on a weary sigh. *It's official. I've finally gone insane. The stress has broken my feeble human brain.*

"Vally, you might want to open your eyes," Dennick calls. The words are garbled, a sure sign of him stuffing his face with more fruit. He eats significantly more than I would expect from someone dead. Good thing we replenished our supplies from the wyrok guards at the last portal.

I shouldn't judge him. Death wouldn't keep me from enjoying food, either.

When he repeats his suggestion, I decide it's best to listen to him before he decides to attempt to pry my lids open with his sticky hands. I wouldn't put it past him to try. One never knows when it comes to Dennick.

When my sight returns, I curse myself for ever closing my eyes in the first place.

"Hello, you adorable little beastie," I croon.

A cherubic creature is perched on Ceraun's forearm. Approximately a foot tall from toe to the tips of its tufted ears and covered in dappled, ash-gray fur, the small primate initially brings to mind a marmoset. Its tiny, ridiculously cute, scrunched-up face is topped with a black brow crest and a pair of perfectly spherical yellow eyes which shimmer like polished marbles.

Ceraun hands me a piece of mushroom, and the creature's round pupils track the movement. I tentatively hold the lemon-sized chunk in the air between us. Quick as lightning, two furry paws tipped with minuscule claws snatch the bright red piece and bring it to the creature's mouth. What follows are the most heart-meltingly adorable nibbles I've ever seen.

I cover my mouth with my hands to muffle my squeal of delight. *What is it?* It doesn't matter. Move over, Conall. I'm in love.

"They're called the cranott," Ceraun answers my unasked question with a small smile. He shifts his arm, earning a glare from the cranott perched atop it. "They live in the mushrooms, building their homes in burrows they create in the caps." When its stick-thin arms lift, I notice thin webbing underneath, similar to a flying squirrel. Which explains how they can maneuver around the mushrooms unseen. "They create family bonds and mate for life, only coming down to the ground to hunt for the softer mushrooms they prefer to eat." He gestures to the black tuft over its eyes, jutting forward in a comically large unibrow. "This one is a male. The females don't have hair here. He's likely hunting for a mate and young ones."

If the adult is this precious, I can only imagine seeing its young. My heart would explode.

The cranott graces us with its presence long enough to chew its way through two more pieces of mushroom. He chitters softly at us when Ceraun hands him a larger chunk to take home. After he scampers away, we settle into a comfortable silence, the forest noises once again becoming our background music. I listen until my ears ring, but am unable to hear any cranott in the caps above us.

Ceraun excuses himself for a patrol, promising to stay within earshot. Despite the lack of predators in the area, he claims it's best to stay vigilant at all times. I purse my lips in a skeptical smirk. The logic is sound, but we all know nothing is coming to eat us with the tiny cranott comfortable enough to be out and about. Prey knows the habits of predators better than we ever could.

"He'd probably just implode if he stayed still any longer," Dennick jokes when Ceraun marches off into the shimmering gloom between the stalks. "His duty demands we get you to the Hearth as quickly as possible, and he's chomping at the bit." He obviously doesn't share Ceraun's sense of urgency. The mocking way he says *duty* is abundantly clear.

I laugh. "He's very...focused. Which I appreciate, but I hope he isn't overworking himself. I don't want him to resent me when we get to his home and he's exhausted from hustling his way across the realms for my benefit." My old insecurities come creeping in, inky shadows in the crack beneath my mind's door. Ceraun has quickly become a close friend. What if I'm nothing more than a job to him?

"Dennick," I say with forced brightness, desperate to steer the conversation somewhere, anywhere, before the mental door crumbles and my mind is overrun. "Tell me about yourself. How did you end up—"

"Dead?" He finishes for me, that cocked corner of his lip firmly in place. His smirk might as well be welded to his face—it's always there, as though the world is one giant comedy for him ninety percent of the time. Must be nice to be confident enough to laugh at the universe itself. "You can say it, Princess. It's not a naughty word."

"Fine. How did you end up dead, Den?"

He sighs. "It's not a pleasant story. You sure it's one you want to know?"

"I'm positive. You're my friend, at this point. If you're planning on tagging along with us for this entire trip, I should know your history, don't you think? You know mine." Days ago, I filled him in on an abbreviated history of my life, my crash course in Avalleans, and how I ended up here at Joran's hands. Ceraun has decided our best option is to take Dennick to the Hearth with us and figure out where he's supposed to be spending his afterlife. As overseers of the Underworld, the wyrok have access to such information in their archives.

Dennick's quirked mouth turns into a full smile, slow and filled with secrets. "The basics, sure, but not the nitty gritty. Maybe one day you'll grace me with the unabridged version of your tale, Princess."

"How about a deal?" I bargain. My head tips back against the smooth curve of the mushroom behind me. Spores rain down around and resemble the seeds of stars. "You tell me yours, I'll tell you mine."

Dennick's laugh is loud enough to scare off anything Ceraun might miss in his unnecessary patrolling. "I prefer that deal a lot more when it's less 'tell' and more 'show', don't you?"

"Watch yourself, Den. Don't toe the line." The last thing I need is Conall fighting my new friend when they finally meet. Because they *will* meet. I'm not losing anyone else, even temporarily. I'll find a way to keep the friends I've made here even when this is over. I swear it.

He shrugs one carefree shoulder, completely unfazed by my warning. "Sorry, Princess, but toeing the line is my favorite sport."

"Fine, Den. It's your funeral."

"A bit too late, don't you think?" Dennick replies. He gestures down his body, then to the world around us with an expression which screams *did you forget where we are?*

A startled chuckle tumbles out of me. "Are you going to tell me your story before I steal a quick nap or not?" I ask around my laughter.

His face falls. I regret asking about his past. It isn't worth it if it's horrid enough to dampen his unending good humor. But before I can tell him not to worry about it, he begins speaking, and I'm stunned.

Stunned, and horrified. Because Dennick's story isn't only Dennick's at all.

It's mine.

CHAPTER 12
Dennick

- VALORIE -

"Before I ended up a wanderer, I was a dehmi on a world full of promise. I'm not sure if you're aware some worlds under our care are more receptive to our influence than others. I hear your homeworld tends to buck the more advanced suggestions we plant, and it's not the only one. There are beings simply too entrenched in politics, or infighting, or tradition to welcome the subtleties our assistance is constrained within." Dennick pauses for a beat, his fists clenching and unclenching in his lap. I'm hanging on his every word, desperate for any kernel of information about the hidden world I'm aching to join.

Provided I can finish this journey in time. Maybe Ceraun is right. Maybe we do need to hurry. There's a sinking tug in my soul, a warning I can't decipher. A headman's ax we need to outrun.

"My Haven was overseen by a dehmi named Chryton. A grizzled hard-ass who was against weakness in any form. Chryton ran our Haven alone for two years after his counterpart disappeared. He was harsh without her around, but fair. I never had a reason to doubt his devotion to Avallea's cause. Never had a reason to question exactly what his involvement was with Lacie's disappearance. Until that night."

Dennick's eyelids shutter. The glow of the spores around us seems to flicker and grow dim as he continues his tale. It's as though the forest itself knows horrors are waiting for him in the end. There is no happy ending, else he wouldn't be here.

"It was spring," he breathes. "I remember, because there was a grove of pink-barked plants outside of the Haven. They became covered in horrid pink fuzz once winter faded. It stuck to everything it touched and was a pain to remove.

"I was returning inside from pruning a few and needed to wash the mess from my hands before Chryton saw. He wouldn't care about how fiercely the damned stuff clung to everything—proper appearances were a must for him at all times outside of our bedrooms. No excuses."

For a split second, Dennick is clear in my mind's eye, hands covered in some alien version of a pink cattail and skulking through the shadowy doorway of another massive Haven. His doesn't sound anywhere near as warm and welcoming as the one I was lucky enough to inhabit for a small while.

He opens his eyes and flicks his hands to dislodge the phantom fuzz. My soundless heart gives a painful clench—I know what's coming when he resumes his story. "Anyway, I digress. In order to enter the kitchen, you had to make your way through a sort of antechamber off the main entryway. The lights were off, so I didn't notice anyone was in there until I was already at the doorway.

"Chryton was standing at a buffet cabinet against the west wall, his back to me. He was deep in conversation with a man. They were discussing ways to subjugate the mortals. Ways to make themselves more than unseen helpers. To make themselves kings, gods." His onyx irises meet my wide stare, and his next words hit my chest with the force of a lightning strike.

"He called his friend 'Joran.'"

My hand flies to my throat, a ragged gasp tearing through my windpipe as I arch backward against the stalk. I was prepared for his story to be bleak, but nothing prepared me for *this*. This abrupt revelation our paths were connected before we ever ended up in the same realm.

"I thought I could walk past them, act as though nothing unusual had been said and report them later. But they stopped me as soon as I stepped foot in the room." Den moves closer to me. Our shoulders press against each other, his right to my left, while he forces his story into the open air. Given the ending we both know is coming, this is likely the only time he's ever had the opportunity to speak the words aloud. He needs to prove they don't hold power over him before they fester and rot.

I'll sit here all night if it's what he needs.

"They attempted to...*recruit* me," he snarls. "And I was horrified, but I was smart. Or at least I thought I was. Not smart enough, though." His bitter laugh is a heartbreaking contrast to the snark-drenched chuckle I'm used to from Dennick.

I bump my shoulder against his in wordless encouragement.

"I told them I understood their point—a lie, of course—but I wasn't experienced enough to further their cause. I asked them for time to prove myself, planning all the while to contact the Haven Program and ask for reassignment. They seemed satisfied, seemed *understanding*." Another laugh, half mirth and half wounded cry, wrenches itself from his lips. "And then I walked to the pristine stainless steel sink in the kitchen, turned on the taps, and they slit my throat."

The world halts for an endless instant. Sound ceases, light quails at midday. I knew it was coming, but the barbed words cut through me all the same.

"Dumped my blood directly into water flowing down the drain. No mess for perfect Chryton, the male I had followed for twenty years as though he was my own father." This time, there's no laugh tempering the pain of his sobs. My heart breaks for him, the same jagged way it broke for me when I crumpled to the damp earth with only the heavens for company, listening as my last breaths clawed their way out of my chest.

The pain hardens into something sharp and tangible. "He's going to die, Dennick. I swear it. I'll kill them myself." My words are ice. Flame. A blade, honed and ready to shove through the hearts of Joran and Chryton and anyone else idiotic enough to stand at their side.

He squeezes my knee. When I meet his eyes, they're surprisingly focused. The haze of pain I expected to find is eclipsed by a soft sadness. "Don't, Valorie. Don't put yourself in danger. You aren't a weapon, you're a remedy. You're salvation."

The word niggles at the back of my brain, an itch I can't scratch. A foggy memory I'm unable to put my finger on. But it doesn't matter, not right now.

"Sometimes," I tell him, my voice gentle but unyielding, a velvet-wrapped sword. "You need to be the killer and the cure."

The balmy air caresses my skin as I emerge into the warmth of a Mid-Atlantic September day. A shaft of buttery light falls over my face. I inhale

the heady scent of the chrysanthemums in the planters by the fitness center entrance.

Oh no. I recognize this pristine afternoon. Its tranquility is a mask laid over wretchedness I never want to experience again, awake or asleep.

I struggle against the grip of the dream, but gain no foothold to hoist myself back into wakefulness. I can only watch myself retrace my steps into the alley and remember how this ends.

I meander my way towards an alley which provides a direct route to the cafeteria. My skin aches to soak in the last vestiges of warmth. I slough off my thin jacket and bundle it up in my arms, exposing my arms and shoulders with the black tank I have on underneath. The shade of the alleyway can't quite pierce the hazy heat of the day. This season is a fighter, clinging valiantly to the remnants of the year, but fall is coming to take her place.

Halfway through the alleyway, a set of footsteps rapidly approaches from behind. A shadow eclipses mine, black against the gray concrete at my feet. Probably a runner or some poor kid late to class.

It's not.

I scream, soundless wails scorching my throat. I know it will never reach the me in the dream, but I can't help it. Whoever said dreams cannot hurt you is a liar.

I move closer to the wall on my left to make room for the other person to rush by me. Instead, a shoulder smashes into mine, crunching me into the rough bricks with enough force to make my arm go numb for a second. Pain explodes through my side.

"Hey baby, long time no see. Did you miss me?"

The voice in my ear sends chills through me. It's instantly recognizable, because it's the one that haunts my nightmares.

My consciousness thrashes against its bindings as Xavier's hands grip my body, as his poison words stain my brain. My soul. I try to shut down, to wake up, to do *something*, but I'm powerless here. As powerless as I was then.

I struggle as he grinds himself against me with a dark laugh. He tangles my hair into his fist and shoves my face against the wall, mashing my mouth and nose into the bricks and muffling my cries for help. Mortar dust invades my lungs, but I scream until my throat aches like I've swallowed knives.

That same pain reverberates through me again. Dream-Val continues to screech, but I grow quiet. It's no use trying to halt the nightmare; I know that now.

I'm a feral animal, flipping and thrashing against the hands keeping me in place. He rips his hand from my head and slides it along my neck in a perverted caress, squeezing my throat until I'm gasping for air. Several mangled, mutilated strands are twisted around his fingers as if they're trying to restrain him. Blood and dust forms a paste, obscuring my view—one of the bricks must have cut me at some point during the attack.

My flailing legs finally meet resistance and Xavier grunts. I manage to gulp the soupy summer air, but his hand doesn't loosen enough for me to make my escape. He flattens me against the wall, using his chest to pin me to the bricks while he works at my fly with both hands. Bloody nails snap and shatter in the flesh of his forearms, and I'm rewarded when a pained hiss flutters the hair above my ear. I redouble my efforts to free myself, determined to make him let go or die trying.

I suck in a relieved breath. Here it comes. Any second now, Conall will charge in and send Xavier scurrying away like the roach he is. It won't work forever—otherwise I wouldn't be dead—but at least *this* scene ends before it's too late.

Xavier's tether on his temper snaps. He hefts another fistful of my hair at the roots, yanking my head backward before his arm snaps forward to crack my forehead against the wall. The blow isn't hard enough to kill, but it sends my head spinning. My limbs slacken for a moment as my world goes fuzzy with pain.

Wait.

The thirty seconds of reprieve from my fighting are enough for Xavier to gain the upper hand. His chest smothers me against the bricks while his hands work at my waist. The slither of fabric against my skin is deadlier than an adder. It may not have venom, but it doesn't need it for the kill. After this, I won't want to live.

No. No, this isn't how things happened. Conall—where's Conall?

My head clears enough to resume struggling, but it's too late. He only needed those few seconds to secure his victory in our battle for my body.

I thrash the entire time. I never give up, not for one second, but it only succeeds in worsening the pain and prolonging the horror. He isn't able to free himself and fully grasp what he came for, but he does enough damage without his pants down. It's nothing I didn't once offer to him under the misguided belief of love, but something freely given once is not an open invitation. He steals a piece which no longer belongs to him, rage at his own impotence driving every brutal twist of his fingers. By the time he finally gives up and leaves me alone in the dirt, I'm bleeding and battered.

Shadowy, ephemeral tears course down my face. I know it's only a dream, a nightmare which will cease to hold me once I manage to awaken. I *know* this. And yet, the comfort rings hollow in the cavern of my empty, horrified psyche. I'm helpless, shackled by nothing more than thoughts, and I hate it.

Quiet steps pad against the dusty concrete I lay shuddering against. If Xavier has returned, I need to stand. To kill him or beg for death, I do not know.

My puffy gray eyes meet a pair of emerald greens framed by obsidian waves.

Conall. He's here, but it's not the same. Everything is all wrong. There's no rescue. No silly talk of giants and nicknames murmured into the sultry summer breeze.

Only pain.

"I was too late," he murmurs, eyes full of tears. His hands are stuffed into his pockets, as though he's afraid to touch me. As though I'm tainted.

No, Conall would never think that. Would he?

"I'm so sorry, Valorie. I couldn't protect you. I can't protect you." He smiles down at me, a sad twist of his beautiful mouth. The mouth that should be granting me a name, a place in his world. His right hand finally reaches out, but only to trace the track of a tear across the angle of my jaw. "You aren't safe with me. This is only one of many possible ways I could fail you. It didn't happen, but it could. Stay there, where it's safe. Where I don't have to spend my time watching over you."

"Stay where?" I choke up at him, too confused to touch the rest of his statement.

His final words swirl through the fog of the dream's end, following me into wakefulness. "Beyond the veil of death, where no one can hurt you."

My lids wrench open at last. They continue to fight, their heavy weight begging to close despite my desire never to sleep again. I drag in a stuttering inhale of spore-laced air, the mild stimulant welcome after the shock of the nightmare. My entire body aches with exhaustion, as though I physically battled my way through my dream instead of being a terrified bystander.

"Shh," a low voice above my head croons. Something feather-light brushes against my cheek, but my quickly-raised fingers meet nothing but my own skin. I turn my head to find Dennick still propped up beside me, hands folded in his lap and his usual carefree grin back where it belongs. The sight is soothing, its predictability a comfort after the strangeness of my unconscious mind.

I scramble to my feet. The soles of my boots slip and squish against the moss, doing their best to send me back to the ground before I manage to find purchase against the slick living carpet. Holding out my hand, palm up, I demand, "Give me a knife."

His grin turns toothy as he reaches down to his side. He palms the hilt of the dagger strapped to his belt, bringing it between the two of us before flipping it through the air. Callused fingertips pinch the blade, and the hilt smacks into my open palm. "Planning to run off and slay those demons right now, Princess? I was under the impression you're already busy, but don't let me stop you. An armed woman is my favorite kind." With a wink, he lets go of the blade and returns his hand to his lap.

"I used to train with one of Conall's brothers," I reply. I test the heft of the dagger with a few practice thrusts. The hilt is carved from a weathered piece of black wood and intricately topped with a clear purple stone. A silver-wrapped pommel leads to a tapered blade. It's the length of my forearm, the razor-sharp edge glimmering in the light of the spore rain. I expected the dagger to be heavy, a decorative item more than a usable weapon, but it's surprisingly light. "I'm probably rusty by now, and he'd hand my ass to me if he knew it, but I was decent before. I can become decent again. I need to practice, to train, to *improve*. And I need to start now, before it's too late."

Dennick doesn't ask any questions. He stays seated, eyes locked on me while I work my way through the forms Finn taught me months ago under the Haven's clear blue skies. My muscles take over on memory, leaving my brain to cycle through the memories of days spent with the two of us doubled over in stitches over my own ineptitude. He'd heckle me worse than anyone, even David, but every joke and jab was punctuated with another lesson, a skill to be mastered. Little did either of us know our carefree days of training would be cut short before I learned more than a fledgling talent with fists and knives.

It will need to be enough, at least for now. I've wasted too much time letting others take blows meant for me in the name of my protection. It's time for me to protect myself.

"What's going on here?" The low pitch of Ceraun's voice is startling. I never heard him coming back from his patrol. If Dennick did, he didn't see fit to share the information. I wheel around, my dagger poised for a strike he would surely block. I'm under no delusions I'd be able to take either male in a fight. Not today—maybe not ever. "I thought you were supposed to be resting?"

"I was resting," I reply. Sweat trickles from my hairline down my temple. I wipe it away and force my screaming muscles to begin yet another round of maneuvers. "And now I'm training."

My boots dig into the moss, stance braced against the oncoming reprimand. Waiting for him to tell me it's not something I need to do. But, he only shrugs and flicks his wings before turning to the packs left across the clearing. "Probably for the best," he says while rummaging through our supplies, "but let's head out. We have ground to cover before we settle in for the night."

With heaving breaths, I slow to a stop at the end of the twisting set of stretches and strikes Finn claimed helps to create proper posture during combat. Why posture would be at the forefront of your thoughts mid-battle is beyond me, but he's the expert. As Dennick passes by, I extend the knife hilt-first.

He sheathes the dagger in a wrapping of supple black leather and presses it back into my palm. "Consider it an investment in your vendetta against them," he murmurs, another wink flashing in my direction. His eyes are full of fire, enough to make me believe he means every word. He may not want me to become a weapon, but he's still supporting my decision.

I give a sharp nod and strap the dagger around my upper thigh. "I hope you've got a spare." I joke as we head off with Ceraun through the mushrooms. "Because you'll be sorely disappointed if you expect me to pick up your slack in a fight."

Dennick laughs. "Maybe it's my turn to be the damsel now, Princess," he quips. But he flips the hem of his jacket up as we walk to present another two short blades at his hip with a longer sword hanging opposite them. I recall the stuffed armory racks of the Haven and assume the weapons craving is universal amongst dehmi. The memory sends a soft, unexpected pang of grief through my chest.

Never expected a handful of pointy objects would make me weepy. But I also never thought I'd be tromping my way through a mushroom fairyland with two companions straight out of a Tolkien novel. Normalcy and its associated comforts are clearly longer applicable in my life. Or afterlife. Both, I guess. Whatever.

"*Kynaira,*" Ceraun breaks my morose self-reflection. "What exactly compelled you to begin training this afternoon instead of taking the time to rest?" His tone is light, but accusation runs beneath the surface.

I open my mouth to formulate some excuse, anything which doesn't involve admitting to another of these bizarre nightmares.

"She had another dream," Dennick says casually, as though it were no more impactful than the mild weather. "Woke up all frightened about half an hour before you returned, as if someone was chasing her from her dreamland."

I hiss and shove my elbow into the soft area beneath the side of his ribs. His breath *whooshes* out of him in a wheezy chuckle. "Oh, was that a secret, Princess? I didn't think it was anything to write home about. You certainly didn't think it was important enough to share."

"Of course it's important," Ceraun snaps. "If she's exhausted from these nightmares, maybe she shouldn't be training after all."

I try to cut in, but neither of them listens.

Dennick scoffs. "It's a bad dream, you overgrown lizard. She's stressed. People have bad dreams when they're stressed."

"Dreams that become so frightening they can't sleep?" Ceraun counters. "Her energy levels are flagging already, and we're only half way to our destination. She needs to *conserve* energy, not waste it swinging a dagger."

At this, Dennick barks a harsh laugh. His hands fly to either side, the left one narrowly missing my eye socket. "An hour ago, you thought training was a great idea. Now, you're against it. Is she never supposed to learn to defend herself? I may call her Princess, but even I know she's no figurehead to be strung up as you please."

Once again, my attempts at interruption go unnoticed. This deep in their battle of wills, I honestly doubt they'd notice if I disappeared entirely. Which is absurd, considering they're arguing about *my* life as though I'm a child and they share contested custody.

Ceraun snarls, teeth inches from Dennick's throat. "Yes, she should be able to defend herself. If those dehmi had taught her proper self-defense, maybe she wouldn't *be* here! But, look at her, Dennick. Each day we wake up refreshed, yet she wakes up weaker. I thought she was sleeping, but apparently she tells neither of us about what goes on when she's unconscious. You *know* why she needs to take it easy. Do not fight me on this!"

"Oh, I'll fight you every step of the way," Dennick seethes. "She can't take it easy, not if you want her to make it to your precious Hearth in time. It's neither here nor there to me, but you're right on one thing, Ceraun. I *do* know why you're in such a hurry. You're a puppet too, and I know who pulls *your* strings. Maybe you should cut them before you're too tangled to save her."

"*Enough!*" My voice fills the clearing we've entered. "I have had it with men thinking they can make every decision for me and I'll just simper and bat my lashes and follow them!"

Ceraun and Dennick freeze, their eyes tracing matching paths from my face to the clearing and back again. In unison, their expressions shift from rage to shame to something colder. Fear.

They should be afraid. I'm done with leaving my fate in the hands of others. I may be a weapon, but I'll wield myself.

Ceraun stretches a clawed hand in my direction. "*Kynaira*, wait."

I take a step backward, shaking my head. "No. It's time for you to wait. You've said quite enough, both of you. And I may only understand half of your secrets and codes, but it's enough."

This time, Dennick pleads, "Princess, you need to stop—"

"No, *you* need to stop, Den!" My throat scrapes the painful words out into the strange circle of open space. The ground here is different, bare of the green carpeting the rest of the forest shares. A piece of my brain warns this should be important, but it's drowned in the cloud of my rage. "You're supposed to be my friends," I choke, embarrassing wetness pooling in the corners of my lids. "We're supposed to be in this together."

"We are," he promises. "We've been horrible, and we'll fix it, right, Ceraun?" Ceraun nods his frantic agreement, his eyes saucers of pure golden horror in his stricken face. "But we need you to come *back*, Princess. Please." His hand mirrors Ceraun's, reaching into the clearing, across the chasm of emptiness between their bodies and mine. Dennick and Ceraun haven't taken another step towards me since I stomped into this empty circle. They wait at the edges, terror growing in their gazes with every step I take away from them. The strangeness of it all is enough to turn down the flames on the hottest of my burning rage. It simmers, but it no longer controls me.

"What's wrong with the two of you?" I ask. Something tickles my ankle—likely another absurd insect. I swat at it absentmindedly.

"Oh no," Dennick whispers. Ceraun's feral roar echoes half a breath later.

Just as the barbed bands around my feet tighten with a painful yank, and stars explode as I hit the ground.

Chapter 13
Ensnared

The bare dirt flies up, meeting my face with enough force to rattle my teeth. A gush of blood coats my tongue with metallic acidity. I must have bitten something in the fall, but I can't pinpoint where the injury is. I can't even pinpoint where *I* am. Everything is shrouded in a disorienting haze of pain. I close my eyes against a rising wave of bile and attempt to take inventory of my body.

My ankles are wrapped in fire, a blaze of seeping agony winding its way up my lower legs. Breaths wheeze from my lungs in ineffectual whistles. They fail to serve their purpose, starving me of oxygen despite my best efforts to wrangle them into something resembling legitimate respiration.

A woman screams in the distant fog—an unending, high-pitched screech of pure pain. The sound of torture.

Fire climbs past my knees. It grazes my torso, wraps its flaming fingers around my ribs, and squeezes.

The screams double in their intensity. Whoever is there must be being roasted alive in this inferno. *I'm sorry*, I think to the mystery victim as I thrash on the floor in an attempt to extinguish my own flames. *I wish I could help you.*

"Be careful," a tremulous male voice barks above my head. "If they touch you, you'll be poisoned too."

"I know," another replies, his response filled with dread. They sound vaguely familiar, the way an old friend from childhood does when you meet again as an adult.

All the while, the screaming continues. Why aren't they helping her? She's dying—even I can tell as much. Are they deaf? Do they not hear her? What are they waiting for, an invitation? If they don't hurry, they'll receive one for her funeral.

"We'll have to pull them out," the first voice says. "Hold her down before they rip her to shreds."

Relief tinges the pain. They're finally going to help the burning woman.

Firm hands clamp around my shoulders in a bruising grip. I open parched lips to beg them to help her first, but nothing emerges. She babbles incoherently, sobbing between fractured pleas for rescue.

"Open your eyes, Princess," the male commands.

His tone gives me no choice but to obey. I force my lids apart and a shadowy face swims in my blurred vision. Slowly, almost as slowly as the fire spreads, his features come into focus. A tousled, nearly black mop. Two obsidian irises devoid of their usual sparkling mirth. A hard-set pair of lips pressed into an unfamiliar line.

"Maybe next time you listen a little better, eh Princess?" Dennick asks. He attempts to smile—or at least, I think that's what his mouth is doing. Everything is swirling and rippling as though I'm viewing the world from beneath several inches of water. Vomit rolls in my throat.

I try to close my eyes, but Dennick *tsks* and demands I keep them open. Gritting his teeth, he tells me, "We're going to help, you hear me? Try not to pass out. I'll miss your wonderful conversation."

He nods to his left, near my feet. Fingertips press into my muscles as a wet, hacking noise echoes through the clearing, the sound of an ax lodging into a waterlogged tree trunk. Several dull *thunks* come from beyond my legs. His fingers flex on my shoulders, their grip becoming even more punishing, his nails digging into the tendons and bone until they feel fused to my body.

And then, for the first time, I miss the fire. I wish it would have consumed me while it had the chance. Anything would be better than this horrific, agonizing *peeling* happening beneath my navel. I'm being mutilated. I'm being flayed.

I'm being killed.

The stranger's screams reach an impossible volume, a pitch loud enough to tear her throat to pieces, and realization strikes lightning-quick and burning. There is no one except for Dennick and Ceraun with me in this beautiful hellscape.

The dying woman is *me*.

Dennick's fingers pulse a tuneless rhythm against my shoulder blades. He murmurs comforting nothings while Ceraun peels the flesh from my bones, soothing nonsense words about how things will be all right, how Ceraun is almost finished, how I'm going to heal up fine. Sweet, pretty lies while I boil in my own skin.

With a final, abrupt wrenching, a heavy weight leaves my lower limbs. My body trembles with a combination of exertion and agony, but the pain has abated enough to quiet my screams. Dennick pulls my head into his lap, cradling my skull against his legs as I shake in silence for several minutes.

"Is she conscious?" Ceraun's drawn face appears over Dennick's left shoulder. His wings are spread wide. Sun lightens the membranes into a sapphire blue the sky could never hope to emulate. We lock eyes, and some of the tension leaves his expression. "Hello, *kynaira*," he whispers. He fashions a makeshift pillow from his tunic, slipping it under my head to allow Dennick to crouch without me hampering his movement.

"Is it over?" I rasp. On instinct, I clear my throat and immediately regret it. The action sends razor blades down my windpipe. Tears line my lower lids, but I force them back before they can fall. If I start crying, I won't stop.

Ceraun slowly shakes his head. The action sends shivers down my battered spine. "What do you mean?" I ask. Ropes of anxiety wrap their bands around my psyche, threatening to clamp down and crush me if I give them any foothold. Instead, I busy myself with testing my range of motion while I wait for his answer. My legs are useless, but my arms are manageable. Stiff and wobbling, but strong enough to grab the hilt of Dennick's dagger at my side and press it into his palm when a slimy *something* appears at his back.

"Behind you!" My urgent croak is barely audible, but thank goodness for supernatural hearing. Dennick and Ceraun whip around in time to slice through the slick, green-and-purple tendril slinking its way through the gray dirt towards our huddled mass of bodies. Sunlight gleams off its barbed violet thorns as the vine writhes and twitches in the dust before falling still.

My heart tries to crawl up my aching throat, but I swallow it down. "What was that?"

"A carnivorous plant. It shouldn't exist in these forests," Dennick replies. He turns to face me, and I let loose a terrified squeak. His features are melting, dripping into waxy designs which bring to mind Salvador Dali's clocks. "Stay here," the Dennick-creature commands through an oozing, misshapen mouth. He lopes off in a shambling mess of sludge and whirling daggers.

As if I'd be able to go anywhere else. I haven't even acknowledged the mess I'm positive is waiting below my waist, but there's no way in this hell or any other my legs will be able to run. I wish I could, because the scene unfolding around me is birthed straight from the mind of Dante himself.

Shadowy limbs stretch from the area below Ceraun's ears and become solid, dark blue arms. Where hands should attach, gaping stumps leak darkness instead of blood. Their twisted, flopping musculature is devoid of any form of bony angles. Like rubber hoses, they flail and whip through the air as he faces off against another of the thorned vines. His sword flashes through the plant in a wide arc. Rainbows reflect off the steel and morph into finger-length snakes when they connect with the now-bubbling ground.

No, not snakes.

Snakes, I could handle. This is much, much worse than snakes.

Miniature wangier worms gnash their lamprey mouths and slither in my direction. Each one is bright rainbow in hue and smaller than a single tooth of their labyrinth-dwelling sibling, yet somehow not a bit less horrifying. The mental image of their tiny colorful jaws boring perfectly circular holes through the soles of my feet and out through my skull plays behind my eyes, sending vomit pouring back into my mouth. I scramble backward on my hands and knees, desperate to escape their hunger. My fingers drag furrows into the dirt in my haste, thin trails for the worms to follow. Gray earth cakes beneath my nails in chalky half-moons, each smiling at my panic like the Cheshire Cat.

They'll eat me. They're faster than I am, so they'll catch me and eat me and—

My flight comes screeching to a stop when a deep chasm opens at the clutching ends of my ragged fingertips. It spreads in a curve through the dusty ground on either side of me until I'm cut off from the worms—and everything else—by a ring of certain death. A backhanded blessing.

I take a moment to suck in a breath, then lean over the edge of the sheer drop before me to check for a path across. Far below the chasm's lip, a thin ribbon of lava flows on a path I have no desire to follow. As I gawk at the distance, *something*, a monster of magma and nightmares, reaches its clawed hands from the crimson river and begins to haul itself up the volcanic rock lining the sides of the gorge. Up and up it climbs, while the sun cries tears of bright gold into the clearing and colors sway around us as the Aurora Borealis shimmered during the weekend I spent with David and Charlie outside of Nova Scotia.

Dimly, reality battles with madness within the confines of my brain. The sun isn't supposed to cry. The air is typically free from odd beams of warbling colors. Friends don't melt and chasms tend to require large earthquakes in order to spontaneously form at someone's feet. Something is not right—not *real*—here.

The realization flees the way I long to when the humanoid thing down below reaches its halfway point and the wangier babies begin throwing themselves into its open maw in perfect swan dives over the chasm's rim. A few more seconds pass, filled with the grunts of my mutated friends and the crunching sound of wangiers hitting whatever substance a lava monster is composed of.

In a swift leap, the fiery being crests the rocky edge, and my world tilts further into calamity. When we lock eyes, the scream I've been harboring in my shredded throat finally escapes.

"Valorie Vargas," Joran hisses in a voice composed of the sound of rocks against metal. He bares his teeth in a facsimile of an indulgent smile, the same one he wore when I begged him for help. When he lauded his plans for godhood at the hands of mortals.

The same one he wore as he watched me die.

Well, largely the same. This Joran gnashes saw-blade fangs, his mouth a pit of boiling flame lined with tiny wangier jaws where his own teeth should be. Thousands upon thousands of whirling needle rings fill the gap between his upper and lower lips. Ropes of magma stretch to breach the opening as though afraid he'll open his mouth too wide and split it in two.

"I've been waiting for you." Joran's cackle is the scraping of boulders, an inhuman, teeth-rattling sound. I shield my aching ears between a hand and my opposite shoulder, using my free right hand to reach for my dagger. It's only when my sweating fingers meet empty leather that the events of minutes—hours?—ago filter back into the present.

Dennick has the dagger. All I've left myself with is the thin blade tucked into my boot, barely more than a fillet knife. Next to nothing against the monster stalking ever closer.

I brandish the paltry weapon. Live or die, I'll go down fighting. Real Joran never expected resistance—let's hope the same applies to this monstrosity. The element of surprise may be my only hope.

I spring up into a stance Finn beat into my brain and prepare to fight for my life against Joran for the second time this year.

But the moment I lunge forward, teeth bared around a scream of rage, hands clamp around my shoulders and freeze my momentum.

Of course he wouldn't fight alone, the coward.

Snarling, I wheel around to unleash myself on whatever lackey Joran has chosen to fight his battle this time. My eyes take in flickers of dark fur, a streak of blue, and dripping, oily limbs in a nauseating jumble. A tumbleweed of slimy tentacles. The image is nonsensical, but I don't need to understand it. I only need to kill it. Then Joran will be mine.

"Maybe you were right," the familiar timbre grunts near my right ear. "Maybe she shouldn't have trained. She's surprisingly nimble for a human."

A short chuckle in another tone, and then the first answers with a sarcastic, "Any day now, you know." The blue half of the tentacle pile brings one oozing whip up to a deep hole in the center of its mass. A billowing wave of silver mist rolls from the opening on a sighing exhale.

It's a mouth, I realize before everything fades into blackness.

Muffled conversation seeps through cracks in the walls of unconsciousness I'm trapped within. I search for the gaps, mental fingertips running over smooth barricades, but the voices fade before I can find the holes they're coming through and escape. My subconscious has shored itself up fortress-thick, determined to keep me locked inside my brain. A frightening place at the best of times, but twice as awful when I have no clue what reality has become on the other side of my heavy eyelids.

Come on, I beg. *Say something.*

There.

The murmurs begin again, incomprehensible sounds beyond the iron veil. But if I can hear them, I can find them. I *will* find them.

Slowly, silently, I coast through the blackness, ear pressed to the uncomfortable hardness of the wall. I creep along in a demented game of "hot and cold". When the voices begin to fade, I make an about-face and hustle as quickly and quietly as I can in the opposite direction. It *should* be me calling the shots in here, but clearly I've been overthrown. Whatever jailer has decided I'm to remain here is to be avoided at all costs.

Finally, after seconds or days, the voices crest to their highest point. A pinpoint of light, tinier than a needle's eye, ekes glorious sound and color into my sightless prison.

I press my pupil to the mote of light and strain for any glimpse of the world beyond. Nothing, only blurred grays and whites. But the voices are coming from here, therefor the real world must be here, too.

Forgetting my fear of the mystery warden, I bash my fist against the wall. Again and again I strike at the fortress without a care for the state of my hands. I can't see them in the blackness—the pinprick of light is nowhere near bright enough to cast any true glow—but their agony is unmistakable.

"Get over yourselves," I mutter angrily. Gritting my teeth, I pound and dig and drive my nails into the tiny divot until I'm finally rewarded.

A crack!

Thin as spider's thread, it snakes outward from the pinprick as though fleeing from the light. The sight is enough to bolster my flagging energy. I hammer on, a feral grin painting my face. When the raw nerves of my hands revolt, I roll onto my back and aim kick after kick at the spreading ruptures. And when those give out as well, I wedge my shoulder into the divot and push my way through, squinting my eyes against the brightness and resisting the urge to shield my ears from the tidal wave of sound.

"Valorie?"

I blink several times, my pupils slowly relearning how to adjust to light after being trapped in total darkness. The sheer volume of stimuli is overwhelming to my newly-recovered vision. I squeeze my lids tight against the onslaught of images.

Dennick quietly calls my name again. I crack open a single eyelid enough to see his brows drawn together as he leans over me. His eyes lock onto the small movement. A relieved smile spreads across his face.

"What the fuck happened to me?" I croak, trying—and utterly failing—to lift myself out of the dust into a seated position. The back of my skull thumps against the ground. I groan.

Ceraun's head pops in next to Dennick's, the two of them hovering upside-down in my view. Their matching, flip-flopped expressions have me wheezing. My tired laughter aches as it leaves my chest, then doubles as they both cock their heads in mirror-image movements. The reaction is likely less related to them and more a result of blunt force trauma.

"When you stormed off," Ceraun begins over my waning chuckles, helping me lean against him in a half-slouched recline, "you were attacked by a carnivorous plant. They're supposed to only inhabit the other side of this realm, but one has evidently found a foothold here." He gestures around us with his free hand, the one not currently supporting my weight.

My gaze tracks his gesture, taking in the clearing we're still hud-dled in. One by one, the abnormalities sink into my tattered brain. The gray, powdery earth devoid of comfortable moss. The circle of sky above us, unhindered by blue-gilled caps. The newly familiar green and purple tendrils wrapping around mushroom stipes at the edge of the ashen circle. Several vines lay hacked apart closer to our resting place. Some appear to be burned or exploded, with blackened pockmarks littering where they've fallen, but none of them move.

Did I imagine it all?

Dennick brushes a lock of my hair away from my face and adds, "The plant's barbed thorns are coated with a thick poison. The concoction is intensely hallucinogenic. It's meant to incapacitate the victim until it can be dragged back to the central bud, where it's dissolved in acid and consumed."

I shudder, imagining being slowly digested while my brain was lost in the demented images concocted by the poison. "That explains the freaky visions during the battle." I pause, thinking. "Was there even a battle at all? I saw the plants attack, and a chasm, and—" I shudder at the memory of Joran, unable to voice the horror, "—was anything real?" My frantic stare locks with Dennick's black irises. My voice drips hysteria-edged panic when I finally whisper, "Was he here? Did you see him?"

His wheels click in his brain as he pieces together who I mean. Who I *need* to know about. The terrible thread tying us together.

He scoops me into a crushing hug, making soothing shushing noises under his breath. I quiet the protests of my aching bones as a small sob slips free, the only one I allow before I bury them deep inside. Joran doesn't get the satisfaction of making me weep. These tears aren't for him. Never again.

"No, Princess" Dennick whispers, "He wasn't here. You're safe." Despite the contradictory state of my half-broken body, I believe him.

One day, I'll take Joran on and crush him beneath my heel. I'll seek retribution for every life he ever thought he could destroy, every soul he sent to this place. One day, he will pay at my hand. But I'm not delusional enough to believe that day is any time soon. So, I take solace in friendship and revenge, and hold them closer than armor around my heart.

CHAPTER 14

On A Desert of Glass

C *lang!*

Deep violet sand shifts beneath my boots, threatening to suck my feet from under me. I twist to block the incoming sword strike and manage to stay upright. Sunlight hits the sharp monoliths spearing up from between dark dunes and refracts into rainbows. The harsh beams lance directly into my eyes. I'll have to work around the blindness—I cannot afford the time it would take to clear the spots from my vision. Another thrust is coming, whistling through the chill air loud enough for me to parry even without sight.

Sun-induced blindness isn't enough to cause my death, but the strike hits the flat of my blade at an awkward, bone-scraping angle. I grit my teeth against the jarring pain in my shoulder and blink rapidly as I shove the attacker away with a riposte. Spots gradually fade from my vision as I bare my teeth at the figure wrapped in billowing gray robes.

"Where do they keep coming from?" Gaius shouts on my left. This is the third skirmish we've encountered since we entered this land. The barbarians seem to appear out of the sand itself as though born from the womb of this arenaceous realm. Wearing the same ashen clothing and head coverings and armed with identical serrated talwars, all individuality is lost between them. Male, female, or neither of the two, it's impossible to discern. We've attempted conversation, but the attackers offer no information before they launch themselves at us with unnerving silence every time we meet. It's disconcerting, to say the least.

Another blocked blade radiates shockwaves up my aching bones. *And it's exhausting.*

"Hell if I know," Finn replies, his vines whipping through the air to snatch the legs out from under his own opponent. "But I wish they'd leave us the hell alone. Or at least tell us what we did to piss them off this badly." He snags a second mystery attacker with a thorny tendril; a throat this time. They flounder in the grainy purple sea as he constricts their airflow until death claims them. The body sinks beneath the scuttling waves of sand the endless breeze has scooped into drifts throughout the desert.

Solail explained lifeforms killed in the Underworld don't technically die, not in the way we would. They'll be reanimated somewhere else within their assigned realm. Only we're in danger here—us, and Valorie. As living souls, our deaths here are final as deaths in any realm. To lose our lives in this world would secure us permanent places within the Underworld, a fate already served to these attackers before we ever encountered them.

My sword sinks into the gut of another enemy. I hiss in frustration before wheeling to begin anew. The knowledge doesn't make "killing" them any more enjoyable, even in self-defense.

Gabrielle whirls into view, her skin blending into the sand around us. She dances through enemies, eyes unfocused as she taps into her Sight. With her power unleashed, she's virtually untouchable. Every enemy blow falls a second late, a hair short. Her rapier glides into neck after neck and our foes topple faster than cards in the wind before her. It's entrancing and terrifying all at once.

Her performance reaches its finale. Gabrielle's sword flicks, cutting the last assailant from sternum to hip. The gash is undoubtedly fatal, but not a quick demise.

It leaves time for action.

With their dying breath, the barbarian thrusts their jagged blade at her heart. If their aim is true, they'll take her down with them. The plan is a good one, given their limited options. Ultimately futile, but they wouldn't know Gabrielle is always one step ahead. It's her blessing and her curse. The Web of Fate carries her along within its tangles, showing her its secrets before they come to pass.

The last time the Web left her behind, Valorie died.

Gaius lobs a brilliant ball of flame into the face of the barbarian. Those flowing robes ignite in a heartbeat, far faster than any normal flame could chew through them. They fall to the indigo sand in a writhing heap.

It soon falls still. The final smoldering embers are dashed into the dunes, carried away on the desert's whispers while we catch our breath.

Gabrielle leans against one of the glassy pillars, catching her breath. The sharp, dark purple spears appear to be formed from the neverending swaths of dark sand, melted and scattered throughout the desert in a random smattering of spikes. A product of ancient lightning storms? Or something less mundane?

She glares at her brother. "I had it, you know. You didn't need to intervene."

"Spare me the anger, sister," Gaius sighs. He nudges her with his shoulder, fishing a bag of dried apples from his pack and holding them out to her with a small grin. "You know I get antsy when you play with your victims. You're terrifying, but you're still my little sister."

"Three minutes. I'm your little sister by *three minutes.*"

"And don't you forget it, *little* sister." Gaius dangles the apples from his fingertips. She growls, snatches them, and shoves two slices in her mouth as her twin laughs.

I scoop a handful of violet sand into my palm, angling it back and forth in the bright sunlight. The grains themselves are translucent. They're not opaque the way sand is on Earth before it becomes glass. Perhaps my assumption is true in reverse—this world was once entirely made of the glass pillars, ground down over eons by storms and wind and time itself.

I dust my hands off on my pants and shelf the mystery for now. Valorie will want to know of it. She may not be here herself, but I'm determined to make sure I'm equipped with plenty of stories and treasures for when we reunite.

There isn't a second that goes by where my head is not full of thoughts of her—her skin, her laugh, the small furrow of her brow before her brilliant mind uncovers the answer to some obscure puzzle. She's my driving force, my heart itself thrust into another body. My wife in my soul—and in the eyes of Avallea in the near future, when all of this is nothing more than cobwebs in the back of our consciousness.

I pray her journey hasn't been as eventful as ours.

"Thinking about Valorie again, aren't you?" Finn's knowing smile is stained lilac by reflected sunlight. He slides down to the sand beside me, our backs propped on another of the glass spears. "You've got that sad, lovesick mug you only get when you've got her on your brain."

He smiles again, but this one doesn't reach his eyes. Their melancholy remains untouched.

I'm not the only one missing my wildcat. Not by a long shot.

On a deep sigh, I admit, "I heard her again last night."

Finn's eyes widen, but he collects himself quickly. I know my siblings think my visions of Valorie are nothing more than simple dreams. Fragments of my subconscious desperately grasping for any shred of her they can find before reality intrudes. They believe these glimpses are a way for me to stay sane until she's in my arms again. But they're wrong.

When his face offers no further judgment, I explain what occurred the previous evening. "I couldn't see her. Couldn't see much of anything, really. Only streaks of color, nothing more than brief sunlight and shadow. But Finn," I pause, a shuddering breath rasping through my lips, "she was afraid. She was sobbing and begging for help. Saying something about how I was supposed to be there.

"And I couldn't get to her. I was there, but I *wasn't*." My voice breaks on the final word. A hot tear rolls down my cheek. It carves a path through the grit dusting my skin. My eyes close, unable to bear the weight of my failures. "Will she ever forgive me for leaving her to die?" The question ekes out before I can swallow it down.

His speech is as waterlogged as my own. "Will she ever forgive you? Brother, you're not the one who was supposed to be there. Gabby and I abandoned her. We're only hoping she'll allow us enough time to apologize before she tells us she never wants to be around either of us again." His hiccuping laugh holds no humor. "But, who are we kidding? It's Val. She probably has some backward reasoning that absolves us of all guilt. And I miss her enough, I might just go along with it."

I chuckle, because he's right. Valorie will find a way. And we'll let her, because neither of us can tell her no.

I dread the day she and Gabrielle find a reason to work together against the rest of us. We're doomed.

Without warning, Finn's arms fling around my body and crush the air from my lungs. His grip is bruising, nearly tight enough to wring the sorrows from between us. But not quite.

We cling clumsily to one another the way drowning victims would grip a life preserver in frigid waters. My forehead connects with his clavicle. His chin knocks against the edge of my ear. Bones creak and protest, but we ignore them. Two battered brothers, cracked in two. Desperately trying to hold each other together.

As time marches on away from us, we remain wrapped in our embrace. Toe to toe, heart to heart. The sand swirls in eddies, stinging our cheeks, yet neither of us lets go. We stand, as unmoving as the obelisks.

And we begin to heal.

Not entirely. No, not anywhere close.

But a few of my jagged shards fuse back together, and I hope his do, too.

"You know," I say as we untangle ourselves with a few thumps on each other's back, "I don't blame you for what happened."

His eyebrows soar. Disbelief is etched into every pore on his face.

"Not anymore," I amend. "You weren't meant to be there until the morning, Finn. How would you have known, especially with Gabby overloaded? I have someone to blame, but it isn't you two." Unbridled rage roils in my veins, begging to be let loose. Rage at Joran and whatever misguided ideas made him think he could get away with murdering Valorie. Rage at our own inability to keep her safe. Rage at the Web itself, for choosing to drag Gabrielle down every thread except the one which would have made us aware of the danger in time to prevent all of this from happening.

His eyes widen further, pupils contracting against the harsh light. I wait for him to protest, to tell me I'm wrong, to say he can scent the fury contained within my smooth movements and gentle smile. But he only smiles and claps his hand on my shoulder as we walk towards our siblings.

He doesn't have to say anything for me to know the truth. He may believe I've forgiven him, but he doesn't agree. Finn might never absolve himself of his guilt. It will haunt his steps forever, the same way it dogs my own. We'll wallow in it together until the end of our immortal lives.

"Nice of you to join us." Gaius' back is turned as he rummages through his pack, but his quip carries easily to our ears. "Mind giving me a hand with this?" He leaves his pack on the sand and walks over, a granola bar in his right hand. The other, he holds out to me.

A deep gash has split the webbing between his thumb and forefinger. Drops of blood from the slowly weeping wound create a divot in the dark grains at our feet. I lean in to inspect the sand-crusted slice. It's immediately obvious both tendons and muscles are sliced in two. The jagged nature of the barbarians' weapons ensured the cut is messy and undoubtedly painful.

My hands hover around his without quite touching. Soft white light envelops the wound and begins repairing as I ask, "How did you manage this one? Block a swing with your palm? I'd expect better, even from you." The subtle glow and pull of my healing magic exacerbates the headache already brewing within my skull. Talking generates more noise to irritate my head, but the distraction outweighs the discomfort of feeling my energy being gradually siphoned the way water sluices through a straw.

"Lucky shot." He grits his teeth and shoves the words through them. Healing magic isn't pleasant for the wielder or the recipient. I can make it comfortable, but it costs me far more strength to manipulate the power into something resembling pleasantness. It prefers to crawl its way through a body, not flow gently down a predetermined route.

The last time I forced it, Valorie was lying at my feet in an alleyway.

"Took two of them on at once. Threw sparks at the first one's eyes—or where I figured eyes would be under those damned robes—but they managed to recover before my fire ate through their buddy. Blocked their slash at the last second but my angle was wrong, so—"

"You caught half of it with your hand instead of your weapon," I finish for him. The light seeps back into my skin and fades.

He twists his healed limb in the light before he grins, all teeth. "Exactly."

We gather our bags and set off, our backs to the blazing sun. Despite its rays, the dark grains crunching beneath our feet never heat beyond a mild warmth. The endless breeze ruffles our clothes and stirs our hair until we all pull hoods up around our faces in a futile attempt to deter it. Maybe the barbarians have the right idea with their cloaks. A reprieve from the chapping winds and grit sticking to my skin would be worth shrouding myself in layers of fabric until I became the desert version of a Halloween ghoul.

Hours later, we break for a small meal beneath the shadow of the largest monolith we've encountered. I settle into the sand next to my sister. "Any luck with Seeing, Gabs?" I ask after checking to make sure

Finn and Gaius are occupied. Without a job to keep them busy, there's no doubt they'd be eavesdropping.

I don't need to specify; she knows exactly what—or *whom*—I'm asking for visions of.

Gabrielle shakes her head. I fight the urge to snap at her when she replies, "It doesn't want to work down here, Conall. I'll keep trying in case something changes, but don't get your hopes up." Gabrielle pats my hand and sighs. There's no way she doesn't notice the slight flinch I'm unable to keep locked down. My body revolts against her worthless words. "If I learn anything, you'll be the first to know, I swear it. I'm sorry. I know you were hoping for better news."

Save your apologies. They're as useless as your "gift". I clamp down tight on my lips to hold back the vitriol before it can spew its taint into the world.

I'm trying. I can't lose them, or Valorie.

With a curt nod, I fall on my meal, eyes trained on the horizon. The wyrok scale vibrates gently in my jacket pocket. It's always in motion, as restless as I am. Some days, the sensation is an angry buzz, but today is a quiet one. Almost as though the scale is growing tired of this journey, too. But, neither of us have the luxury of resting. Not now.

Food flies into my mouth as fast as I can swallow. Valorie's out there, somewhere. The less time we spend eating, the quicker we can find her.

CHAPTER 15
Forbidden Fruit

- VALORIE -

"It's possible they're a side effect of being in the Underworld. My dad would have crazy dreams whenever we went on vacations because of how terribly he slept in hotel beds—maybe this is the same type of issue." A poorly-timed puff of air sends a cloud of spores directly into my nostrils. Eyes and nose streaming, I only hope these mushrooms reproduce asexually. Logically, I know their method of reproduction changes nothing about the situation. But my brain would prefer to avoid images of inhaling globs of fungal sperm. And I happen to think my brain is due for a pass after the multitude of other horrible realities it has had to face lately.

When my fit of sneezing abates at last, two pairs of confused eyes are locked on me, heads cocked as though they're wondering if I've finally gone mad. "Oops, do you guys not know what hotels are? Is there some cute medieval fantasy term you use instead? Inn? Hostel? Tavern with one room in the attic and you've got to share the only bed, inevitably leading to all sorts of impromptu romantic revelations?"

Ceraun shakes his head slowly, chuckling. His stare doesn't lose its "she-could-be-completely-nuts" quality, however.

"No," Dennick stretches the word into several syllables. "We know what hotels are, Princess. Although, let's revisit your last part about romance later. I'm intrigued." He winks.

Of course that would be the part he's focused on. Ceraun's elbow connects with his ribcage, forcing Dennick to stop and catch his breath with a wheeze. Dennick winces and rubs his side. "Anyway. What we *don't* know is what exactly you're talking about. What do you think is a side effect?"

Oh. "The dreams."

He tilts his head. "Ah, I understand now. Couldn't it have been a byproduct of the toxic plant you decided to wrap yourself in?"

My middle finger flips upward. His answering snort proves he either already knows what it means or understands context clues enough to piece it together. "First of all, I didn't choose to 'wrap' myself in the damned plant. Nobody told me the cute mushroom forest would also be home to a demented version of the piranha plants from *Super Mario*. And second of all—" Dennick's mouth opens. I rush to finish before he can interrupt and derail this conversation further. "It couldn't be from the plants, because the weird dreams started before we found them, remember?"

"Well," Dennick waves his hand dismissively, but his words splutter from his lips. "I'm sure it's nothing important. You said it yourself—maybe you're sleeping poorly. Maybe," he pumps his eyebrows until I huff a small laugh, "you need one of those romantic attic beds."

Ceraun's elbow connects with another *whumpf*. "Don't be disrespectful, transient." He ignores Dennick's glare, instead locking eyes with me while we pass through the shade of an extraordinarily large mushroom. Our faces are shadowed for several seconds as the house-sized cap blots out all light beyond the glittering dust in the air. "*Kynaira*, I don't think you should dismiss the dreams. Something is amiss. You need to be on your guard."

"Isn't guarding her your job, oh great and powerful lizard?" Dennick's jab drips with sarcasm. It's evident to all three of us he puts no weight behind Ceraun's caution. "To be her guard?"

"Even I cannot protect her within her own mind." The admission hisses from Ceraun's mouth as though the admission physically pains him.

"I'm going to scout ahead," Dennick announces suddenly. Walking backward into the spore-speckled gloom, he calls, "You'll see, Princess. I can guard you as well as Old Lizardpants over there."

I laugh. Ceraun does not. He keeps his head on a swivel, silently observing even after Dennick disappears from view. His wings rustle behind him, readying themselves against an unseen, imaginary foe.

"Oh, come on," I nudge him with my shoulder as we walk, earning a clip from one wing in response. "You have to admit, he can be funny sometimes."

"He does add a certain crass humor to the trip," Ceraun concedes. "But he's entirely too forward with you. And I find it hard to trust him, despite his eagerness to help." He says *eagerness* as though it's a detriment to Dennick's character. "Please, watch yourself around him. He's an unknown factor, a mystery. He never should have been in that area to begin with. If he betrays you, I will drag him to the Pit myself."

"And I'll lock his shackles myself if it comes to it, Ceraun. But I couldn't leave him there to rot alone." Visions of stars and blood flash before my eyes before the sun banishes them.

We fall into silence. Ceraun's words echo in the snarled mess of my head. Does his desire to protect me stem from the fact we're friends, or because he feels he has to out of a sense of occupational duty? The thought is a sobering one. It rests heavily in my gut, an uncomfortable weight I can't shake. How many of those close to me are there because of obligation? Once I'm no longer the weak link, will they be proud? Or will my friends, this family I've cobbled together for myself, drift away once they know I'm no longer in need of protecting?

"Ceraun?" I ask. The call is bordering on inaudible, but he hears me. His head immediately swings until his topaz irises with their slit pupils bore into mine. "Am I a burden?" My voice breaks around the words. I bow my head, embarrassed to find crystal droplets of liquid on my clenched hands.

Without me, Finn doesn't have to spend his days training a human to protect herself instead of enjoying his bread and plants. Without me, Gabrielle has less to strain her Sight. Without me, Marguerite and Domenic have no need to open their home to someone outside of their circle. Without me, my parents can focus on their lives, and David and Charlie can begin theirs together, freed from worry for their third wheel.

Without me, Conall is free.

The demons in my mind are feasting. They cavort and celebrate with each depressing revelation that slices through me. They dance within my skull, claws tearing at my confidence, my pride. My steel spine I've worked so hard on hammering into a straight line begins to bend and crumble under the weight of their revelry.

Until a single finger, warm against my cold, clammy panic, lifts my chin. The tapered claw at the tip dents the soft skin under my jaw. Those honey-gold irises burn brighter than flames. The demons flee in terror, deep into the recesses of my subconscious. Not defeated, but subdued.

"No." It's a complete sentence. A benediction. A condemnation.

"No?"

"No," he repeats sternly. "They do not get to win, *kynaira*. You know your strength. You know your kindness, your pain, and your joy. You know what you've given, what you've been through to get this far. Do not insult your friends, your love—do not insult *me*, by thinking us too stupid to comprehend your worth. Everyone is a work in progress, a sculpture half-finished, but do not diminish our intelligence by insinuating we cannot see the masterpiece hiding beneath the dust."

The tears fall, and I let them. They flood and wash away the stains on my heart until I am lighter than I have been since I woke up without a heartbeat.

"You're right," I agree on a tremulous breath, "I'm being silly."

"Not silly. Overwhelmed. You've been through a lot, or so I've heard." A gentle smile softens his features.

Ain't that the damn truth.

"But," Ceraun leaves one arm around me and marches us back into the stalks. "You're not alone. I have a feeling you never will be again."

And isn't that a miracle all on its own?

We weave our way between cream-colored mushrooms for probably fifteen minutes before Dennick materializes from behind a large, off-white stipe in the middle distance. His lips are pursed and a small crease dents the space between his eyes.

"There's a grove of trees up ahead. Some sort of plaque is attached to one," he informs us.

"Trees?" I ask. "Actual trees? Not fungi? Not man-eating hallucinogenic plants?"

He shrugs. "Well, I didn't get close enough to confirm or deny the man-eating part. Want me to go ask?"

"Shut up." But he earns himself a laugh. Ceraun's cautious words from before dampen my mirth. I push them to the back of my mind. Dennick has given me no reason not to trust him.

Yet.

We follow Dennick through the forest. The moss along the ground weakens beneath our feet as we walk ever onward. It continues to blanket the grown in emerald swathes, but the cushioned comfort it's offered over the past two days has diminished significantly. Much to the displeasure of my calves and ankles.

The air ahead seems to thin. As we step into the clearing surrounding the grove, I realize what's missing and my mouth falls open.

No spores drench this area in shimmering curtains of golden rainfall.

Because you can't have the spores without the mushrooms.

And Dennick wasn't lying. There isn't a single mushroom here.

There are *trees*. Massive, arching canopies filled with broad-leafed branches tapering down to thick, brown trunks. Roots dipping in and out of the ground in gnarled curves as big around as soda cans. Shaped similar to oaks, but with the height of a redwood, seven sentinel trees stand at attention in an otherwise untouched space, the moss at their base covered by patches of a sparse layer of leaf litter and splattered with light and shadow through their canopies. Their wide boles are arranged in a ring of six, with the largest alone in the center. Odd growths bud from low branches on the central tree, several different hues of rounded blobs I can't discern at this distance.

"There," Dennick announces. His finger points through a gap in the ring of boles, on the side closest to where we've stopped. "There's the plaque. No clue what it says, though. I couldn't make out the words from here, and I didn't want to have all the fun without you two."

I squint at the central trunk, the one wide enough to swallow my childhood home whole. Sure enough, there's a bronze plate embedded into the umber bark approximately five feet up. Light gleams off the burnished surface as though it's been freshly polished. Do these trees have a caretaker? Someone waiting to ambush us when we step foot within the ring? My head swivels left and right, searching but finding nothing.

When I share my concerns, Ceraun sniffs the air for a tense moment. "Nobody but us has been here for a long while," he finally answers. "Long enough for time to wear down their scents." My shoulders fall in relief. I'm far too tired for another battle this soon after Lava-Joran and his wangier babies. He may not have been real, but my aching muscles and sore head didn't get the memo.

Dennick hums. "Well, if nobody is here to get angry..."

Without waiting for Ceraun and me, he skips between the trees and approaches the plaque.

"Den!" I shout, running after him. Not my brightest idea, given what happened the last time I rushed into a random gap in these woods.

After a quick lap to scout the grounds from all angles, Ceraun joins us in front of the plaque, wings raised in a stiff position I've learned means he's irritated. When he narrows his eyes at the two of us like we're children who've run off into a crowd, I know I've read him correctly. And when the groaning crackle of wood precedes the snarls of roots springing up around the outer ring and caging us into the grove before we can escape, his glare turns withering.

I point an accusing finger at Dennick. He shrugs with a sheepish, *"what can you do?"* grin. He's right, what *can* we do?

A glint of sunlight on bronze draws our attention back to the plaque in front of us. It must hold the secret to escaping the roots.

We study the symbols etched into the metal for several minutes. No matter how hard I squint or what angle I tilt my head, the combination of swooping curves and harsh lines never manages to form discernible words. They hover out of reach of my brain's grabbing hands, taunting me in the company of catchy songs I've heard once in a shopping mall hallway and overly complicated graduate-level organic chemistry lab compounds. Virtually definable, but falling just this side of gibberish.

Dennick isn't much more enlightened than I am, if his severely scrunched brows are anything to go by. "It's a wyrok tongue, yes?" he asks with a tilt of his head towards Ceraun.

Guess he knows rather more than I do, after all.

Ceraun nods without taking his eyes off the etchings. His lips move soundlessly, mouthing words in a tongue only he knows while his finger drifts above the words. He traces the symbols three times before finally speaking the final line aloud. *"Havariath maran espiral daqar eirath."*

"Mhmm, yeah, that's wonderful. Very pretty, and also about as useful as a raincoat in the desert, Ceraun." My sarcasm is thick as tar. Dennick snickers beside me.

Ceraun chuckles. "I don't understand the problem, *kynaira*. I thought you loved mysteries."

"Scientific ones, sure. Logical puzzles? I love them, too." I retort. I reach up and flick the tip of his left wing, laughing when he hisses and recoils from my touch. "But I'm not about to learn an entire language in two minutes, am I, *dragon*?"

He smirks at my old nickname from our earliest days together, several weeks ago. I'm reminded of the lighter, more comical Ceraun from before Dennick joined us. Part of me misses when it was only the two of us, but a larger part hopes Ceraun and Dennick will mend their fences soon and stop tearing at each other's throats. Our journey will continue to shove them together, two magnets with opposite polarities. I pray it doesn't end in someone's blood being spilled.

"I suppose not. Very well," he acquiesces, "I will translate for you." His clawed index finger moves over each line of swirling text as he recites the poem carved into the metal of the ancient tree.

"'Neath the branches lies your test.

Pick correct—we'll acquiesce.

Only one with health aligns,

The others cause a swift decline.

Form and flavor, hand in hand,

Will save you from this hallowed land.

Spice alone is favored fine,

If our company is your design.

Bitter green is forest's ire,

But sweet emerald is your desire.

Sour goes the same as sweet,

But only if red and blue meet.

Consume the chosen; be set free.

Choose another—we will feast.'"

Silence reigns when his recitation fades into the leaves overhead. My cogs whir as the part of my brain molded specifically by mornings spent with my dad and the *New York Times* crossword section flickers to full power.

It's a riddle. One which may get us through the roots and out of this place, should we pass the test.

Dennick's gaze slides sideways. He nudges me with his elbow, but I hold up a palm before he can speak. "Hold on," I whisper, afraid speaking louder may break my concentration. "I'm working on it."

'Neath the branches...

I crane my neck to peer at the lowest branches above our heads. The other trunks are straight for at least one hundred feet up, where their branches explode from them in bottle-brush fans of green leaves. This center tree, however, has several lower boughs. They protrude a few feet overhead, and hang heavy with—

"Fruit!" I gasp.

Dennick and Ceraun jump at the sudden sound.

"The riddle, it's about fruit!" The more I think about it, the more I comprehend. The riddle mentioned colors and flavors, and I'm positive there was a line about consumption somewhere near the end. "Ceraun, can you read it again, slower this time? I need to check something. Den, hand me that branch by your left foot."

He obliges. I jot notes into the earth as Ceraun repeats the riddle at half speed, pausing between each line. When he's finished, I sink back onto my heels and study my scribbles.

"All right," I begin. "It says we need the correct form and the correct flavor. I'm assuming by 'form', they mean color, since color is also referenced later on." Ceraun nods. His approval darkens my cheeks. Fighting may be new to me, but logic is where I shine.

Don't worry, Finn, I silently swear, *I promise I'll keep working on the combat part, too.*

My word vomit continues, working the puzzle aloud in case they have input I might overlook. "We don't want any of the spicy fruits—"

"But I thought they said spice was good?" Dennick interrupts.

I shake my head. "They said spice was good *if you want to stay here.* Planning on making a break from us, Den?" My smile is bright, high on the joy of being useful for once. He chuckles in return, ruffling my hair before I can swat him away.

"As I said, no spice. No bitter green ones, either. *Sweet* green ones, though, they're good to go. Let's keep an eye out for green fruits."

We pace around the gargantuan trunk, eyes trained on the branches dripping with globular fruits. Most of them shine in enticing shades of pinks and reds, but every possible hue in the rainbow is represented. I even spy a smattering of gray and black fruits high in the tangle. Good thing the riddle didn't mention those. Even the three us stacked end-to-end wouldn't be tall enough to grab the lowest of the shadowy spheres.

"I found one," Dennick calls from the other side of the tree. He meets us back at the plaque, an apple-sized green fruit clutched in his grip. "It smells sweet, definitely not sour or bitter. I didn't taste it, though." He offers it to us and Ceraun and I both sniff. He's right. The fruit is cloyingly sweet, without a hint of other flavors to mellow the sugary aroma.

"One down, two to go," I count with forced levity.

Ceraun sighs. "The only green fruits I found were undoubtedly bitter. They smelled of bile." My upper lip curls at the thought. "I could attempt to fly to the higher boughs and search, but I worry the tree will somehow consider flight to be cheating. Perhaps this trap was not meant for winged ones."

It occurs to me Ceraun could attempt escape at any time, if he left us behind. He's here because he doesn't want to leave us to die. I squeeze him in a quick hug. At my whispered thanks, he pats my head and sighs. It's his pleased sigh, though, not his pissed off sigh or his "you're-be-ing-an-idiot-by-not-sleeping-enough sigh. I could fill a dictionary with nothing more than his exhales.

My heart sinks as we continue with my notes. I was hoping to find all three fruits straight away, or at least two. The closer we get to the bottom of the poem, the more nervous I become, especially with the way the light has shifted while we've been searching. In the dark, mistakes will be more likely. What if we choose incorrectly?

"There was another option," I recall, brightening. I scour my writing, jumping to my feet when I get to a scribbled line near the bottom of the list. "Sour fruits are good too, but only 'where red and blue meet'. Red and blue make purple. Let's find some sour purple fruits."

This time, Ceraun is the winner. He finds a pair of purple fruits ten feet in the air, dangling from branches close to the trunk itself. I attempt to climb the rough bark, but stop when Ceraun bursts into laughter behind me. He lifts me onto his shoulders with the ease of a parent hoisting a toddler into the air. I stand on tiptoes, held fast by his large hands, and stretch to reach the fruits. The second my fingers close around them, he lowers me to the ground.

This is it. We have our fruits. Now, all we've left to do is eat them and hope I haven't doomed us all.

Nobody volunteers to go first, not even Ceraun. We count down from three, then begin to chew in unison. The soft purple flesh of my orange-sized fruit gives way beneath my teeth with little effort. A burst of mind-numbingly sour pulp hits my tongue.

My mouth floods with saliva. I was expecting at least a hint of sweet—it is a fruit, after all—but there is nothing but pure sour tang. A decade of eating Sour Patch Kids did not train me for this at all. Guzzling citric acid by the beaker in Chemistry lab wouldn't have prepared me for the unified revolt of every single taste bud. I force myself to go in for another mouthful, again and again until my fingers are coated with juice and my tongue has blissfully become numb.

The three of us finish every last bite, and the roots slink back into the loam as our fruit pits fall from sticky fingertips. I beam, the pleasure of a puzzle solved lighting up my brain brighter than a tree on Christmas morning. The boys clap me on the back, Ceraun's heavy palm sending me stumbling forward and nearly colliding with the tree. Laughter sparkles between us on the beams of the setting sun, relief making us buoyant and giddy.

We did it—*I* did it. We're free.

"Hey, Ceraun?" I ask when we're well beyond the ring of trees. The mushrooms are back in full force. I've never been more excited to see fungi in my life.

He hums a wordless response.

My yawn splits my jaw in two. "How much longer until we make camp?"

He laughs loudly into the spore-filled evening air.

I grit my teeth against the sound of his mirth. I wasn't joking, but I can't tell him.

Keep going, I think to myself, urging my throbbing legs to take another faltering step, begging my flickering energy reserves to draw more from some untapped portion of my body we haven't razed yet. Maybe there's a pinky toe I haven't drained. *Don't let them see. We've so much further to go.*

173

CHAPTER 16
Wraith

– VALORIE –

"*It's beginning to look a lot like Christmas...everywhere you go...*"

The crackly sound of Christmas music flows from Dad's old record player in the far corner of the living room. White lights twinkle on a ten-foot artificial tree in the corner, scattering pinpoints of soft light off ornaments and the French doors to the backyard. We still have a little over a week until Christmas, but the tree skirt is already buried under gifts I've accumulated for family and friends. The mantle over the electric fireplace is filled with a carefully staged Department 56 Christmas town. I've been collecting since my grandma gave me my first piece at fifteen—additional buildings and warmly-lit set pieces spill over onto the bookshelves on either side.

I smile at the scene, familiar as my own skin. The carefully preserved ceramic church always sits in a position of honor on the corner of the mantle, small bottle-brush trees lining a path through cotton snow to connect it to the rest of the minuscule village. Grandma may be gone, but a piece of her will always be in that village. The comforting thought is nearly enough to mask my trepidation over being thrust into another memory-dream. What will my demons destroy in this enchanting place?

174

Buffalo-checked blankets and cozy, themed throw pillows are over-flowing off of the couches and chairs. We can never have enough—winter is the perfect season for every surface to become a comfy place to curl up and nest. Real pine garlands twine around the banister, filling the house with their crisp scent. There's even an antique silver menorah on the dining room windowsill for Charlie.

Bing Crosby is right, it's beginning to look a hell of a lot like Christmas.

Not that I can see any of it right now behind my closed eyelids. The tree could catch fire and burn the whole festive display down without me noticing. Maybe it has. Maybe that's where this fire in my veins stems from. Or maybe it's the immortal currently devouring my mouth as though it's his last meal.

Our breaths mingle together as he murmurs against my lips, "You're going to drive me insane, looking like this all night when I won't be able to touch you."

Something about his voice sets tiny alarm bells ringing in the back of my brain. My thoughts, hazy with lust and longing, move too slowly to grasp the oddity. It's gone before I can decipher it.

Clenching his fingertips into my hips for control, he grinds against my pelvis, the hard length of him rolling against me. He's impressive enough through his jeans to make my brain short-circuit. Liquid heat pools in my core, spurring me on. In the heat of the moment, my leggings are somehow both barely there and much too thick for the ideas he's planting in my head.

Another roll of his hips positions him right where I need him. My head lolls back to thunk softly against a hard, unyielding surface. He presses me against the cold wood of the front door, the flares of heat from his body against my chilled skin causing me to erupt in goosebumps.

This is right—amazingly, achingly right. And yet, not. What am I missing? The phantom sensations flood my system, hazing my ability to comprehend patterns and reason. Focus, Valorie!

I groan, seeking the friction he's dangling in front of me. The thin sheath of satin is all that separates me from him.

There shouldn't be anything between us. Conall stole my underwear the night this happened, pocketed them as a lewd trophy. Why would my subconscious change this? What does it mean? And how will it be used to hurt me later?

"Please," I moan, half plea and half protest.

If the me in my dream would only open her eyes, maybe things would be clearer. I curse the twist of logic which allows me to think independently of her, yet only offers sight in inconsistent drips and drabs.

"Shhh," he whispers. The vibrations shoot through me in bolts of lightning, wrenching a moan from my lips. But he hesitates, and the grip on my hips shifts into something less passionate.

He's a thunderstorm, a hurricane, and I'm standing straight in the path of destruction. If only he would give in and not pull away.

"Please," I moan again.

I get no verbal response, only a physical one. His hands clench against my hips as though something has upset him. He finally raises his head.

I gasp as I finally comprehend exactly how this place has changed. My subconscious crawls away from the scene, scaling the walls of this prison in an attempt to escape this betrayal, even as the hands of dream-me cling to him as though they've been molded for holding his body.

Green eyes have become black. Hair has lightened a single shade and receded into a tousled tumble my hands have tangled themselves into in the throes of ecstasy. A dimpled quirk rests in one corner of his mouth. A mouth I know every inch of in real life, but not like this.

"Hi, Princess."

My bones grate against each other as I drag my feet under me with a groan. A mushroom stalk provides welcome assistance to haul myself to a position vaguely resembling standing. I'm drained. Lately, sleep siphons as much energy as it provides. Especially with dreams as awful as the one I've hauled myself out of again this morning.

The boys are bustling around, rolling up bedding and tamping the small fire from last night's meal. A small plate near my pack holds an apple, a small hunk of hard cheese and a heel of bread. Breakfast.

"Are we ready to move?" The question rasps from my dry throat as I pull on my shoes and jacket. Rasping coughs claw through my chest. Thankfully, a full canteen rests beside my morning meal. I help myself to several large gulps before I tuck in.

Dennick and Ceraun pause their packing. In unison, their eyes trail my figure from my now-booted feet to the tips of my bedraggled curls. I know what they're cataloging. Stooped posture, mussed curls, dull eyes, wan skin. My face is reflected in the steel surface of my camp plate, and the figure staring back at me isn't one who screams, "Don't be alarmed. I've had a wonderful night's sleep and am totally capable of pulling my weight on this journey."

I can do this, I tell myself as I polish off the last of my food. The weight of my meal hits my stomach, my body relishing the promise of calorie-fueled energy. *It can't be too much longer, right?* I have to keep moving, keep fighting the dragging exhaustion attached to every one of my bones. Keep pulling my own weight, lest they decide it would be easier to leave me behind and cut their losses.

Ceraun tips his chin. His gaze is soft, mouth turned down at the corners. "As soon as you're ready, we'll head out." He hikes a thumb across the long open rectangle of mossy earth. At the far end, the portal waits. The swirling vortex of blue and gold produces the same low hum a generator would back home. Could we connect it to wires and produce electricity?

"What're you thinking about, Princess?" Dennick tugs on a lock of my hair, pulling me from the puzzle. I cringe and immediately feel horrid as his grin flickers. It's not *his* fault my brain decided to use him as a stand-in last night.

When I force a smile and offer up my draconic electricity musings as a distraction for my behavior, he chuckles. "Portal power, huh? What a thought. Maybe you should bring it up with Ol' Scaley Ass over there, see what he thinks."

A quiet *crack* sounds when my hand meets the flesh of his biceps. I school my expression into stern flatness. "Be nice, Den. Ol' Scaley Ass is sweet and helpful. Just because he's not the reincarnation of an ancient trickster god like you doesn't mean he's no fun." Dennick raises an offended eyebrow. "What? It's true! He picks on me almost as much as you do. Honestly, I'm the aggrieved party here. You should be ashamed—you, and Ol' Scaley Ass." My snort ruins the severe facade I'd been trying desperately to hold onto.

Ceraun calls a dry, "Thank you so much for your glowing defense, *kynaira*. But, I can assure everyone my ass is not scaled...in this form," and the three of us burst into laughter. The gaiety chases away the last vestiges of my morning's pall and leaves me feeling lighter. If only it could imbue me with some stamina as well.

Still chuckling, we shoulder our packs and head through the portal. The tornado of colors whirls around us. I'm filled with the same sickening sensation fun-house fair tunnels always gave me as a child. Before the nausea can become overwhelming, we're spat into the next stop in our string of destinations.

It's the complete opposite of the shimmering vale of mushrooms we've left behind, yet every bit as captivating.

"Wow," I breathe. My eyes devour the landscape, threatening to escape from their prison of bone and wander off on their own adventure if I don't feed their ravenous appetite quickly enough.

The portal has deposited us on the edge of a vast field bordered in the distance by snow-topped gray mountains. A shag carpet of lush green grass dotted with white flowers waves in a brisk wind beneath a perfect robin's egg sky. It's picturesque, a Swiss Alps postcard scene fit for Sophie and Howl or a Julie Andrews musical number.

Ceraun tugs on my wrist. "This way, *kynaira*." I spin around, and the scene before us is equally as beautiful and much more shocking. My jaw hangs open.

A *village*.

Ceraun leads our little trio forward into the first settlement I've seen since I dropped into this world. Rows of two-story cottages built from earthen brown bricks border a main cobblestone thoroughfare. Smoke puffs merrily from chimneys slouched on their slate roofs like squat dragons belching into the blue. Flower pots hang from windows, their rainbows of petals waving as shutters clack beside them in the wind. Peering down the main road, I can spy smaller side streets branching off in haphazard angles, each of them filled with chattering people milling about. At the far end of the thoroughfare sits a sprawling jumble of stalls with hawkers shouting the virtues of their wares beneath the bright yolk of the sun. Everyone is talking and laughing, moving from place to place with a vibrancy I wish I could bottle up and inject directly into my sluggish veins.

Sweat beads on my forehead as we move deeper into the village proper. The houses block most of the wind's power, leaving the sun free to beat down on us and reflect off every shiny surface and wavy glass window pane. *Cylinder glass.* I remember the name from a historical architecture course I took for a freshman year elective. A small chuckle escapes me as I stare. Mr. Franklin would be in heaven here.

We weave our way through the throng, their bumping elbows and brushing sides shifting around us without more than a passing "pardon" or "watch it" when someone's hard angles meet another's softer spots. The jostling isn't chaotic, but keeping upright in the tide of people is draining. By the time we're deposited on the edge of the market, the crowd splitting into three sections down the main aisles and becoming marginally less claustrophobic but still thick, I'm wavering on my feet.

In the chaos, Ceraun and Dennick have been deposited across the lane from the row of shops I'm standing beside. They catch my eye and begin shoving their way through the gaggle of shoppers, but the crowd is ten feet deep and their progress is slow. I take the opportunity to catch my breath and will my body to remain upright before they can get close enough to notice how fatigued I am.

"I'm sorry," I gasp when my left leg buckles for a moment and I career into the corner of a stall. Several of the sparkling trinkets slide across the smooth wood table, but nothing crashes to the ground. Thank goodness.

The saleswoman flashes a motherly smile and waves my apologies off with a suntanned hand. "It's no trouble, dearie. Nothing broken, no harm done." Her gaze narrows, becoming shrewd. "Are you all right, though? You seem rather flustered."

My eyes flit over my shoulder. Dennick and Ceraun are likely close enough to hear by now. Oh well, I'll take my chances. "Actually," I admit, "I'm feeling a touch under the weather. Is there someone around here who sells medicines?"

She pins me with an oddly pitying stare. "Mikael's is halfway between my shop and the lake, on this side of the row. His pennant is white and blue." She points to a pointed flag flying above the wooden awning keeping the sun's rays off her stall. I notice every stall has one, each with its own design—some of the larger shops have two or three. "He sells remedies, though I don't know he'll have anything for you."

Her last statement chafes against the back of my mind, but I don't have time to ask her more about it before a dark brown mop and a sleek head of glowing blue appear over each of my shoulders. "Boys," I drawl. "Nice to see you again."

"What are you up to, Princess?" Dennick asks in my right ear.

"Everything fine?" Ceraun questions in my left.

I sigh. "Yes, Tweedledee and Tweedledum." When two blank stares are all my joke earns me, I huff and start walking in the direction the shopkeep indicated. "Let's go, I have a stall I want to visit."

They pepper my back with questions about where we're going, but I ignore them. It makes no sense, since they'll learn as soon as we reach my destination, but I'm holding my cards close for a few more minutes before they find out how much I'm struggling. Maybe I can spin the medicine as a preventative.

At last, a white pennant flutters in the breeze, blue stripes creating arrow-shaped patterns along its length. I veer straight for the light wood of the stall it's attached to, catching the eye of the older man selling a paper-wrapped parcel to a woman who looks to be in her mid-30s. The tail end of his explanation of the medication—something about headache relief for chronic pain—ends as I belly up to his table. He shifts smoothly from wishing the woman a good day to greeting me with a friendly tilt of his lips that reaches the lined corners of his eyelids.

"How can I help you, young one?" He asks. His voice is mellow, calming. A plain white jacket in some type of light fabric covers his torso and arms to the wrists. Despite the sun's heat, he seems cool and comfortable.

I lean in, as though the motion will do anything at all to keep the sensitive ears behind me from hearing my admission of weakness, "Sir, do you happen to have any medicine for fatigue? I've been a little...run down lately." The words sting as they slither their way out from where I've kept them locked up deep inside my chest. Their barbs cut my throat and tongue, the ache reminding me I'm sharing knowledge which could leave me stranded here when my friends abandon the weak link.

He smiles, but it's a sad one. My heart sinks, a ball of hot steel tearing through my feet and burrowing into the stones beneath us. "I have several medicines for fatigue, but nothing to help you, dear. My remedies are made for the people of this area, along with a handful of tinctures for the odd wyrok who might pass through on their duties. What I do not carry, unfortunately for you, is medications for wraiths. My apologies, and good luck." He offers me a final head bob and turns to his next customer, leaving me blindsided.

Ceraun and Dennick hook their arms into my elbows and steer me down the lane. The sparkling surface of the lake draws nearer. Sun reflects off it to a near painful degree. I long for a good pair of sunglasses. "What did he mean? What's a wraith?" My voice warbles under the heavy weight of my disappointment.

Dennick's face is stony. "He shouldn't have said a thing," he answers in a heated hiss. "Wraiths are weak. You're not weak, Valorie. He doesn't know what he's talking about."

"But what *are* they?" I push. Ceraun pulls ahead of us as the crowd thickens, forcing us to walk single-file.

Dennick doesn't answer.

We stop at a stall with red and black pennants flapping at either end. Buyers jostle each other in a large group, each vying for the attention of the lone employee manning the entire establishment. He flips skewers over a charcoal flame and baskets of food in hot oil without breaking a sweat. The sound of sizzling meat drowns out any conversation below a yell.

Ceraun elbows his way to the front of a cluster of customers, ignoring their protests and meeting fierce glares with cool indifference. Several buyers motion to his wings before stepping back to give him the scant few inches which pass as personal space here. With a few inaudible words and a clawed finger pointing at the grill in front of him, he places an order from the grizzled man with a shock of white hair stationed behind the counter. Three woven baskets piled high with steaming foods appear on the countertop's high ledge. Ceraun nods and tips a handful of what appear to be polished blue and pink acorns into the man's callused palm. Are they some type of currency? A barter system? A pit-master doesn't strike me as the type to have a side business gardening, but you never know.

While Ceraun forges a path out of the melee of the food stall, another hungry patron takes his place at the counter. My eyes strain to catch what they hand the salesman. A cluster of striated rocks earns them two skewers of dark brown meat. At the shop to our right—an establishment selling teas and spices—a customer walks away with a parcel of dried leaves as the shopkeep pockets two rectangular pieces of shining gray wood etched with sharp lines. There's no rhyme or reason to what constitutes payment except everything is natural in origin.

My unanswered questions rattle in my head as Dennick and I follow Ceraun's winding route between the press of bodies. The masses gradually thin, and I plan my attack for the moment we're relatively free of the cacophony of the market. Once we have the peace to speak without shredding our vocal cords, I'll have my answers.

They can't deflect forever.

When the shimmer of sun on water comes into view, I'm unable to hold back my grin. The lake's surface is a placid, clear blue, ruffled only by the subtle push of the wind and the wakes of several distant boats. Four wooden piers—two bare and two with small sailing crafts attached—jut from a harbor as bustling as the market we've escaped. Sailors throw nets to one another, fishmongers examine the day's latest catch, and captains strut along their decks, all while a group of rowdy children chase each other up and down the planks.

Is there anywhere in this village not clogged with people? The racket is bothersome, but the sheer happiness pouring from everyone we've passed is enough to temper the irritation of the headache thumping steadily behind my brow. If this is what the afterlife is, maybe death isn't so bad, after all.

A beam of sunlight bounces off a metal container at the end of the leftmost pier and spears into my skull. My headache gobbles it up like a starving man, growing stronger as it feeds. I suck a pained grunt through my teeth before I battle it back into submission.

This corner of death may be beautiful, but it's going to have to wait its turn. I know I'm on its doorstep, but I'm not knocking yet.

We settle ourselves onto a patch of sandy beach beyond the harbor. Here on the outskirts of the village, the hubbub dials down to a pleasant thrum of life—or afterlife—on the fringes of the lake's peaceful aura. A few scattered couples wander near the water's edge, far enough out of earshot to make me comfortable beginning my interrogation.

Ceraun passes a basket to each of us. A pair of the skewers of brown meat I saw earlier steam faintly in the cool air off the lake. Beneath them, thick medallions of a pale fried food resembling potato or yucca are nestled in the bottom of the basket alongside a purple root vegetable. Everything is drizzled with a creamy white sauce flecked with colorful spices. It smells heavenly, especially after weeks of trail rations and scavenged fruits.

"What is a wraith?" I ask again after half of my food disappears down my gullet. Restful sleep has abandoned me, but food still provides the energy I desperately need to continue on. For now. "And don't feed me some half-answer about how I'm not one. Answer the question."

Dennick sighs. "A wraith is a soul in the Underworld who hasn't come to terms with their death yet. They wander, refusing to assimilate into the Underworld and be at peace, because such a thing would require admitting they're dead."

My stomach churns around the lunch I inhaled. "Isn't that exactly what I am, then? A wraith?"

"No," Ceraun replies. "There isn't a word for what you are, but it's not a wraith. You aren't meant to be here, *kynaira*. Not as a deceased soul, anyway. Your path is different."

Well, what a relief, though I don't entirely grasp what he means. "And while we're on the topic of words I don't understand, what does *kynaira* mean, anyway?"

Ceraun's face freezes. He turns away, and my eyes must be playing tricks on me, because there's no realm possible where Ceraun would blush. "There isn't a direct translation in your tongue, but a possible meaning for the word would be...'princess,' I suppose."

I snort a surprised laugh. "All this time, you've been calling me 'princess', too? The two of you are more alike than either of you want to admit." They glare at one another, mirrored expressions of offended denial, and my laugh multiplies until I'm close to tears. My vision is blurry, but I catch tiny, grudging smiles on both their faces.

"Now it's our turn to do some asking." Ceraun leans his hands on his bent knees. The relaxed posture is bizarre on his frame. He's always on high alert, but here on the shore he acts almost carefree. "Why did you hide the fact you're getting weaker?"

I cough and splutter on my own spit. The question catches me by surprise, despite knowing they're both upset over me hiding my affliction. "I was...afraid," I admit quietly.

"Afraid?"

With my face aflame, I explain, the words rushing out of me as though I've broken the dam holding them back, "I thought if you found out I was growing weaker you'd want to cut the dead weight, you know? I've already gotten the 'stop training' speech—which isn't happening, by the way—and that was before you even knew the full extent of everything. You wouldn't want me dragging you down, so you'd leave me behind and continue on without me to get home faster. I can't make it to the Hearth without you, so I hid everything. I pretended to be fine when I'm actually completely wiped." Even the lunch in my stomach isn't helping as much as I hoped, but I keep this tidbit to myself. They know enough to make their choice.

"Well, that wasn't necessary," Dennick drawls, picking beneath his nails with a wooden skewer from his lunch. "For two reasons. One, we've known you've been getting worse for weeks."

My spine stiffens. "You have?"

"Yeah, Princess. You're not very good at pretending, and believe it or not, Ceraun and I do talk to each other on occasion. It would've been nice if you trusted us enough to confide in us, though." Ceraun nods. It may be the first time I've ever seen the two of them agree on anything. The fact it's their disappointment in my deception that's brought them to the same side has me sick to my stomach. "Because, reason two is we're a team, aren't we? Can't be a team without trust. We would never leave you behind. You're stuck with us, even once we get to the shining city itself."

I hang my head, ashamed of how I've allowed my anxiety to poison our relationship. I need to keep my demons locked behind iron walls. I'll build until my hands grind down to bloodstained stumps if that's what it takes to win back control of my own psyche.

On the sandy beaches of this far-off land, our bond shining bright as the sun above, the three of us twine our fingers together and make a vow.

Chapter 17
Across the Lake

- Conall -

I would happily kill for a pair of sunglasses.

When a puffy cloud moves lazily away from the perfect disc of the sun above, allowing it to resume its cauterization of my corneas, I make a mental note to add protective eyewear to every packing list we have at the Haven. There is no need for us to settle for discomfort simply because we have accelerated healing capabilities. Between the desert we've finally left behind and now this meadow, my eyes are begging for relief. The steely gray mountains with their white caps in the distance are much too far off to provide any respite from the sun.

Gabrielle pirouettes up ahead, her straight, silver locks flowing around her in the wind like a dancer's long skirt. She's been flitting through the delicate white blossoms and thick, calf-length grass since we arrived, clearly pleased by our new location. I understand why. At least this one doesn't have a surplus of barbarians trying to slice us in two, or skulking animals searching for their next meal. A major point in its column over several of the other realms this scale-turned-lodestar has traipsed us across. It took us five days to leave the glassy sands and dark monoliths behind. None of us would choose to go back there again.

My sister dances in the closest approximation to bliss I've seen from her in a long while, and I wonder. Does she prefer it here? Is it easier for her to exist in a world where her "gift" isn't beating down the doors to her mind, dragging her in and out of timelines without her consent? My gaze snags on her twin and the questions dry up and drift away on the petal-scented air. Gabrielle and Gaius are inseparable. He's the only thing she would never give up, even if the trade-off was a world where she could feel closer to normal. He would follow her here in a heartbeat, yet she would never ask.

But a part of me puzzles over what she would choose if she was no longer tethered to the living realm.

We crest a rise, far too gradual and slight to be dubbed a hill, and a charming scene reveals itself on the other side. The waving grass continues its flow straight to the pebbled bank of an enormous lake. The calm oval of water stretches for miles of pristine mirrored surface, reflecting the blue and white sky without interruption. It's entirely too large to traverse around. Swimming its diameter would undoubtedly lead to a watery grave, even with our stamina.

"Well," Finn huffs. His hands rest on his hips and he surveys the water's edge as though expecting a port to magically reveal itself. There are a handful of ships on the water, but they're mere pinpricks in the distance. "We have a bit of a problem."

Gaius snorts. Leave it to Finn to describe a lake big enough to swallow three Havens whole as "a bit of a problem."

Nevertheless, we wade through the sea of grass and its islands of flowers to dead end at the pebble-strewn shore. My eyelids contract in protest against the bright glitter of the sun on the lake as we draw nearer. The water laps gently at the stones, their surfaces rounded and smooth from centuries of liquid eroding their sharp edges. There's minuscule ones the size of my smallest fingernail, mid-size stones an inch or two across, even a handful of flat pieces of shale large enough to roast a chicken upon, if we had one available. And a fire pit to place it on. But the lake shore is devoid of anything resembling poultry or dry wood.

Or boats.

After half an hour of pacing the damp rocks, we're no closer to crossing the lake. "Now what?" Gaius asks with a groan. Palms flat against his thighs, he crouches in the shallows, watching minnows dart to and fro.

Gabrielle bends down beside him. Her fingers trace paths in the water, and minnows flock to nibble at her skin. "Too bad we can't ride these little guys," she says with a soft laugh.

"Ride them?" Finn scoffs, jostling her shoulder as he peers over it. "We can't even eat them."

We trade ideas on how to cross the water as the sun meanders its way through the sky. Each suggestion is more far-fetched than the last, and they quickly devolve into a way for my siblings to pass the time rather than any real brainstorming.

My jaw pops with the force of my teeth grinding together—anything to keep my frustration from vomiting itself onto the shore. I swipe a palm-sized rock from the shore and clench my fingers around it, imagining for a split second it's their necks. The thought is vile, but I'm losing the will to keep my temper controlled these days. How can they sit and joke? We're at a dead end. A beautiful, picture-perfect dead end. One Valorie would sell her kidney to experience, and I won't even be able to tell her about it if we don't find a way across this damned lake.

The stone groans within my grip. Stinging pain shoots through the middle of my palm, and I unfurl my fingers to find a line of blood stemming from a gash along the center of my hand, courtesy of a jagged protrusion on the underside of the rock.

So much for the water's ability to soften edges. Even the lake can't do its job properly.

With a grunt, I hurl the bloodied rock into the water. It sinks beneath the surface with a splash. Ripples fan from its impact point, the motion turning the reflection of the setting sun into flickering flames. I rip open my pack and remove the last two items Solail entrusted to us. A bag of colored seaglass and an ancient, looped rope of pearls. Two tools remain, without a shred of a clue as to what they're for.

Shoving the glass back into the pocket of my bag, I pace while my fists connect and separate in front of me, pulling the rope taut with a sharp clacking sound. My temper flails against its ever-weakening bonds. I count backward under my breath, willing my heartbeat to slow and my veins to cool the blood within them. My chest expands and contracts in time with the rope's crisp noise, and as the water returns to normal, I begin to believe I might be successful.

Until the surface begins to ripple once more, and a scalloped slab of glass pierces the placid lake from below. The four of us scramble away from the lake. Smaller pebbles roll into the frothing water as we beat our hasty retreat from whatever the hell is slowly rising from the depths.

About ten feet from the shore, the mysterious fragment continues to shoot upward into the creamsicle sky. Clear ribs shoot downward from the edges into the curved pane, glowing faintly in what's left of the sun's rays. Light refracts and splinters into rainbows as it passes through. Up and up the glass rises, the end broadening and thickening until it finally connects to a curving base which breaches the water in one smooth motion.

A truck-sized oval, its ends tapered to blunt points, bobs halfway out of the water. The scalloped pane is embedded into its top, while a similar structure is attached to the rear end of the structure. A subtle, repeating pattern covers the entire body. Within the transparent exterior, globular masses pulse in various colors. The hues shoot along pipelines and span the interior in a web of light. Churning water near its middle continues to move even after the rest of the lake returns to stillness—an unseen flotation or propulsion system beneath the surface. On the end without a fluttering sail, a shutter opens and closes over a circular lens the size of a wheel. The craft moves in figure-eights along our end of the lake, the nose of its structure cutting cleanly through the water with barely a disturbance.

What is this creation? There's no questioning its beauty, but there must be some type of utility involved. A submarine, perhaps? I lean in, but there's no sign of anyone inside the craft. Maybe it's autonomous? But who would manufacture a vehicle with such obvious mastery only to leave it alone in a lake?

When Gabrielle speaks, the sudden sound sends me leaping out of my skin. "It's a fish," she breathes. A wide-eyed expression of awe is painted across her features.

It's as if her words wipe a film from over my eyes. The strangely fluttering panes of glass? They're *fins*. And it isn't a pattern etched into the somehow transparent skin of the being—those rounded, U-shaped lines denote the borders of scales running the length of the creature's body. It blinks once more, and I peer into its dark pupil. The fish's gaze is filled with unmistakable intelligence. This is no mere happen-stance—this magnificent denizen of the lake is here for a reason.

But why?

"Conall," Gabrielle glances at me, the thick grass waving around her calves. "What's in your hands?"

The rope dangles limply between my fingers, its knobbled length forgotten in the chaos surrounding the majestic fish. I hand it over for her inspection.

"Why would a fish be interested in a rope?" Finn asks. His blond head pokes in next to Gabrielle and he runs the long end of the rope through his palms while she examines the loop at the other end. Gaius watches her work, as though their twin bond offers him a direct window into the workings of her mind. Maybe it does.

The pieces fall into place within my brain, and the picture forms. "It's not a rope. It's a lasso."

For a moment, no one speaks. We stare between the lasso in Gabrielle's hands, to the formidable being drifting lazily in the water.

"We're going to ride the fish? Sweet." Gaius and Finn exclaim in unison. They snicker and slap their palms together. My gaze meets my sister's and we shake our heads. Their antics never change. Sometimes I marvel at the fact they're both older than I am, if only barely. It often feels as though Gabrielle and I are the eldest siblings rather than the youngest.

We agree Gaius should be the one to wrangle the fish. He has the best throwing arm by far between the four of us. Valorie once showed me a movie where vampires played baseball, and she joked Gaius would fit right in. "Immortal, ghostly pale, and a fan of the so-called Great American Pastime?" she joked. "He's three for three. We could get him some body glitter and his Halloween costume would be set."

The memory shreds my tattered heart into smaller pieces.

I welcome its ache and indulge myself for a moment. It ricochets through me while I cling to the recollection of her laughter and the kiss I stole to capture the sound and swallow it whole.

With a firm shake of my head, I banish the wisps of my past back into the recesses of my brain where they lurk and wait to torment me. Now is not the time.

Gaius stands at the water's edge, poised and ready. His arm cocks back under the spreading dusk, and he heaves the length of pearls over the surface a handful of times, testing the trajectory and force needed to close the distance between him and a row of swirled spires protruding from the apex of the fish's head. On his fourth throw, the lasso glances off its mark. Gaius' stern expression morphs into a feral grin. A vicious chuckle curls out of his throat into the evening, and he flings his arm forward once more.

The lasso loops over the largest spike, smooth and simple as a child playing ring-toss. Gaius whoops as we thump his back and congratulate him. Beneath the loop of pearls, the fish stills and turns its giant eyeball in our direction. It assesses us as if to ask, "Are you coming?"

"Okay, the lasso allows us to control it, and we can use it to climb up its side. But, how do we get to it?" Gabrielle wonders. I have an inkling she knows the answer and is hoping for another option.

No such luck, sister.

I smile at her as the stars wink into life overhead and ask, "Come on, Gabby. Don't you fancy an evening swim?"

CHAPTER 18

A Lead

- CONALL -

Spray pelts every inch of exposed skin as we fly across the water. The night sky glitters above us, stars splattered across it like paint flicked off an errant artist's brush. The breeze, gentle and soft on the shore, is a crisp gale that lifts our hair into flapping banners behind us and chaps the places the spray has drenched. Between my legs, the unyielding coolness of the fish's odd skin pulses with those strange inner lights.

Riding on the back of the glass fish is an assault on the senses, an overwhelming maelstrom of sensation. For a moment, everything else falls away. Every part of me is focused on maintaining my precarious seat as the world churns around us and threatens to slide us off into the inky blackness below. The body of the creature has no give to it whatsoever, and at this speed any impact with the water's surface would be akin to hurtling into rock. We're forced to keep our limbs tightly clenched and grip each other's shoulders for purchase, with Gaius at the front of our line clinging to the slippery pearls and the spike at the fish's crown.

It's terrifying, exhilarating, and achingly beautiful. How I wish—for what must be the millionth time—Valorie was here to experience this.

The fish turns in a sudden, sweeping curve, and we all inhale a collective gasp as the slick surface shifts to the right beneath our bodies. We lean

196

dangerously to one side before righting ourselves and sinking back onto the slight ridge along the creature's spine. It's uncomfortable, cutting into places beneath my waist which should really be handled with more care, but straddling the pointed line of scales gives us a modicum of traction.

"You think we'll have this much fun when we're back in Avallea?" Finn calls on the wind from where he's seated directly in front of me.

The corner of my mouth ticks upwards. Thanks to the collective memory purge administered to every dehmi when they leave our home-world behind, our knowledge of Avallea is largely limited to history and government. We know little of the specifics of the world itself beyond the fact it's suffused with magic and peace. We'll reclaim our memories when we make it there, in order to facilitate a smooth transition back into Avallean society. But until then we're left with guesses and hope.

"Personally, I think we'll find a way to make some fun no matter where we are. If we managed it on Earth, we can do it anywhere, right?" He laughs, the sound briefly making its way to my ears before the gale snatches it away.

As the shore rapidly approaches, Gabrielle points towards a cluster of dark objects hunched against the lake's edge. A soft glow emanates from rectangles and pinprick spheres within the jumble. A minute later, laughter and music reaches us from the distant village.

"Maybe they'll have information," I shout loud enough to make my voice crack. Hopefully they can hear over the roar of wind and water. Gaius shoots a thumbs up back with his pearl-wrapped left hand. If he heard me, I assume they all did.

A weak flutter starts in the shadowed depths of my heart. It's possible whoever inhabits this place may truly have news. We've been following Solail's instructions religiously, but a confirmation we're on the right track would be a relief.

Sand twinkles in a field of glitter beneath the light of the stars and full moon as the fish slows to a stop in the shallows of a sliver of beach. It's only been approximately an hour of riding, based on the position of the silvery orb in the night sky. If you ask the sore, partially raw skin on the insides of my thighs, it's been long enough.

The four of us emerge from the waters and collapse on the sand. We likely resemble a pile of waterlogged seals, groaning and whining about our aches and pains. Finn vows never to leave his bed after this is all over. I have to agree with him. With Valorie in my arms—clothes preferably not included—never leaving bed again is a fantastic idea.

Crackling orange fire sprouts from Gaius' palms. With a wave, he sends a softball of flames hovering around each of us until our clothes are dried and everyone is pleasantly warm. Once we're finished and he's satisfied none of us will complain about mildew or blisters in the morning, he dumps the fire into a divot near where the sand shifts back to grass. It will burn all night in a merry blaze without needing fuel. The warmth of the enchanted bonfire battles the lingering chill in my bones. It nearly wins. But, deep within their marrow lies a cold the fire couldn't touch even if I threw myself on top of it.

We settle into the cushioning green and make our camp for the night. From around a curve in the beach, the sounds of partying and general life drift in from the village. Bowls of thick stew filled with the last of our more palatable provisions make their way around our circle of bodies. Hopefully this village is as bustling as their nightlife makes them appear. If not, we'll be traveling the rest of the journey on hardtack, jerky, and whatever edible plants Finn can cultivate on the move. Hunting is off the table. It's not safe for the living to eat the beings of the Underworld, according to Solail.

Bowl scraped clean and washed with a scouring handful of sand at the river's edge, I barely wrap my blankets around me in the grass before sleep claims me for the night.

The edge of the village bleeds into the endless grasses as though born of the field itself. Postage stamp rear yards are fenced between houses built of brown brick, their outside edges left open to the flora beyond their boundaries. Cobbled streets divvy up the residences and storefronts into neat parcels. Several of the larger streets extend into the meadow itself, becoming dirt roads which weave their way into the waving green. Gray predawn light mutes the world into a watery replica of its normal vibrancy, but the early hour has done nothing to diminish the liveliness of the town itself.

We'd packed up our meager camp at the first sign of light on the horizon, determined to slip into the village unseen near the docks and formulate a plan of action before the morning rush began. But it seems this village never sleeps.

Dockworkers and sailors shout to one another, their burly arms filled with boxes, barrels, and nets, ready to snag the day's catch and be back in time for supper. On their ships, boatswains ready the rigging to set sail the moment their crew is finished preparing. Urchins scurry underfoot through it all, but they lack the haunted eyes and gaunt figures of neglected orphans. These children are tidy and clearly well-kept despite their mischief. Their laughs fill the pungent air as they cavort along the time-worn wood, their shrill giggles becoming piercing when a muscled workman with a faded tattoo along one forearm jokingly threatens to string them up as bait.

We weave through their chaos and head in the direction of a lively market. Flags attached to stall roofs flutter and snap in the air's current, each one different than its neighbor. Our ears trade the gruff timbre of the sailors for the calls of shopkeepers hawking their wares to early morning shoppers. The din is no less painful here, especially with the vestiges of last night's headache clinging to my temples, but at least the smell is vastly improved. A myriad of sweet and savory aromas intermingle in the market's air with the tang of metal and a spicy, fresh undercurrent I'm guessing comes from a tea shop or herbalist.

"Which one of these do you think would be most likely to know about travelers?" Finn asks Gabrielle as we wander up and down aisles.

She points to a stall with a large crowd already formed around it. A twin set of flags dyed crimson with dark squares lined end-to-end whips over its awning. The unmistakable sizzle and pop of cooking meat emanates from the front of the disorganized line of patrons. "That one."

It's a wise choice. A crowd means conversation. Conversation means a flow of information which may lead us to news on Valorie.

"Sweet," Finn replies with a grin. "We can grab breakfast too. Kill two birds with one stone." Gaius leans in for a high five. The loud clap of their palms makes us all wince. I offered to heal everyone before we left the beach, but nobody wanted to deal with the crawling discomfort of the healing process for a handful of aches and pains likely set to fade by lunch.

I didn't say it, but I was relieved not to have to spend the morning nursing my power reserves back to health. My brothers can work their magic for much longer before it begins to affect their constitution, since their affinities deal with the natural world. Gabrielle and I suffer for our more complicated gifts, but I wouldn't trade my powers for another's.

I doubt she would say the same.

We enter the line and wait—patiently, on my siblings' parts, not as much on mine—until we finally reach the front. Behind a warbling shield of hot air from the grill in front of him, the cook's stern face is lined from decades of life. He flips kebabs and empties fry baskets without breaking eye contact as he waits for our order.

I step forward. "We need to ask you a few questions about a girl who—"

Finn grabs my collar and jerks me backward. Coughs and splutters explode from my bruised throat. He steps into my forcibly-vacated position and his elbow catches me in the gut in a swift move I'm positive is anything but accidental. I wheeze ineffectual curses at his broad back.

He ignores every one of them. "Good morning, sir," Finn leans against the counter with a casual, easy smile as if he's been friends with the grizzled man for years. "We're on the hunt for some delicious food and a smidge of information on a friend, if you wouldn't mind helping us."

If his warm expression and friendly blue gaze have any effect on the shopkeep, it doesn't show. One bushy gray eyebrow raises over an impressive scowl. "Are you buying or not?" the male growls.

Finn's grin grows impossibly wider. "We'll take four of everything."

The male finally cracks a smile. His brown eyes twinkle as he grabs a wooden tray and begins piling it high with baskets of fried foods and small bowls of pickled vegetables. "What do you want to know, boy? Let ol' Branson see about getting you some answers to go with your patronage."

"Mmm," Finn hums with a hand on his stomach. We're arrayed around a four-top table in a small square in a less crowded section of the village. Discarded baskets and bowls are stacked between us. "Branson is my new favorite person in all the worlds. Who even are you guys, again?"

"I'll be sure to tell Margie the next time she bakes cinnamon banana bread," Gaius quips. The three of us snicker as Finn splutters about how Margie is his true favorite and could never be replaced and how could we insinuate such blasphemy, conveniently forgetting *he* was the one who started this.

Insufferable though he may occasionally be, Finn's carefree attitude is the reason we sit here with full bellies and the only information we've received since we left Solail.

Valorie was *here*.

She walked these streets a scant handful of days ago in the company of a wyrok and another male. They bought food at Branson's stall, but he only spoke to the wyrok before they headed towards the water.

He said she seemed tired, dragging alongside the males without sharing their enthusiasm. My heart aches with the information and the fear it stirs within. Valorie isn't great at sleeping under the best of circumstances, and I doubt her nights have been comfortable on the road.

Just hang on a little longer, Wildcat.

After the shopkeep told us everything he knew, we detoured into the port and asked around. None of the sailors or captains recalled a trio of outsiders requesting passage, but a handful remembered seeing a wyrok with his companions on the beach about three days prior. Since nobody had given them a seat on their crafts, they must have left on foot.

"Next step: We buy ourselves some provisions and continue on to the next portal as soon as possible." I rest my elbows on the table and palm the bag of seaglass resting in front of us. Half of it is empty, the colored chips having bought our feast from Branson. According to him, this village only deals in natural items as currency. They believe true wealth is what can be given back to the land when its usefulness is spent. An admirable philosophy, one the Avallean society would certainly support in the living realms. I assume—based on how these people spend their afterlives in *our* Underworld—we already do.

"Hey," Finn mutters. His hand covers my own, and I notice my fingers have been drumming into the wooden table hard enough to bruise. "We're only a couple days behind them. That's huge."

I inhale and exhale slowly through my nose, determined not to explode in the middle of this peaceful place. "What if those few days are the difference between life and death, Finn?"

"It won't be."

My gaze slides past him to connect with Gabrielle's. She gives a microscopic shake of her head, her mouth turned down at the corners. No new news. Another dropped ball. "We don't know for sure, Finn," I sigh. "We don't know anything."

He squeezes my hand. "We have to keep trying and stay positive. Wallowing won't get us to her any faster."

I nod and smile up at him, but his words are useless. I'm not wallowing without her.

I'm drowning.

CHAPTER 19
Fading

- VALORIE -

A pair of suns—one harsh, one a watery shadow of its brother—throw the scene beneath me into harsh relief. Clods of dry, tan dirt crunch beneath my feet as I inch closer to the edge of the cliff I am perched upon. The drop is sheer and deadly, but the carnage on the valley's floor draws me, a hopelessly entranced moth enticed to its flickering demise.

Where am I?

This isn't like the other dreams. There's no haze of memory softening the sharp edges, no warped sense of self to contend with. I'm not a phantom observer, I'm as real as the fighters crawling ant-sized on the sun-baked earth down below. They connect and repel each other again and again. A chorus formed from the steely clang of their weapons mixed with cries of pain and fury reverberates up to my vantage point with every collision. It sets my teeth on edge.

I hold my hand against my forehead to block the worst of the suns' glare and crouch at the crumbling rim as though closing those three feet between me and the battle one hundred feet down will have any effect on my ability to discern who is fighting for their lives on the cracked and dessicated plain. I focus and, in the odd way dreams ignore all science and reason, my eyes begin to pick out identifying features on the toothpick combatants.

Near the edge of the fray, a silver-topped stick figure encloses its op-ponent in an earthen cage. Beside it, a taller one capped with a shorter bit of blackness conjures a veritable fire hose of water to drown an enemy. Closer to the center of the melee, a cluster of fighters is battling a team twice their size. Two opposite sticks, one with a white braid and another with the barest midnight fuzz atop its pinprick head, work in tandem as though they share a mind. A larger figure to their left flings green whips. They wrap around their targets and constrict until bodies split in two. And on their other side, a minuscule head of obsidian waves wields a sword in one hand. His other is wreathed in white light—when it flares, a body falls to the ground. Flare. Thud. Flare. Thud. The magic sucks the life from one assailant after another, but the wave of enemies rolls on without end.

By the time the third body lies lifeless around him, I'm on my knees, rigid fingers tangled in my hair. Because I know those matchstick warriors down below, each of them small enough to cover with the tip of my pinky. I know them as well as my own family, because that's precisely what I consider them.

My entire body is absorbed in tracking the fate of each of the dehmi as they fight for their lives. So much so, I don't notice the solid, stabilizing weight of his arm around my shoulders until he speaks.

"I can't tell you how glad I am you're not down there, Princess," Den-nick murmurs. His voice is low, practically drowned out by the cacophony of the war at our feet. And yet, I still startle at the sound. I'd likely tumble over the edge and into oblivion if he wasn't holding me in place. "Words can't express how grateful I am you're safe with me and Ceraun, far from Joran's clutches."

"Joran?" I ask. My sight shifts of its own accord once more, bringing another of the tiny people into focus. His cold, lifeless mien sharpens and

becomes clear, and I glimpse my murderer cut down three faceless dehmi in one swoop of a bloodstained greatsword.

A gasping inhale wheezes into my lungs. "No, we have to help them!" I scream at Den. "They can't stay there! He's coming for them!" Because I can spy every shift and pattern from this distance, and Joran's trajectory is aiming straight for the ball of fighters containing my heart and soul.

"We can't help them, Princess," Dennick's low tone is remorseful, but it carries none of the panic suffusing my own. Only resignation. "They have their course already set, but we can change yours. You're safe with us. Joran will never find you here. He'll either find his victory and stay in the living realm as their new god, or he'll finally be defeated and cast into the Pit where he belongs. Either way, we'll keep you safer than their group ever could." He gestures to Conall's family with his free hand, somehow knowing exactly who to point towards. Maybe the dream gifted him the knowledge the same way it gifted me sight. "They want to drag you into danger, but we only want to keep you protected."

I shake my head hard enough to rattle my eyeballs in my skull. "You're wrong, Den," I whisper.

With a morose expression close to tears, he extends his hand in front of us again. "Look, Princess."

My gaze follows the path of his finger. When the scene warps and refocuses, my palm flies to cover my mouth and I choke on bile.

Next to Conall, there's another figure I'm positive was not there before. A girl, with a halo of onyx curls frizzed around her head. She whirls and pivots to meet each approaching enemy, but even from this distance I can tell her movements aren't as smooth as the others. She moves as though she's still learning her own body. As though something fundamental had recently been changed, down to her bones and sinew.

The two groups collide, and everything becomes clear. It isn't Conall who Joran has had his eye on from the moment he walked onto the battle-field.

It's me.

Sobs wracking my body, rivulets of tears coursing down my cheeks to soak the parched earth, I'm forced to observe as the me who isn't me fights for her life. She ducks under his sword, a dagger wrapped in black and silver flashing in her grip as she closes in.

"Thanks for keeping that, by the way," Dennick murmurs. I ignore him, too focused on the path this thread of my own fate has taken. Is this how Gabrielle feels, helplessly forced to follow a strand in Fate's Web as it's woven into existence?

My dagger connects, but the blow is glancing. It only serves to throw Joran further into bloodlust. He roars, the sound piercing even from this distance. Piercing the same way his sword slashes and runs through my chest as though my bones are nothing more than water. I fall, and the thread snaps as the life leaves the eyes of the me in the valley.

Conall screams. I sob. And Dennick holds me to his chest as Joran summarily fells every dehmi I know, one after another. Their bodies crumple to heaps beside the small pile of flesh and fabric that was meant to house my soul for millennia.

"It can't happen," I wail, tear-filled eyes begging him to agree. "It won't, Den. Gabby said the Web can be rewoven." A sudden revelation gives me enough hope to draw a breath. "This is just a dream, it's not the true future. This isn't real. Right?"

Small shushing sounds rumble his ribcage beneath my ear. Dennick rubs soothing circles on my back while he whispers words that gently slice my heart to tatters with their truth. "You weren't made for that life, Princess.

They were doing fine down there, before. They might have even won. But your death? It was the distraction that broke them. Don't you see? Everyone is safer with you here."

You know the sensation of being stuck in a nightmare, desperately trying to make any sound at all, to call for someone to please fucking *help*, and your damned pons and medulla oblongata shake metaphorical hands with each other and say, "Let's keep her locked down tighter than a bank vault?"

Well, not this time. Jokes on you, brain.

My scream knifes into the morning air, taking my soul with it. Ragged sobs carve holes into my chest, ripping chunks off my dwindling, sputtering energy reserves, ones I can't afford to lose. My vision blurs and darkens with a terrifying combination of lack of air and mind-altering exhaustion, yet the keening wails keep coming. Something cracks and crumbles inside me. A crucial part of my armor rusts and atrophies, leaving a gaping hole behind.

"Valorie, stop! You're hurting yourself!" The *real* Dennick, not my dream one, has to yell to be heard over the animalistic sounds erupting from my chapped lips. He yanks on my hands, their harsh angles thrusting my nails deep into the flesh of my arms. Blood wells beneath the short half-moons and drips down my skin to the grass. "Snap out of it!"

Words shove themselves between my screams, but they make no sense. I'm not even sure I'm the one making them, but they sound like my voice. "They can't—I can't—no, please!" I shove against Dennick's iron grip, desperate to be free. To do what? I have no clue, but I have to find a way to fix this. My dream can't become reality. I won't let it.

"What have I done? What's going on?" Dennick's whispered voice is as hoarse as my own, and I'm fairly sure I mishear at least half of his words, but I'm too far gone to care. Behind him, Ceraun's wide gaze flickers between Dennick's shocked expression and my feral struggle to break away and run. It's instinct—an inhuman, base desire to be anywhere but this place. I'm an animal, a piece of prey, and the wolves are closing in. I doubt I have the energy to make it twenty feet, but my body says I'll run until my legs give way, and then I'll crawl until I die. There's no fighting this, because there's no *this* to fight, but try telling that to my nervous system.

Something hardens behind Ceraun's pupils. He shoves Dennick with an elbow as though he weighs no more than a child. "*Kynaira*," he murmurs. His voice, barely above a whisper, somehow wends its way to my eardrums. I thrash in his grip. "I'm sorry. I'll fix this, I promise."

Just as I lick my lips and prepare to tell him there's no way for him to solve this problem, to just let me *go*, a familiar mist exits his mouth. It drifts over me in a mint-scented cloud and settles itself in my lungs. As the world dims, I get the hazy impression of Ceraun hissing at Dennick, his clawed hands infinitely gentle as they lift me from the earth. And then I know no more.

I wake to a rhythmic jostling emanating from two bars beneath the curve of my back. For a brief moment, I'm reminded of horseback riding, but the angle is all wrong. My heavy lids fight every step of the process I go through to force them open and figure out what is going on. I win the battle, and am rewarded with sunlight and the underside of Ceraun's clenched jaw with a background of sunlit leaves. Apparently, I'm being carried.

The telltale heat of an embarrassed flush creeps its way up my neck. "You can put me down, Ceraun," I croak. "I'm okay now." Mentally and physically tapped out, sure, but I'm back in my right mind at least. A single tear rolls down my cheek and runs along a line of scales on Ceraun's arm. His eye tracks the sparkling drop on its lonely path. Of course. Ceraun never misses a thing.

His gait doesn't falter. "I think you're going to stay right here, actually," he replies. I protest, but Ceraun shakes his head. "Conserve your energy, *kynaira*. You're no heavier than a youngling, and I could use the workout before we return to my people and I am ridiculed for slacking on my fitness." His tone is light, but I know better. I can read between the lines quite clearly. This is his way of letting me know he's not going to listen to arguments, making it apparent I shouldn't waste my breath.

Instead, I busy myself with taking in our surroundings. Sometime during my slumber, we must have entered a new realm, because gone are the windswept grasses and white-capped mountains of the cute little Alpine lakeshore meadow. Now, we're wandering along a dirt path dotted with transparent stones in a variety of colors. To our right, a grove of odd plants looms. At first glance, they remind me of a standard deciduous forest on Earth, albeit with deep blues and purplish burgundies in place of the normal greens and browns. On closer inspection, something about the trees appears almost...incorporeal, despite clearly being solid. It hurts my head to peer too closely at them.

To our left, a cliff descends into nothingness, as if a butcher cleaved the world itself with one swift slice. A shudder rolls down my spine at the thought of falling forever down the never-ending drop, and yet I find it hard to tear my eyes away.

The delicious scent of grilled meat and bread hits my nostrils. A second later, a sandwich comes into view beneath my nose, Dennick's long fingers wrapped around it. "Eat up, Princess," he says with a faint smile. It's smaller than his usual one, less cocky and self-assured. "You gave us quite the fright back there. How about you don't do that again, huh?"

Well, at least his attitude hasn't changed.

I swipe the sandwich from his hand, stick my tongue out at him, and take a hearty bite. Yeasty bread, slightly spiced meat, and a hunk of hard cheese vaguely reminiscent of cheddar. Fresh provisions we bought from the village by the lake. It's simple, but the flavors explode across my tongue. My stomach roars its approval and demands more. I wolf the rest down in under a minute.

An ominous red glow off the cliff's edge to our left drags my attention away from licking the remnants of my meal from my fingers. I crane over Ceraun's arm, stretching my neck until the tendons protest in an effort to take in more of the harshly beautiful, hellish sight. Far below, mountains of black shale glint wetly in the crimson light of lava flowing through the valley between them. Despite the molten river, something about the obsidian crags is cold. Lifeless. "Is that the Pit?" I ask, dragging my eyes from the foreboding sight to peer up at Ceraun.

When he nods, I call to Dennick, a goofy smile plastered across my face, "Hey, Den, look. It's Joran's future neighborhood."

"I'm sure as hell not helping him house hunt," he replies between barking laughs. "The Pit is a horrid place, designed to ensure its inhabitants never have an ounce of comfort. A dome of magic, maintained by the Paragons of Death themselves, creates a dichotomous system—simultaneously burning hot and glacial. The light from the lava burns their eyes and skin, no matter the species. Even within the caves dotting the mountain's walls, there is no relief."

His explanation is near identical to the one Ceraun once gave me. Sounds like the perfect place for Joran to spend eternity.

"Dichotomous, huh?" I smirk. "Look at you learning how to use your big boy words."

He snorts and shoves my shoulder. "What can I say, Princess? You're rubbing off on me."

A disgruntled rumble vibrates my right arm. "We should be arriving any second," he growls. His expression starts out soft when it flickers down to my face, but finishes with a glare in Dennick's direction. Guess the two of them didn't kiss and make up. If anything, he seems even less trusting of Den than before. What *happened* while I was unconscious? "There are guards hidden within the trees, but they won't appear unless they're needed," Ceraun grunts, his eyes flicking back to Dennick. His glare is daring Dennick to give the phantom guards a reason to show their faces.

I draw in a breath to ask what the issue is, but my inhale morphs into a gasp as we round the corner.

When Dennick and Ceraun called it the Crystal Forest, they weren't exaggerating.

Wide trunks sweep upwards from the ground in graceful curves, their spiraling branches arching over the path and intertwining up into the hazy distance beyond. Their bark is smooth and unblemished, the colors ranging from the deep blues we've passed by already to bright cerulean and teal. Lush plants in pinks and emerald greens blanket the spaces between their bases, while broad indigo leaves twinkle merrily in the sunlight.

Every bit of flora from the earth to the sky is made of purest crystal.

"You live *here*?" I ask Ceraun in a breathless whisper, unable to tear my gaze away from the majesty. It's pure magic, a wonderland you'd have to drag me away from kicking and screaming. "Why would you ever leave?" *Oops.* That question was meant to stay in my skull, but oh well.

Ceraun chuckles. "Yes, though the home city of my people lies further in. And I leave on occasion for one reason or another. This time, I left to find you." He jostles his arm beneath my shoulder blades, punctuating his sentence with a small wink.

"Thanks for that, by the way," I reply. "So, what are we waiting for?" My chin lifts towards the crystalline trees. Their light refracts and sends small rainbows across my skin, reminding me of Ceraun's scales in his dragon form. "Let's get going!"

But Ceraun doesn't budge. "Maybe it would be better for us to make an early camp," he says. He gestures to a small space free of plant life at the edge of the forest proper. Dennick wanders over and peers through a translucent, fern-like plant in a pleasant shade of baby pink. "You could use the extra rest."

Please, no. I fight the urge to shudder, sending a grin his way instead. Hopefully, it'll mask my trepidation. "I'd really rather not. Let's keep moving." *And stay awake,* I add internally.

No luck. Ceraun's head cocks one way, then the other. His lids narrow slightly, and I know he's seen right through me.

I sigh. "I'm afraid, okay?" The admission drags its feet and emerges in a garbled grumble.

His eyebrow arches. "Of?"

"Of falling asleep?" My sentence rises at the end, turning itself into a question. I deflate. "I think something is breaking inside of me, Ceraun. Something fundamental. I'm afraid I'm falling apart, and the dreams are a sign something is seriously wrong with me." Our eyes connect. The telltale sting of tears begins behind my lids. "What if we're too late?"

"That's crazy," Dennick calls. He strides over to where Ceraun stands, me still nestled in his arms. "There's no way that could be the reason. Maybe the dreams aren't a negative thing, Princess. Maybe they're a sign. Maybe this is where you're meant to be." His words are composed, assured. Delivered with his usual quirked grin and a firm pat on my forearm. There's no way for him to know which one of us is correct, yet he speaks as though he has all the answers.

My brain is still puzzling over Dennick's overconfidence when Ceraun suddenly stiffens beneath me. Slowly, too slowly, he walks several paces away, clears a patch of short, lavender-colored brush, and sets me down under the boughs of an apple-green tree with sunlight filtering in rainbows down through its center, a living stained glass sculpture. "Stay," he commands in a low, hard voice.

His back fills my view as he turns. Ceraun's posture is always impeccable in a ruler-taped-to-your-spine way a human could never master, but this is different. He's gone completely stiff, his hands clenched into clawed fists at his sides. Light hits the spread membranes of his wings and lines the delicate bone structure like a radiograph. The scales on the backs of his arms are flared, and I swear his skin is halfway on its way to the deep blue of his dragon.

What's going on?

"Ceraun?" I whisper, but my question is drowned out by his growled threat. One which makes no sense, but curdles my blood all the same.

"Give me one reason why I shouldn't flay you where you stand, dreamtreader."

CHAPTER 20

A Dream By Design

- VALORIE -

"Ceraun?" I call into the heavy silence. It hangs cloyingly in the wake of his accusation, begging to be broken. "What do you mean? What's a dreamtreader?" I wrap my brain around the word and digest its pieces. My stomach sinks.

I have a foreboding sensation I already know, but it can't be true. There has to be a link in this chain I'm missing, a piece to the puzzle which would make everything clear and calm. Because right now my mind is bathing in a churning sea of fear.

"I should have known." Ceraun stalks across the bare patch of grass towards Dennick. His voice is a feral, rolling thunder.

Den's hands fly up, palms splayed in defense. He makes no other moves as Ceraun enters his personal space and towers over him to growl, "Your scent has been shifting, twining with hers for a long while. I assumed it was due to proximity, but you smell more of her than yourself today. There's only two ways such an occurrence would come to pass, and you certainly aren't mates. So, tell the truth, *transient*. Tell her how you've broken the trust she placed in you. How you've broken her own *mind* with your horrors. *Tell her!*" he finishes in a roar loud enough to chase birds from the treetops.

Loud enough to chase my shocked soul from its mooring.

"I didn't," Dennick whispers. Broken coal-black irises lock with mine from a dozen feet away. Their edges swim under a lining of liquid. "Valorie, I swear, I didn't mean to hurt you. This was all to keep you safe! Joran will kill you. He killed me! I was a fighter, born and bred and *beaten* to be a warrior. I was at the top of my game, and he cut me down like a calf at slaughter." Tears pour down his cheeks as he speaks. They mirror my own, my heart fracturing as I fill in the blanks between his words.

"You deserve to be safe," he whispers. "You should be safe, and they're failing you. They're all failing."

Ceraun isn't moved, not one bit. "And that gave you license to take it upon yourself, as her *savior*, to enter her mind without her permission," he yells. A taloned finger jabs into the scant inch of air between the two of them. "To skew her dreams, morph her nightmares, until she reached the point where sleep itself terrifies her? You want her to stop fighting, to retreat into the eternity of this place? You, who knows her story, who knows who she *is*?"

My head aches as I follow the two of them in their battle. Only half the words make sense, and none of them are comforting. A horrific clenching within my chest tangles with the fiery constricting of my throat, with the burning in my eyes. And beneath it all, the ever-present fatigue begs me to say it's all too much. To just give up.

"I don't give a fuck who she is!" Dennick's tether on his emotions snaps quick as a sun-dried rubber band. Sadness and rage war across his expression. He leans forward and screams into Ceraun's face. "Who she is? *Who she is*? Do *you* know who she is, Ceraun? Beyond your precious job, your duty to the Paragons? Is she even a person to you, or is she nothing more than a pawn? Because I know who she is. She's my *friend*, and I'm tired of losing those to the Web of fucking Fate. She's safe here, with us! They can't hurt her here! Don't you think she's been hurt enough? Wasn't your whole job to keep her safe? Or does your oath mean nothing to you?"

He turns his back on us, then makes an abrupt turn and dashes past Ceraun before my guardian can recover. Dennick skids along the crystal grass to kneel at my feet. With my hands grasped between his sweating palms, he begs, "Please, Princess, you have to believe me. I never meant to hurt you, I swear it."

"What did you do, Dennick?" I ask lowly. "Did you really—did you really send those dreams to me?"

"I didn't send them," he says, a thumb rubbing circles on the back of my hand, "but I did change them. I was hoping—" he coughs to clear his throat, "—I was hoping you would experience the beauty of this world—and the terrors of theirs—and choose to stay. Before our lives collided, I was doomed to loneliness, and you were doomed to death. Joran won't let you live—he'll cut down every one of your friends on his way to you and never stop until you're in his clutches. But here? Here he can't touch us. Here, we're *free*. You're my best friend, Valorie. I want you to stay, please. Can't you understand what I mean?"

His eyes hold so much hope. So much desperate hope.

Hope becomes pure horror as I pull my hands from his grip and cast my tear-filled gaze onto his. "How could you, Den?" I choke. "I'm your best friend?" He nods frantically, and a sob escapes the iron vise I'm keeping around myself. "Friends don't manipulate their friends. Friends don't hurt friends. They don't try to scare each other into making a decision that would change their forever. They *talk*. You should have fucking talked to me, not tried to scare me into submission!"

"But you would have said no," he whispers in a broken voice. It claws at my heart, but I don't relent. "You would have said you needed to leave."

"And I do. I can't spend forever glancing over my shoulder and wondering what could have been, had I only been braver. I can't spend forever waiting for everyone I know to die so I can be with them again. I can't spend forever without Conall, Dennick. Not without at least *trying*. But I would've seen you again, some day. Our friendship would have had its eternity. I would've come back and found you, because friends don't forget." I hiccup through another sob, then focus on Ceraun in the background, his face stony, his eyes filled with my own sorrow. "I'm ready to go, please."

Ceraun lifts me into his arms without a word and turns his back on Dennick, taking a few steps toward the path. I don't fight his desire to carry me. There's no energy left in me to walk. Every bit I have is focused on not falling apart.

"Valorie, wait!" Dennick is still on the forest floor, crying in earnest among the crystals' multicolored glow. One hand claws itself into the dirt beneath him, while the other reaches for me as though he can breach five feet of distance with a single arm.

Part of me wishes he could.

"I'm so sorry." His whispers are broken, shattered like a crystal under someone's boot. "This isn't what I wanted. I just wanted you to be happy. I'm so, so sorry."

"I know, Den," I weep. "That's what makes it so hard to say goodbye."

And as we walk away from him, as the crystals close in around us and block him from my tear-drenched view, I hear him.

"I'll fix this, I swear. I'll never stop watching out for you, Princess. When you need me, I'll be there, because friends don't forget."

221

CHAPTER 21
I'm Fine

- VALORIE -

It takes Ceraun a whole two minutes of tense silence before he asks if I'm all right. His skin is still two shades closer to oceanic than it has been since the day we met, and I swear it darkens one step further when I shake my head and blink furiously against the fresh prickle of tears threatening to unleash themselves on my raw cheeks. A shuddering exhale crackles from between my lips before I press them tightly together to keep a sob from following suit. Nestling into Ceraun's arms, I close my eyes and try to breathe deeply, but the combined weight of losing Dennick and the sickening, unending exhaustion makes it hard to draw in more than reedy bits of air.

Do not cry, I chant internally, even my mental voice dripping with sluggish lassitude. *Keep it together.*

A large part of me wants to beg Ceraun to turn around. It would be all too easy to return to my friend, to lift him from the dirt and dust him off and tell him I understand. Because I do. If anyone can comprehend the mind-numbing grip fear can have over every facet of your life, the abysmally stupid decisions it can cause you to make under the guise of preservation, it's me. It doesn't make what he did acceptable, but he knows that.

I hope our paths cross again some day.

But Den is going to have to hold on for a while, because I'm not sure *I* can hold on much longer. My body trembles as though it's made of dandelion fuzz, and every step Ceraun takes dislodges a few more wisps of my soul and sends them floating away into the ether.

"Am I going to die, Ceraun? Are we too late? Was I too slow?" My voice is a whispered rasp, barely audible. I shake with the effort required to force it from my parched throat. But he hears. He always hears.

His golden orbs reflect my haggard face back at me, slitted pupils contracting in the multicolored light of the crystals. "We're almost there, *kynaira*. The Paragons will know what to do." he replies.

I don't miss the way he avoids actually answering any of my questions.

Afterwards, we don't speak for a long while. Ceraun focuses on catapulting us deeper into the forest as fast as his legs can take us. I focus on matching my breathing to his own, the smooth cadence reminding my faltering lungs of their necessary job. When his increased speed turns the crystal flora into whips of smeared color across my field of view, I squeeze my eyes shut and pray to these absent Paragons I don't waste any of my precious energy vomiting up the contents of my stomach.

I must fall asleep, because the next time my eyes open, it's to the sound of quiet conversation above my head. I close them again and focus on the murmured voices.

"...here yet?" It's the tail end of Ceraun's question, and I have no idea who—or what—he's referencing.

A low, androgynous voice answers, "Not yet. I've heard they should be here soon, but there was a hold up of some sort topside."

"The Council, if rumors are to be believed," a third voice, this one high and feminine, cuts in.

I feel more than hear Ceraun's sigh. "How long?"

"A couple days, maybe?" The first one replies. "They haven't given an exact time to expect their arrival."

Ceraun's grip clenches around me. His next words are soft, but they send a chill straight to my heart. "I don't know if we have a couple days, Ixiran."

The female voice speaks, and I struggle not to jump and blow my cover. The sound is much closer than before. "Is this her?" A pause, and then, "Take her to the temple, Ceraun. They'll know what to do until the Paragons arrive."

Ah.

My stomach clenches. Anxious sweat pools in my palms as I slowly reprocess their words. No matter how I rotate and rearrange, there's no other possible meaning.

Esraa and Amon aren't here yet.

"You're right," Ceraun replies. He begins moving, and I crack my eyes enough to peek as we pass under an arch of glowing golden metal. "Thank you, Ixiran, Mephys."

"See you soon," they reply in unison at our backs. I tilt my head to face forward, and gasp.

A brilliant cityscape sprawls in front of us. Tiers of pristine stone buildings in shades of gold, opalescent white and a rainbow of pastel climb the mountain the city butts up against. Crouched over it all is a temple, a gargantuan Grecian structure gleaming a blinding white with whorls of shadowy gray bleeding through it as it basks in the light of the sun.

I have approximately three seconds to admire the magic of Ceraun's hometown before my vision blurs and blends back into nothing but streaks as he rockets forward yet again. I groan, the heels of my palms pressed over my closed lids in a futile attempt to keep the nausea at bay. "Ceraun, do we have to move so quickly?" I want to explore, to soak up the vitality of this place and force the thickened blood crawling its way through my veins to accept it. Surely it would be enough to bring me back from the brink of whatever chasm I'm slowly slipping into.

He doesn't answer, but I'm almost positive he speeds up. If I wasn't running on fumes and wrestling with my own gut, I'd smack him. As it is, all I can do is cling to him and count the seconds until this is over. Whispered questions and friendly greetings get left in Ceraun's wake—several voices call to him, but he doesn't stop until the glaring sunshine morphs into cool shadow.

I crack a lid to find the beautiful temple's columned overhang looming, a fanged maw waiting to swallow us whole. A pair of breathtaking wyrok, one robed in luminous alabaster, the other in a shade of black so deep the light itself appears to flee in fear of being consumed by its darkness, stand sentinel on either side of the temple's closed entrance. It's a flawless work of art my eyes ache to absorb. Intricate carvings displaying scenes of carnage, of mercy, of birth and life and death and joy, are etched into the solid opal double doors standing a dozen feet taller than even Ceraun's dragon form. The more I stare, the more I find smaller scenes tucked within the larger ones. Most of them feature wyrok, both in their humanoid, winged forms, and in their draconic ones. However, there are plenty of Avalleans, and a handful of other species I can't name interspersed throughout as well. I get the feeling I could stare for all eternity and never find every secret image hidden within the surface.

The wyrok pair moves in our direction as one, their steps in perfect, effortless sync without as much as a glance swapped between them. The white-robed one speaks first, her soft, melodic voice filling the handful of feet between us. "Ceraun, how lovely to see you returned to us safe and sound." Her violet eyes lock with mine. She blinks first, turning to share a long look with her companion before returning to Ceraun. "Is this her? The *kynaira*?"

The nickname feels wrong coming from another's lips. Belatedly, my brain wonders why she would know to call me *kynaira*, but the thought comes too late to ask the question aloud. Ceraun has already nodded and asked for us to be given chambers, to which the wyrok female laughs before responding with, "Of course. We've had them prepared for ages."

Her companion pivots on a heel and silently gestures towards the doors with a sweeping arm. They open on a wisp of shadow in time with his movement. At my startled gasp, the female giggles. "It's rare for us to get newcomers in the Hearth. Forgive my brother for showing off."

The interior of the temple is as magnificent as its facade. Now that Ceraun is finally moving at a speed more compatible with the human body, I soak up the intricate surroundings as he carries me through the innards of the building. The layout is open, with endless swaths of the same smoke-swirled white stone on all sides of us. Several sunken, wall-less "rooms" pepper the main chamber. Some are filled with cozy seating areas, others with flowing water features, pocket gardens brimming with flowers and miniature trees, or small altars lit by candlelight. Columns dot the area, their bodies stretching up to a ceiling lost in indistinct darkness high above us. And every one of them is carved with more of those same scenes from outside. Even the banister curving beside us as we ascend to a higher floor is etched with frolicking animals and fairies the size of my palm.

"Are all the buildings decorated like this, or is this one special?" I whisper as the black-robed wyrok leads the way down a royal blue carpeted hall.

The wyrok in white giggles again. "Yes, and also yes," she replies. "We wyrok love our arts as much as the Avalleans do, maybe more. But, the temple is especially intricate. The High Paragons are revered by our people."

My brow scrunches. I rack my brain in an attempt to recall Conall or his family mentioning "high" Paragons, but come up empty. Finally, I ask our new companion.

"Those who rule over Death itself," she clarifies. "The highest of all Paragons, for they are the ones who maintain this realm. We owe them our lives and our home itself." Her perfect face breaks into a beam, sharp cheekbones softening as her full lips spread and her pert nose scrunches.

Ceraun answers my next question before I have a chance to ask. "The wyrok aren't originally from the Underworld. Long before any of us—or even our great grandparents—were born, wyrok lived in another world entirely. Nobody remembers our origin point, and even our oldest texts barely mention its existence. But, we know it was destroyed in a cataclysm, and the Paragons of Death who ruled at the time decided to harbor us here. We would have gone extinct in an instant without them."

Our little party comes to a sudden stop before another set of doors. These are midnight blue, swirled with iridescent sparkles like galaxies in the night sky. A twin pair of golden handles in the shape of planets turn beneath a brief look from the silent, shadowy wyrok. He enters the room first, robes swishing behind him, and we follow suit, Ceraun still refusing to put me down despite me having insisted several times I'm perfectly capable of walking. It may or may not be a lie, but I don't particularly care for these new people seeing me being carried as an invalid.

The room is, of course, immaculate. Plush blue-black carpeting with unfamiliar gold constellations covers the floor, while matching blue and gold curtains frame a bay window on the far wall, complete with a wide ledge outside holding several potted flowers. There's a low coffee table and loveseat facing a small fireplace crackling quietly in the corner. A pair of single doors in the same style as the entryway line the right-hand wall, standing open to reveal a walk-in closet and an en-suite bathroom.

But it's the massive canopied bed along the opposite wall which dominates the space. Easily bigger than a California King and draped in sapphire silk, I could fit six of me under its down comforter without being cramped. It is there Ceraun finally decides to set me down, inching his hands from beneath me as though I'll shatter into dust if he moves too quickly.

I sit up, struggling to contain my yawn long enough to ask, "Can we please go explore now?"

"No, you need to rest," Ceraun admonishes. When I pout, his expression softens. "You're more asleep than awake right now, anyway. I doubt you'd notice any of the sights if I did take you."

Another jaw-cracking yawn splits my face in two. I have to admit defeat. "All right," I acquiesce, snuggling beneath the covers. "But tomorrow, you promise we'll go explore? Sounds as if we have time to kill before it's show time, anyway." *And maybe someone out there in all that magic can help me,* I add silently.

He nods and brushes a lock of hair from my face before settling himself into the couch by the fire. Guess he's waiting here. Honestly, given Ceraun's propensity for overreacting, I'm surprised he's not curled up at the foot of the bed like an overgrown, scaled guard dog. He and Conall are going to feed off each other when they meet, I just know it.

My eyelids begin to sink shut, slowly obscuring the view despite my best efforts. The two guards make their way to the door and tell Ceraun to call if we need anything. When I garble my thanks for their help, they offer twin smiles in return.

"Sweet dreams, *kynaira*," the obsidian-cloaked one murmurs. He stops to talk to Ceraun for a moment, but their voices become a low hum I can't decode. His companion sees me struggling to stay awake to eavesdrop—though is it truly eavesdropping if they're in my room?—and sits next to me on the coverlet. She starts to braid my curls on the pillow, humming a soft melody I don't recognize while her deft fingers sort through tangles and snarls.

It's the last thing I hear before sleep carries me away.

CHAPTER 22
(I'm So Not Fine)

- VALORIE -

T he morning light glittering off the myriad colorful stones and metals in the city below us would be breathtaking if not for the piercing ache behind my eyeballs. I squint, willing my brain to stop turning to mush for a little while and allow me to appreciate my first real taste of the magical metropolis outside my window. The temple's position high above the city offers the perfect vantage point for observing the Hearth, and I'll be damned if my body's dramatics are going to prevent me from enjoying it.

The tiers of the city cascade down the mountain like a giant's staircase. Each level is blanketed with life and culture. I long to be down there among it all. The left third of the city looks to be homes, smaller two-to-three-story structures vibrantly iced in swaths of color, with front-facing balconies over the thoroughfares and doll house gardens behind. On the right-hand side of the city, an amphitheater sits surrounded by smaller buildings. They appear shorter than the houses, but this could be due to the open-air theater complex dwarfing them. From this distance, it's impossible to discern their purpose.

"What are you?" I whisper as my fingers tap on the ledge.

"The entertainment district."

"Shit, Ceraun!" I yelp, jumping halfway out of my skin. "I'm serious about putting a bell on you. You're a hazard!"

Ceraun chuckles. "It's not my fault you become incredibly unaware when you're observing something." He leans over my shoulder, pointing in the direction of the amphitheater. "Entertainment." His finger slides to the center of the city. It's teeming with tiny, ant-sized bodies moving up and down the streets and through an open square filled with stalls. "Artisans. Shops, stalls, an open marketplace—anything you want to purchase can be found in the center of the Hearth, although there are other shops throughout the city which sell necessities like food and clothing."

Next, he confirms my assumptions were correct; the left side is reserved for living spaces. Some of the artisans and shopkeepers have homes above their stores, he explains, and the priests and priestesses are allowed to reside in the temple if they wish. But the majority of the Hearth's citizens live in the picturesque neighborhood below, or in the Crystal Forest beyond the Hearth's official borders.

I think that's the end of it, but he directs my attention to a section of the city I didn't notice. Directly below the temple, there are a handful of tiers with buildings sporting larger, more austere facades. Fewer people walk the paths between them, and the ones that do move with a quick step, their movements less carefree than the shoppers in the center of town. "The official facilities," Ceraun explains. "Our citizens decide the city's fate based on an equal voting process, but these buildings house the entities designed to enact those results, as well as a barracks for younglings being sent on missions or unmated wyrok working as peacekeepers."

My head nods while my mind spins with the influx of new information. When Ceraun holds his hand out to me, I blink at it in confusion. He sighs through a smile and takes pity on my poor, overloaded mush-brain. "Aren't you the one who made me promise to take you to explore the city today? I vaguely recall saying yes being the only way to get you to agree to rest." His smile droops. I know what he's going to say, and I'm shaking my head before he even begins speaking. "You really should be in bed, *kynaira*. You don't have much strength left, even I can tell. You should conserve it."

"Please, Ceraun," I beg. I'm not above getting on hands and knees, but I don't think I'd have the energy to get back up. And if Ceraun found *that* out, he'd strap me into the bed himself. He may be aware I'm getting weaker every day, but I've managed to hide the full extent of my deterioration.

I've been through worse; I can overcome a touch of fatigue. Excitement and fun are what my body needs, not a week of holing up in a room with only my thoughts as company.

"I can't handle being cooped up for days. It's jarring to be stuck indoors after all this time. I'm asking for a quick peek around, a light walk to stretch my legs, and then I'll come back and you can tuck me in and read me bedtime stories for the rest of the day. Promise." I stretch my pinky out to him with a grin, and he has me wait two tense seconds before sighing and wrapping his own around it.

"This cannot be broken, you remember?" he admonishes, as though he was the one to teach me about pinky promises and not the other way around.

I nod rapidly, my smile broad. He sighs again—I'm beginning to worry he's developing a breathing condition—and we begin the long trek down into the city of the wyrok.

I wish I could say I spend the entire walk down the mountain brimming with energy. That the city of magic and crystals pours its life into me and fills me up. That I'm skipping merrily, full of joy and wonder, without a shred of exhaustion left inside my tiny five-foot-one body. That we languish our day away frolicking through the streets full of beautiful, winged people, and I return to the temple sated and rejuvenated.

I wish I could say any of those things, but I'm not a liar. In reality, I'm panting, haggard and out of breath before we've even cleared the quiet streets surrounding the white-walled official sector. Sweat rolls down my back beneath the light clothing I've been provided with, despite the morning's relatively mild temperature. I'm dragging my feet along the path, inch by torturous inch, too damned stubborn to ask to turn around and go back to bed.

I knew this was a bad idea, knew it before I—quite literally—dragged myself from bed this morning while Ceraun was briefly out of the room. I waited until he left because there was no way I was going to leave the bed without being a decrepit mess. My intuition was right then, and it's right now. I don't *quite* have the energy for this, but I don't have the mental fortitude to sit in a bed like a child with the flu until someone comes to fix me. I'm fine, despite what my muscles would have you think. They like to lie, anyway. Always told me I couldn't handle the mile run in high school gym class, and they were wrong then, weren't they? So they can shut up and be wrong now, too.

With my elbow in his hand, Ceraun tows me to a stone bench situated beneath a tree with weeping boughs low enough to sweep the cobblestone pathway. I collapse onto it with a groan. The cold surface leeches heat from my sweltering skin, and I resist the urge to lay flat on the smooth gray stone and roll around until it touches every exposed bit of me.

"Ceraun?" He turns in my direction, but I jerk my head away. My questions are spoken into the verdant grass at our feet. "What will happen if the Paragons don't show?"

"They will, *kynaira.*"

A sigh escapes my nostrils. "All right, well what happens if they don't get here *in time,* then?" I don't tell him the reason behind my questions, the black and purple-green splotches at the edges of everything. They remind me of the way my vision blanks when I stand too quickly, but I've been sitting as still as possible for several minutes, trying to wrestle control of my body.

Trying, and failing.

One fang indents itself into Ceraun's bottom lip. His hands wring in his lap. I've never seen him this uncomfortable. It's endearing. "I...don't want to answer," he admits quietly.

"If they're too late, I'll die for real, right?" My voice is an almost inaudible wisp of fear given form. "Will I have to leave you behind?" *Will I be truly alone?*

Ceraun pivots on the bench and grips my shoulders. "You don't have to do anything you don't want to. I promise you." His left hand slips down to mine. Ceraun's clawed pinky wraps around my own, squeezing the limp digit.

With all my strength, I manage to bend my finger around his and give him a sleepy smile. "That's good," I whisper. My head lolls forward onto his shoulder as my neck finally gives out. My spine follows suit, slumping down into itself and tumbling me into Ceraun's chest.

"*Kynaira*, are you all right?" He shakes me, gently at first, then frantically, stopping abruptly when my limp neck snaps back and forth with a horrid crackling sound. A large palm cradles the back of my head as my face presses against his shoulder.

"Ceraun?" The words slur, dripping and bleeding through numb lips. "I don't think this was a good idea after all." A delirious chuckle. "You're going to gloat about being right, aren't you?"

My question startles a short laugh from him, but it dies before I can congratulate myself. "I swear I won't, just stay with me. Keep your eyes open. *Please*," he begs in a voice that cracks and shatters. When I remain silent, the effort of speaking suddenly too much to overcome, Ceraun's plea rises to a broken shout. "Wake up! Valorie!"

I think that might be the first time you've said my name since the day we met. I mean to say the words, I swear I try, but I don't think they make it out of my mouth. Everything flickers between shades of monochrome and overexposed vibrancy. Back and forth they war across my vision: life and death, existence and nothingness, the endless struggle of consciousness versus the blank emptiness of purgatory. All while Ceraun begs and pleads in the background, calling for help to anyone who can hear. Not that it will accomplish more than driving him hoarse.

When it becomes clear the gray is winning, I rally enough energy for one last moment of clarity. One pair of breaths, inhale and exhale. A singular instant to spend on my guardian, my friend I never expected to find in this place.

I hope he's right about what comes next.

"Ceraun," I breathe, "thank you...for everything."

I tell myself I'm fine, the mantra I've repeated countless times over the past few weeks. Over and over, while my friends marched on without knowing I was deteriorating, falling to pieces beside them. My eyes are still open, the world is still there, so I'm fine. It's colorless and staticky, barely visible behind the bruise-colored speckles and blotches of shadow, but it's there, and so am I. If I had a heartbeat, it would still be thumping away, because I'm fine. I'm completely fine.

I'm so not fine.

Then the darkness descends and I know no more.

CHAPTER 23

Waiting

- CERAUN -

"Thank you...for everything." Valorie's words, breathed into my shoulder without any of her usual fire, curdle my blood. This cannot be happening. It *cannot*.

"Valorie, *kynaira*, you have to wake up. Come on, wake up!" I repeat the words over and over as I sprint up the path, scarcely realizing they're exiting my lips. Her head lolls limply over my forearm, the too-fragile bones in her neck creaking with each jolting bound I take across the sun-warmed stones. I constantly forget how delicate humans are, how easily they can be irreparably damaged. If I had remembered, if I had fought harder against her simple yet disastrous wishes, maybe we wouldn't be here.

It's all my fault. She was my charge, my kynaira, *and I've failed her and the Paragons. I've failed my people.* The words scald my brain in a wave of acid and vitriol. My claws flex against her skin, threatening to puncture the alarmingly sallow flesh before I hastily soften my grip.

What will happen to our world without her? What will happen to her love when he discovers what I've done? Will he leave without completing his ceremony? What will happen to *me* without the friend I never thought I'd make? This was supposed to be a simple duty, nothing more than another job, but it became the most fun I've had in a century.

And now, I've lost it all. I should've pushed us to move faster, should've stopped her from training and forced her to conserve her energy. The thought would be laughable under different circumstances. As if anyone could stop Valorie when she sets her mind to something. She's a spitfire—or she *was*.

"No," I snarl. This is not the end, not if I have anything to say about it. And I have a lot to say. Innumerable desperate words roil around in my throat, attempting to burrow their way out and into Valorie's brain to shock her awake. But there's no time to waste—begging won't work.

I tuck our *kynaira*, the future itself, securely against my chest and move her head into the crook where my arm and torso meet. My wings flare behind us, their navy expanse muting the sun's glare. With one flap, then another, I gauge the change in airflow with the addition of her limp—but *not* dead—weight in my arms. I raise my chin and roar a warning into the morning air. Then, eyes trained on the window to her room on the temple's highest floor, I fly.

"You need to take a break, Ceraun."

I grunt. Deina continues to stare at me, her violet irises glowing lightly as her magic pours another wave into Valorie's prone form lying on the bed.

I remain perched near the footboard, unmoving. Deina can keep staring; it will not work. I am not leaving this room. She doesn't scare me. Neither does her brother standing in the corner, nothing more than a raven-cloaked shadow. Daros somehow manages to avoid the sunlight streaming in through the open curtains. Curtains covering the window I crashed through with Valorie in my arms, scattering a starscape of crystalline shards in our wake.

I haven't had the motivation to fix it. The sharp slivers feel appropriate—we're all broken.

Deina hums and removes her palm from Valorie's forehead yet again. She turns to face me, hand on her white-robed hip. "It's been two days, Ceraun."

I don't know what the point in her statement is, but I am certain I am going to find out momentarily.

Sure enough, she continues with a heavy sigh. "You haven't bathed. You've barely picked at the food Daros has brought in for us, and the only time you sleep is in the brief moments after I've assured you she's stable. You're falling apart at the seams." Her gaze leaves my own and moves to Valorie. Still and lifeless, even the minute rise and fall of her chest is undetectable beneath the blankets. Only Deina's assurance Valorie's consciousness is trapped somewhere inside her mind keeps me from tumbling over the edge into pure panic. "Would *she* want you to be like this? Our *kynaira*?"

Another grunt rumbles my chest. "It's listening to what she wanted that got us in this situation in the first place. If I had only pushed her to rest more—"

"Nonsense," Deina interrupts curtly. Her slitted pupils contract and flash with the draconic fire we all store deep within. Maybe I should be afraid of her, after all. It's easy to forget she's as formidable an opponent as any of us, hidden beneath her gentle exterior. "You know this wouldn't have been solved with a few more hours' rest," she says in a softer tone. "The Paragons should have been here six days ago, but they're not. Their absence is the issue, not a hiding game or a few sword sessions." Deina may have received a frantic, guilt-ridden recount of our entire trip during her initial exam of Valorie. I was worried, certain this was my fault and yet desperate for someone to confirm my inability to say no to my small friend was not the cause of her demise. Deina has been attempting to convince me of this fact for the past two days.

I still only partially believe her.

A loud knock rattles the celestial door to the hallway. Three pairs of eyes snap in its direction. A head of teal spirals peeks into the room. "Is he ready?" Mephys asks, her high voice as familiar in my ears as my own.

With a groan, I roll my eyes at Deina. "You called my cousin?"

She shrugs. Daros chuckles from his corner, smiling darkly when I face him. "You knew, didn't you?" I accuse.

"You've been a mopey bastard for days," he replies with a shrug. I bare my teeth and resist the urge to rip his wings off when he adds, "There's nothing you can do here, you're simply annoying my sister."

"No he's not," Deina protests, a faint blush coloring her cheeks. She glares at her brother. A look passes between them I cannot decipher, especially on two days of no sleep.

Now it's Daros' turn to roll his eyes, their violet shade the exact same as his twin's. Younglings are not easily created among our people—twins are practically unheard of. Their birth was a celebration for our people, and they've been a pain in my scales ever since. "Well, he's annoying me, then."

"Come on," Mephys whines. Her small hand tugs relentlessly at my elbow. I must have missed her entering the room during my conversation with Daros.

I snatch my arm away and clip the back of her skull with a wing tip. "Have I gone through a portal into the past? Are we children once again?" Mephys pouts before baring her fangs at me. I turn away—any reaction will only spur her on further. But I cannot resist muttering, "Some of us never grew up, it seems."

"Ceraun," Deina says sternly. "Go. Get some fresh air and food beyond the fare from the temple kitchens. You will hear from me if she awakens—which she *won't*," she adds as I lean forward, this exact question poised on the tip of my tongue.

My cousin leads me to the exit. I do not drag my feet, because sulking would be unbecoming of the *kynaira's* personal guardian. They simply move slower, coincidentally. And happen to scuff the floor on their way. When we reach the two doors of midnight stone the color of my deepest scales, as though I was destined to be assigned to the *kynaira* from the moment of my birth, I pivot on my heel. "You swear she'll be fine?" I ask, panic lacing my voice.

Deina nods. Her smile is the only invitation my cousin needs to sweep me back into the world. The door shuts behind us on Daros' shadow magic before I have the chance to rush back inside. I know without checking he's locked it and won't open it again until we've spent what he—or his sister—deems a suitable amount of time away from Valorie's chambers. But I have no desire to walk amongst my people. Not now. I don't deserve their company, their joy.

As we leave the temple, Mephys suggests taking our midday meal by the gates, where we can soak up the peace of the forest while also checking in on Ixiran and his trainee on duty. Apparently, he brought a new guard with him today in order to give my cousin the freedom to spend her day babysitting me. I'll have to remember to "thank" him for his role in their meddling.

Regardless, Mephys' plan is a decent enough one, and it satisfies my desire for privacy. I grunt my assent. We turn down a quiet side street winding its way in the general direction of the food shops.

Mephys' hand skates down my upper arm to my elbow. "You're not yourself, cousin." She offers a small, soft smile entirely unlike the wide beam she wears in public. My cousin is wild and free, but only those close to her know her gaiety is a front to cover the bleeding heart beneath. "It's not like you to question Deina's assessments."

A long, tired exhale *whooshes* from my nostrils. She's right. Deina is the best healer we have in the Hearth, despite her scant century of life. The four of us—my cousin and I, Deina and Daros—studied together as younglings. We were inseparable before our callings bit a large chunk out of the time we have to spend together. Now, we're lucky to scrape together one or two evenings of revelry in a lunar cycle.

"I don't know what to do, Meph," I confess. "I'm at a loss."

Mephys cocks her head, her curly teal locks swishing midway down her back as she saunters at my side through the crowds. A full foot shorter than me, yet she carries herself with the confidence of a wyrok twice her size. "Well, what's she like, the *kynaira*? By the time you brought her, she was half d—" She cuts her statement off with a gulp, but not fast enough. I know what she was going to say.

Dead.

A snarl attempts to force its way out of me as we round the corner into the market district. I resist the urge to snap at my cousin and force the snarl down to a rumbling growl, but it's difficult. Instead, I pour my torn heart into detailing our trip, the way our *kynaira* showed her bravery, her unwavering, occasionally misplaced kindness, her stubborn force of will which made me want to bash my head against a tree on more than one occasion. I spare no detail, good or bad, only pausing to order a meal when we finally reach the new food shop Mephys demands we try. By the time we spy the golden archway of the Hearth's entrance half an hour later, my cousin has heard every twisted step of the journey it took to bring Valorie to our home.

"She sounds like one of us," Mephys responds when my tale is through. "I can't wait to meet her properly. I'll be sure to tell her all about the trouble you got into as a youngling. What better way to welcome her than to pull back the curtain on her stoic, oh-so-professional guardian?" She smirks and wiggles her shoulders back, marching in a stiff circle around me until she falls to pieces laughing.

My shove threatens to send her tumbling to the ground beneath the glimmering archway. She squawks in alarm as her food lists dangerously in her arms. "If I remember correctly, *cousin*, you were as much a part of said trouble as I was."

The shadow of the gate's curved apex passes over us before blending with the dappled colors of the weak shade from the crystal boughs above. Their translucent leaves don't offer much in the way of sun protection, but the hazy rainbow of light seeping through is subdued and comfortable compared to the glare off the city's buildings. And the quiet of the forest is a welcome change from the Hearth's bustle and abundance of inquisitive stares.

"Mornin', Ix," Mephys chirps. She bounds forward to their side as I peer around the patch of sparser vegetation directly opposite the entrance to the city. It's peaceful, but something is...off. Out of place. Nothing beyond the ordinary catches my eye, though.

Until I turn to the left and stop dead in my tracks. My wings flare and contract behind me, torn halfway between a defensive stance and a looming offensive position.

"What is *he* doing here?" I snarl.

Ixiran glances at the sparse encampment nestled into the edge of the forest as though they've forgotten it exists. "Oh, him? He's been here since the day you arrived. Showed up that evening and begged to be let in. Which clearly was not happening on any guard's watch, yet he refused to leave. Kept asking to be taken to the *kynaira*."

Of course he did.

"When we said she wasn't available, he said he would stay until she was." They shrug one shoulder. "As he's not harming anyone or impeding our duties, I don't have a reason to force him to leave until the *kynaira* or the Paragons say. Plus," they add nonchalantly, "he's interesting company."

I splutter. "He's been here since—" Suddenly the time line connects in my head, and I whip towards my cousin, who has been standing silently at Ixiran's side for several minutes now. Mephys is never quiet unless she's trying to hide something. "You *knew* he was here," my voice is a deadly growl, "you knew during my entire story, and you didn't see fit to tell me about this?"

She flashes a saccharine, innocent smile. One single-handedly responsible for saving her from the wrath of our family and the peacekeepers several times as a youngling. "Oops?"

Insufferable female.

Fallen crystal leaves crunch into multicolored dust underfoot. My footsteps spawn a tiny cloud with each furious stomp in *his* direction. Peering down at where he's seated against an amethyst tree trunk, wings flared wide and claws glinting, I wait for him to cower.

But, he barely acknowledges my presence. Electricity crackles along my scales and lifts the lines of short fur along my limbs and spine, but still Dennick remains impassive, his stare boring into the middle distance. A single dark eyebrow lifts over black eyes overflowing with sorrow. Not an ounce of fear dwells in their depths. I would be impressed, were I not currently preoccupied with resisting the urge to turn him into a lightning rod.

"*Leave*, transient," I hiss through elongated fangs. My scales ripple with the force of resisting the change of forms. Our mind remains intact upon embracing our other state, but certain *urges* become less controllable. Were I to shift now, I would likely incinerate him before I had the chance to stop myself.

His voice is lifeless, a shell of the flamboyance I became grudgingly familiar with during our travels. "Where is Valorie?"

The misery infusing those three quiet words cuts through my rage. He asked, yes, but the question feels rhetorical, as if he knows the answer but wants me to refute it. "She's...asleep," I reply softly.

A slow dip of my chin. "Yeah, that's how I thought you'd phrase it." His eyes flicker to mine. They're dull, as devoid of life as his voice. "If she's dying for real—" his voice cracks, and he clears his throat before continuing. "If this is as close as I can get to her when she's in trouble, this is where I'll be. She would do the same for either of us." A sad, humorless chuckle. "Who are we kidding? If it was one of us, Valorie would have found some way to beg, bribe, or sneak her way into the center of the city by now."

Despite everything, I find myself sinking to the ground beside Dennick. We stare at the city gates, avoiding eye contact but bonded by regret. "Never takes no for an answer, does she?" I huff as the tree's bark scrapes against my upper back.

He simply snorts. It's answer enough.

"I'm pretty sure she's forgiven you already," I tell him quietly.

"She shouldn't," he replies. "What I did—I had my reasons, but I still went too far. Fear is a cause, but not a justification." His gaze meets mine. "I know that now, for all the good it does."

"I agree, but forgiveness is not up to either of us. If it were, I'd make you grovel for at least a year before throwing you a bone."

His eyes widen in shock at the small smile which accompanies my comment. "That may be the first joke I've heard you make with me, Ceraun. I thought you hated me."

I shake my head slowly. "I didn't hate you, I simply did not trust you," I explain. I can't resist adding, "And I was at least partially right in my assessment, wasn't I?"

His shoulders slump under the weight of the truth. "Yeah. 'I didn't mean to' doesn't count for much in the grand scheme of things."

Climbing to my feet, I keep the knowledge I've also begun to, if not *forgive* him, at least comprehend his decision, tucked away for now. He can stew in his transgressions a while longer, especially considering I guarantee he's continuing to plot ways to convince her to never return to Avallea. Instead, I promise, "I can't let you into the city without her or the Paragons saying they're fine with it, but you can stay here until then. I'll send word, if there are any...changes."

"Do you think she'll pull through?" His chin lifts with the question we're all asking these days. But his face falls once more with my answer.

"I don't know." A deep sigh rumbles my chest. "I'm not sure exactly what's going on, to be honest. I don't know if she's trapped in her own skull, or floating around in some great beyond we can't reach. I pray it's the latter."

"She would hate to be trapped," he whispers into his lap.

With all the sudden brilliance of a lightning bolt, an idea strikes. I ask Dennick if he's able to sense whether or not Valorie is dreaming. If he could contact her, maybe he could ask her what she needs in order to awaken.

When his head begins to shake, my hope plummets once more. "Not from here. If I were in the room with her? There could be a chance, maybe. But not from this distance."

I can't risk letting him inside the walls. Not before the Paragons arrive.

We lapse into a somewhat companionable silence as the sun crawls across the sky. Familiar birds and small creatures chitter as they move unseen between the multihued plants around us. I soak in the peace of the forest and pray it clings to my bones upon our return to the Hearth.

Mephys swoops in and smashes my peace to smithereens when she—loudly and repeatedly—demands we head back into the city for dinner. As we reverse our path back into the neverending throng of wyrok buying food and trinkets, I find myself wondering how furious Deina would be if we brought our food back to Valorie's chambers and ate there. A few of her favorite sweet bean buns might assuage her anger. Wyrok live for food, and I know for a fact Deina is no exception.

When she swings open the starry door to find Mephys and me waiting on the other side, the scowl on her face slowly melts into a wide grin. Turns out a dozen of the city's best buns are the price of entry—one I'll gladly pay for my forced "reprieve" to end a few hours early.

I dash to Valorie's bedside, nearly upending my basket of food onto the pristine coverlet in my haste. I bought extra in case she was hungry, but it's apparent my foolish, hopeful purchase was in vain. Valorie is unchanged, her skin the same uncomfortable shade of paste it was when I left, eyes sunken slightly behind lids spiderwebbed with blue veins.

"*Kynaira*," I whisper fervently, "please wake up."

But, as they've done a thousand times before, my pleas go unanswered.

CHAPTER 24

In the Land of Dragons

- CONALL -

This is it. The final stop.

Three hours ago, the final portal opened onto a hard-packed dirt path bordered by an oddly insubstantial forest on one side and a bottomless cliff drop on the other, exactly as Solail said it would. Even without her description, the group of five dragons now flying overhead would suffice as a clue. They soar several miles in the air, yet are impossible to mistake for any species of bird.

The wyrok scale has been vibrating frantically in my pocket since we arrived. I'm worried its friction may burn a hole through the thick fabric. The longer we walk, the harder it jitters, like a dog who knows home is waiting around the next corner.

My siblings point and crow about the wyrok high above us. They observe the dragons' maneuvers and displays of magic backlit by the bright blue sky and muse over the differences between their magic and ours, whether we have similar origins or developed our powers along diverging lines of evolution. A subject Valorie would no doubt jump headfirst into with theories and postulates at the ready, full of evidence none of us picked up on but she somehow amassed and categorized without any tools besides the one between her ears.

Fates, I miss her.

I pray this winding path is a short one. If the Hearth awaits us at the end, and if Valorie has indeed beaten us there, I could have her in my arms by nightfall.

My palm rubs absentminded circles in the center of my chest, but it does nothing to ease the stabbing pain I've had hounding me for the past five days. There was a brief moment where it seemed to lessen several days ago, but it quickly returned tenfold. It's as though my organs are being strangled within my ribcage, squeezed by an iron fist until they're ready to pop. I've turned my healing abilities inward more than once, to no avail. Which shouldn't be possible, unless the pain isn't coming from me at all. Unless it's coming from somewhere else. Some*one* else.

Someone like Valorie.

"You're spiraling." Finn's elbow nudges my side.

"I'm not in the mood, Finn," I grumble. I twist away from him as we pass under a swath of overhanging branches in shades of maroon and violet. The trees and leaves here seem to be becoming less...solid than they should be. I reach my hand out and brush my fingertips around the edge of a feathered leaf. Definitely corporeal—rock hard, in fact—yet somehow the faint outline of my fingers and the sunlight itself shows through. Crystal Forest, indeed.

When it's clear I'm not paying him any further attention, Finn snaps his fingers in front of my face. "Conall, hello?" He cups his hands around his mouth and calls as though I'm yards away instead of a scant few inches. "You're acting weird. And this is coming from someone who spends every day with you. You're always weird, but you're acting *weird* weird."

"Thanks for your glowing commentary," I drawl. "Want to tell me anything else about myself? Is my hair messed up? Do I have a rip in my pants? Dirt on my face?"

"I mean—" he twirls his index finger in a circle, motioning for me to turn for him. I don't oblige, but he remains undeterred. "You could do with a bath, but the same goes for all of us, frankly."

In typical Finn fashion, he pivots from joking to serious faster than a traffic light turns red. "Seriously, what's going on now? I thought you'd be ecstatic, sprinting ahead and rushing back to yell for us to get a move on. But you're not. And what's up with the hand thing? You're acting the way I do when I get heartburn after inhaling Mrs. Huang's fire noodle platter." Finn motions to where my palm is still rubbing my sternum hard enough to bruise.

My face heats. Both hands drop to clench into fists at my sides. "I have this odd ache in my chest. It's been getting worse for almost a week now."

He tilts his head and purses his lips in thought. "And your healing can't fix it?"

"Not at all," I respond on a sigh. "I'm worried it has something to do with Valorie." I hold up a palm before he can interrupt. "I know it makes no sense, but since when has sense mattered?"

Finn opens his mouth to respond—likely with some platitude meant to be comforting, but which won't help at all—when the crystal branches beside us part, and movement stirs within their colorful, shadowed depths.

A tall, thin figure steps from the shadows to our right. His bright crimson hair is shorn to the scalp in a severe style. Deep green eyes glow as he reaches the edge where shadow meets sunlight. A stockier wyrok—this one a female with bright blue eyes and straight locks a shade of blonde bordering on white—mirrors his stance on the left side of the path.

We've been flanked.

"How did you make it to this place?" Right asks with a deep scowl.

Left interjects, "Avalleans aren't permitted to access this realm without a wyrok escort. We have received no notice of visitors. Who authorized you?"

I pull the wyrok scale from its fabric prison, my grip tight to keep it from buzzing out of my hands. Its surface glitters in every shade of brown, from darkest umber to a pale tan shade reminiscent of the iced caramel lattes Valorie used to grab before her early classes. The warm weight shivers in the sun's glow, setting the colors swirling in a kaleidoscope of earth tones.

The sentries stagger backward away from the glimmering oval, lips curled as though I've unwrapped a rotting corpse at their dinner table. "Where did you get that?" The red-headed one snarls as the other shouts, "It's the Seer's scale! What have you done?"

Gabrielle tries to explain but her words fall on uncaring ears. The two advance in lockstep, towering over us with fangs bared and wings unfurled to cloak the sun. Flames to match his hair wreath the hands of the right wyrok. I silently plead Gaius doesn't decide to match him with his own conflagration.

Of course, that's *exactly* what he does.

Gaius steps forward with a dark smile, sparks dancing around his head. Twin whips of pure blue flame snap in his hands. Finn squares off at his side with a set of chakrams formed from thorny brambles. The guards' snarls morph into feral grins. I get the impression they want nothing more than to have the excuse to rip us apart.

I have no choice. With Valorie somewhere on the other side of this blockade, I'm not going to stand here and lose another second I could spend with her. If a pissing contest between my siblings and a pair of puffed-up lizards keeps me from her, they'll wish they'd torn each other to bits when I get my hands on them.

"*Stop!*" My shout rings out over the crackling of flames and creaking branches. Not a single head turns in my direction. No one banishes their weapons.

Oh, well.

I turn my sights inward, stepping into the pool of my magic deep within my soul. Around my mind's eye, an array of specks of life, distilled to pure light, ebb and flow as each creature moves. Gripping the life forces of the wyrok pair and my brothers, I *pull*. The four of them stagger to their knees, clutching at their chests and choking on thin, ineffectual breaths. The technique isn't one I use often, and for good reason. I've been told the sensation is akin to cardiac arrest.

I stand over the four bodies and wait until I'm certain they're in no state to be causing unnecessary fights. Slowly, I release my magic's fist on their souls. My brothers rocket to their feet a second before the wyrok—likely because they've trained against this technique before. They sneer down their noses as the guards rise.

It's Gabrielle, always the peacemaker, who breaks the stalemate. Her voice never rises above a conversational tone, but the low volume doesn't prevent it from dripping with ire and condescension. "The scale came from Solail, who was told *by the Paragons* to assist us in getting to your home. If you don't mind, we are under a time constraint and would love to end whatever dick measuring contest you've got going here and be on our way."

The pair of sentries blink. Inexplicably, their demeanor shifts. The red-haired male grins sheepishly with a hand on the back of his neck. His blonde companion offers a bashful chuckle and a shrug as she dusts off the seat of her uniform. Gone are the pair of fierce warriors thirsting for blood. Instead, they're practically friendly.

"Well, why didn't you say so?" Red asks. "Your story is easy enough to confirm."

I resist the urge to remind him we weren't given a chance to speak. He moves forward, touching the scale with his head bowed for a long moment before nodding and stepping back.

"Good. You're telling the truth."

And how would he know? I'd love to ask, but I doubt I'd get an answer. And we don't have the time.

After informing us of his name—Shadar—and the name of his partner—Rethya—he ushers us down the path while she melts back into the forest with a two-fingered salute.

Our group follows Shadar quietly as the trail weaves through the crystalline plants. We're still in shock over their sudden shift in personality. Gabrielle falls back to talk to Gaius in the rear of the pack. Based on the hissed conversation, she's berating him for jumping into a fight with the sentries. *Good.* They're friendly now, thank the Fates, but a brawl could have ended horribly.

Finn walks alongside me, directly behind Shadar. His eyes flick to where my left hand is once again rubbing circles on my breastbone. "Still hurting?"

I confirm, and he calls, "Hey, Shadar, any news on a human around here recently? She's short, has curly black hair, green eyes? Likes to talk about cool science concepts I can never quite grasp?" He snickers when his last sentence draws a snort from me.

Finn loves to listen to Valorie's "cool science concepts" as he called them. On more than one occasion, I've caught him searching up surface-level explanations online afterwards. He claims he doesn't want to interrupt her "flow" by asking for her to explain the basics, so he researches them for the next time she broaches the subject.

I suspect he doesn't want her to know he's surprisingly inept at biology for a male who spends most of his day with plants.

"The *kynaira*?" Shadar responds without turning around. "Yes, they passed through here a few days ago."

My footsteps stutter and stop. Only Finn's hand flicking to grasp my elbow keeps me from falling over completely. He drags me along for several steps before I recover. "How many is 'a few', Shadar?" Finn asks.

He hums thoughtfully. "Five, I believe. Her and her two attendants: the guardian and an Avallean."

Five days? Wait—

"Who?"

"Her guardian, as in the wyrok assigned to her? And the spirit of an Avallean. His origin is unknown, we were not expecting a third." He turns to meet my stare over his shoulder. "The three of them were incredibly close. I assumed he was a loved one of some sort, since other spirits aren't typically allowed into this realm. It's not our place to question the *kynaira*. He was with her, so we didn't stop him."

My mind blanks. *A loved one?* Valorie doesn't have any dead Avallean loved ones. She was unaware Avallea existed before she met us.

Who the hell is tagging along with her, and why?

"How is she?" I struggle to keep the frustrated grumble from my voice. I'm not entirely successful.

Shadar pivots back towards the path before he answers. "That's...classified."

Did I call him friendly? I take it back. This time, the frustration boils into rage. "What do you mean, classified? How the fuck is my *fiancée* doing, Shadar?"

He jolts. I'm not sure whether it's from the raw fury in my tone or the revelation of my relationship with Valorie, and frankly, I do not care. "It's *classified*, Avallean. You may be welcome here, but you're not entitled to anything more than what the Paragons and the *kynaira* have decided. And if you are not yet mated, your word holds no power here."

My hands shoot over my head. I shout, "Her name is Valorie! Not *kynaira*! What the hell is a *kynaira*, anyway?"

Shadar answers with only a smirk and a flippant, "Guess that's classified, too."

My blood churns, writhing with the force of a thousand snakes in my veins. They leech their venom, infecting me with the desire to shred the world to pieces until I find her. The telltale glow of magic wreaths my hands. I itch to send him to the ground for the second time today, to twist his life within his body and force him to tell me everything he knows.

Finn shoves me into the pinkish shade of a translucent willow on the side of the trail. His palm connects with my shoulder, forcing me against the bark. "Get yourself together, Conall, and then we'll catch up." I open my mouth to protest, but he silences me with a palm over my lips. "Don't bullshit me. I was right next to you, and I'm not stupid. You were lit up like a glow stick, and you've been able to control the light of your magic since before we met. You need to take a couple damned breaths before I douse you in pollen and put you to sleep until we get this over with."

He releases my face but remains in the way. The second I start to speak, Finn *tsks*. A plant begins to form in the center of his palm. "I'll do it, Conall. I won't have you jeopardizing everything because you're pissy and want to have a little power trip. Keep your shit together or you'll take a nap. That's final. And you know Gaius and Gabby will hold you down while I do it."

He's not wrong—a betrayal I'm still muttering about as we jog to rejoin the group. Thankfully, Gabrielle informs us we're approaching the city gates. The path turns and widens into a clearing draped in a faint dusting of crystal sand. At the opposite end sits a pair of open golden gates set into a protective wall of crystal. Its colors shift in an aurora, endless blues and pinks and greens with a pearlescent sheen overlaid along the entirety of the ten-foot-high structure. Two more wyrok—one with a head of blue curls and another sporting a violet Mohawk—stand guard beneath the entrance's gaping archway. They nod to Shadar before moving aside, leaving the way open for us to proceed.

Shadar pats my shoulder and heads back the way we came with a cheerful, "See you around." As he approaches the edge of the forest behind us, I hear him say, "Oh, sorry, didn't notice you there. Avalleans are everywhere these days, I swear."

Avalleans?

I spin to find a new male standing in the center of the path. Crystal dust curls up around his boots with each step. He prowls towards us until we're nose-to-nose. Tall, with a build ranging between mine and Gaius', the stranger's hopeless, melancholy expression appears to absorb and erase the colors of the light filtering weakly through the trees at his back. His black eyes scour my face, clearly searching for something I cannot provide.

When they flare wide in shock, I step backward. A hand shoots out to clap around my shoulder before I can escape. His fingers dig into my skin as though he's afraid I'll disappear if he lets go.

"It's you," he whispers in a voice as broken as my own. "You're here." He twists around without loosening his grip, until his gaze connects with each of us in turn. "You're all here."

CHAPTER 25
Too Late

- CONALL -

"**Y**ou need to hurry," the stranger rasps. His fingers continue their attempt to burrow their way into my upper arm. I grit my teeth as pain lances through the muscles. "She doesn't have much time left."

My heart plummets through the ground beneath us and lodges somewhere far below with a sickening lurch. "Who?"

The strange Avallean releases his bruising grip and steps around our group. With a shove against the center of my back, he propels me towards the open gate as though it was my idea for us to dawdle here. "You know who. Now *go!*"

The shorter of the two gate guards falls into step with us as we rush beneath the archway. "My name is Mephys. I'll escort you," she asserts in a high, clear voice. Her toothy smile glints in the light thrown off the golden gates.

Mephys sets a pace just shy of a jog. Despite needing two steps to match one of ours, she's bouncing along without a shred of effort, coiling a teal curl around her finger in a carefree gesture. In comparison, we must resemble a herd of elephants in her wake. Buildings impeccably constructed of glittering stones in a variety of light colors line the streets we hurry down, flashing by too quickly to discern their purposes.

"I would take you to guest lodgings," Mephys calls as we round a sharp corner and begin ascending the slope of the mountain the city is built around, "but I assume you'll want to be taken straight to the *kynaira*." She points to a white building at the peak. Clouds have rolled in to obscure the sun, but I imagine the alabaster stone shines as a beacon over the city when the light hits its surfaces.

A short huff—part exhaustion, part frustration—hisses from my nostrils. "Why does everyone keep calling her *kynaira*?"

"It's—"

I groan. "If you say 'classified', I swear..."

To her credit, she offers a sheepish grimace and apologizes for the secrecy. It makes me like her a trifle more, at least more than Shadar. With her small stature and riot of curls, she reminds me of Valorie. The similarities ache as much as they comfort.

I focus on Valorie's image in my mind and glance at the massive temple waiting above, praying she's waiting for me there. Praying she can somehow read my thoughts. I hope she knows every one of them has been about her since the day we met. I hope she can feel the distance between us shrinking with every step.

See you soon, Wildcat.

After zig-zagging our way through verdant terraces, around sharp switchbacks, and through a handful of carved tunnels, our path comes to an end at the temple's colonnade. A muscular figure paces between the benches lining the far sides of the shaded space. His hair, shoulder-length and a shade bluer than our escort's, is disheveled. As we stand at the edge of the line of columns, he spears clawed fingers through the straight locks and continues a fit of agitated mumbling.

Mephys jolts towards the wyrok. She grasps his wrists with gentle hands, pulling them free from the tangled mess. Her wings flare behind her to offset the effort. "Oh, cousin," she croons softly, "you have to stop this. Look, the other ones are here now. Take heart." Her head tilts in our direction. She angles him to face us, and the sight of him face-on sends us staggering backward.

His honey-gold irises overflow with pain and sorrow. Their slitted pupils are dilated, blown wide enough to swallow the topaz surrounding them. His fangs are bared in a rictus of pain from some unknown source. Internal or external, I do not know. Whatever the case, he's clearly a second away from losing his grip on reality.

"Meet my cousin, Ceraun," Mephys murmurs. "The *kynaira*'s guardian and close friend. He's...not usually like this."

My first thought is, *How could Esraa and Amon trust her safety to this mess of a male?*

But my second is the one which curdles the acid in my stomach. *What happened to make him this way?*

"I suppose I'd better take you up," Ceraun sighs. His voice is strained, yet surprisingly composed. "Go back to the gates, Mephys. I'll be fine."

She nudges his side with her shoulder. "You sure?" When he snaps his teeth at her in response, she chuckles. A brief kiss brushes his cheek before she flits back down the path and out of sight.

The carved doors behind Ceraun open on a silent wind. We follow him into a large central chamber draped in soothing darkness. Soft lighting illuminates a multitude of sunken spaces within the gargantuan room. A quartet of columns mark the corners of each pseudo-room and spear straight to the shadowed ceiling far overhead. Ceraun ignores each of the alcoves, instead heading for a staircase spiraling around the edge of the room. My steps are flagging, but my excitement grows with each heavy plod up another stair.

Just a few more, I encourage myself. *Another few steps and then we'll be together again.*

Ceraun reaches a high landing and exits the staircase. He stops before a room near the end of the plush-carpeted hall. Not a single sound can be heard beyond the deep sapphire doors. They're carved from a material reminiscent of lapis lazuli, but with variations within that bring to mind galaxies and starscapes. They're beautiful, somehow soothing. The perfect entrance to the spacious, elegant bedroom suite revealed when Ceraun raps twice and they finally open.

My head swivels hard enough to make my neck cramp. I take in every corner of the room at lightning speed.

Where is she?

The lounge space by the fireplace holds a pair of wyrok in black and white contrasting robes, but no sign of Valorie. The cushioned seat at the bay window is empty, same as the breakfast nook nestled into the corner, surrounded by bookshelves on two sides.

Is she in the restroom? No, the door to the en-suite stands ajar. The space is impeccably clean, but unoccupied.

My eyes land on the bed and the diminutive lump beneath its linens.

I'm running before I have the chance to think. I collide with the bed frame at a force hard enough to bounce me backward. I ricochet off the wall of my siblings' bodies behind me and rebound against the edge of the mattress.

"Valorie? Wildcat?" I'm yelling far too loudly for the silence in the suite, but I cannot stop. "I'm here, love. We're *here.*"

My siblings crowd around me, pressing in close to her. "I'm so sorry," Finn sobs. He grips over the covers where her knee is wrapped in crisp linens. "I'm so sorry, Val." Beside him, Gabby leaks soundless tears in Gaius' arms.

"She won't wake." The short, mumbled sentence coming from the other side of the bed is almost incomprehensible. Four sets of confused eyes must make this apparent, because Ceraun quietly clarifies, each word strained as though being pulled from him. "Valorie. She won't wake up. It's been three days, and still she slumbers. The Paragons are arriving in the next few hours—you barely beat them—but I—" he chokes. "—I fear they may be too late for even their magic to save her."

My entire world tilts sideways and blackens at the edges. *No.* I can't have found her only to lose her again. I won't survive it.

Never in my wildest nightmares did I picture this.

CHAPTER 26
Paragons

I spend four hours motionless at Valorie's bedside.

My siblings array themselves around me in a wall of flesh and hide us from the prying eyes of the wyrok. Everyone speaks in hushed whispers, though we could scream every horror imaginable and it wouldn't wake her. The healer, Deina, is not sure whether Valorie is able to hear us or not. We keep the conversations to bland, safe topics, just in case.

I hope she can. I hope she hears every whispered, "I love you," I've been repeating into her ear since we arrived. I hope she can sense my clammy hand clenching hers beneath the layers of linens. I hope she knows we're here for her, waiting for her to open her eyes.

I *hope*. It's all I can do.

Gaius sends a twinkling array of sparks to dance their way through Valorie's hair and across the bridge of her nose. Pinpricks of red, blue, orange, and yellow flicker and play across her features, the only joy in the room. Their light brings a modicum of false life back into her pale complexion. "You'll be fine, little Christmas tree," he whispers when he thinks nobody is paying attention. "You've got this."

Tears sting the back of my eyes. I duck my head until they've dissipated.

At one point, Finn suggests I lie beside her on the bed, but I refuse. My travel-stained clothes keep me perched at the edge. To the eye, she's pristine beneath the crisp white sheets—I don't want to sully the illusion.

The meticulous care of the wyrok is evident. Valorie is spotless, her flyaway curls braided in an intricate style she would never have the patience to do herself. If it weren't for the green tinge to her skin, sickening against the blue of the veins under its pallor, I'd believe she was merely napping, ready to awake at any moment. But she remains locked beyond our reach, my own Sleeping Beauty. If only a kiss were enough to wake her. The prince had it so easy in their tale. He was practically handed the antidote, neatly packaged in a pair of lips, a swapping of touch.

Behind us, the subtle *snick* of the door opening barely registers in my head. The wyrok have filtered in and out of the room on occasion throughout the evening. About an hour ago, the black-robed one—Daros, I believe—brought in several large baskets of food on a magical wind. He and his sister arrayed a spread across the circular breakfast table and any other flat surface they could find. Gabrielle brought me a plate, claiming the meal was delicious. Finn agreed, already on his second helping.

It tasted of bitter ash on my tongue, but I don't blame the chef.

It's not until Ceraun speaks I realize the door was never closed. They always close it as quickly as possible to retain Valorie's privacy, though I expect the entire corridor outside has been declared off limits while she is...indisposed.

"They've arrived."

My spine stiffens. Finn, Gaius and Gabrielle jump to their feet. I don't bother.

Ceraun clears his throat. "They're in the repository, if we would like to—"

"Tell them to come here," I demand. My voice is quiet, but unyielding. "Tell them to meet us *here*, in this room, where they can observe exactly what their lack of punctuality has caused."

"*Conall*," Gabrielle's admonishing whisper rolls off my shoulders without sticking. Her small bit of shame cannot touch the mountain I already hold in my heart.

With a firm shake of my head, I say, "I'm not leaving this room until she gets up and leaves with me, so either they come here or they can talk to you all without us present. They've had no issues with making everyone else's decisions thus far." I'm done with talking about this. I know it's unreasonable—downright idiotic, frankly—to make demands of the two strongest Paragons in existence, but I'm beyond all caring now.

I'm not letting my wildcat out of my sight.

My mind flashes back to the last time I left her in a room alone. The phantom scrape of the cold stone of the altar beneath the Haven bites against my palms. She was *dead* then. A part of me is terrified were I to turn away for even a moment, she'd be dead again.

I brush the backs of my fingers across Valorie's cheekbones to reassure myself she's here. She's real. The firefly sparks Gaius created weave around my pinky in greeting. They jitter on the wind of my heavy exhale.

My siblings slowly settle back to their positions. Finn locks eyes with Ceraun over his shoulder. "You heard the man. He's a hard-ass, especially where Val is concerned. I suggest you tell the Paragons we're waiting.

Respectfully, of course, because I don't want to die," he adds with a low laugh.

"There will be no need for a messenger," a melodic voice drifts into the room from behind Ceraun. Despite its gentleness, it carries a commanding presence, one which instantly has every set of shoulders in the room snapping straight. "We're already here."

Ceraun hurries out of the way. He takes his position on the far side of the massive bed and bows low as the Paragons of Death sweep into the room. Gabrielle gasps and drops to a knee, Finn lowers his head, and Gaius sketches an intricate bow with several unnecessary flourishes. His action draws a scathing glare from both Ceraun and Daros.

I've spent more time with the pair of Paragons than any of the other members of my family, making me more familiar with the shocking effects of their powerful presence. I shift to face them, offer a terse verbal greeting before turning back to face Valorie. My eyes search for any infinitesimally small sign of movement she may have made while I wasn't looking.

Nothing.

The rulers of this realm have not changed since the last time we saw them, the morning my siblings and I stepped from the stone chambers beneath the Haven and through our first portal to this realm. Esraa's sunset skin glows in pastel shades of rose, periwinkle and lavender where it peeks out from her flowing garb, while Amon stands stalwart and stern at her side in deep brown leathers with a crimson one-shoulder cape. If Esraa embodies the clouds at sundown, Amon is an inky, starless night lit by the fires of vengeance. Even the shadows cling to him as if seeking their home.

I know not what his innate affinity was before the power of the Underworld was passed to him and Esraa, but I can guess.

With every sedate step the pair takes across the constellation-spangled rug, the flames of my rage stoke higher and higher. They circle the bed, examining Valorie as though she's nothing more than a perplexing piece of artwork in a museum gallery.

My fists clench into the comforter until my knuckles pop with the effort of biting my tongue. I'm surprised the fabric doesn't rip, but I assume a clawed species would prioritize durability.

"She won't wake?" Amon poses the question while peering at her closed lids. He raises a perplexed brow, as if he thought he could force her to open them through willpower alone. His lips turn down at the ends with a disgruntled huff when Deina details the past few days of futile healing attempts. A hand slips beneath the blankets and my vision glazes scarlet, but he merely extracts one limp wrist and uses two fingers to check for a pulse.

My composure begins to flake away like wind-battered paint on an old house. A decrepit, haunted house, possessed by the demons of what I used to be before every strand in the damned Web of Fate knotted into a snarled tangle between the rest of my body and my heart lying asleep in this bed. "You already know she has no heartbeat. You can hear as well as any of us," I grumble under my breath. And I know he hears that, too.

"He's checking her life force, dear," Esraa explains softly. "He's gauging her ability to survive." She crosses to my side, nodding her thanks to Finn as he grudgingly shifts enough for her to settle between us. Her hand lands on my shoulder with a squeeze undoubtedly meant to comfort, and she hums a vaguely familiar tune under her breath.

My efforts to shrug her off are half-hearted—it's nigh on impossible to be rude to Esraa, but Valorie's state is as much her fault as it is Amon's. Either of them could have rushed here and saved her.

"Survive what?" I glare as she shifts to crouch next to me at the bedside. "She wouldn't be in this state if you would have been here on time. I think you owe us far more than mere scraps of information."

Gabrielle admonishes me again. She leans against a carved post on the footboard, shaking her head as though I'm a petulant child with a tantrum.

Esraa's smile turns melancholy. "We were caught up in meetings with the Council and couldn't escape, unfortunately. Believe me, we tried. Few things are less enjoyable than discussing subterfuge and strategy with the other nine, you know." A chuckle punctuates her statement, one echoed with a startled snort by Finn. I've spoken to Esraa and Amon enough times to know they observe the lower nine and their infighting with the fond annoyance one might feel towards a gaggle of younger siblings.

The pair have always had a curious habit of showing up with assignments for me themselves instead of having them passed along by another Paragon, but I've never questioned it. They're calm, comforting...except for when they're the reason my love is lifeless in a realm built for death.

"Strategy for what?" Gaius asks. His sparks flare around Valorie's face. They brighten into tiny sunbursts, spinning faster in their endless dance, but they never burn her delicate flesh.

Finn interjects, "Is it Joran?"

Esraa's eyes flit around the room before she gives a barely perceptible nod.

My siblings burst into a flurry of questions, but Esraa says it's not the time to focus on Joran and his cronies. I agree. My only focus is the woman lying in front of me and my desire to have her *open her damn eyes.*

I lean my head against the soft silk of Esraa's shimmering opal robes, suddenly pummeled by the exhaustion of the past few days. The past few months, honestly. Her arm spans my shoulders, tucking me into her side. "Why is this happening, Esraa?" I whisper.

"Her soul and body have been separated overlong. The soul is only meant to be disconnected from the body under one particular—and permanent—circumstance." She tips her chin towards the darkened scene through the open bay window. The city below, lit by the light of dancing bands of colors overhead, with the forest of crystal plants beyond. Beautiful in an otherworldly way, this realm meant for the eternity of the afterlife. The realm of death. "She's worn out, dear. I'm so sorry this has happened. The tether between body and soul is flickering. Her soul is searching for a way to be a part of this world, instead."

"A way to die, you mean." It isn't a question, but she dips her chin.

Amon's head finally lifts from where he's been bowed over Valorie's wrist. His gaze locks onto Esraa's and he nods. "If we're going to try, it needs to be soon."

"Try what?" I ask.

Are they going to save her? Sweat coats my palms at the thought. Bathed in the soft glow of the bevy of enchanted sconces scattered around the room, her skin appears warmer. More alive. It's a peaceful lie.

Amon shifts his stare to me. His blazing irises cut directly into my shattered soul. The fire welds a handful of fragments back together when he replies, "What you've asked for all along."

My breath turns to lead in my lungs. If wishes had weight, I would be crushed. "You mean—"

Esraa's hand clenches on my shoulder once more. Her gentle smile is a parent's comforting hug, a bandage on a child's skinned knee. It's the life raft of hope I've been holding onto through tumultuous waves. "We're going to try to turn her," she explains, pulling us both to our feet. "With any luck, Valorie will become an Avallean. It's time."

Chapter 27
The Ceremony

I worry they will demand we move Valorie to some vast, frigid chamber for the ceremony which resembles the one beneath the Haven where we were set to bind ourselves together before everything went wrong. A room I used to love, yet now the chilling rush of memory causes my stomach to lurch and my palms to bead with sweat. I may never be able to return without images of Valorie's corpse hounding my every move.

The wyrok putter around the room, silently clearing the dinner dishes. Daros tidies the scattered papers he brought to leaf through while we awaited the arrival of the Paragons. Beside the open bay window, Esraa and Amon have their heads together as they sit on the royal blue cushion, speaking in hushed tones even my hearing cannot wholly discern. The room is busier than it's been since we arrived, everyone working at once. Through the hustle, my siblings stay glued to me, and I cement myself against Valorie. I brush my hands against the two ridges along her crown, tracing the knobs of braided curls as I whisper all of my plans for our life together into her ear.

A dainty cough breaks my focus. "We're ready," Esraa announces. She and Amon must have made their way over while I was absorbed in detailing exactly what type of house I wanted to have with Valorie. Or maybe they crept in early enough to hear me ask her whether she would prefer a home in the forest or closer to the beach. She loves both; it'll be a tough choice for her, but no choice at all for me. I'll follow her anywhere. I followed her straight into death's domain—anything else will pale in comparison.

"What do we need to do?" Gabrielle asks, her hand on my back. Beside her, Finn and Gaius nod in unison. Finn's hand hovers near Val's, and Gaius shifts his body closer. They're sending a clear message: We're a unit. Where one of us goes, we all go. And "all of us" includes Valorie.

Esraa smiles, a benevolent curve of her lips. "In essence, the ceremony is a transfer of pieces of soul between two individuals. It is not normally done, for several reasons, but this is a special circumstance which has been given express approval."

We incline our heads. This information isn't new—it was given when we initially agreed to the ceremony.

"Amon and I will remove a small portion of Conall's essence, and swap it with a similar section of Valorie's. It imbues the two of them with a link between souls. They'll be able to sense each other's emotions, and there may be other changes we aren't aware of. As I said, it's not a common event.

"But, if all goes well, Valorie will wake up as an Avallean. If you would prefer, you can have a formal Bonding ceremony later, as two Avalleans normally would. However, this procedure encompasses everything a Bonding would entail and then some. The formal ceremony would honestly be no more than that: a formality."

"Provided they both survive," Amon adds from behind Esraa.

I choose to ignore him. His statement is irrelevant—we'll survive. I square my shoulders. "What do you need me to do?"

After a brief, not even remotely reassuring explanation of the specifics, I find myself settled on the bed beside Valorie. A trio of over-stuffed pillows cushions my reclined back. Our intertwined hands rest atop the blankets, her pale skin lifeless between my bronze fingers.

My siblings have been instructed to stay close, but never touch. Apparently, there's a small chance their souls could be plucked instead of ours, were they to have physical contact with Valorie or myself during the procedure. The thought of one of them being Bonded to her in my place makes my teeth grit. My jaw twinges under the strain.

The tension in my jaw multiplies as Esraa's hand comes to rest atop my head. Her other hand twines with Amon's across the bed. Foreign magic twists and slithers through my skull and down through my torso like a horde of snakes searching for a meal. The squirming energy coalesces into a globular mass of fire within my breast, its intrusive burn squeezing the air from my lungs until stars whirl at the edges of my vision. I gasp against the painful heat inching its way up my throat. My back arches involuntarily. It's as though my spine may snap in two before the molten power carving a chunk of my soul can escape.

My tear-lined eyes find Amon's hand resting on Valorie's head in a mirror of Esraa's pose. His fingertips blend with the onyx rows of plaited curls and disappear within them. Despite the two Paragons working in unison, Valorie's body remains motionless as ever. I pour all my remaining energy into praying she's too far inside her own mind to experience the agony I'm experiencing as our souls are slowly dragged from our bodies.

After several thousand years' worth of unending, burning pain, something shifts within me. Esraa and Amon suck in a joint breath a second before two glowing spheres appear over their clasped fingers. At first glance, the two appear identical, outshining the dimmed lamps in the room with their brilliance. Two amorphous balls of pure light lined with wisps of shadow and wreathed in fire. But as I look on with rapt attention, Valorie's piece drifts closer, trading places with my own, and the differences between the two become apparent.

There is no corona of white flame surrounding hers. No powerful threads of magic orbiting the mass the way a planet's rings orbit its body. Her soul is naked, unarmored. Delicate. And yet, inexplicably, it holds strength. A perfect encapsulation of my wildcat. The sight sparks my first true smile in eons.

As her soul slowly sinks into my chest, directly over my heart, I feel *everything*. The objects in the room become sharper, the hushed susurration of breathing becomes a pressing white noise. The faint summer pear scent that's uniquely Valorie becomes a heady perfume. My brain steams and my blood ices over, day and night shake hands and swap houses, and gravity itself decides to stand on its head. For an instant, nothing and everything collide.

Then the dust settles within me in new, unimaginable patterns.

My life is forever changed the moment I behold the tether between my soul and hers.

I bolt up in the bed, ignoring the startled exclamations of my family and the Paragons hastily demanding I relax. My only thought is finally seeing Valorie's eyes light up when she realizes we're together again. Beaming, I turn my body to face hers.

But her stormcloud eyes remain hidden behind closed lids, same as they were before we began.

Unmoving, unchanged. Lifeless.

"What's going on?" I shout. My frantic stare bounces between Esraa and Amon. "Why isn't she awake?"

The room falls into silence. It's then I notice the icy terror lurking within a corner of my mind I wasn't able to access before. An antechamber connected to our newly formed Bond.

My entire body seizes. "She's terrified," I whisper. Blazing hot tears ooze down my face as the blood drains from it. *Why haven't they woken her? She's in danger!* "What are you waiting for?" I scream at the Paragons. "Wake her up! She needs help!"

Amon stiffens, but Esraa reaches to brush her fingers against my cheek. I twist away and repeat my demand.

Her soft words will haunt my nightmares for years. "We cannot."

Finn wraps his arms around me in a bear hug while Esraa speaks. Whether for comfort or restraint, I do not know. Likely a mixture of both, and for good reason. I'm torn between wrenching at my own hair and lunging for a being who could shred me to ribbons with a thought. Broken sobs shake my body as Esraa explains how Valorie's body is stuck deep in stasis. How they hoped her change would give her the strength to awaken, but the power a standard Avallean, especially a dehmi, holds is clearly not enough. How any further attempts for them to rouse her could push her body into giving up entirely.

The quiet words pelt hard as bullets.

"But why?" Gabrielle asks quietly. "Why isn't the power enough? Correct me if I'm wrong, but it should have been more than enough to revive someone who was previously human."

Esraa shares a loaded glance with Amon, who inclines his head." We believe it is because this is part of her Testing." She slowly replies.

My siblings' shocked gasps echo through the suite. Even the wyrok close in on the bed at her words, though their raised-brow expressions are more confused than shocked.

"Isn't that a bit unorthodox, though?" Ceraun grumbles from Valorie's side. He lurked behind Amon for the entire ceremony, close enough his breath mingled with the Paragon's. Neither complained. "Shouldn't the journey have been enough? I believe it was more arduous than your own Testing," he adds, softening the accusation with a demure bow.

I wish one of them would explain what they're discussing. If I could draw enough breath to form words, I'd demand an explanation for this "Testing" everyone appears to know about but me.

Esraa bobs her head at Ceraun, but it's Amon who replies, "I agree. But, although the *kynaira* and *kynairar* are our choice as the reigning Paragons, the Testing is from the Web itself. It would appear she has one final hurdle to surmount, unfair though it may be." He brushes an invisible mote of dust from her face. The gesture is surprisingly soft, one I would have expected from Esraa, not Amon.

"*What is going on?*" I force the words through gritted teeth and gasping sobs.

Gabrielle opens her mouth to speak, but Amon cuts her off, "It's not important right now. We will explain after we've seen whether she can overcome this or not."

I'm spared the agony of forming a reply by the wyrok healer's approach. Deina nudges her way through the group surrounding the bed and hovers her palms over Valorie's body. One stops several inches above her face, the other rests directly over her heart. Her healing magic pulses over Valorie, the intensity of it several times stronger than my own.

After a tense moment, she says, "I worry she won't know where to begin, given her lack of knowledge of our customs. I assume nobody was given leave to explain this particular chain of events to her?" The statement tips up into a question at the end. Ceraun shakes his head in answer. "Then she may become trapped purely by her own ignorance. If only we could reach her within her mind, explain to her the importance of finding a way out before it's too late. We don't even know what's going on in there. We're practically as ignorant as she."

"If someone doesn't explain, I swear—"

A distant, hollow crashing sound emanates from the open window. We all turn in the direction of the disturbance and freeze. Because there, crouched on the window's wide stone ledge, is the strange Avallean from outside the gate. He is windswept and disheveled, but his gaze is brighter than when we last met.

"Dennick?" Ceraun asks, his voice heavy with accusation.

Before I can ask how they know each other, the black-robed wyrok steps forward into a menacing half-crouch.

"What are you doing here?" Daros growls. "This room is off-limits. How did you even get into the city?"

The Avallean—Dennick—ignores him completely. "Ceraun," he pants with wide-blown pupils. His words tumble in a mad rush, likely aware he's running on borrowed time before he's forced back out of the city permanently. "I had to see her. You understand. You *know*. And I'm glad I talked your cousin into believing Valorie—" my spine stiffens at his casual mention of her name "—would want me here. Because I heard your problem. And Ceraun?" He squares his shoulders, hope shining in his stare as he locks eyes with the wyrok charged with guarding Valorie. "I can do it. I can try to find her. I can help her get free."

279

CHAPTER 28
Dreamtreader

- DENNICK -

Yeah, I expected my sudden appearance would throw them for a loop.

I ran through countless scenarios as Mephys ushered me through the gates two hours ago. I promised not to mention her name if I was caught, but I was fairly confident this particular scenario would not come to pass. Scene after scene rolled through my brain on a loop as I crept through the less populated city streets on silent feet. I tried desperately not to recall memories of Chryton teaching our band of dehmi how to be soundless on any surface. Instead, I busied my mind with contemplating how to broach the subject of my helping Valorie to a room full of what I fully expected to be angry immortals brimming with agitated power. By the time I began to scale the temple's stone walls, eyes on the warm light pouring from a broad window alarmingly high up, I was locked in on my chosen plan of action.

A plan which flew right from my head and ran screaming the second I scrambled onto the window's ledge and knocked a damned terracotta planter to the ground.

I could practically hear Valorie's laughter-filled voice in my head saying, *Way to go, Den,* as I watched it tumble for an eternity, soil and sprigs of some flowering thing cascading from its opening in an arc of brown and green.

Good thing I think quickly on my feet. Or in this case, on my haunches. Which are not thrilled with my uncomfortably perilous perch on this foot-wide slice of stone, two hundred feet in the air.

"Mind if I come in?" I ask with forced levity, cheeky grin on full display. It flickers as they continue to stare without answering. My gaze flits from face to face, studiously avoiding one in particular. If my eyes land on Valorie for too long, I'll break. Every horrible insult my brain has hurled down my throat and into my heart these past few days will crush me under their weight.

My eyes land on a statuesque, rose-eyed woman in the back. Her elegant fingers rest on the arm of the Avallean Valorie is besotted with. Con-something. Conrad? Connor? Con...valescent? He needs to be. The male is an obvious mess, all haunted eyes and haggard grimaces.

But, aren't we all these days? I've been a mess for years. These last few weeks are the most whole, the most *sane* I've felt since Chryton and Joran held me over that sink and drained my blood into the swirling water like I was nothing more than livestock. Sue me for trying to protect my friend before she leads herself to the same fate on the arm of a pretty boy with a death wish.

I sigh, clear my throat, and ask again. We don't have time for their mouths to catch flies, and I tell them as much.

My callousness finally breaks their stupor. Ceraun waves me over to their group with a quiet invitation. The stick usually living rent-free in his rectum whenever he speaks to me is seemingly absent today. If I weren't already terrified by the way Valorie's eyes have sunken into her skull, this change alone would have my palms sweating. I don't think

Ceraun hates me anymore, not after our conversation beyond the gates, but I doubt he'd invite me to be his drinking buddy.

Not yet, anyway.

Don't worry, Princess. I'll wear him down.

"She's going to be so proud of your progress towards being a real person with complex feelings, big guy. You're not even grumbling at me," I whisper with a patronizing pat on Ceraun's upper arm. He responds with a growl, and I chuckle quietly. "There you are, Ol' Scaley Ass."

The nickname—or the memory attached to it—makes him flinch. I immediately regret bringing it up. It was a poor effort to lighten the thick, soupy fog of depression clogging this room, but I can't stand how everyone is gathered around her bed, wringing their hands and moping as though it's a coffin. Valorie would be mortified. How has her *soulmate* not realized that yet?

"You believe you can reach her, dreamtreader?"

It's been a long while since I was face-to-face with any Paragon, but Amon isn't someone you can easily forget. His red irises scour my heart and dredge up every transgression. Does he find my soul as lacking as I do?

I nod, a swift dip of my chin I hope hides my nerves. "I can find her, sir."

"And you're aware you cannot give her assistance, only information?"

"Yes sir," I respond. "I know the limits. I can explain the situation, encourage her to rally her strength, but no more."

"Why?" Ceraun interrupts. He glares at me, his brows low over narrowed eyes. "Why would you help her with this, Dennick? You, who so badly want her to stay, who believes she would be safer here within our walls?" The angry Avallean—*Conall*, if I remember correctly—jerks, but wisely keeps his mouth shut. This isn't about him. It's about my friend having the freedom to choose her own fate, even if I hate it.

I shrug. Nonchalant is good, right? Best to pretend the choice isn't gnawing its way through my insides with razor-blade teeth. "She's my best friend. I love her enough to want her to be happy. I'm used to being alone, I'll survive out there for a while. Who knows, maybe it'll give you and I time to bond while we wait for her to come back, eh Ceraun?"

My exaggerated wink doesn't fool him for a second. That's the insufferable thing about Ceraun—besides his stick. He's incredibly adept at discerning when you're lying through your teeth. He knows this is tearing me apart. But, we both know he won't stop me. Not if it helps everyone else get what they want at Valorie's expense.

The Paragons intrude. "We are aware of your transgressions," Esraa chides.

Damn. I was hoping they weren't.

As though she can read my mind, the corner of her mouth turns up. "We are aware of many things within our realm, dreamtreader. We know the hand you were dealt, and how it affected your soul. We remember when this realm received you. You slipped through the boundaries then, too." Her head tips towards the open window. A small smear of dirt mars the surface where the potted flowers once sat. "It's becoming something of a habit for you, isn't it?"

I smile. "Yes, ma'am. I'd say I'll try not to do it again, but I wouldn't want to be a liar *and* a sneak."

Her chuckle is melodic, light. Comforting. She motions me to stand beside her, close to Valorie's head. Valorie's usual chaotic halo is tamed into a complex crown that wraps around her unmoving head. The style should be pleasant, but instead it's out of place, offensive. It emphasizes her absence.

"If you do this, Dennick, you are absolved in our eyes. We will not punish you further, nor will the wyrok. You will have a home in this place, one of the few non-wyrok to receive the honor." Esraa pauses, and I wait for the *but*.

After a moment, it hits. "As far as *we* are concerned. But, the girl has the final say. We cannot force her to forgive you."

My silent heart clenches as I offer my agreement. It's only fair, truly. I tried to twist Valorie's fate with my own hands, and now *my* fate rests in hers.

"Are you ready?" Amon asks. My chin lifts in assent. He motions the others to move away and give me space. Not that I need it, but I appreciate the gesture. The wyrok fill the couch in front of the fireplace, content in their waiting. The other Avalleans settle themselves into the breakfast nook in the corner much less patiently. It only has two chairs, but Conall and an absolute mammoth of a male with kind blue eyes stand next to the table. Conall's foot taps incessantly against the floor, a metronome in fast-forward. The burly one whispers to him under his breath.

Light and shadow play across Valorie's empty expression. The peaceful picture of repose they've painted is the biggest lie I've ever been privy to. I can sense the pull of her subconscious, the insidious tug of an unending nightmare. It's a twist in my gut, the same sickening, lurching spin of your innards before you vomit.

And it's powerful, terrifyingly so. When she was human, her psyche wasn't weak, but it was more contained. A human mind only needs a drop of power to function properly. Now, she's part of a species which builds worlds and spans realms. Her mind has changed, becoming *more* in order to comprehend the multitude of realities Avalleans are connected to. With it, her nightmare has grown as well. It had to, otherwise she would've been free the second her soul touched *his*.

There's a non-zero chance neither of us gets through this, but I don't tell that to my audience. I should probably say *something*, though. Just in case. Last goodbyes, and all.

My fingers touch Valorie's frigid forehead. The clammy tips rest gently against her skin as I turn to Conall and say, "She loves you, you know? Make sure you don't take it for granted, because she'll stay my best friend whether she wants me around or not. If you fuck with her, I'll be waiting for you."

Before he can do more than open his mouth, my eyes find Ceraun's slitted pupils near the fire. "Hey, buddy," I croak. "Help her out after this if I...can't, please? And—" a shuddering breath keeps the tears at bay. Fates, this hurts. "—try to help her remember the parts where I wasn't so horrible."

When his chin lowers, I steel my nerves, close my eyes, and dive in.

Ready or not, Princess, here I come.

CHAPTER 29
Friends Don't Forget

- DENNICK -

Oppressive darkness immediately engulfs me. Complete and utter blackness, the kind where you can't see your own hand an inch from your face. Where the entire world fades into nothingness so thick, you could slice it with a blade. The world is a void—a terrifying, isolating totality of emptiness with no beginning or end.

The second sensation I'm struck by is the soul-crushing cold billowing in endless, frigid waves from up ahead. Because of *course* we couldn't do this on a sunny beach somewhere. When we're free of this nightmare, I'm having a little talk with Valorie about her subconscious, because this is ridiculously unwelcoming. Frankly, I'm offended.

Speaking of the woman of the hour...

"Valorie?" I call around chattering teeth. *Damn, it's fucking freezing in here.* If I didn't know she was safe in a warm bed in the real world, I'd be cursing myself for not bringing her a blanket or twelve.

Regardless, this is real to *her*, and I know she can't be comfortable after being here for this long. I've been in here for two minutes and certain sensitive cargo below my belt is already trying to crawl its way back inside my pelvis.

When my repeated shouts produce no response, I begin to trudge my way towards the origin of the freeze. Without usable eyesight, it's the only point of reference I have for direction. The ground is smooth and featureless beneath my boots. A blessing in disguise. Wouldn't want to trip and fall into a hole in Valorie's subconscious when I'm supposed to be helping her figure her way out of this mess.

Deep in the distance, a flickering bit of color catches my squinted eyes and causes them to widen. "There you are," I mutter under my breath. The arm I was holding in front of my face in an attempt to keep my nose from falling off drops to my side as everything speeds up.

In the confusing way dreams move, with spurts of motion only attainable in a place where pesky laws of physics and mass are blurry and blendable, the distance between myself and Valorie is eaten up in a couple of steps and icy breaths. A blink, maybe two, and I'm stumbling to a halt a handful of feet from her. My steps end at the edge of a dim circle of light.

I've been dreamtreading for decades, dipping in and out of fantastical scenes and horrifying memories without batting an eye, but nothing has prepared me for the way the Valorie appears right now, trapped within her own psyche.

She's crouched close to the glossy onyx floor, black curls limp and stark against her ghostly complexion. The formless white pants and matching tunic she's wearing hang loosely from her frame, as though she's somehow lost weight while she's been a prisoner in her own mind. They're ripped and shredded in several places. Her irises are a flat gray, a far cry from the deep, clear storms they usually hold.

Before her is the beast the Testing has crafted. A menacing humanoid with dangling arms and fingers tipped with daggers. I try to ignore the way several of them glint deep crimson in the faded blue-white glow of this place.

Its face has a hideous split for a mouth, a too-wide grinning facsimile of a smile complete with gnashing silver fangs. Above the maw, features twist and shift between two faces. One of them is a young male I recognize from her dream in the alleyway. When his likeness drips away and is replaced, my stomach lurches and my fists clench.

The other face belongs to Joran.

Valorie stumbles to the left to avoid a slashing blow from one of the monster's razor-tipped fingers and she...flickers. In and out of existence, like a television image caught between channels.

Shit. We don't have time to waste.

"Princess," I call in a voice dripping nonchalance despite every tendon in my body being wound tight enough to snap. Fake it 'til you make it, right? The last thing Valorie needs right now is someone else spiralling. "I've got to say, you're always beautiful, but this isn't your best outfit. Dingy cream rags are very last season."

Her eyes fly to me, a small scream bursting free when the distraction gives her opponent an opening. She rolls backward in a clumsy but effective dodge and scrambles to her feet. "Dennick?" she pants. "How the hell? Where did you come from? What are you doing here?"

I smile at her, suffusing the expression with every ounce of warmth I can muster. "Unlike your current mess, shining armor is an outfit I always pull off."

The weary hope on her face is painful. "Are you here to get me out of here? Thank fuck, because I can't do this, Dennick." To my horror, fat tears roll their way down her cheeks, leaving tracks in the grime covering her battered skin. "I'm fucking tired, Den. I ran away for a while. I figured I'd wake up soon enough, but he kept following me. I tried pretending he didn't exist, and I got this for my troubles." She lifts her left shoulder, and I spy a deep gash running down to her elbow before she ducks past another blow. "I keep telling myself to wake up, but it doesn't work. I thought that was what you were supposed to do in a dream, isn't it?"

I steel myself for the way her face is going to crumple when I explain what's happening. "Normally, yes," I answer gently. "But this isn't your typical dream, Princess. I have a feeling you won't be able to leave until he's dead. And I can't be the one to do it."

Her head whips back and forth in violent denial. "No. No, Den, *please*! You're here to help. You said you would!"

"Shhh," I try to console her while she continues to cry, barely staying beyond the being's reach. An index finger's bloody blade catches the back of her neck on a mistimed dodge.

I wince. Valorie doesn't even notice the cut. It blends with the dozens of others littering her flesh.

"Fight, Princess! You need to fight!" My shout is hoarse with fear.

Valorie holds out her right hand without stopping. A plain, thin-bladed sword forms in her grasp. She jerks it in front of her in time to block a razor-lined slap from the monster, but the blade flickers and dies in her hand before she can raise it again. Another frantic roll carries her away long enough for a pair of daggers to materialize. She sweeps them towards her nightmare.

My jaw tenses as I study their battle. Valorie's blow is sloppy and misplaced, filled with fatigue and nerves. It misses his face by several inches, but manages to carve a deep line along the beast's forearm. Inky black blood drips and sizzles as it hits the floor.

A harsh breath hisses through my teeth when the nightmare opens another shallow cut. This one follows her cheekbone as though tracing the delicate line of her skull. The thing cackles with glee as her blood beads.

She can do this. She has to.

I rack my brain to dredge up images gleaned from her fainter memories I once traveled. Friends, family, anything. It's the only way I can think of to help.

There was a young man in an early dream with blue hair not unlike Ceraun's, on the arm of another male with glasses and an indulgent smile. I draw them up to the forefront of my mind and keep digging.

A trio of older humans, their faces lightly lined by time's caress. The mischievous dehmi with flickering flames, and the burly one playing with a tendril of vine. The white-haired, sad-eyed beauty I glimpsed at Valorie's bedside. Two older dehmi watching the younger ones with keen eyes and pleased expressions. Conall himself, smiling at Valorie as though she's hung every moon and star.

Each recalled person steps from my memory and into the dreamscape, becoming nearly as real as we are. Only the slight wavering of their borders, the hint of transparency around the edges, keeps them from being entirely corporeal. With spread arms, I send the apparitions to ring the circle of light Valorie fights within.

She gasps, her irises darting as she takes them in between parries and haphazard swipes of her current weapon—an ax which is already beginning to fade from of her grip. "Are they real, or yet another lie?" The words are soft, likely meant for her ears alone, but they still drive barbs beneath my skin.

"They're real beyond this place, Princess, but we need to get out of here if you want to see them again."

From the corner of my eye, I catch sight of the nightmare before she does. The beast rears backward and prepares to strike, taking advantage of Valorie's preoccupation. What was meant to give her strength has become a distraction. *Fuck.* "Watch out!"

She spins with a shriek, stabbing her knife forward as the Joran-faced creature slashes his claws where her head was a split second earlier. His blow misses.

But Valorie's connects. It's not enough to kill, but it sends the horror scuttling backward, offering her a moment's respite.

Her bloodshot, wide stare locks onto mine in a rare moment of quiet. The beast slowly stalks forward, gnashing its teeth. Savoring her panic. "Den, *please*! I can't do this! I-I didn't have enough time to train, I'm not prepared!" Valorie's eyes speed back and forth, searching without actually seeing anything. She's spiraling, her brain working against itself as time ticks down and the monster slinks closer.

Her agony is a blade between my ribs. This is what I was trying to avoid, what I wanted to save her from. I broke every rule, shattered every trust she placed in me, all to try and prevent this.

And look where that landed us.

My words are low, but they rush out of me. It's a race between us and the monster creeping towards Valorie. "I can't touch him, Princess. Only you can. He's your nightmare, your Test, but he's built from the old you. The you who, through absolutely no fault of her own, and despite her very best efforts, was a victim. A victim of Fate itself, which we both know is unfair bullshit. But you hung on, Princess. You told the Web to shove itself. You aren't a victim anymore, are you?" I cock my head and wait with bated breath and sweaty palms, prayers to nothing and no one rushing through my skull. If this doesn't work, her life is forfeit.

Her pupils widen. "No," she breathes.

I lean in and whisper into her ear, "What are you, Valorie Vargas?"

Narrowed eyes and an iron spine answer me before she opens her lips. But when the words finally emerge? They ring like music in my ears. An anthem for change. A battle hymn.

"I'm a weapon."

"That's my girl."

Valorie turns to face her demon. Exhaustion still lines every plane of her body and dogs every footstep with snapping jaws, but a new light now glimmers in her eyes. Her head tilts, surveying the monster before her. Cold, calculating, calm.

My stomach plummets as I realize she's no longer planning her escape.

She's planning her *assault.*

Valorie's fingers flex open and shut at her sides, a reflexive movement. I watch, waiting for weapons, but no blades appear. No axes, no spears, nothing but dead air. A sinister, half-crazed grin lights up her face with a manic energy. I can't help but smile along with her, my heart lodged in my throat as she waits in silence for the shifting-faced creature to slink forward.

The nightmare prowls closer, hunched on its too-long limbs. All pretense of humanity in its stance is long gone. Only the beast remains, wearing the faces of her two killers. The boy and the man, the human and the dehmi. The spineless wretch and the sanctimonious worm, both unaware of their impending death standing before them.

Vengeance disguised as a woman. Victory given form.

My smile grows teeth. When she's done with Joran, even immortality won't be enough to save him. And personally? I can't wait.

Valorie bounces lightly on her heels, a pugilist awaiting her opponent's strike. When the beast's dagger claws swipe, she spins easily out of its range. The silver blades sweep the empty air beyond her shoulder, then again above her tucked head. I bob along with her, a ringside fan mirroring her moves as she ducks and swerves her way through each of its attacks, closing in tight against the creature's gangling body.

Too tight.

Despite my best effort to stay silent, I can't help myself. She's going to get herself beheaded. "What are you doing, Princess?" I shout anxiously. "Stop toying with it!"

Her only answer is a feral chuckle. Gone is my sweet-natured, trusting friend. In her place, a finely honed warrior stands, the force of a thousand souls at her back. She's terrifying as she steps close enough to embrace the demon before her. If I were her opponent, I'd be running for my life.

From this angle, all I'm able to make out is her back and the flailing limbs of the demon as she closes in. Slices and scrapes mar this side of her as well, and her shirt hangs in tattered ribbons over her sickly pale skin. Her right arm flicks forward, towards the beast. The elbow swings up, then wrenches down and away.

And the creature slumps to the floor.

As its body crashes into an unmoving heap of flesh and metal, I sprint. Rounding the scene, I stand face-to-face with my friend. My stare roves from her bent head and parted lips to her heaving chest, her raw skin. It follows the rivulets of black blood dripping down her right arm and sizzling in a puddle on the ground. Down, down my gaze crawls.

To the heart clenched in her lowered fist.

She tosses the lump onto the carcass at her feet. It hits the pile with a wet squelch and rolls down to splash into the puddle on the floor.

Valorie raises her head and her expression breaks into the brightest beam. "Fuck. Him." she pants.

Relieved laughter bubbles from us both, barely this side of hysteria. I pull her into a hug and grip the back of her skull before holding her in front of me at arm's length. "Why didn't you conjure up a sword or something, Princess?"

She winks—fucking *winks* at me while that thing's blood still drips from her fingers. I swear my heart cheers when she replies, "You don't need a weapon when you *are* one."

"For my own sanity, maybe use a damned blade next time. Got it, killer?"

"It would be cleaner, I guess," she jokes, holding up her gore-drenched hand. Thick black coats it in macabre paint up to her elbow. Gobs of viscera are stuck within the drying layer, and cracks spiderweb across it as she lowers her arm.

Valorie tips her head to the side and studies me. "Why did you save me?" she asks. Her voice is quiet, with no trace of anger or suspicion. Only curiosity. "I left you behind. Why did you come back for me?"

"You're my best friend." My reply comes with a small shrug. "How could I not? Even if—"

The breath wheezes out of me when her body barrels into mine. Slim arms band around my torso with surprising strength. Strength she hasn't been able to muster for weeks.

Valorie's frizzed head lands on my shoulder. "Thank you, Den," she whispers. A quick peck of her lips brushes my cheek. "You're one of my best friends, too. And don't worry," she adds, pulling back enough to meet my eyes, "we'll always be connected, even if we're apart."

"Careful, Princess. Someone might overhear and think you've forgotten how you're supposed to hate me."

"Oh, I'm still furious," she chuckles mirthlessly. "And I'll hand your ass to you one of these days for what you did, mark my words. But, I also understand you, Den. It's hard to be alone, and even harder to be lonely. We all do stupid things for those we love, especially when we're afraid they'll be hurt." She levels me with a stern glare. "That doesn't excuse what you did, though. And you're going to have to work like hell to prove yourself trustworthy again."

Her stern expression softens and her hand squeezes my upper arm. "We'll discuss this further when we aren't wading through the most disgusting puddle ever created, got it? But, in the end, you came for me when you could've sat by and had exactly what you wanted fall right into your lap. You earned yourself a huge point in the 'forgiveness' column. You'll get there, I have no doubt. You're too stubborn not to."

Her wink is the last thing I see before I wrap my arms around her and squeeze. If I try hard enough, maybe I can form my body into armor for her when she heads back into the living realm. She'll need it.

With a sigh, I pat her head. The springy locks bounce beneath my palm. It reminds me of the moss-laden forest we played in all those weeks ago. "I've never had an annoying little sister before, you know? I'm beginning to understand the appeal."

She barks a startled laugh as I cackle into her ear. Valorie's foot connects with my shinbone and sends a sharp pain radiating through my leg. "Ouch! Or maybe not, hellion! You better not be getting demon blood on my pants. It won't follow me back to the real world, of course, but it's the principle that matters."

Laughter fades gradually until the two of us are left together in a soft, comforting silence. Our breathing is the only sound left in this dark, fathomless space. We need to return home, but I sense she needs a moment to collect herself before facing everyone—and everything—waiting for her.

Our embrace breaks apart, but we don't go far. Quietly, I explain the basics of what she'll encounter when she opens her eyes for the first time in days. I keep the information Esraa and Amon are waiting to share to myself. They'll tell her soon enough. Likely the second she's fully awake, knowing the Paragons.

You'd think eternal beings would have endless patience, but that's apparently too much to ask for.

"So, Princess, are you ready to go back? You've got a lot of people waiting on you, and you've gone way beyond being fashionably late."

Valorie inhales deeply. Her lids fall shut and stay closed. Is she finding the words to ask for more time? I'll grant that wish, if she voices it.

But when her eyes open, they're steady and resolute. She thrusts out her hand. When my fingers wrap around hers, her chin dips in a firm nod. "Let's go."

CHAPTER 30
Avallean

- VALORIE -

Hope is a dangerous thing. It's enough to keep a drowned man swimming into nothingness far beyond when his body should realize the water has won. It keeps breaths moving in the flatlined long enough for life to claw its way back into their veins. It drags people through mud and muck for the mere possibility of a better existence at the end, real or otherwise.

It keeps a dead girl's soul together as she wanders the Underworld.

I may be a weapon now, but hope is a weapon, too. And as I lie here, wrapped in softness and willing my eyelids to crack open, hope is a herd of razor-bladed butterflies slicing my innards to ribbons.

Muffled voices drift through the haze behind my shuttered lids. Dennick's hits me first, saying I should be waking up any moment now. Several others provide overlapping responses. Some are familiar, scratching at the back of my mind without fully revealing themselves. Others are entirely new. Their lilting accents remind me of Ceraun's, but the pitches are all wrong.

Their words fade away without sticking in my brain. In and out, here and gone. Until two ragged, wish-drenched sentences grow barbs and embed themselves in my eyelids, forcing them wide open.

"Wildcat, can you hear me? I hope you can, because I desperately need you to wake up, *please*."

How could I ever say no?

I suck in a wheezing breath as the world explodes into color.

Oxygen rushes through my lungs and chases away the last vestiges of slumber. Faces swim into focus above me, a pair of emerald irises shining brighter than the rest. A single tear coasts down his cheek, followed closely by another. I reach up to swipe them away, and my hand lingers against his jaw, savoring the rasp of his stubble against my skin, the sheer, radiating warmth of him. He turns slightly and presses his lips to my palm before they find my own.

His tear-soaked kiss holds a million apologies, but I need none of them. I'm finally home.

"Hey there, magic man." My voice breaks in a hoarse croak when his forehead touches mine. It's raspy from disuse. I cough to clear my dry throat. Someone presses a glass of water into my free hand, and I drain it in one gulp.

My eyes reluctantly pull away from him to roam the sea of people clustered behind him. We all seem to be in the opulent suite I used my first night here. That night may as well have been a lifetime ago.

Each person is pressed against the next, as though they all needed to be as close as possible to where I am. Every face is painted in a wide-eyed, furrowed-browed mixture of concern and cautious optimism.

I smile. "Why the long faces?"

A harsh laugh bursts from Finn's lips and abruptly morphs into a sob. He rushes over and crushes me in his arms, lifting my back from the pillows. I brace for the squeak of air being forced from my lungs and the creaking ribs which usually accompany his hugs, but they never come.

"Finny, did you skip a workout day or three? You're not breaking every bone in my body."

"It's not him," Conall answers. His hands never leave my skin. They roam every inch of me, presumably checking for injuries. Thankfully, none of the ones I suffered in my nightmare have followed me to the waking world. In fact, my skin is completely unmarred, smoother than before I fell asleep. "It's you."

"Me?"

Ceraun rests a gentle hand on my shoulder. The small scales along his forearm glimmer like sapphires under the soft light of a sconce over the bedside table. "Do you feel any different?"

I glance down, taking an inventory of my body. Two arms? Two legs? Check and check. Fingers and toes are all accounted for. My head buzzes strangely, as though it's been packed with electrified steel wool, but a quick brush of my hand across my face confirms all's normal there, too. Still, an intangible *something* remains. A burr in the rear of my skull.

I close my eyes and a jolt barrels through my body. I'm used to the blackness behind my lids being occasionally interspersed with swirls of purple-green or a flash of yellowish orange when I take a peek at the sun despite knowing exactly what it does to my corneas. Whatever, beauty is pain and the sun is a prime example. My eyeballs doth protest too much, in my opinion.

No amount of retina-melting glimpses of our flaming star could have prepared me for the riot of colors ricocheting behind my eyelids. Brilliant fern and magenta chase each other along glowing pathways tinged with purest gold a shade away from ivory. The energy coalesces into a mass of scintillating hues, rays shooting from it in firework bursts. Dwarfed by the corona is a more diminutive lump of light, this one bedecked in rings of blue-white. Mysterious, inexplicable warmth emanates from it. A twirling thread connects this smaller piece to the larger mass. A matching string spears off into the darkness without end.

It's beautiful. Comforting and intimidating in equal measure, and entirely foreign.

My eyes open. "What happened to me?" I whisper.

A woman—Avallean—steps forward. At her side is a stern-faced male who would be at home on a battlefield. I assume these are the Paragons I've heard so much about. "We have finished what we started long ago," the female says in a melodic voice. Her smile is wide and welcoming. "You are now an Avallean, Valorie Vargas."

"I am?" I turn to Conall. "They did it? We're Bonded?"

His beam could cut glass and set the universe aflame. Let it—I'll dance in the sparks until the world is nothing but dust in deep space. "We are, my love. And if it's all right with you, I'm hoping Esraa will be the last person to call you by that last name."

All I can do is nod and hope my joy shines through my tears.

Conall pulls me into his arms with a sigh. My chest twinges, a deep sense of relieved happiness flowing from the mass I noticed before. Suddenly, I understand the smaller, warm knot in my chest is *him*. My fragment of his soul, and the tether binding us for eternity.

Over his shoulder, I make eye contact with his siblings—my own siblings, now. There isn't a dry eye among them. The ornate mirror behind them reflects the new and improved Valorie over their heads, wrapped in love and complete with tear tracks over her rosy cheeks. "I hope you know you're never getting rid of me, now," I say with a watery chuckle.

The three of them jump in and pile onto the bed with us until we're nothing but a tangle of limbs and laughter. "Fates, I'm glad you're back, Val," Gaius says over the ruckus as we gradually settle down amongst the pillows and churned up bedding. "I don't know how much longer we could have handled Conall."

When I ask what he means, Conall's blush deepens. His hand rubs at the back of his neck and he suddenly finds his lap intensely interesting. "I may have been a bit...over the top when you were missing."

Gaius snorts. "A bit? You were bat shit crazy and you know it. Even Gabby was tired of dealing with you, and she's more patient than the three of us put together." Gabrielle shrugs. The boys break into snickers again, pushing and shoving each other until Gaius careens over the edge of the bed and lands in a heap on the floor, one foot suspended in the air by a coiled sheet wrapped like a constrictor around his ankle. Laughter flows around us without end.

I find Conall's hand among the chaos. Our palms connect and I squeeze. When his eyes land on mine, I mouth, *Missed you, too.*

There's no sign of tense shoulders or thinned lips in the tangle of Avalleans surrounding me. Not anymore. They're practically rapturous.

Which is why an anxious pair of slitted pupils catches my attention when they appear over Finn's golden brown head. I pat the scant few inches of empty bed beside me with my best soothing smile and scoot to make room for my guardian.

Ceraun dashes to my side, tripping over a discarded throw pillow in his haste. With how he's acting, you'd think I'm about to die. I guess I can't blame him, given the state I was in the last time we spoke.

With one hand firmly grasped between Conall's, I sling the other around Ceraun in a one-armed hug. He crushes me into his side, pivoting to better wrap both arms around me. A wing bends to cradle my shoulders in blue warmth. In the early dawn light of the open window, the tears lining his lids glisten like diamonds.

"I failed you," he croaks in my ear. "I had one job, and I failed you."

I make an overly dramatic show of sweeping my gaze through the room. "I don't know, Ceraun. Seems I ended up exactly where I'm supposed to be." My finger taps against his nose. I giggle when he jerks his head away. "Aren't those lizard eyes of yours supposed to be powerful? Maybe you need to get them checked. Do wyrok have ophthalmologists?"

"You're insufferable," Ceraun chuckles. His body relaxes against mine, the stiff set of his shoulders collapsing into a relieved slump. His features are soft and unguarded as he says, "Glad to see you're still you, *kynaira*."

We chat quietly between us for several minutes. I listen silently as he recounts the events that transpired while I was asleep. Afterwards, Ceraun clears his throat to breach the din in the room and introduces me to the trio of wyrok standing near the fireplace in the room's far corner. Two are vaguely familiar from my pain-hazed early days in the city. The third is a stranger despite the familiar curve of her jaw.

Ceraun calls her Mephys. His cousin and close companion since childhood, along with the other two wyrok. Which explains the family resemblance.

Mephys is an instantly contagious ball of excitement. The petite wyrok bounces on the balls of her feet, her spiraling teal curls springing to and fro around a bright expression in the same cerulean tone as Ceraun's. Her slitted pupils are framed by irises in a bright shade of pink no human could ever achieve without colored contacts. She zips around the room, flitting back to my bed every few minutes with another question for me or joking comment about young Ceraun.

We're going to be good friends, I can tell.

Nestled in a darkened corner, an aloof Daros nods a greeting from his shadow shroud. I give him a small wave. The dark wisps of magic ebb and flow around him like harmless smoke. Intuition tells me there's nothing harmless about him, though. I vaguely recall how he used his shadows as extra limbs when we first arrived and resolve never to make an enemy of him.

His sister, Deina, beams beautifully beside him as she did when we first met. Her violet eyes and olive complexion blend perfectly with her twin's. His obsidian mane, a perfect match for hers, is tied up in a severe bun at the back of his head, making it impossible to discern its length.

Ceraun said earlier she was the healer who kept me alive while we waited for the Paragons. I dip my chin and mouth my thanks when I catch her eye, which earns me an even larger and twice as radiant smile from the female wyrok.

The deep blush drenching Ceraun's entire face when Deina grins doesn't escape my notice for a single second.

He *likes* her. I'd wager all my money on it. And when his elbow jabs into my ribs, I know he's aware his secret is out. I pump my brows at him and mime zipping my lips. I'll keep my observation in my back pocket until we're alone, but you can bet I'll hound him for details some time soon.

Without warning, all my thoughts screech to a halt. Everything turns inward, searching for something I didn't remember until this moment.

"Wait a second," I whisper as realization floods. Mind whirring, I don't notice my hand is raised in the air until Finn snickers and slaps it in a high-five. I shove at his shoulder and repeat myself at a higher volume.

The chatter dies down instantly, as though a deity's grasp has turned the room's volume knob to its minimum. All eyes on me, I ask the question childhood Valorie would kick me for forgetting. "If I'm an Avallean now, do I have magic? Do I get a power?" I'm close to vibrating in hopeful anticipation. *Please say yes.* Frankly, I deserve one after all this.

"Of course you do," Conall replies with a cocky flick of his wrist. He glances at Esraa and Amon and his overconfident facade cracks with uncertainty. I'd laugh if we weren't discussing the possibility of me having actual magic for all eternity. "She does, right?"

According to the brief explanation Esraa provides over the next minute or two, complete with the occasional interjection from Amon, I do in fact have powers, same as every other Avallean. Score one for preteen Val.

And I have a sneaking suspicion the two Paragons know what my powers are. They simply refuse to tell me. Not so awesome.

Preteen Val would be throwing a fit, waving her hands around in grand sweeps while she wailed about unfairness. Emotional stability wasn't anyone's strong suit at twelve years old. But I'm a mature adult now. I don't throw a fit.

I beg.

My pleading and attempts to barter fall on deaf ears. Neither Esraa nor Amon will budge on fast-tracking me towards discovering what type of magic I now have within my grasp, no matter how many times I play the "I died and then almost did it again because you were late" card.

Instead, after entirely too long, Esraa tells me to close my eyes and search inside myself for the second time since I've awoken.

"There should be a sphere of color," she explains softly. When I confirm, Esraa continues. "Envision yourself reaching out to touch it. Be gentle. It's your first time."

Distantly, Finn cackles and mutter under his breath, "Yeah, Val. Be *gentle* for your *first time*." A *thump* echoes in my ears, then his pained groan.

"Focus," Amon admonishes when I snicker. "What does it feel like?"

I brush the softest of mental caresses along the vibrant halo. My vision buckles inward, hurtling past me as if I've stepped off a cliff into the abyss. The screeches of terns and eagles assault my eardrums. They vibrate through my skull and mix with roars and chitters and odd words blended together in a mishmash of nonsense phrases. Animals of all sorts, furred and scaled, large and small, flit in short glimpses down the endless tunnel of my sight.

"Enough." Amon's command breaks through the tumult and calls me back to reality. I suck in a rasping breath and snap my eyes open wide. "What did you feel?" he asks again.

"It felt like...like when I would work at the Conservatory? I don't know how to explain it. There were animals everywhere and all their cries were overlapping with these warped humanoid voices. It was madness—yet comforting. Like I belonged among the chaos." I blush. The explanation sounds ridiculous, but from the nods of the Avalleans around me, I'm guessing the sensation isn't uncommon. "But what does it mean?"

"A wildwalker?"

The room pivots in Gabrielle's direction. She faces the Paragons. "Is that what she is?"

Esraa nods. An irritated sigh hisses through my nostrils. Having people talk *about* you instead of *to* you is exhausting. I'm tired of it.

"They're one of the rarer affinities," Gabrielle explains after a quick apology, "along with dreamtreading and shadow magic. I haven't heard of a new wildwalker being born in ages, come to think of it. They can speak to animals and assume their form, although I've read the latter is very physically draining." She shrugs. "It would make sense, given your previous calling before you were mixed up in all this."

"I'm a fucking shapeshifter?" The words are a barely discernible squeak of rushed air. I may have stopped breathing entirely. "A shapeshifter who can talk to animals? You're serious? Because I swear, if one of you says 'just kidding', I will cut you." My glare could slice glass into ribbons.

I wait with bated breath, but nobody starts laughing. There's a complete lack of Ashton Kutcher popping from under the bed, and nobody has a camera pointed at me for the moment It's revealed I've been Punk'd.

Nobody is denying it.

Reality sets in slowly, and then suddenly, I believe them.

I squeal. My feet flail under the bed linens. I scramble to my feet, pulling Conall along with me. I'm already planning on begging everyone in the room to help me train, the wyrok included.

When I round the edge of the bed for the first time since gaining immortality, I spot him. My feet stop abruptly enough to leave skids in the thick carpet.

"Den?" I whisper.

He jolts, though I couldn't possibly have startled him. His stare was locked on me already. Dennick is curled in a patch of shadow beside the breakfast table, his back plastered to the far wall. Knees drawn up to his chest, arms banded around them as though fighting to keep still.

I approach slowly, arms held in front of me the way I would placate a cornered animal. His body tenses impossibly tighter with every step, each muscle and tendon strained taut enough to snap. "What are you doing down here, Dennick?"

His gaze flicks rapidly, from me to the door and back. "I tried to leave, but I couldn't. I had to make sure you were alive. Had to make sure you were safe. It's kind of my thing, you know?"

As his final word catches in his throat and breaks, so too does my composure. I bend down and embrace him. "Don't leave, Den. Don't go." The words are whispered for his ears alone.

I pull back and meet his eyes. I need to make certain he understands. I don't know how much time I have left in this place. "We still need to have our conversation, and we will. But please don't leave. You belong here with us. Without you, I'd still be trapped in there, alone and struggling uselessly against death once again." I shudder, the memories of the two-faced creature cold as ice in my veins. *I got out,* I remind myself, *I'm free.* "You've more than earned your place at our table, Dennick. I only wish I didn't have to leave you and Ceraun behind. It's hard to mend a friendship between worlds."

A throat clears behind us. Over my shoulder, Amon looms, his shadows adding to the darkness of Dennick's hiding place. "You will not be leaving this place behind."

"What?" For a split second, my heart soars at the thought of more time with Dennick and Ceraun.

And then it plummets as his words sink in. "What do you mean?" My breathing accelerates. Sweat pools in my palms and between my shoulder blades. I sense as Dennick grips my arms, but the sensation is distant, muffled behind the all-too-familiar haze of panic.

I hardly notice when Conall and his siblings surround us. Conall pushes through to my side. "Am I still dead?" I wheeze. "Did the ceremony not work? You said it did! You said—"

"What's going on?" Conall drips with confused rage. "You assured us everything worked. Her magic is present, the Bond has been formed. There is no reason to keep her here."

Every Avallean seethes, avenging angels arrayed around me. Only the wyrok lounging in the rear of the suite are visibly unfazed. Ceraun catches my eye and motions with twirling hands for me to take deep breaths. As if such a thing is possible in this situation.

"You misunderstand," Amon says. "Valorie Vargas is indeed alive and well. And she will rule the realm of death."

Chapter 31
A Bombshell

A mon's revelation explodes through the room, leaving silence in its wake. A pin dropping three rooms down would make more noise than any one of us. We're frozen, statues in a still-life manifestation of shock.

My head sluggishly pivots to take in the startled expressions on each of my siblings' faces. Valorie is pale as milk, all the newly-found color drained from her face in abject horror. We're all thinking the same thought—it's written across our scrunched brows and between our bulging eyes: Certainly we must have misheard him?

Esraa's dainty chuckle is the first sound to break the cloying quiet. "I think you've broken them, dear." Snorts erupt in the cozy corner the wyrok have claimed as their own. "Maybe you should explain. Gently. I think a feather could knock the whole group over."

She's not wrong. My knees are trembling hard enough to send tremors through my teeth. I lock them in place and wait for Amon to speak.

"I assume you're aware of the fact most of the lower Paragons are chosen by the Avallean populace from a pool of qualified candidates chosen by the reigning Paragons. There are several factors taken into account, none of which matter right now." The Avalleans in the room quietly confirm. In the corner, there's the quiet scraping of a wyrok filing their claws in boredom. Likely Daros. "The Underworld's rulers are chosen by a different process entirely. The sitting rulers choose their heirs without outside input from the lower Council. To prove their suitability for the role, the Web of Fate itself provides a challenge for the heirs when their time comes. We call it the Testing."

Amon faces Valorie's frozen form. A rare softness smooths his harsh face. "Your Test began the day you died, and ended when you awoke as an Avallean."

Valorie's eyeballs are in serious danger of falling out of her head. I give her hand a firm squeeze and pray to the Web for a moment's peace.

I don't know how she's managing to take all of this in after what she's been through.

I'm desperately trying to think of anything but how close I came to losing her forever. The simple beat of her heart thumping within her chest is a marvel. How inexhaustible and constant it sounds at my side! How it scoffs at the mere notion of ever ceasing its rhythm! It's my favorite instrument, the soundtrack to every memory I hold close and every dream I dread waking from. The little liar, I love it so.

"You're saying I'm...you?" Valorie asks Esraa. She scrubs the heel of her palm across her forehead with a sigh dripping with exhaustion. "It's been a long day, what with the whole 'new species magical transformation' thing on top of the 'evading death *again*' thing. My fancy upgraded Avallean brain is basically soup at this point. I'm going to need you to explain this in very small words."

"The short answer is yes. It is time for me to step down as a Paragon. For both of us to retire, truly. I will stay on as an adviser until you are more comfortable, and Amon will still reign for the time being. There must always be two Paragons of Death, and his heir has not yet passed his Testing." Esraa tilts her head and pins Dennick and Ceraun with an admonishing glare. "I'm surprised you weren't already aware of the situation, to be honest. Did neither of your companions explain?"

An overlapping chorus of "Well—" and "I thought—" and "The time was never right—" begins.

Valorie whips around. She stabs a vicious finger at the pair. "You told me it meant '*princess*' you assholes. Don't even try to pretend you actually explained. Nobody had the thought, 'Oh, I should probably tell my incredibly overwhelmed friend she's on her way to become the ruler of an entire *realm*' at all during the weeks we spent traveling? Males," she scoffs. The two cower, suitably chastised.

Better them than me. If I never find myself on the end of her rage again, it will be too soon. I haven't completely recovered from the last time.

"Why me, anyway?" Valorie asks Esraa. Her words tumble in a frantic ramble. "I really think you should keep the job. I've been an Avallean for about thirty seconds, how could I possibly be qualified? And who is taking over Amon's position? The two of you are Bonded, which I'm sure is not a prerequisite, but I'm not about to have *that* kind of relationship with a random Avallean. Clearly," she adds with a brief, soft smile in my direction.

Valorie's soft curls brush my neck as she leans into me and catches her breath. My brain short-circuits temporarily. I circle my arm around her waist and pull her further into my side until her fresh summer scent envelops me. I want to bottle her up and drink her down, coat my every cell in *her* until we're inseparable.

My blood heats at the simple press of her soft skin against mine. One brush is all it takes for me to want her, even after all this time. I release a rough breath and curse my body's horrible timing, but I can't help myself. If we didn't have an audience, I would have us across the room, tumbling into the massive bed we only just vacated.

It's been far too long since I held my wildcat in my arms. Last time, I was weeping over her corpse. I need to feel her, taste her, banish every memory of that day beneath an onslaught of new sensations.

Absorbed in fantasies, I nearly miss Esraa's answer.

"You had been our top choice for my successor for some time. But, we finalized our decision shortly after your death. Your soul was fresh, it had not yet made it to the Underworld itself." Esraa shifts on her feet as she speaks, her motions becoming more animated. "Your decision to become an Avallean initially drew us to consider how your unique perspective could benefit the position. Especially considering who we had already chosen as Amon's heir. But, for a mortal-turned-immortal who rules over Death to have walked the roads of the Underworld? How could we resist? Think of the benefits, the one-of-a-kind viewpoint only you could offer on behalf of other souls." The way she speaks—she muses about Valorie's life as if she is a particularly fascinating puzzle piece finally slotted into position.

I fight the urge to tuck Valorie behind my body and shield her from view. They would never hurt her, but I don't enjoy hearing about how her death benefited them. Esraa has a point, yet I can't entirely forgive them for their callousness, even if it does aid the realm of the dead and all the souls housed within. Being an Avallean is about self-sacrifice; we're all taught this from infancy. Serve the Web, then take your place among our people back home.

My willingness to serve stops the second anything touches Valorie.

"And as for your second question, Valorie, I would think one as intelligent as you would have figured it out by now."

A snort, then, "Humor me."

"Why, our son, of course," Esraa replies.

Valorie blinks twice. A blank expression and a snark-laced, "And who might *that* be?" are all she offers the two people who could wipe this whole room off the map with a wave of their hand.

I doubt I've ever been more attracted to her than I am in this moment.

Amon's severe scowl crumbles into a laugh. His gaze traces the arm I've wrapped around Valorie. He follows its line up to my eyes before saying, softer than I've ever heard him, "He's right beside you."

"I still think it's a strange call to pick your son for an heir. Dehmi aren't even supposed to know who their parents are until they arrive back in Avallea. Won't people call you out for it? Judge Con—and by extension Val—for not earning their positions? Nepotism doesn't seem high on the list of sought after qualities for Paragons," Finn chatters incessantly around a mouthful of roasted meat and herbed potatoes. He points his fork at the Paragons, a chunk of crisped, honeyed carrot dangling from the tines.

Several of the wyrok glare at him from the far end of the lacquered wood dining table. We've finally escaped the confines of the suite to take over a small dining room a few doors down the hall. Royal blue curtains hang heavily to the parquet floor. They flank floor-to-ceiling windows open to the cool midday air. Sun shines above the city, but clouds roll in the distance—a harbinger of rain in the future. The distant bustle of wyrok down in the streets is overlaid by the clinking of cutlery against silver plates piled high with meats, vegetables, and thick slices of toasted bread rubbed with garlic and butter. A slew of pastries cover an ornate sideboard to our left.

Esraa and Amon, seated at the head of the table, acknowledge him with a glance. "We didn't set out to hand Amon's position to our son," Esraa explains between dainty bites of apple tart. "However, he's become a clear choice. He has a spotless record and additional benefits, especially considering who he's chosen to Bond himself to. The Underworld must be ruled by a pair, and a Bond affords certain benefits which, while they aren't necessary for the station, are certainly advantageous.

"Ultimately, the decision was ours to make, but we had the same fears you've described. But, we asked. The Council of Paragons has given their blessing to both heirs and agrees with our choosing."

"Spotless record until Val came along," Gaius mutters under his breath. He flashes a wide smirk at Val, who smiles sweetly in return and scratches her eyebrow.

Neither I nor Gaius miss how she chooses to scratch the area with only her middle finger.

"We're both going to be Paragons now?" Valorie asks. "Since Conall made it through the Underworld too?"

My hand squeezes hers between our plates. I haven't let go since we left the room, despite her repeated complaints over how it's difficult to eat without the use of both her hands. She can complain all she wants—I love it when she's feisty.

Esraa shakes her head. "Not yet. Only those who have overcome Death itself can become its ruler. While Conall may have survived his trek, he was never faced with Death's finality. His Testing will come in time, and then he will assume his role alongside you."

Of course it couldn't be simple.

After that annoying bit of information, chatter falls to a lull as everyone finishes their meal. I try to avoid the sick churning in my gut at the thought of Valorie and I being separated once again, this time by duty.

No. I'll simply remain by her side until my Testing comes along. Then, she can be with me while I face it. She had Dennick's and Ceraun's company for hers.

Wood screeches against marble as the Paragons stand. The wyrok rise to their feet and remain standing until Amon waves them back to their chairs. "We must be going. We will be back in a week for the Crowning, where Esraa will formally step down and Valorie will assume her place as Paragon. It must happen within a fortnight, or the Web will move on and choose another on its own. Ensure you're ready."

"Enjoy your week," Esraa adds cheerfully. She faces Valorie and I, hand-in-hand in our chairs near the table's head. Her gaze focuses on our clasped palms atop the table for several seconds. "Become accustomed to the newness of your change and your Bond. Enjoy its...benefits." A hoot from Finn causes Valorie to grin. A blush crawls up her supple neck, one I long to lick until the rosy tint covers her whole body. "Take some time to begin working with your powers, and don't fret over what is to come."

Valorie's snort and mumbled, "Sure, that'll happen," cause a ripple of chuckles to flow down the tables. Even the wyrok join in the laughter. Except for Daros, but I doubt he's ever laughed before in his long life.

A portal opens a few feet from the table. The swirling vortex of light blocks the window behind it with a mercurial sheen. Amon's arm wraps around his partner and the two step toward the oval of power waiting to take them back to Avallea. "Oh," Esraa exclaims. She spears me with a stern look from over her shoulder. "Don't bother pestering poor Gabrielle over your Testing. Seers can't foretell that specific weaving of the Web."

My frustrated groan chases their retreating forms through the portal until it snaps closed at their backs.

CHAPTER 32

Finally Alone

- CONALL -

After the Paragons' departure—and the shocked mutters following the revelation of Conall's parentage—the rest of us agree to meet up for dinner this evening. Ceraun and Deina offer to play tour guide and show us the sights of the city tomorrow, but for tonight they correctly assume we would rather stay in and relax.

I appreciate their perceptiveness. I have no desire to be around anyone except Valorie for the next several hours—a long tour would be a nightmare.

If we could only make our escape from this room.

Valorie, my siblings and I mull around the dining hall with Dennick, waiting for guidance. I know where I want to be—a celestial-spangled room two doors down—but we have no information on whether the rest of our party will be offered lodgings in the temple or need to procure some in the city proper. The wyrok are gathered in deep conversation in the corner.

Well, two of them. Daros merely lurks in the shadows once again, glowering as though he would prefer nothing more than to evacuate the gathering from the room entirely.

"Uh, where should we go?" Finn garbles in their direction. His lips are stretched around a large crust of bread he's shoved in his equally large mouth. He swipes another hunk of the brown loaf from the table and tucks it into his pocket. Two pastries from a platter in the center of the table follow suit. If I didn't know him, I would think he's afraid we'll be starved during our time in the Hearth. But this is typical Finn behavior.

Deina finishes her whispered conversation with Ceraun and confirms smaller suites have been prepared for everyone. The wyrok healer graciously gathers my siblings near the exit to show them to their rooms.

Ceraun's booming voice echoes against the high ceiling. "Deina, you've missed a duckling."

She turns around, robes billowing like petals. Faint pink blush tinges the bridge of her nose. A smile bursts across her face when their eyes meet. Several seconds pass before she gasps and blinks, as though coming back to reality. Their infatuation is hilariously obvious, yet Valorie whispered over lunch Ceraun never mentioned the attractive healer during their trip.

Of course, my wife already has plans to interrogate him.

My *wife*.

"Come along, then," Deina beckons Dennick with a curl of her fingers. "We wouldn't want you to get lost. It's a maze in here."

"Oh, I—uh," Dennick splutters. "It's all right, you don't have to—"

Valorie takes a single step towards where he's waffling in the center of the room. Likely because it's as far as she can go with my arm around her waist, and I have no plans on letting go any time soon. "Den," she calls gently. He meets her eyes and she nods once. "Go."

He sighs and slinks forward to join my family at the door with no further argument. Smart male.

Finn loops an arm around his shoulders and pulls Dennick into the throng. With her charges all in place, Deina claps her hands and ushers them from the dining hall to the left.

Thank the Web—Valorie's suite is in the opposite direction.

Ceraun trails after Deina. His movements are slow—I don't know if he even notices he's making his way in the direction she led her group. Upon reaching the doorway, he jerks to a stop and spins back in our direction. "Do you require assistance finding your room?" he asks with a slight frown. His body sways to the left.

The question is clearly directed to Valorie, but I butt in before she can speak. "Ceraun, I will never be able to repay you for taking care of my wife when I could not." He dips his chin. "And I appreciate your friendship. But let me make myself crystal clear. If you follow us to our room and interfere with my plans to finally have her to myself for a few hours, I will siphon your soul from your body and use it to repair someone's colon."

Ceraun bristles for an instant before his shoulders drop down and he throws his head back in laughter. Valorie turns a shade of crimson so deep, I'm surprised I can't bask in the heat off her skin. She manages to blush even further when Ceraun pats her obsidian curls and vacates the room with a chuckle and a shake of his head.

He heads left, of course.

I reach my hand towards Valorie. The caretaker of my soul. The woman I braved the realm of death for.

My wife.

In the bright, natural light through the windows, it's hard to re-member she was dead this time yesterday. Her palm lands in mine, and I pull her from the room.

I rush us down the hall until we arrive at the lapis lazuli doors with their golden stars and gilt trim like the night sky itself is trapped within them. A doorway fit for a goddess. *My* goddess. And I want nothing more than to worship at her altar.

Yet when the doors shut behind us and we're alone at last, I find myself as frozen as those gilded stars at my back.

Valorie spins in a clumsy pirouette, arms flung to her sides. She collapses backward onto the freshly made bed, giggling the whole way down. The clean white and royal blue linens swell in plush clouds around her. She calls for me to come to her, beckons with raised hands for me to revel in the comfort she's found, but I am powerless. I want nothing more than to be at her side, but my limbs rebel. I remain glued to the chilled stone of the double doors.

"Conall?" She calls. My beautiful bride sits up amongst the linens and stares. Her face falls when her gaze traces my expression. I'm sure it's a mess. "What's wrong?" Valorie trips over her own feet and tangles herself in the sheets in her haste to cross the room. Her fingertips trace wet tracks down my cheeks.

I wasn't aware I was crying.

"Nothing is wrong, Wildcat," I croak. My fingers circle her wrists. They drift down her arms and up to cup her cheeks between my clammy palms before retreating to grasp her wrists once more. I need to feel her pulse thrum beneath my skin. "That's just the thing. Right here, in this very moment, this sliver of eternity? Nothing is wrong. Everything is gloriously perfect. And I'm finding myself a bit overwhelmed at the beauty of it all."

I tilt my face to press a kiss to the inside of her palm. "There was a part of me which believed I would never see you again." Another brush of my mouth, this time at the pulse point on her inner wrist. "I thought I had lost you." My lips find the junction of her elbow. "I was going mad, consumed by my fear." The silk of her short, ice-green dress whispers beneath my kiss as I coast along her shoulder. "What if you were gone forever?" She shivers when I find the soft skin of her neck with my teeth. A gentle nibble turns her shiver into a gasp. "I would have embraced death with open arms, were it the only way for us to reunite," I whisper against her parted lips.

And then I claim them.

Everything between us distills down to pure feeling. The pillowed cushion of her lips against mine. The slip of silk, now warmed by her blush and my roaming hands. The thunder of her heartbeat where her chest presses against my own. Her coiled cloud of onyx hair as it sifts through my fingers.

I grip a fistful of it, angling her head to devour her more thoroughly. My tongue tangles with hers and she nips playfully at my bottom lip.

It's a battle with no losers, a war I never want to end.

My fingers trace the hem of her dress. I drag it upwards until it puddles to the ground in a flutter of sage. Two scraps of fabric join the pile, leaving her milky skin free for me to access. I couldn't tell you what they look like if you threatened my life.

All I see is her.

A soft whimper reverberates from her mouth and spears down my spine with an electrical zing when my hands cup her bare breasts. I corral her towards the plush mountain behind her with slow steps and deep kisses, overwhelmed with the need to consume her, to envelop her, to tangle us together over and over until our scents merge as deeply as our souls are intertwined and the entire universe knows of our Bond.

The stars themselves must learn I will never lose her again.

Valorie's inner knees hit the golden frame of the bed. She falls backward in a billow of fabric. Draped in nothing but the sparse beams of afternoon sunshine through the open bay window, she's starlight given form, sent from the heavens to torture and tantalize in equal measure.

My clothes fall to the floor as fast as I can remove them.

I drape myself over her. Body to body, skin to skin, heart to heart. My palms coast up her inner thighs and ease them apart. Nestling myself between them, I dip my head and capture one of her nipples between my teeth. Her head lolls as I roll my tongue around the taut peak. "I don't think I can take this slow, my love," I whisper raggedly. She shivers as my breath wafts over the damp skin. "Not now, anyway."

"We have all of eternity for slow," she replies. "Today, after everything, I just need you."

She truly was made for me.

I line my aching cock up with her soaking heat and drive into her in a single hard thrust. Instant bliss sends stars whirling before my eyes. There's no way I'll be able to last long.

Her back arches in my grip and her mouth opens in a silent, perfect circle. "I'm sorry," I groan, seated completely inside her. I drop my forehead to her chest and struggle to remain still. I should have tried harder, should have found a way to be gentler.

"Conall?" she breathes. Our eyes connect along the perfect length of her body.

"What do you need, love?"

She reaches towards my face and places a single finger against my lips. The tip slips between them, and I bite down. Her thighs wrap around my hips, ankles tucked tight against my spine. "Shut up and move, *husband*."

The title has fire rippling through my veins. *Husband*. It's the purest sin, the simplest pleasure. A word dripping with enough lust and possession, it should be illegal for her to utter it outside of the confines of this room. I would be happy if she never said my birth name again.

My response is a low rumble of pure desire. "It would be my pleasure, *wife*."

I pull backward until only the crown remains wrapped in her warmth, then snap my hips forward. Over and over, I drive into her with abandon. Valorie throws her head back and grips my waist, meeting me thrust for thrust. Each time our hips collide, a throaty moan tumbles from her swollen lips. She's immaculate, incredible. I could fuck her until the universe collapses around us.

Valorie's fingernails dig into my skin, the tiny pinpricks heightening the ecstasy rippling through me. I tilt the angle of our joined bodies and drive into her, making sure to brush her clit with every deep stroke. It doesn't take long before she's writhing beneath me, gasping and begging for me not to stop.

As if that was ever a possibility. I'd weld us together if I could.

Liquid fire barrels down my spine and ignites, but I refuse to finish without taking her with me. I roll my hips faster, drawing out her pleasure until she crests and finally explodes beneath me.

And then I'm gone, powerless against the inexorable pull of *her*. With a hoarse groan, I empty myself inside of her. I barely have the presence of mind to roll us onto our sides and avoid crushing her when my limbs give way. I drop onto the mattress with a sigh.

"Fates help me," I breathe into the crook of her neck as we lie tangled together atop the haphazard duvet. "I think you may have killed me."

Valorie chuckles. She drags her hands up and down my back, the motions light and teasing. My muscles jump beneath her dancing fingertips. "How odd," she murmurs sleepily, "because I've never felt more alive."

With the sunlight streaming over us in a warm blanket and her sweat-slick limbs tangled with mine, I can't help but agree.

Chapter 33
Hearth and Home

The evening's dinner is a tired affair, with everyone's energy levels flagging despite brief naps in the afternoon. Conall and I spend the meal fighting the urge to doze off and collapse headfirst into our plates of pot roast and potatoes.

Our brief afternoon rest was largely spent tangled atop the sheets. It included two more bouts of lovemaking, ensuring any energy we recovered was thoroughly and deliciously spent well before Ceraun's swift knock at the door announced dinner. When we trudged our way into the room, it was to a score of cat-calls and whoops led by Finn and Gaius. It didn't escape my notice they've taken Dennick into their fold.

Fates help us all.

"How does it feel to know who your parents are?" Finn asks over a mountainous slice of pie topped with thick cream. Every Avallean in the room waits for Conall's answer, their eyes trained on him. Until today, none of them knew their parentage.

So many changes in one day. So many bonds forged and reforged.

Conall swallows a bite of pastry and replies, "I don't think it's entirely real for me yet. Looking back, they were actually quite obvious, but I never picked up on their hints."

"They did always come to meet with you," Gaius agrees. "It's odd for those two to give tasks, yet they were constantly seeking you out for something or another." He turns to his twin. "Did you know?"

Gabrielle's mouth turns down at the corners. "Of course not. If I did, do you think I would have kept it a secret?"

"Of course not," Gaius soothes.

"What do I do with parents?" Conall's question is small, uncertain. The ageless worries of a child hoping they measure up.

My hand finds his where it rests on my knee, and I squeeze softly. "You don't have to do anything," I whisper. "Just be you. If they're smart, and I believe they are, they already know how amazing their son is." I press a kiss to his cheek and chuckle. "A son and a husband? Big day for you, huh? Lots of new changes."

He grins down at me, eyes sparkling brighter than a forest under the summer sun, "The start of a wonderful new chapter, I hope."

Morning dawns clear and bright, and finds us all gathered once again in the dining hall, bleary-eyed and yawning as the first bits of gold light drip their way across the floor. Ceraun and Deina warned us breakfast was scheduled for sunrise, and they weren't exaggerating. I'm weighing the benefits of an extra hour of sleep versus a full stomach.

The two have planned a full day's tour of the city, and the promise of finally exploring the ins and outs of the Hearth is the only thing keeping my eyes open. I shovel fluffy eggs, thick slices of honeyed ham, and sweetened cornbread muffins into my mouth at record speed, praying the calories will do their job quickly and provide me with some much-needed energy.

Dennick smirks in his chair on my left, his gaze slanted to where my fork is working double time. "Hungry, Princess?"

"I thought being an Avallean meant I'd have more energy," I grumble through my overfull cheeks. "Guess that was a lie." With a grunt, I spear another slice of ham with the silver serving tines and haul it onto my plate. My fork and knife descend on the innocent slab of marinated meat, hacking it into hunks barely small enough to be considered bite-sized.

Seated on my opposite side, Conall's hand rubs circles on my back. I'm sure he thinks his loving touch makes up for the way he's chuckling along with Dennick and his brothers, but he's wrong. I'll get him back for it later, once I've got more than a thimbleful of strength and my eyelids aren't waging a losing battle against gravity.

Ceraun and Deina sweep into the room as I'm scraping the vestiges of the ham's glaze off my plate with a crusty roll. Perfectly put together and well-rested, they approach our table and stand at the head.

Damned dragons and their poise. I likely resemble a gremlin.

"Is everyone ready?" Deina asks. She's draped in another immaculate set of robes today, this time a pale sakura pink instead of her usual ivory. Her sleeves are short and the thin fabric brushes the tops of her sandaled feet. Beside her, Ceraun wears a dark pair of pants with an open cerulean vest on top. The stiff fabric matches his scales, and his chest is bare beneath it.

They warned us to dress for warm weather. After witnessing their attire, I'm glad I went with a pair of peachy linen shorts and a fluttering sky blue tank. I have no desire to end our tour early by melting in the heat.

Our group rises in a mass of scraping chairs and shuffling feet. I frantically scoop the last of my breakfast onto my fork and inhale it, coughing as a piece of egg threatens to choke me.

"Rookie move, Val." Finn's massive fist pounds my back until I can breathe again. "You don't struggle to eat it all at once." He snags the largest biscuit from the bread basket, splits it in two, and stuffs copious amounts of egg and ham between the two halves. A dollop of honey butter and a splash of hot sauce completes the perilous stack.

Once the boulder of a sandwich is safely wrapped in a napkin, he places it between my palms. "You take the food with you. That's how us experts work." When he pats his bulging front pocket with a wink, I realize I'm not the only one leaving with a Hobbit's second breakfast packed to-go. Tolkien's characters would be right at home around Finn.

We file out of the hall, past my suite, and down the winding staircase to the temple's entrance. The sky-high doors open and their ornate carvings catch the blinding sunlight. Glinting bits of precious gems within the stone reflect perfect rainbows of light like a giant's sun catcher.

Daros peels away from the pair of attendants at the temple doors and joins our party by Deina's side. He offers a raised hand in greeting. From him, that's practically gushing.

We gather along the edge of the terrace in front of the temple's portico. The city is laid out before us in a sprawl of riotous color. Each district is distinct from the next while managing to maintain a cohesive appearance for the city as a whole. Their names have escaped me, a fault of my muddled brain in my final days of humanity, but I vaguely recall their functions a second before Deina lists them. Commerce, regulation, entertainment, and housing, each with their own style and throng of happy, ant-sized citizens moving through their winding streets a mile below our feet. The sounds of the wyrok bustling through the city find their way to our ears even at this height. Down in the thick of it, they must be deafening.

Dennick fills the empty space at my side as Conall steps aside to speak to his sister. "Surveying your new subjects?" His question drips with mirth.

The joke makes my blood chill and coagulate.

I didn't even consider what the wyrok of the Hearth may think of me. Do they know I'm about to take over for Esraa all too soon? Are they aware of how absolutely unprepared I am? How their world is being partially handed over to a former human who couldn't even manage to keep herself alive, not to mention one who knows nothing about the newfound magic twisting within her?

Anxiety stirs from its slumber deep in the recesses of my skull. It trails demonic fingers down the walls of my mind, claws scraping tattered strips from my fragile self-confidence. My stomach lurches in revolt. My palms moisten and my heavy breakfast turns to lead. I'm suddenly wishing I had forgone food entirely. I wish I would have stayed in bed. Locked the doors and hidden away from a city full of judging eyes who will find me lacking in every possible way.

Dennick must notice something in my frozen rictus of an expression. His smile falls and he kneels to meet my glassy stare. "Hey," he soothes. "What did I say?"

"They're all going to be judging me, aren't they?" The questions fall fast and frantic from my numb lips. "Will everyone be watching me, waiting for me to screw something up? Will they be wondering why I was picked over someone more qualified? What if they hate me?"

Dennick's mouth opens, but the voice answering me comes from over his head. "They're already aware of who you are," Ceraun says in the same tone one would use to calm a skittish animal.

Maybe I am an animal. A small, overwhelmed one, ready to bolt.

"It's not their first time seeing you, remember? You're in a much better state now than you were when you arrived. Nobody will judge you. They're excited to meet you properly." His stern face promises a swift retribution to anyone who would dare to challenge his word.

Has he already gone up against others saying these things? Or is it merely Ceraun being overprotective?

"Yeah," Den adds. "If you managed to charm the most frustratingly surly wyrok in the city months ago, the rest of them will be no problem." When the comment pulls a chuckle from me, his dimpled smirk makes a full appearance.

"I didn't realize she charmed Daros," Ceraun grumbles. His sullen frown has Den and I howling with laughter. Even Ceraun cracks up after a few seconds of pretending to be grouchy.

My demon sulks back to its hole, banished in a blaze of warm sunlight and camaraderie.

Deina's pleasant lilt recaptures our attention. "Come on, then, let's be off! Trust me—we don't want to be descending the mountain when the sun is at its highest."

We follow her to the edge of the path leading down the side of the peak and begin our descent in a rowdy group. Gaius shoves Finn near the rail-less edge of the pathway, close enough for a handful of pebbles to skitter down the mountainside to the polished stones below.

Finn counters with a flurry of heavily pollinated blossoms which sends Gaius—and the rest of us—sneezing until our eyes stream.

Shading my eyes with my hand, I glance at the cloudless morning above. Sure enough, the full, golden orb has already climbed over the rooftops and is steadily inching through the sky. The heat is enough to cause sweat to bead along my spine. It's not even close to noon, but the morning is already sweltering. After last night's storm, the air is heavy with humidity, making each thick inhale a sensation closer to drinking than breathing.

We'll melt if the sun gets much higher before we reach the shade of the colorful awnings and overhangs stretching across the city's winding streets. Several of the marquees have bold patterns painted or stitched onto their tops. The sight of rich decoration on the upward-facing surfaces is puzzling until I remember, between the winged citizens and the mountain itself, the tops must be seen as much as their undersides.

The gray cobblestone path winds down the mountain's face in a gradual zig-zag. We follow Ceraun and Deina while the latter gives brief explanations of the functions of the various official buildings we pass on our way down to the city proper. Tidy copper plaques shine on pristine white columns or directly on the stone facades of the buildings themselves, proclaiming functions in subjects ranging from infrastructure regulations to resource management. We even pass a smaller building devoted entirely to a guild for wing modifications.

A palatial structure, its Gothic architecture at odds with the Grecian style of the temple and most of the regulatory buildings, sits at the edge of the official sector. Dozens of intricate stained-glass windows in a variety of shapes line the building's umber exterior walls from base to the gabled roof. Their rainbow reflections line the walkway in beams of color, a welcome mat of light on our way into the lower city.

According to Deina, it's officially a hospital, though most of the space is devoted to assisting new mothers and providing care for the handful of incredibly elderly wyrok who prefer not to live alone. The species' fast healing and natural resistances to disease eliminates the need for a large, long-term care space. A wing of the building contains extended stay rooms for the rare case of chronic illness, mental infirmity or extreme injury, but Deina assures us these circumstances are few and far-between.

We spend the day bombarded by sights and sounds in the packed shopping district. Each one is more fantastical than the last, flooding my system with beauty, color, and life itself. A downpour of vitality to replenish the drought our harried journey here left within me. Shopkeepers hawk their wares from a slew of glittering storefronts. The crown jewels of the Hearth.

I'm propositioned by dozens of eager artisans thrilled at the prospect of displaying their products for the *kynaira*. My shoulders start off hunched around my ears, but they quickly relax when it becomes apparent Dennick was right, as much as I loathe to admit it.

Not a single wyrok greets me with anything less than eager enthusiasm. Several press samples into my hands despite my protests, until I have no choice but to purchase a cyan-and-ivory woven shoulder bag from a bright-eyed, stammering wyrok teen working the counter at his parents' textile shop. I crouch on the street's edge near the shop's entrance to organize my spoils. The sack, large enough to hold a pizza box, is quickly stuffed with my armfuls of bangles, bolts of fabric, and other trinkets.

"Quite the haul you've got there," Conall remarks. "And you were worried they wouldn't like you." He slings my bag over his shoulder as if it's no heavier now than it was while empty, and finishes the action with a peck on my cheek before I can warn him of its weight.

Not that he needs a warning—none of us do, myself included now. How many years of being an Avallean will it take before I remember I no longer play by the rules of humanity? A decade? A century, or longer?

Maybe I'll always suck in a deep breath before lifting something which once would've taken all my strength. And won't Finn and Gaius love picking on me for it.

"I don't get *why* they like me, though" I grumble. "They don't even know me. I'm an interloper."

Ceraun twists around near the teeming crowd and answers, as though the answer is as obvious as two plus two, "Wyrok sense energy, *kynaira*. They value power—and a pure heart to wield it—more than anything else. You have both."

The setting sun chases us into a brightly lit, two-story restaurant on the corner of the main road. Swooping overhangs tilt up at the corners over open walls on both stories, with only a low railing separating the diners from the outside world. Chefs are preparing dinner for their guests throughout the space at large metal tables with seating arrayed around them. Scents of tangy marinades, charred meat, and pungent spirits permeate the open rooms while diners fill the restaurant with chatter and the clink of cutlery on ceramic.

A smiling server in a black dress chats with Deina and Ceraun on the way to our table. Slits are cut into the dress' back for her brilliant amethyst wings. She returns with drinks before we're even settled into our plush seats. Food follows quickly after, and we eat and drink until the moon is high in the sky and our stomachs are full to bursting.

Deina ushers us to a series of spellbound lifts cut into the mountains for when wyrok are too elderly, intoxicated, or bogged down with packages to make the journey to the top on their own wings or feet. Why we couldn't use them this morning, I'm too sleepy to question.

We ascend at a speed guaranteed to—were I still human—have made me experience my delicious dinner in reverse. Thankfully, becoming an Avallean seems to have cured my motion sickness.

The temple's interior is blessedly cool and quiet after the chaos below. We trudge to our respective rooms in tired, sated silence. It's not until the others have peeled off to their beds and only Conall and I are left outside our door that someone speaks behind us, their voice quiet and hesitant.

"Princess, do you have a moment?"

CHAPTER 34
Making Amends

"**G**o on," Conall urges. "I'll be here."

Dennick and I pad down the hallway in complete silence. At the end of the hall, a silver key opens a cherry door carved with birds in flight.

He begins babbling the second the door clicks shut. "I'm not here to waste your time, I swear. I only wanted to let you know I'm leaving in the morning."

I take a moment to survey the suite while he speaks. It's richly decorated, though smaller and sparser than my own, with a small bathroom visible beyond an open doorway in the rear of the main room. There are no personal effects scattered on the surfaces—no comb resting near the gilt mirror on the dresser, no toothbrush drying in the cup near the sink, not a single sock or rumpled shirt thrown over an armchair or footboard. A set of folding doors rest ajar along one wall to reveal a bare closet, empty hangers wobbling gently in the breeze from the open window. The only sign of any inhabitant at all is the small stack of packs and camping gear waiting by the exit.

"No, you're not."

Dennick rears back and blinks as though I've grown a second head. "Y-yes, I am," he stammers. "I'm not going to intrude any longer." He trails off into a mumbled, "I don't deserve to be here."

I cross the room and settle into the overstuffed burgundy chair by the unlit fireplace. My chin tips at the matching seat next to mine, arms crossed in my lap. "No, you're not. You're going to sit in this comfortable chair, in your pretty little guest room, and you're going to give me a heartfelt apology." His mouth opens, but I hold up a single finger to stop him. "After I graciously accept, you'll let me say my piece, ask a couple questions, and then you'll unpack your shit. Because—my god, Den—this empty bedroom is depressing. We slept on the ground for weeks; I know you're not ready to do it again."

He gapes silently for several long moments. With tears lining his lashes, he finally forgoes the chair to kneel in front of my bent knees instead. "Valorie, I am so sorry," he chokes. "If I have the privilege of your friendship for another thousand years, I'll never stop apologizing for what I did. I let my fear get the best of me, but there is no excuse for my actions.

"I swear, if you cast me out right now, I will walk away and never darken your doorstep again. It will be as though I never existed, as though I never allowed my own horrors to infect yours. You would be free to live your life, and if my endless apologies occasionally found their way to you on the wind, you'd know I spent eternity regretting my betrayal of our friendship."

My own tears threaten to spill down my cheeks. I forgave Dennick long ago—if anyone understands how fear-driven decisions can overrun your life, it's me—yet we've both needed this closure. But now the sorrow-tinged air in the room is far too heavy after the joyful day we've had. So, I do what needs to be done.

"Oh my gosh, Dennick." I roll my eyes with a grin, trying desperately to pull him back to the present and out of his guilt. "That was *so* dramatic. Get up! You're denting the carpet. My knees hurt just looking at you."

I'm rewarded with a waterlogged chuckle. Dennick rises to his feet and sweeps me up in a bone-crushing hug. At last, all of these fragmented pieces are beginning to fall into place.

And what a glorious picture of the future they form.

"Frankly, I need you to stick around, Den," I whisper, arms locked around him. "If I'm going to have to take up this mantle, I'll need a good schemer by my side. A spymaster. A *friend*," I add with emphasis.

His face lights up like a fireworks show. "Anything you need, I'm there."

"There is one thing I want to talk about." I force my tone to remain light, conversational. Inside, I'm cringing, my pulse hammering harder than the blacksmith we visited this afternoon. But I need answers. "About the Christmas dream…I'm going to need an explanation of exactly what went down when you…well, went down." A snort escapes my nostrils and blush colors both our cheeks as we hold back laughter. I can't help myself; I've been spending entirely too much time with people whose minds occupy prime real estate in the gutter.

"Ah," he sighs once we contain ourselves. Light from the sconce behind him gilds his inky head as his head hangs, his words muffled as they're spoken into his lap instead of eye-to-eye. I don't ask him to lift his gaze—it's easier for both of us if zero eye contact is maintained during this topic. "First of all, I love you dearly, Princess, but not in *that* way. We share a connection, and yes, there was a brief moment where I wondered if this meant we were fated to be together. But, then I realized a connection doesn't have to be romantic to be real. Which is fantastic," he adds, "because I see you as a sister. A hot sister, sure, but a sister nonetheless."

My laughter bursts free. "You're disgusting," I exclaim around heaving breaths.

"Speaking of hot sisters, the tall one with the white hair is a looker. What's her story?"

"Focus, Den," I admonish. "We can discuss Gabby later."

He nods. "Right. The Christmas dream was...unfortunate. Did I get the chance to explain to you how my gift actually works?"

I shake my head. We never had the time for a real conversation after everything went to shit outside of the Hearth. I've been dying to ask since I awoke, but there's been no opening without a dozen witnesses.

"A dreamtreader literally walks through dreams. Observation is our primary power, with only the stronger ones being able to influence anything. I trained for years under the strictest circumstances—" his eyes cloud, and I know he's thinking of Chryton "—to be able to exert a measure of control over the dreams I inhabit, but even I have constraints. My actual influence over them depends on several factors. First, I have more ability to change dreams created entirely by a subconscious than ones dredged from memories. Memories are more concrete. Your brain knows how they should be, meaning I can only change small things without your psyche attempting to reject the irregularities and damaging itself in the process.

"When you fell asleep that night, I attempted to sway your body to choose something happy. Something to lift your spirits and bring you comfort. And apparently, it listened, in a way. But you always have to be difficult, don't you?

"Your subconscious picked the setting, and I had to work with what I was given. The power does what it can to seamlessly place me into a dream, often implanting me directly over another person if I can't disappear into the background. Of course I didn't realize it was, well, *that* type of dream until it was too late. Unfortunately, your recollection was pretty ironclad, which didn't give me much wiggle room, and I can't always force someone to wake up, or force the dream to spit me out. The more obscure Avallean gifts are imprecise and have a will of their own, as you'll soon experience. I kept things as chaste as possible, made some changes where I could, and hoped your brain would figure things out quickly enough."

The underwear. "You left my underwear on," I muse. When his eyebrow raises, I blush and mumble, "They weren't on when it actually happened."

"You dirty girl," Dennick laughs. "Right there by the front door?" The sound of his joy morphs into a grunt when my toes connect with his shinbone.

The two of us settle in and spend the next hour reconnecting. Our separation was brief, but busy for both of us. I tell him about my last few days of consciousness before I was pulled into the nightmare. He trades stories about Ceraun and the gate guards outside the city's entrance, as well as his trek through the dark streets to save my life.

Things are easy, fun. The way they were before, but stronger. Tempered steel, when before our friendship was newly forged and untested.

A small, dark bird alights on the window sill. Round, moon-bright eyes and a smiling beak on a heavily domed skull remind me of a potoo.

Its head cocks to the side with a small coo as it examines us without an ounce of fear. The warm light of the bedroom illuminates its wings in shades of gray and black, from a dove gray ruffle around its neck to sooty, near-black downy fluff beneath flight feathers in a dark shade of blue-black. Our eyes lock, and it gives another tiny, friendly-sounding peep.

"Talk to it," Dennick whispers at my side. I jump, having momentarily forgotten he was here in my fascination.

"Hi there, little one," I coo quietly. My hand reaches out, then snaps back as Dennick's light slap cracks across the back of my head.

He scoffs under his breath. I catch his eye roll in my periphery. "No you idiot. Who's a big, bad Avallean now? You wanted magic powers, didn't you? Well, *use them*."

Oh. *Duh, Val*.

"I don't know how. Haven't had the chance to learn," I remind him.

Dennick waves away my protestations with a flippant flick of his hand. As the night bird watches with a peculiar intelligence, he coaches me through steps virtually identical to the ones Esraa and Amon used to show me my magic. But this time, I grasp hold of the luminous globe of energy and sink my consciousness into it until the core of who I am is wrapped in strands of gold-tinged green. I breathe in deep, the musky scent of fur and feathers suddenly suffusing the air.

When my eyelids part, Dennick has returned to his chair. His eyes are on me, his upper body tilted in my direction.

I face the bird hopping its way along the sill and clear my throat. My lips part...

And nothing happens.

Not a whisper of sound emerges, animal or otherwise.

A chill races down my spine, waves of sweat chasing it along my back. *Where is my voice?*

I cough, trying desperately to dislodge whatever is preventing me from speaking, but nothing feels out of place. Something must be wrong, something hidden, lurking beneath my skin.

Is my magic tainted? Did I break it? Did I break myself?

Cool fingers wrap across my hands and peel them away from where they've fastened themselves around my neck. Quick pinpricks of pain sting the delicate skin of my throat where my own nails embedded themselves. The small half-moons are tinted red. My bulging eyes flick between the crescents of blood and Den's expression. He's calm, his small smirk in place as though my reaction is amusing.

Oddly, his lack of fear soothes my own, his deep, even breathing prompting my lungs to match. My heart gradually ceases its galloping assault on my ribcage, and the cold moisture on my palms begins to dry.

With my demons shoved back in their cage, I raise my brows in silent question.

He better know how to fix this. I don't need a voice to pummel him into the ground, or at least make a valiant attempt.

"I'm no wildwalker," he hedges, grin still firmly in place, "but I'd guess you're speaking, just not in a language our ears can pick up. Maybe you're calling every fish in a thousand meters, or coordinating a mob of bats outside the city. Who knows? But you need to relax. You and your magic, you're still strangers. One day you'll be best friends, and it will know exactly what you want without any effort, but you have to walk before you can run." He chuckles at my sullen frown. "Cheer up, Princess. You've got forever to get your tweets untangled from your barks. Now, try again, and this time focus on the bird."

The ball of feathers on the window ledge becomes the only being in the universe. All else falls away, including me. My eyes follow the edge of every feather, trace every talon and the curving curl of his wide beak as it leads up to those round eyes, incredibly large in its bulbous head. Its tail flicks reflexively when the wing of a moth fluttering in the low light brushes one of the long, straight feathers. It breathes in, and I follow suit, again and again until even our heartbeats are matched.

Only then, when I am more bird than woman, do I begin to speak.

And when a sooty gray head swivels and I receive a sweetly chirruped, "Finally!" in response? I spend the next five minutes in awestruck conversation with a bird, something I've dreamed about since I was a child pretending to be Snow White in the forest behind our backyard. A squirrel sat in my lap that day, and I sobbed for half an hour.

Tonight, I only cry for ten minutes.

CHAPTER 35
The Coronation

- VALORIE -

F our days.

Four impeccable, glorious days perusing the endless streets of the Hearth with Deina and Ceraun until it's as much my home as Sycamore Heights. Four days' worth of rowdy dinners and complicated wyrok board games after our stomachs are stuffed and the fat moon has risen in the clear night sky. Four days of dodging pranks planted by Gaius, of watching Finn pilfer food from any unattended table in the temple. Four mornings where I wake up wrapped in Conall's arms, his head nestled on my chest as though he needs the reassurance of my steady heartbeat even in sleep. Four afternoons crouched in the crystal dust outside the city gates as Dennick helps me grasp my new powers.

After the first night, speaking with animals has progressed quickly.

Shapeshifting, on the other hand, is on an indefinite hiatus as of two days ago. An unfortunate blast of overconfidence led to three hours spent under constant cover of my friends' laughter, thanks to the cat's whiskers I had grown, but could not remove from my face. They eventually faded, but not before my pride took a heavy hit.

The chaos and comfort of the past four days has already birthed some of the most memorable moments in my newly immortal existence.

All in a vain attempt to avoid the clock ticking inexorably down to this exact moment.

"Stop fidgeting, you'll wrinkle the fabric." Gabrielle swats my hands away from the front of my ceremonial robes for the third time in the past hour. Her fingers smooth invisible pleats from the heavily embroidered lilac silk. I highly doubt wrinkles would be visible beneath the daedal scenes of mountainous landscapes, windswept plains, and pristine wetlands covering every inch of the carefully draped swath. Minuscule wyrok are sewn throughout every embroidered environment, their scales glowing and glimmering with a lifelike shimmer through some twist of artistry or magic. Likely both. Their active poses are portrayed in such detail, I wouldn't be surprised if one decided to take flight and leave the ensemble entirely.

I survey myself in the floor-length gold mirror I'm seated before, its edges carved with comets and stars. Gabrielle stands reflected at my shoulder, fussing with another carefully constructed sweep of silk. Behind her, Deina and Esraa have their heads together in the corner beside the door to the bathing chambers we used earlier this morning.

When the three women arrived at my door before dawn's first light had touched the city's rooftops, I was too exhausted to question exactly what "ceremonial bathing and dressing" would entail. I pictured stiff-backed nuns and cold tubs of water, painful scrub brushes and yards of shapeless, unadorned linen. Not the scalding hot springs and this laughing trio of women bathing each other before slathering me with soaps smelling heavily of blackberries and roses. And definitely not the supple bolt of pale purple silk draped and ruched strategically around every curve of my body in a sensuous waterfall.

Beneath the long train, simple gold sandals are ready to protect my freshly-lacquered toes from the flagstones of the city streets I'll walk along after the ceremony is complete. Deina trades places with Gabby and places several crystal pins in my curls to complete the ensemble. No makeup is allowed after the cleansing ceremony, but my skin glows with the magic now flowing in my immortal blood.

"You look wonderful," Deina coos, her hands on my shoulders as we gaze into the mirror's image. I smile up at her reflection, secretly plotting ways to get Ceraun to take the next step with her. They'll be perfect together. And if this morning's gossip is to be believed, their mutual hesitation is built on nothing more than a lack of confidence on both their parts.

"Absolutely radiant," Esraa adds as she rises to join us in front of the mirror. She's resplendent in the matching ivory satin shift dress the three of them are wearing. My nerves around Esraa have all but disappeared after this morning. There's been a carefree beam glued to her face since we entered these chambers. She laughed and joked along with us as if this was a girl's night in and not the preparation for the most terrifying workplace on-boarding in history. She's one of us now, despite her being my mother-in-law and saddling me with her full-time job after I technically died under her jurisdiction.

None of us are perfect.

Gabby's pink eyes have a mischievous glint to them. "The boys will have to tie Conall to his chair," she snickers. "I should try to get a message to Finn and have him wrap Con's ankles in vines before you arrive. Otherwise, he might ruin the ceremony. Could you imagine?"

Laughter fills the roughly hewn stone cavern. It echoes off the thick walls and bare floors, no windows in the underground chamber to allow its escape or textiles to dampen the sound.

Which is how we nearly miss the quiet chime of the timepiece on the mantle signaling the turn of the hour. Fortunately—or unfortunately, if you ask the riot of bees buzzing below my diaphragm—few sounds go completely unnoticed in a room full of various immortal species. The laughter peters out, my attendants flank my sides and rear, and, with one final shaking breath, I ascend the twisting flight of stairs in the corner of the room, a direct route to the temple's apex and the crystalline room where I'll become a Paragon.

"Why are there this many people?" My whisper slices through the antechamber. From the golden decorations, to the multitude of wings beyond the door, to the polished crystal surfaces of the chamber itself, color abounds in this room and the next.

Sweating feet slip inside sandals gripping a floor of semitransparent sapphire. The limpid walls fade upwards from deep blues into heliotrope, from lavender to rose and citrine near the perfectly clear diamond adorning the domed ceiling's apex fifty feet above my head. Bright shafts of multicolored light spear through sections around the room and paint the space in watercolor rainbows saturated with coruscating motes of dust twirling through the air. The entire experience is akin to standing inside of a giant's shaken kaleidoscope, one which would be ethereal if my attention was not wholly trained on the centimeter-wide gap between the doors to the main chamber.

Deina laughs, a musical tinkle. "It's three dozen wyrok, a handful of esteemed guests, and your companions," she says in a tone meant to soothe. It is unsuccessful. "Less than fifty people, all told. Esraa and Amon did not even give the other Paragons leave to enter the Underworld for the coronation."

I send a *thank you* to the universe for the small miracle. I'll meet them eventually, but I fear even my vastly improved Avallean reflexes would not be enough to save me from embarrassing myself if the nine other Paragons were in attendance today.

Deina leads me away from the threshold to where Gabrielle leans against a lustrous section of amethyst. A golden diadem dangles from her hand and throws sparks from its teal stones when it catches a beam of light. She nestles the aurum semicircle atop my head, and the three of us turn to face the doors, waiting for the signal.

Esraa left us here half an hour ago with strict instructions. She needed to take her place at the head of the ceremonial room, but our orders are clear: When the chimes sound, wait three seconds and then proceed into the chamber. I must go first, followed by Gabrielle and Deina. An Avallean and a wyrok, to represent the traditional melding of the Paragon's life with the lives of those who dwell in the Underworld.

A low, clear tone reverberates through the crystal surrounding us. We each draw a breath as complete silence descends on both chamber and antechamber.

One. Two. Three.

With a sweep of my right foot, our march begins. The doors part of their own volition. Whether they're enchanted independently or controlled by a force akin to Daros' shadow tendrils, I'm not sure. Contemplating the possibilities allows me to proceed halfway down the long aisle before reality sinks in and threatens to drag my feet to a standstill.

The room is the larger, grander sibling to the space we were sequestered in, with a ceiling high enough to house an oak tree. Twin sections of seating line an aisle covered in intricate whorls of gilt paint. Still-life animals cavort within the painted design, an homage to my newly acquired powers. Esraa and Amon wait at the far end, bedecked in matching robes of charcoal gray. My own robes shine against their backdrop as our trio reaches the pedestal upon which the two Paragons stand. Deina and Gabrielle peel away to the front row with a silent signal to Ceraun. He leaves his post by the dais and takes the now-vacant position over my right shoulder.

Muscle memory, honed by hours of practice with Esraa, directs my movements as my courage flags under the crowd's scrutiny. My right hand reaches into the space between us of its own volition, sweating palm facing the crystal ceiling.

Esraa takes a single step to meet me. A silver knife with a hilt wrapped in metallic tendrils of vining plants rests in her grip. Marble-sized emeralds adorn the pommel, each perfectly round and smooth. Its long, curved blade descends toward the flesh of my palm as though eager for its meal.

Her voice is a toneless, formal chant as the point of the thin knife begins to split my skin. "Blood of the *kynaira*, given in knowing sacrifice."

I hold my spine ramrod straight and refuse to flinch. The cold metal sinks effortlessly into the heel of my palm. It drags upward until a crimson line wells from my wrist to the webbing between my middle and ring fingers. Fat drops of my blood splash audibly against the crystal below.

"We receive the offering," the crowd replies as one.

Next, Esraa pulls a rumpled lump of tattered fabric from a hidden pocket in her robes. She unfurls the mass, and everything within me tightens until I'm a drawn bowstring, ready to snap. Ceraun must sense my shock and horror, because he leans closer as if ready to catch me. Or hold me back.

"A life, unknowingly sacrificed. Witness how your *kynaira* has over-powered the forces of Death itself. Only one who has fought Death and won may have power over it." Esraa intones.

My bloodstained tee shirt, the *Grease* logo almost entirely obscured by dollops and spatters of gore, flutters in the air. The shirt I was wearing as I fought for my last breaths beneath a moonlit sky all those months ago.

Again the crowd chants, "We receive the offering."

I'm frozen in place, locked tighter than a bank vault so as to remain outwardly emotionless while my entire being rages within me at the sight of my happenstance death shroud. My soul snarls and snaps, rattling the bars of its cage, baying for Joran's blood to coat the entire world the way mine coats the scrap of fabric.

Soon, I soothe as I lock her in tight. *Soon.*

She'll have her feast, but she needs to be patient. Now is not the time. Today is a day for joy.

Ceraun pads forward on bare feet. The familiar sight brings me back to earth, locks another deadbolt on the cage housing my inner beast. He spreads his wings and rises ten feet above our heads. "The power of the wyrok, ready to serve," he declares.

Ceraun's eyes focus on me before he points them skyward. His mouth opens, and a great gout of pure white flames wreathed in lightning pour forth. Beautiful in their deadly power, the mixture sprays upward in a fountain of death before sprinkling harmlessly over my skin, light as the last ashes of a fireworks display.

As he lowers back to the ground, I turn to face the crowd for the final portion of the ceremony. Tinted sunlight bathes them in washes of diffused color. A patch of periwinkle here, a great splash of cyan there. A rainbow of life.

I smile at the gathered assembly, and my voice is clear when I promise, "The power within me, ready to serve as you do."

At my words, Deina and Gabrielle release a flock of radiant white songbirds from the back of the room. The birds wheel around, tweeting and chattering in a raucous discord. Several swoop down to pull at ornamental gems woven into the various hairstyles of the assembled guests, and their disgruntled protests only set them off further.

I spread my arms at my sides and call, "Leave them be, and come sing for us. Be welcome here, friends!"

A chorus of gasps and wondrous exclamations fills the room when the birds gather and perch themselves on my outstretched arms. Their chattering melds into a symphony, and Esraa has to shout to be heard over them. "Behold," she cries, "for the transfer of power is sacred and unbroken. As one falls, so does the next rise."

"So does the next rise," the crowd responds.

I gasp and my hand flies to clutch at my chest, dislodging several of the flightier birds. Dimly, I notice Finn and Gaius holding Conall into his seat in the front row. The scene is clouded as though observing an old film through a dingy window pane.

My entire soul reels as a second ball of magic bursts into existence and joins the one I've only recently come to be familiar with. Icy and molten, soft and spiked, the second globe pulses with dichotomous urges, comforting warmth and feral power. It races through my veins in an attempt to free itself, barreling down every capillary and burrowing into my atoms themselves.

The magic thrashes as I slowly wrestle it into submission, force it back into the confines of its ball and wrap it in my own magic until it ceases its seething and purrs beneath my mental grip. All the while, the crowd continues to watch with breathless interest. Have they been here for seconds or hours?

"It is done." Esraa sounds at once exhausted and lighter. As though the foreign addition to her power I now hold had once strengthened her, but at a cost. Left her a capable master of its force, yet beholden to its call.

While the cheering crowd sweeps me up and out of the chamber in their joy, while Conall's hand slips into mine and my friends' revelry assaults my sensitive eardrums on our way down to the city itself, I cannot help but question.

Will I feel the same, after a thousand years of rule?

Spirits and Spice

"**S** orry, sorry!" A wyrok babbles slurred apologies, his eyes widening into headlights as he realizes exactly whose front his beer is sloshed across. He grabs a handful of napkins from the table and dabs frantically at the amber splash darkening the lake scene on my chest. Icy froth sinks through the thin silk faster than he can mop.

I hope these robes are washable. Maybe there's a charmed version of stain remover?

Conall's hand flashes out, gripping the poor wyrok's wrist like a vise. "She's fine, but you won't be if you continue," he growls. His glare flicks pointedly between the ruddy-cheeked male's face and the place where his napkin-wrapped hand remains pressed against my breasts.

I try—and fail—to hold back my chuckle. Horror slowly dawns on the drunken wyrok's hapless expression. His palms fly up in front of his face, shielding his eyes. "I'm...going to leave now," he stammers, backing away three steps before spinning and fleeing through the crowd. Several revelers shout as he careens into their tables, sending snacks and drinks flying in his haste to disappear from the scary new Paragon and her overprotective husband.

Our friends and family have sprawled over three round dining tables on a raised platform at the back of the packed room. I'm fairly certain its original purpose is a stage for evening performances, but the owners of this bar quickly improvised when they heard our procession was searching for a place to settle for dinner. By the time we made it to their section of the city, they had filled the platform with wooden tables, plush chairs, and enough food to feed an army. Finn and I took one look at the overflowing platters of roasted fowl, battered fish, steaming heaps of potatoes and root vegetables with tureens of gravy stationed at the ready, and the separate long table in the back devoted entirely to desserts, and we were sold. Much to the joy of the ancient wyrok proprietor, who personally escorted us into his business. His heavily wrinkled face split into a brilliant grin which made him appear decades younger as he skipped off to tell his staff to prepare for the onslaught of people who would undoubtedly be following us into the bar.

And follow they did.

Finn slides a platter of pillowy cookies under my nose. "Try these."

I snatch two, and warm strawberry blooms on my tongue as I survey the teeming party. Bodies press and writhe on a makeshift dance floor in the center of the main room. Music pumps from somewhere unseen, an ethereal rhythm which thumps in your chest and overpowers your own heartbeat until the music is all you are, and all you can do is succumb to its call. Along the burgundy papered walls, dark oak tables I'd assume usually populate the central space are pressed end-to-end, each blanketed in plates and baskets of food interspersed with tankards, glasses and the occasional fish bowl filled with brightly colored alcohol.

The throng spills through the open doors, blending seamlessly with the mass of people partying in the streets. Children with tiny wings ride on their parents' shoulders, waving glowing sticks in every color imaginable. Sprays of magic and handheld sparklers light up the spaces between the welcoming lights of buildings open long after their normal hours. Every door in the Hearth is thrown wide, boundaries ceasing to exist as the world around us churns in one city-wide celebration.

The bar's owner bustles around our table, clearing empty tankards and replacing them with milky green shots in tiny glasses. I tap his hand and smile up into his brilliant blue eyes when the cool, sour liquid coats my throat. "Thank you." I have to yell to be heard over the din, despite the old man being six inches away.

He shakes his head and squeezes my shoulder, the grandfatherly gesture so at odds with the pomp surrounding today. I struggle not to weep at the casual affection. "Welcome to the city, dear. The Hearth loves its Paragons, but wyrok party as hard as they train. If you ever need an escape, this establishment is yours. We have private rooms in the rear of the house in case our more...enthusiastic citizens become overwhelming."

Conall leans in and murmurs, "We may need to take you up on your generous offer sooner rather than later." His warm breath caresses the shell of my ear. A shiver runs down my spine, cool against the heat of his body pressed against mine. One finger trails up my inner thigh beneath the table, and my insides go liquid as the silk I'm wrapped in, even as my cheeks flame with mortification.

The wizened proprietor's face creases in a conspiratorial smile. "Of course. Take the door behind the curtain, and I'll ensure you aren't disturbed. If I may offer one suggestion?" Conall nods for the male to continue. "Try to make your way back to us before the next hour's chime.

Your Bondmate's disappearance may be noticed when the pyrotechnics begin."

Conall's victorious grin makes me choke on my drink. "Say no more, sir," he replies with a formal incline of his head, his artfully rumpled waves begging for my touch.

I shriek when Conall's arms sweep me up from my chair. His throaty laugh rumbles against my side. Cradled to his chest like a bride on her wedding night, I can do little more than hide my head in his shoulder and flip a single finger at our howling friends as he carries me through the brocade curtain and down a shadowed hall draped in rich wallpaper and carpeted thickly enough to muffle Conall's rushed footsteps entirely.

He chooses a seemingly random door and shoves his way in, slamming it behind us hard enough to rattle the unlit chandelier overhead. Cool wood assaults my back through the silk robes and my toes brush against another thick rug. I gasp and arch away from the sudden cold.

Conall seizes this moment and covers my mouth with his. Our tongues tangle and plunder while his hands roam a frenzied path down my body to the tabletop he's laid me upon. He brackets my head with his forearms and looms over me, breathing in heaving drags.

"I can't wait," he pants. Scalding fingers slip beneath the fabric and climb my legs as Conall sinks to his knees in front of me. My pulse ratchets when the soft fabric of my underwear slips down to my ankles. He twirls the drenched lace around one finger before flinging them into a darkened corner, his fiery gaze never leaving mine. "All those plates of food, but my favorite meal was tempting me the entire time, just out of reach. A delectable tease. So spread your legs, Wildcat, because I'm ready for my feast."

But he gives me no time to react. In the next instant, my legs are over his shoulders and the flat of his tongue sweeps across my core. My back arches off the table on a long moan when two fingers sink into me. Fire torches every neuron, flaring higher with each thrum of his tongue and thrust of those curved fingers. I'm already close, still high on his touch after being apart for far too long.

He rolls the tip of his tongue around my clit, and I combust. I can't speak, can't think, can't *breathe* with him lapping at me until I believe I truly am his favorite treat. Sparks and stars whirl behind my eyelids as my orgasm barrels into me with all the force of a truck with no brakes.

Once my glazed eyes open to find his smug expression, cocky and wholly confident in the mind-numbing pleasure he delivered, a plan blooms into being.

He may be my husband, the literal holder of a piece of my soul, but nothing about that means he's allowed to *win*.

I force my legs not to shake as I rise to my feet. I toe my sandals off and use one bare foot to nudge the center of his chest. His face blooms into a confused but excited grin.

Oh, you silly, innocent man. You have no idea.

"Take off your shirt and lie back," I command. He follows the instruction without hesitation, stripping and reclining until his bare back dents the red carpet. Lust-blown emerald pupils gleam in the pops of colored light filtered through the sheer curtains covering the window. His smile turns molten when I flick the line of buttons holding his pants closed and ease them down his legs. They slip off with his shoes, leaving him clothed in nothing but darkness and desire.

"Wildcat, what are you—" his question dead-ends in a rasping groan as I straddle his hips and sink onto his cock. My fingertips dent his chest, small crescents peppering where my nails dig into the smooth copper skin. I lift my hips until only the tip remains notched within me, then drop back down completely, locking our hips together.

He swipes his tongue along the pad of his thumb and reaches up to run it across my peaked nipple. I choke on a moan, rhythm faltering before I raise my hips again and ride him with reckless abandon.

Conall bucks beneath me, meeting every plunge of my hips with his own thrust. His body curls so he can plant wet, open-mouthed kisses against my skin, but I press him back down to the floor. The slap of skin against sweaty skin erupts and dies against the rich furnishings. I doubt anything below a shriek would ever be heard over the raucous party outside.

"You're incredible. I'm so close," he pants, words turning jagged when another undulation plunges him fully inside of my core.

And then, a wicked grin gleaming, I do the unthinkable.

I *stop*.

It takes every ounce of self control to halt my rhythm at its apex, his cock barely resting within, but I do.

Conall chuckles breathlessly, undulating beneath me. When his movements produce no results, his eyes darken with lust and challenge. His lips and teeth speckle red and purple marks across the sensitive skin of my lower abdomen, each one a proclamation and a plea. He growls, grips my waist, and thrusts upwards, to no avail. Every one of his movements is matched by an opposite one of my own, a dance of passion on the edge of oblivion's bliss.

"Next time," I croon. One nail traces a slow, tantalizing swirl across his nipple. He shudders beneath me, his gaze rapt and rabid. "Refrain from embarrassing me in front of the nice old person, *husband*. Or I'll leave you high and dry and finish myself at home. And I won't let you watch." I lean down and follow my finger's path with my tongue, eyes glued on his. My teeth close around his skin, and his lids clamp shut with a frustrated moan.

"You're killing me," he groans beneath me. "I'm dying, and I don't even care. Take me out, my love, and carve the story of your body over mine into my tombstone. Let the universe know it was the agony of ecstasy which felled me. Let them be jealous for all eternity."

Little does he know, I'm dying too. My thighs are slick with how much I want to give in until we both hurtle over the edge. But the combination of him writhing beneath me, desperate for friction, and the heady power I feel hovering above him is intoxicating.

I'm a queen, a goddess. Of course I can rule this realm. I could rule the entire cosmos with Conall's cock as my throne.

"Say please," I tease, tutting when he twitches at my entrance.

His smile turns feral. Callused hands clamp over the dip of my waist, and the world spins. Suddenly, I'm staring up at the glorious face of my love as he drives into me. Neck stretched, back arched, he bottoms out in one stroke, my body giving way under his onslaught as though it was made for him. Maybe it was. Wrapped up in him, I can believe our souls were fashioned from the same bits of stardust and hope, destined to occupy the same corner of the universe and make it perfect, if only for a moment.

"Ready, Wildcat?" he asks.

I'm powerless to do anything but nod.

Conall captures my mouth in a sweeping kiss in the same moment his thumb finds my throbbing clit. With one brush of skin against skin, I fracture. Pure ecstasy ricochets through my body. Every muscle tightens, every nerve fires at once. He captures my scream with his lips, embracing it with his own roar as he jerks and pulses deep within me, and we climb together until we crest among the stars.

Slowly, so slowly, we come back down from our high. Conall dresses quickly and leaves for a moment, returning with a soft cloth and a bowl of warm water. He dabs at the sticky mess we've made between my thighs, then gently tugs me to stand.

Weak as a newborn fawn, my legs tremble as he carefully adjusts my robes back into a facsimile of formality. The gesture is sweet in its futility. Our entire group knows exactly why he carried me off like a barbarian.

Fifteen minutes later, with mussed hair and flushed cheeks, we emerge into an empty restaurant.

"There," Conall calls, pointing.

I follow his line of sight and spy our family among the even tighter crowd outside the doors. We rush to join them.

I hope my antics in the back room haven't made us late. I'll never hear the end of it.

We reach the exit as the city's lights flicker off and plunge the crowd into darkness. The first fireworks bloom in a navy blue sky to earsplitting cheers and applause. Their flares reflect off the beaming smiles of my friends, the wide eyes of children, and the knowing wink of the old bar owner nestled into the alcove by the door, his hand held in the grip of an aged female wyrok who smiles up at him while the sky explodes above us.

Chapter 37

Calamity

- Conall -

An incessant, painful drumbeat reverberates within the confines of my skull and echoes into my teeth. Last night's celebration did not end until the first gray touches of dawn inched over the horizon, chasing bleary-eyed revelers back to their beds for a paltry few hours of sleep. We cavorted and drank our way through the night, and now we reap what we've sown.

The lights in the dining room are far too bright for my eyes. Squinting, I slide into a seat across from my brothers—Gabrielle has stationed herself in a quiet corner of the room, far from the food—and cringe when the small motion jostles my queasy stomach.

Thankfully, the temple's acolytes have heaped the usual hearty fare down the lacquered table. Consuming my body weight in eggs, bread rolls and cured meats sounds like a wonderful hangover remedy.

"Is it possible to think too loudly?" Finn's groan is muffled. His forehead is pressed into the tabletop and his large arms are slung around it as though he can hold his aching head together and keep it from exploding. An empty plate rests on the table by his elbow, decorated with smears of red jam and several discarded specks of ham and biscuit.

"It's possible to *talk* too loudly, and you're proving it right before our eyes." Valorie throws herself into a chair with vehemence. It scrapes on the hard floor, and she grits her teeth against the harsh screech.

My wildcat is evidently not a pleasant person when she's overindulged and underslept. She's been grousing and snapping at any inanimate object she's deemed offensive in the thirty minutes since we were dragged from our bed.

It's adorable, but I won't be telling her so. Not when it would mean her crosshairs angling in my direction. Better to let Finn take the brunt of her wrath. It's only fair—he's the reason for half of the alcohol she consumed.

"I thought being an immortal would mean I didn't have to deal with this shit anymore." The grumbled complaint earns Valorie a chorus of quiet amusement, more huffs of breath than actual laughter. It's all any of us can manage.

Gaius glances over from where he's been toying with a candle's flame next to Finn's portrait of exhausted misery. "Even immortality can't fix stupid decisions," he replies.

Valorie groans, then winces and grabs her temple. "I'm never drinking again."

"We'll be back at the bar in two days," Finn stage-whispers. A biscuit bounces off his disheveled head with surprising force. Valorie sticks her tongue out at his answering snarl.

Sedate footsteps announce the arrival of Ceraun and Deina, together once again. To my surprise, Dennick is on their heels, chatting amicably with the wyrok pair as though they've been friends for years.

"Settle down, children." Dennick calls, flopping into a chair next to Valorie and scooping up a muffin. He flicks a crumb at her with a wink and a grin.

Valorie hisses at the offending piece of pastry. "Where did you disappear to last night?" she asks with a raised brow. Dennick shrugs one shoulder, but I don't miss the way his eyes flick to my sister's before he wrestles them back under control, or how she blushes and turns to face the window beside her chair.

Valorie doesn't mention the interaction. Did she not notice, or is this not new information for her? I'm guessing option two—Valorie notices everything. She could write a dossier on any one of us.

We've been gathered in this room for yet another meeting with the Paragons. Well, Paragon and former Paragon. It's still hard to wrap my mind around the idea of my sweet spitfire of a wife entering our world and promptly being thrust into a position most Avalleans have lifetimes to prepare for. She's outwardly confident, greeting wyrok citizens and training with Esraa with amazing tenacity and patience.

But she forgets about our heightened senses, despite now having them herself. I hear her in our bathroom when she believes she's alone, whispering to herself beneath the shower's spray.

Valorie has no idea I went to my mother a week ago and begged Esraa to reconsider abdication. I pleaded with her, going so far as to get on my knees beside her chair and grip her hands in supplication, but to no avail. Once the transfer of power from a reigning Underworld Paragon to their *kynaira* or *kynairar* has been commenced, nothing short of death can halt it.

I worry Valorie's pushing herself beyond her limit between mastering her new magic and the duties of a Paragon, but she assures me everything is under control each time I beseech her to relax. Seeing her last night, vibrant and unchained for a few short hours, was overwhelming the way an entire bottle of liquor overwhelms an empty stomach.

A smile paints itself across my face at the memory. My hand finds her thigh beneath the table, and her fingers tap against the back when I squeeze gently. Her joy in the bar was potent, a drug in my veins. I was powerless to resist its song. It's no wonder I had to have her in their private dining room like a teenager with his first crush.

I'll be searching for back rooms for a thousand years or more. The universe will collapse into dust, and they'll find our sparks in the cosmos' broom closet.

A portal appears in the room's entrance, cutting through quiet with the clap of lightning splitting a dead tree. Esraa and Amon step through the swirling silver vortex, holding hands as if it's no more than a doorway between rooms in a bed and breakfast instead of one spanning realms.

"You've all made it through your first Hearth celebration unscathed. Congratulations." Esraa's words are laced with her tinkling chuckle. Even Amon's stony visage cracks into a small grin.

Finn grunts, "Tell that to my brain, if you can find it. I'm pretty sure I left it on the bar's floor last night."

The pair settles into chairs at the head of the table, the same ones left open for them during our first meeting in this room. It's hard to believe barely a week has passed since that morning. So much has changed in seven short days. Mostly for the better, but my gut continues to churn when I'm reminded of Valorie's impending role.

We could have happily lived without that particular change.

Morning light plays on Esraa's pastel hands as she spreads them, palms down, on the table. "We're here to discuss plans for the immediate future, since Valorie's ceremony is complete."

"Is Conall going to have his Testing soon?" Valorie asks anxiously. She turns to Amon and adds, "No offense to you, of course. I'm sure you'll be lovely to work with."

"Though not anywhere near as exciting as the prospect of working with your love. I understand the appeal," Amon replies. His right hand finds Esraa's left atop the table, and the two are lost in each other's eyes for a handful of seconds before someone—likely Gaius—clears their throat. "Unfortunately, none but the Web of Fate knows when a Testing will occur. I will receive a signal when it is about to commence, but I will be unable to convey said information to you until the Testing is complete. If I were to break that rule," he adds when I open my mouth, "you would no longer be eligible for the role, and my life would be forfeit as punishment."

Of course. The Web loves its damned rules and consequences. "Understood."

Esraa's fingers tap inaudibly against the polished wood as she speaks. "Because Valorie is still relatively unaccustomed to this city, and seeing as how you have been separated from one another for quite some time, we believe it would be best if you all remain here for the foreseeable future." The room swells with a round of excited murmurs. Gaius and Finn high-five, hangovers momentarily forgotten. Beside me, my wildcat beams with relief.

Amon speaks once attention returns to the pair. "Your duties as dehmi will be paused, but this time assisting the new Paragon's transition will count towards your service period. Consider it a special assignment.

A trip to Avallea will be necessary for Valorie in the next few weeks. Your presence will be allowed, despite the general rules against dehmi being allowed in the homeworld before their assignments are completed. However, you must stay with Valorie at all times as her personal guests. You may not roam, nor are you permitted to leave the capital. Failure to follow these rules will result in your expulsion back to Earth, with an additional century added to your necessary time of service."

Complete silence falls as we all process this information. We each slip into the training hammered into us by Dom and Margie since we were young. Every dehmi in the room straightens in their chair and dips their chin at Amon. "Understood," we respond in unison.

"Does somebody want to tell me what this is?" Valorie's high, nervous tone breaks our collective focus. Above her empty breakfast plate, a palm-sized whorl of light is forming in midair. Tiny threads of lightning crackle along the surface of the rotating disc, more violent than the calm swirls of Esraa and Amon's portal. It spits a rolled sheaf of paper onto her plate, narrowly missing a tureen of white gravy, and disappears with a sharp *snap*.

Valorie's trembling fingers close around the cylinder and unfurl it. The scrap is a scant few inches square, with room for no more than a handful of lines of text. But it's evidently enough space to hold a message which drains every drop of blood from her face.

The scroll furls back onto itself when its bottom edge slips from her fingertips. She holds the unassuming roll pinched tightly between two fingers, as if it may break away and run the second she lets go. "I think you should read this," she whispers to Amon. "Please. I know I'm technically on equal footing with you now, but this is so far above my pay grade it's not even funny."

The scroll changes hands with Amon's gentle, "Of course." He tosses it into the air and it opens at his eye level under the foggy grip of his magic. I scour his face while he reads, my own falling further as his smile drips away into a frown. Over his shoulder, Esraa gasps behind a raised palm.

Amon drops the scrap of paper. It flickers out of existence in a lick of shadow.

His veins strain against the skin of his forearms, and a single tendon twitches in his clenched jaw. A sour tang coats the back of my throat, threatening to choke me with dread.

"Plans have changed," Amon tells the frozen room in a cold voice which leaves no room for arguments. His stony gaze finds the wyrok in the back of the hall. Ember-drenched eyes rove over each of us in turn before ending on Valorie.

Her clammy hand spasms around mine beneath the tabletop. She read the missive before any of us. She knows what's coming, and it is clearly not good.

My heart slowly descends through the marble tiles. I resist the primal, childlike urge to cover my ears to drown out Amon's next words. *Not yet*, I plead to whatever scrap of the Web is woven closest to us. *Not again.*

But the Web has never deigned to weave in our favor before, and it won't start today.

The dining hall bursts into furious activity, yet I'm glued to my chair as Amon's horrid revelation sinks in.

"Joran has infiltrated the Kraal. The Titans have awoken. Prepare for war."

Epilogue: The Awakening

The last guard slid from Joran's blade to the parched, rocky soil with a meaty *squelch*. A full moon overhead gilded his gore-drenched sword in pale light, casting the gobs of viscera dangling from its point in silver-lined shadow.

Joran knelt and ran the blade over the jerkin of one of the corpses at his feet. With a swift kick, the body rolled to rest alongside the three other deceased Avalleans at the edge of the outcropping. A single arm flopped limply over the cliff, sending a rain of moon-bleached pebbles tumbling to the churning waves a mile below.

Blade sufficiently scrubbed and sheathed, Joran scoffed and tilted his head at the imposing set of doors before him. Carved directly from the mountain's gray face, the Kraal's massive entrance towered one hundred feet high, its face etched with runes in a long ago tongue designed to prevent entry by any except the guards currently lying in a heap, their blood puddling in the lifeless dirt.

Poisoning their rations had been an embarrassingly easy feat, in Joran's opinion. The product of a people too complacent in their flaccid idea of peace to suspect treachery.

"Bah," Joran scoffed. He whirled around and began to pace the length of the outcropping, muttering to himself. "Peace. Such a paltry desire. Why should we strive for peace at the expense of our own time? Why should we serve, when we could rule? Mortals deserve no part of our power. We owe them nothing. Their resources should have been ours from the beginning."

His path plumed dust off the cliff and into the sea far below. Stopping before the doors, Joran raised his hands and pushed against their handleless exterior.

His feet slid backward in the grit, but the doors did not budge even a single inch.

The crunch of grinding teeth filled the air as he kicked the door with an impotent scream. "Open, damn you!" Joran shouted over the crashing waves. His enraged stomping carried him to the corpse pile, but his rough, furious examination of the bodies yielded no keys. Blood and entrails caked his fingers and turned his nails to red-black slivers, yet no solution revealed itself.

Would he be forced to return to his Brotherhood without their weapon? Joran shook his head violently at the idea. *No,* he thought. No one must learn of this, especially not his brothers. He must succeed in this task.

If only he had taken the time to question the guards before cutting them down. But he could not.

The bloodlust was one of Joran's best-kept secrets, hidden even from his closest comrades for decades upon decades. The mindless desire to consume, to bathe in the life of those inferior to his greatness as they flickered to nothingness beneath him.

As his magic waned within his chest, the obsession grew exponentially. Most days, Joran could no longer experience the caress of his power. But where magic deserted him, his blade never failed to provide him with what he craved.

He sensed his tenuous grasp on his control flagging even now. Once, he was the pinnacle of restraint. That was before he saw the truth, the reality of how Avalleans should be.

How they *would* be under his rule, if only these damned doors would part and show him his well-earned prize.

Open-palmed slaps rebounded off the stone beneath his abraded palms. "Open, damn you!" His shout seemed to sink into the granite, and the doors shuddered before slowly scraping inward. Joran stumbled forward, catching himself before he could tumble to his knees. It worked! But why? Was it the commanding majesty of his godlike voice? Did the Krall sense he was destined to rule?

A bloody handprint on the left door caught his attention in the moonlight. *Of course*, he thought with a high, manic chuckle. *Blood is always the answer.* The three vials in his pocket seemed to tinkle in agreement. "Soon, my dears," he crooned to the glass tubes, held securely over his heart. "Soon, you will finally be useful to our cause. I hope you consider yourselves honored."

As the slabs of granite finally slotted into place, twin rows of torches mounted high on the roughly hewn walls flared to life. Their magic was older than many worlds, born of the desire to contain what he had come to release. And as he raced down the winding corridor into the core of the mountain, their power called to him, so close he could taste its sweetness on his tongue.

One final, skidding sprint brought him face to face with the glorious monsters who had done their best to destroy half the mortal realms. The treacherous beings who had consumed scores of Avalleans before their reign had ended.

The Titans.

Behind bars of liquid magic said to have been formed of the freely-given lives of mortals and Avalleans working together, three towering bodies waited, slumped in stasis. Joran's lip curled at the thought of mixing his life force with a mortal's. The very cage the beasts were held in was an affront to Avalleans. Why contain that which could be controlled? With the Titans at his side, Joran would be unstoppable. Mortals would line up and beg to do his bidding, would give their resources, their *lives* for his favor. Avallea would finally see him for the savior he was.

The thought was enough to make him salivate.

Joran's gnarled fingers twitched with the recollection of wrapping them around mortal throats and squeezing until their eyes went as dim as their inept, inferior brains.

He dove a hand into his front pocket, freeing the three vials. Each was filled three-quarters full with thick liquid: one a bright red, one chartreuse, and the third a darker, nearly-black cousin of the first. They sloshed up to their corks with his erratic movements.

"Three vials," Joran muttered wheezily under his breath. His teeth descended, and the first cork skittered along the ground as he spat. It hit the empty air below the lowest bar of the cage and rebounded backward. "One, two, three. Three mortal lives from three mortal worlds." Two more vials popped in time with his count, until three open mouths glinted in the torchlight.

With a grunt, Joran's arm reared back and snapped forward, his clenched fist blurring in the flickering shadows. The vials struck the bars with a splatter of liquid and the crisp shatter of thin glass. Before the blood had reached the floor of the cavern, a thin, palm-length dagger had made its way to Joran's grip.

"One immortal's essence, the final component," he chants. A hiss forced itself through his teeth when the steel tip dipped beneath the first layer of his flesh. Joran swore, embarrassed with the show of emotion. Pain was weak, and gods were *never* weak.

The blade drew a straight line of crimson from his elbow down towards his wrist, its end wavering to the left at Joran's flinch. He balked, then swore again, when the knife hit his delicate wrist bone, but he did not dare remove the dagger from his arm until the line was completed.

When the blood fell in a clean sheet of wet red down the side of Joran's forearm, he pressed his weeping limb directly to the center bar of the prison. His breaths quickened into the whimpering pants of an injured animal as the strange metal heated under his arm, rapidly becoming unbearable. An instinctual urge had him mindlessly attempting to yank his burned flesh from the prison's enclosure, but the fatty layer beneath his skin was crackling and popping, stuck to the bar like a slab of meat on a grill's fiery grate. He could only watch in horror as his left arm disintegrated to dust.

And the beings behind the bars began to stir.

"What have we here?" A mammoth figure, vaguely humanoid, spoke in a low, smooth timbre from the blackness of the cell. Deep blue skin stretched tight over bones the size of tree trunks as the Titan rose to its feet for the first time in millennia. Scraggly gray hair hung limply over broad shoulders. The monster's head had the bone structure of an ape, but with a lizard's slitted nostrils and forked tongue.

"Who would be so foolish?" hissed the orange monstrosity to its right. Craggy, boulder-like flesh was lumped into a bipedal form far wider than any Joran had laid eyes upon before. A wall given life, its body dotted with small embers from the magma which ran in its veins in place of blood.

"It is not even enough for a meal," the final Titan responded. It had no solid form. Only a pair of pupil-less yellow eyes in a tumult of thick, swirling smoke. The roiling blackness, far darker than any natural shadow, whipped itself into one shape after another as it spoke lazily to its kin. "We used to be given the choicest morsels of life, and now they send this scrap to our table, brothers? We, who were once more than gods?"

His arm no longer holding him hostage, Joran drew himself up to his full height. He leveled an imperious stare at the trio, despite them being ten times his stature. In the tone of one far beyond sanity's grasp, he called, "I am no meal. I am your new master."

Two seconds of silence, broken only by the cracking of magic powering the sconces, answered his declaration. Then, a horrific, discordant combination of three inhuman laughs rang through the cave.

Joran's ears bled under the onslaught, but he refused to cower. He was destined for greatness. This was only a roughened stepping stone in his brilliant plan, needing the briefest of polishes before it fell in line. "I have fulfilled the demands of the spell containing this place. You will now follow me, and we will wage war against mortals and immortals alike until they succumb to my rule."

Joran leaped back as the door to the cell swung open and clanged against the rock. "Fool," the first Titan jeered. It crowded into his side of the cavern. "Bold words you babble, especially from one who used twisted blood to trick the seal on our temporary den without our request. Insolent, lying little bit of flesh, did you think we would not scent the girl lives?"

"What?" Joran spluttered.

Confusion swirled in his skull. Their den? Twisted blood?

And then it hit him. *Impossible.* "You mean the human girl? But I watched her life leave her with my own eyes. There's no way."

"That is the second time you've been wrong tonight," the shadowy third Titan rasped. "We will align our cause with yours for a moment's time, foolish one. For long we have slumbered, and worlds have a disgusting habit of changing over time. But suffer no delusions of what transpired in this place. You do not control the Titans, and we will one day claim your life as payment for your folly."

Joran bowed his head, hiding his sneer behind a mask of servitude. "Of course," he simpered. "Our alliance will prove fruitful, I assure you."

The Titan's horrible laughter brought several small chunks of the ceiling's stone crashing into rubble around them. Joran flinched, then clenched his one remaining fist until blood pooled between his fingers. He could not show weakness to these *creatures*. They would learn to fear him, too.

Dusty earth trembled as the moonlight touched the Titans' forms for the first time since this mountain was hollowed. History quailed, sensing the return of those who scarred its pages long, long ago.

Three faces stretched to the heavens, mouths split wide in nightmare grins.

"Brothers," the half-smoke Titan hissed, his voice suffused with bliss. Incorporeal wings sprouted from its back, featherless and translucent in the moonlight. Its siblings gathered close, each with a hand sunk deep into its shadow-skin. "Let the fun begin."

The Playlist

Please enjoy a sampling of the amazing music that inspired Shards in the Void. For the complete playlist, visit my social media or website, or search Shards in the Void on Spotify. All songs are property of their respective artists.

Lost My Mind - FINNEAS
Lullaby - The Spill Canvas
Believe - The Bravery
Body - Sleeping At Last
Ships in The Night - Mat Kearney
Die Alone - FINNEAS
This Is How I Disappear - My Chemical Romance
From Where You Are - Lifehouse
Crossfire - Brandon Flowers
Save My Soul - Jonah Kagen
I Will Follow You into the Dark - Death Cab for Cutie
Sky is the Limit - Mark Ambor
Repent and Repeat - Mayday Parade
Made Up My Mind - Jonah Kagen and Lily Meola
Ghosts - Mayday Parade

Fantastic - King Princess
Pollution - Jonah Kagen
Low Fidelity - The Spill Canvas
The Memory - Mayday Parade
The Mountain is You - Chance Peña
Neptune - Sleeping At Last
The Roads - Jonah Kagen
Midnight Prayer - Thirty Seconds To Mars
The Darkness - John Michael Howard
Stay With Me - Anson Seabra
Far Too Young to Die - Panic! At The Disco
Never Say Never - The Fray
Saved - The Spill Canvas
Still Breathing - Mayday Parade
Moon - Jonah Kagen
Emergence - Sleep Token
The Line - Twenty One Pilots
Wasteland - Royal & the Serpent
Chokehold - Sleep Token
New York to California - Mat Kearney
Where You Are - Mayday Parade
hill that i'll die on - Jonah Kagen
The Apparition - Sleep Token

Thank you so much for reading!

If you enjoyed your time in the Underworld, please don't forget to leave a review to help my books get into the hands of more readers! Reviews on websites like Amazon, Barnes and Noble, and Goodreads are essential for small authors, and every one of them helps in the fight against the evil algorithm.

If you would like a pronunciation guide and cheat sheet to help you keep track of important places and characters on your journey, you can find a link to a continuously updated one via my website or the linktree located on my Instagram profile. Book clubs can also find lists of discussion questions for my books at the same location. See the "About the Author" page at the end of this book for more information on where to find me online.

Thanks again; I'll see you in Avallea!

ACKNOWLEDGMENTS

Phew, this one was a beast of a story, wasn't it?

I thought Strands in the Web was a massive undertaking—and it definitely was—but creating the entirety of the Underworld and all of its intricacies while also running two side-by-side stories and corralling multiple narrators was a whole new ballgame, one which never could have happened without my own veritable Haven full of people.

First in line and first in my heart are my husband and daughter. Are you helpful when it comes to actually getting work done? Absolutely not. In fact, you're frequently the reason I have to work overtime to meet a deadline. But you mean the world to me, and your endless support and unwavering belief in my abilities are worth more than gold. And sweetheart, keep writing your stories. Mommy is endlessly proud of you.

To the rest of my amazing family: I will never stop appreciating the way you've rallied behind me in this crazy endeavor. You've bought tickets to conventions, convinced coworkers, hairdressers, and friends to purchase copies of my work, talked me up to everyone and anyone, and never failed to remind me I'm loved and supported. Thank you, and I love you.

To my friends, both in person and online: Some days, you are a large reason why I'm still an author. This world is tough. It's harsh, and disheartening, and unforgiving. But, having you all in my corner to make me laugh and let me vent about the struggles of being an indie author gives me the push I need to not give up when sales tank and I feel like a fraud. Keep being weird, and I'll keep writing stories that make you yell at me.

To my beta readers, Amanda, Katiria, Dakota, Mara, Shannon, Melissa, and Austin: You guys rock. Thank you for taking time out of your busy schedules to read Shards and give immense amounts of feedback. Truly, this book would not exist without you and your unhinged commentary.

And to those of you who loved Strands in the Web enough to follow me into the Underworld: You're the best fans an author could ask for. Even if I wake up and sell a million copies tomorrow, you'll always be the ones I write for. Thanks for sticking around, for leaving absolutely feral comments on my posts and in my messages and chats online, for leaving reviews and recommending my work to others, or for just quietly reading and supporting me in your own, quiet way. I hope Shards in the Void was everything you've been waiting for. Did you bring enough tissues for all your tears? Don't forget to hydrate, and I'll see you in the next one.

ABOUT THE AUTHOR

K.T. Host has been writing in some shape or form since she could hold a pencil. From poems, to stories, to scientific papers and professional statements—if you can create it with words, she's probably done it at least once. She has a bachelor's degree in biological sciences with a side focus in sociology, which gives her unique insight into the inner workings of world-building and character design and helps her flesh out her stories for maximum emotional damage. K.T. lives with her husband and daughter in a secret cavern in the deepest recesses of the cosmos, where she beams her books directly to you via a complex linked system of teleporters closely guarded by various international police agencies.

Find K.T. online for exclusive content, sneak peeks, helpful information and general mayhem:
Instagram: @k.t.hostauthor
TikTok: @kthostauthor
Tome: @kthostauthor
Web: kthostauthor.wixsite.com